HOUSE OF
BONE
AND RAIN

ALSO BY GABINO IGLESIAS

Zero Saints

Coyote Songs

The Devil Takes You Home

HOUSE OF
BONE
AND RAIN

A BARRIO NOIR

GABINO
IGLESIAS

MULHOLLAND BOOKS

LITTLE, BROWN AND COMPANY

NEW YORK BOSTON LONDON

Copyright © 2024 by Gabino Iglesias

Mulholland Books / Little, Brown and Company
Hachette Book Group
1290 Avenue of the Americas, New York, NY 10104
mulhollandbooks.com

First Edition: August 2024

Mulholland Books is an imprint of Little, Brown and Company, a division of Hachette Book Group, Inc. The Mulholland Books name and logo are trademarks of Hachette Book Group, Inc.

Book interior design by Marie Mundaca

ISBN 9780316427012
LCCN 2023950965

Printing 1, 2024

LSC-C

Printed in the United States of America

To Borikén

HOUSE OF
BONE
AND RAIN

1

GABE

—

Two bullets to the face
The wake
A baquiné
Brotherhood of the gun
The church of anger

The last day of classes, our last day as high school students, marked a new era for us. We wanted it. We feared it. We had plans for it. Then Bimbo's mom hit the sidewalk with two bullet holes in her face, and the blood drowned out all those plans.

Bimbo called to tell us the day after it happened. His real name was Andrés, but we mostly called him Bimbo because he was brown and chubby and looked like the mascot bear of a brand of cookies. It's normal for people to report the death of a parent. Old age. Cancer. A heart attack. Whatever. Old people die and we expect it, accept it even. It's normal. Murder is different. Murder is a monster that chews up whatever expectations you had regarding death and spits them in your face. Murder is an attack on someone's life, yes, but also an attack on those left behind.

When Bimbo called to tell me about the death of his mother, María, I felt attacked. "They shot my mom, man." Five words about the recent past that were heavy enough to crush our future.

I said nothing because there was nothing to say. Death swallows words, or at least shows you how fucking useless they are.

María had been working the door at Lazer Club for a few years. All she did was check IDs and yell at the gorillas inside if anyone got belligerent. At least that's what everyone thought. What most people didn't know — and we knew only because we were Bimbo's best friends — was that she also dealt on the side. But no judgment: mothers are sacred. Mine definitely is.

In the pregnant silence that followed Bimbo's words, María's coarse laugh came to me, a ghost made of sound. I wondered what would happen to the spaces that laugh was supposed to fill in the world, the ears it was meant to touch, the conversations it was supposed to decorate with its humor. I saw María climbing into the shitty Chevy Malibu she drove everywhere, Héctor Lavoe screaming nasally from those busted speakers, his voice leaking out the window like the perfect soundtrack to María's perpetual smile.

When my pops died, when I was ten, I didn't want to be home, because he haunted every corner of it. He'd hung every picture on our walls. The kitchen table smelled like his aftershave. He'd painted my room. He was everywhere, so I spent a lot of time at Bimbo's place, and María had welcomed me then, fed me arroz con salchichas and asked me about my mom while scolding Bimbo that only assholes hit girls after he had pushed his sister.

I wanted to tell Bimbo about these memories, to let him know that I'd loved his mom, too, that he didn't have to carry the pain alone, but I couldn't say shit. Any question I asked would be stupid, and anything I said would fail to bring María back, but I had to say something, so I mumbled the same thoughtless sympathy I'd utter at anyone else. Bimbo made a noise that was a *Yes, okay,* choking on it.

Then Bimbo cleared his throat and said he'd be in touch. As we were hanging up, he paused. "She loved you, man." I sat there on my unmade bed and thought about never seeing María again. Then I imagined my own mom dead on a sidewalk outside a club in Old San Juan. My insides filled with something so heavy it was hard to breathe. If someone killed my mom, I would burn the world to cinders.

Soon after Bimbo called us, we called each other. Xavier, Tavo, Paul, and me. Along with Bimbo, we were a crew. Brothers, really. You know, like the tight-knit group of kids in a Stephen King novel, except with three brown dudes and two Black ones running around and getting in trouble. We didn't have much to say, but we needed to know the rest of us were still there, that we still had each other. Their voices were a familiar place where I could hide from whatever Bimbo was feeling and the awful way in which we all imagined ourselves in his shoes. Just hearing each other that day was enough to get us through. Men are weird when it comes to love, but sometimes a *You good, man?* on the phone is as good as *I love you, brother.*

After the phone calls, I walked out of my room and told my mom, who was sitting at the little kitchen table while watching over something she had on the stove. "Virgen Santísima," she said, her hands covering her mouth. Then she crossed herself, kissed her fingers, and stood up to hug me. I hugged her back a bit too hard, feeling very lucky that she was still with me, and wishing I could crack my chest open, put her inside there, and keep her there forever so nothing could touch her the way it'd touched my father and María.

"Déjame saber si Bimbo necesita algo," she said. She didn't ask any questions, only told me to let her know if Bimbo needed anything. She knew that María led a life that flew too close to danger, but she had never said anything about it or about her, and had even gotten the cops off her back a few times with a few lies and a big smile. They were women raising kids by themselves, and that brought them together in a way only other women like them would understand.

My mom let me go and sat down.

"María…," she started, then stopped. She took a deep breath. "María came to see me a few times after your father passed away. She asked me if I needed money. Then she said her brother…would take care of things if any man tried to take advantage of me. She was a good woman. Don't let anything you hear now distract you from that, okay?"

I nodded, but I'd had no clue. María had been good to me, but knowing she had also reached out to my mom made me feel a different, bigger love and respect for her. It made me hurt for Bimbo even more.

Two days later, we sat in Bimbo's living room and he told us what he knew: a couple of dudes with Scarface dreams had approached María at the club and asked her to sell for them. She'd refused. Whoever owned Lazer paid her to work the door, but as far as María was concerned, her brother, Pedro, was her one and only boss, and María was comfortable with that. The men who had talked to her apparently didn't like that answer, so they drove by again the next day and rained down bullets on María and three other unlucky people standing near the door. The other three had survived. María left a hole in the world. Of course, as with everything else in life, what we knew could have been a pebble at the bottom of the mountain of everything we ignored, and there was a chance at least half that pebble was bullshit.

The wake was on a Thursday. We all went. Xavier picked me up. He was a good dude. Smart. He played tennis, a bit of soccer, and had full-ride offers from a few colleges. He was a bit taller than me and good-looking. He was dark, but he had what folks on the island call "good hair," so he was seen as an indio instead of Black. He was a thinker, too, methodical. We relied on him to figure things out. While we watched action flicks and horror movies, he watched documentaries. He wanted to get a degree in electrical engineering, like his big sister. We knew he'd do it. Some folks have everything they need to win at life regardless of where they're born. He lived with his parents in a neighborhood so bad it didn't have a name, right behind the largest housing project in the United States. To the outside world, it was tierra de nadie; a lawless, violent place you stayed away from at all costs. For Xavier, it was home.

We ran into Tavo in the funeral home's parking lot. Tavo was a surfer. Taller than the rest of us. Blond with green eyes, which made him stand out. He was a pure soul, like he was made of ocean and clear blue skies instead of the shit the rest of us are made of. He'd been waiting around for someone else to show up because he didn't want to go in alone. The three of us strode in like dudes in a Tarantino movie, but as soon as we saw Bimbo, we all melted into a weepy mess.

Once we had collected ourselves, Bimbo said he had to talk to the other people and left us there, feeling hurt, sad, and awkward, so we went up to the casket because it seemed to be the right thing to do. We had to pay our respects.

María's casket was closed. That was fine by me. Next to the casket, mounted on a wooden easel, there was a big black-and-white photo of her with Bimbo and Bimbo's younger sister. They were in front of a Disney World castle. Bimbo's father had never been in his life and neither had his sister's father, so I guessed they'd asked some fellow tourist to take their photo. The big smiles on their faces seemed out of place, like diamonds in a catacomb.

María had been a loud, rotund woman who used to scream at us whenever we turned her house upside down looking for quarters so we could go to the corner bar to play the old *Pac-Man* and *Street Fighter II* arcade games. I wanted to remember her that way, so I tried to think about her laugh instead of wondering what her face might look like in that casket. My brain refused to cooperate and served up the ugliest, most painful image possible. Two bullet holes in her face, leaking blood onto the grimy sidewalk, and her eyes open but not seeing anything.

We moved a few feet away from the casket and watched silently as people came and went. They were all part of the ritual, just like we had been when we arrived.

Paul showed up about an hour after we got there. He had some relationship drama going on, as always. If there was ever a line on his forehead, it meant he was in one of his dark moods and we knew not to press him.

Some people showed up to talk to Bimbo about helping him and his sister, who was also called María because that's how we Latinos do it. They said the church near the high school would ask for donations for them. We almost laughed. Everyone knew giving money to the church was as good as burning it. Bimbo nodded, but I could tell he wasn't paying attention.

Paul, Tavo, Xavier, and I moved to a corner in the back and kept quiet. Over our heads, the room's AC unit made a racket as it struggled to keep the room cool while the Caribbean sun pummeled the building with its relentless rays.

I thought about Francisco Oller's *El Velorio,* a painting everyone knows even if they went to the shittiest school in the country. *El Velorio*—"The Wake"—is arguably the most important painting in the history of Puerto Rican art. At some point, every kid in the country is thrown on a bus with no AC and taken to the University of Puerto Rico in Río Piedras to stare at the massive work of art.

The painting depicts a baquiné—a wake or celebration after the death of a child—which, like many other things in the Caribbean, has deep roots in Africa. Basically, the baquiné celebrates the fact that kids are innocent and thus become angels when they die. The painting had seared itself into my brain the moment I laid eyes on it. It featured folks laughing and partying, a few dogs and other animals frozen in memorable poses, a kid running around, some jíbaros drinking and playing music, and in the middle of the whole thing, an old man with a cane standing in front of a table where the dead infant lies. The old man is alone, and you can tell by the way he's looking at the dead child that he can feel Death itself starting to creep into his bones, singing to him from beneath the ground, calling him home.

There was none of that here. This was just a wake, not a baquiné. The AC's hum and the smell of disinfectant and the unnatural lighting engulfed the whole place and seemed to declare Death the winner. I hated it. I wanted to go back in time and reclaim the festive nature that had been part of my culture years ago. I wanted to cry for María but also to celebrate that we who had survived her were all still alive, ready to enjoy life for at least a while longer.

About half an hour later, the room had emptied, everyone going back to their little worlds, probably already in the process of forgetting María.

Tavo, Xavier, Paul, and I were still sitting together in a corner in the back, not saying much and keeping our voices low when we did because the one thing we knew —driven into our thick skulls by parents and grandparents alike—was that the dead deserved respect.

Bimbo closed the door to the small room as soon as the last two people left. Then he walked up to the casket without saying a word and opened it. The lid was split in two pieces, but it still looked heavy, and Bimbo struggled a bit with the top half. The casket was made of dark brown wood and the insides were white. A pretty thing to hold a dead woman. I wondered if Bimbo had picked it. I'd been too young to take care of anything when my father died, and I couldn't imagine having to pick a big box for my mom's body.

Losing my father had broken me and built back a strange version of the kid I'd been. It ended up strengthening my bond with my mom —something I'd do anything to preserve—but I'd had to learn to live with a ghost. Bimbo didn't have anyone in his family to lean on other than his uncle, who was always busy, and I wondered how much that contributed to the monstrous pain that was surely eating him up.

With half the lid raised, Bimbo looked our way and asked us all to come closer.

María's face looked like a dollar store version of the one she'd had in life. She was a dark woman, darker than Bimbo and his sister, but now looked a few shades lighter, like a vampire had sucked the life out of her. And you could tell the undertaker had used some kind of plaster to fill in the two bullet holes, one under her left eye and one just beneath her hairline on the right side of her face. The filled holes were different in texture from the rest of her skin and had sunk in a little. She looked like a cheap doll and I knew then that this version of her face was going to show up in my nightmares soon enough.

"Look at her," said Bimbo. We were already looking at her. It was impossible not to—death and curiosity made good dancing partners. Bimbo was telling us to look at her, sure, but he was also begging us to *be* there, to bear witness.

"Fucking look at her!" Bimbo's scream made us all jump. He started sobbing.

Xavier took a step toward Bimbo, probably to hold him, but Bimbo pushed him away with his left hand while pulling out a gun with his right one. If his scream had pushed us all back a step, the gun—a black, blocky thing—doubled whatever distance we'd previously put between Bimbo, the casket, and ourselves.

"What the fuck are you doing, man?" asked Tavo, his voice climbing an octave. Tavo had always been the voice of reason. He had come out to us about two years earlier, and because we had all grown up deep in bullshit macho culture, his being gay made him smarter in our eyes, like he had a bit of that sixth sense. We all knew any change in his tone usually meant he was worried, sad, angry, or scared, and if Tavo was scared, things were bad.

"This doesn't end here," said Bimbo. "We're gonna make this right."

I thought about trying to calm Bimbo, to tell him that the cops would take care of it, but we all knew they never would, because one more dead woman — a small-time dealer at that — on a tiny island that sees hundreds of murders every year isn't anyone's priority, so I kept quiet just like everyone else. We had to let him have this moment, had to let this righteous anger consume whatever Bimbo needed it to consume.

A good minute went by before Paul broke the silence. "What are you talking about, man? What do you mean, 'We're gonna make this right'?"

Bimbo looked down at the gun in his hand. "We're gonna kill the motherfuckers who killed her."

It was a fucking awful idea, but it made sense. An eye for an eye and a tooth for a tooth. It was part of how we did things. It was part of how the whole fucking country did things. We all knew that, but we also knew that stealing or beating people up or destroying someone's car — all of which we'd done more than once — were very different things than murder. We should've said no right then, but Bimbo was suddenly a preacher at the church of anger, calling us to partake in some sacred ritual of righteous violence.

"I'm with you," said Paul. "They deserve to die."

Fucking Paul. His anger was like a leech, always looking for something or someone to attach itself to. He was always the first to throw a punch, the first to hurl an insult, the first to ask someone if they wanted to take it outside. Maybe not having a father had made him that way, the constant fight to be as manly as he thought he needed to be to survive. However, I knew all about not having a father, and I wasn't like him, so maybe it was just something that same missing father had left him with.

Bimbo nodded at Paul and then turned to the rest of us. Our awkward silence seemed to give him a resounding yes, and he placed his gun on top of his dead mother's chest. When he looked at us again, his eyes were bloodshot, his dark face streaked with tears. He used both hands to wipe his cheeks before reaching into the casket again and placing his right hand on top of the gun. We were all watching him, wondering what weird ritual we were witnessing, being a part of. Bimbo kept his eyes glued to his mother but moved his head sideways. He wanted us to put our hands on top of his. When you spend enough time with someone, you can more or less read their mind. We all took a step or two forward, reached into María's dark brown casket with the lacy white interior, and placed our hands on the gun resting on her chest. Then we stood there, huddled over María's body, shoulder to shoulder like the brothers we were.

None of us knew exactly what Bimbo meant by making us put our hands on his gun, what words had died in his throat, but I know we all thought he was making a promise on our behalf. We didn't care. We loved him.

2

GABE

—

Bad spirit in the storm
A father's death
Parking-lot pigeons
Natalia
La casa grande

They put María in the ground, and her murder went from being a hot topic to something folks mentioned as a warning or a sad story about the state of our country. Then people stopped thinking about it at all. I knew how this went. We'd all grown up surrounded by death.

When I was ten, we'd locked ourselves in the house, listening to the wind howling outside. My abuela always stayed with us during hurricanes. She was convinced bad spirits came with each storm, that the angry winds birthed demons and pulled dark things from the bottom of the ocean. "It's out there," she'd say, wringing her hands as we all sat at the kitchen table. "It's always out there. I don't know where it goes when hurricanes stop, but I know it's always...somewhere."

I sort of laughed at her. "You think that?"

"There's nothing to *think* about, Gabe," my dad said, giving me a swift kick under the table. I yelped and got up to look out the window. Respect your elders was big in our house, but that didn't mean I had to buy every ghost story. The water was coming up fast, covering our street and threatening to get into cars.

Our street sort of dipped a bit, and the drainage was shit, so heavy rains always brought flooding our way. It was normal. Then came a shriek unlike anything I'd ever heard, and I saw a dark figure standing outside right next to my dad's car, seemingly impervious to the wind.

"Get away from that window and sit down with me," my dad said. I looked back at him. His eyes were wide.

"Dad, there's a guy out there. I think, maybe, he's trying to steal your car."

My dad stood up, shaking off my mom, who pulled at his sleeve. My grandmother started saying a rosary and I wished I could grab my last sentence out of the air and swallow it whole, but I also wanted to know what the world looked like during a hurricane, so I followed him to the door. My dad lifted his bloodshot eyes and grabbed me by the shirt. "I said, stay inside, Gabe." The move made me shrink back and we all waited at the door, holding it open against the wind just an inch and looking at the chaos beyond.

I watched my dad lean hard into the wind, like something might rip him away from the world, but he made it to the car. The other man seemed to be gone, but instead of turning back, my dad pulled his keys out of his back pocket and got in the car. He managed to drive it up the street a bit to where it wasn't flooding. He parked under a big tree my friends and I sometimes climbed when we were bored. The car's brake lights flicked on and off as the wind howled.

The trees were doing a mad dance that made it hard to figure out which way the storm was blowing. I watched my dad struggle to open the door against the wind. Then there was a huge *CRACK!* and the tree my dad had parked under shook like an agonizing giant before it all came crashing down on top of the car in a loud metallic crunch.

I ran out of the house with no raincoat or shoes. The wind knocked me down as I reached the sidewalk.

My mom screamed behind me.

Only the back half of the car was visible.

Then my dad emerged from the foliage. Blood was running down his face and he was holding on to the car like he was weak or dizzy, but he was alive and walking and I'd never felt relief like that before.

But the tree must have brought down the power lines as it fell, because when my dad took a step, still holding on to the car, his body shook like it was possessed by a demon. A sound like bees rose off him. The transformer at the end of the street exploded, sending wild sparks into the air right above the fallen tree.

My mother had to drag me back to the house, where my abuela called 911 and then held me the entire eight hours between watching my father die and the moment my mom finally went out to meet the paramedics. All I remember of that time is my abuela's strong, gnarled hands wrapped around me tight so that I wouldn't try to go out to see my father.

The weeks that followed were hot and dark, same as after every hurricane. We didn't have power or water for a few days. I couldn't sleep. I had no idea how to act, what to say, how to turn back time. There was so much death everywhere on the island that no one cared that much about my dad's fate in particular. Also, I was left with a big secret only he and I shared; a thing that gave me nightmares and that had pushed me away from baseball, a sport I'd loved. Without my father around, the weight of that secret threatened to crush me. A month or so after his death, school started again. I got into fights. My grades dropped. I got suspended. I lost the year.

That was also when I started hanging out with Bimbo, Paul, Tavo, and Xavier. We each had holes in our lives that were shaped more or less like the rest of us. We fit together. We stuck together. We had each other's backs. When I was with them, I was less alone. Maybe that's why I always went along with anything they said.

* * *

High school was done now, and a strange kind of desperation had set in. The end of summer would also be the end of an era. Xavier, Tavo, Paul, and I took that desperation and tried to drown it in good times. We had a party at Paul's house, where everyone got a little too drunk and little too high and we talked about the things we'd gone through that had changed us, throwing in as much humor as we could. We went fishing twice, camped at our favorite beach in Guánica for a week. At night we smoked weed and looked up at the stars, talking about the possibility of life on other planets and making plans to move there if the apocalypse finally came.

Bimbo never made it to anything, never picked up his phone, and never called or texted any of us, and that had somehow planted a chunk of ice at the center of our souls anytime we hung out together. We had always been a group, a crew, a family. We had been for years. Bimbo had moved from Puerto Rico to Florida and then back to the island the year before and had gotten caught selling weed at his previous school. Tavo moved from New York with his family to live on the island early that year and was just starting school. Paul's mom was too busy to care about his fights and suspensions, and Xavier was absent so much that he flunked a bunch of classes. That meant we started the fourth grade all over again as older kids. Bimbo, Tavo, Paul, Xavier, and I didn't have much in common to start off, but we were all lost and angry, so we gravitated toward each other and soon became inseparable. We became brothers.

After a few weeks, as July ran toward its end like a spooked horse, dragging the last vestiges of our childhood with it, we spent a few nights in Old San Juan, playing dominoes and listening to music that meant something to us—Joaquín Sabina, Fito Páez, Silvio Rodríguez—as the scorching Caribbean night outside did its best to warm up our insides. Not having Bimbo there felt weird.

Xavier and I drove by his house a few times. We knocked on his door and rang the doorbell, but no one came out, and Bimbo's car, a shit-brown Dodge Neon, was never outside. We wondered if he was out in María's Malibu and told ourselves and each other that he was just processing shit, that he only needed time to let his wounds heal, then he would return to us. When four weeks became five and then six and seven and no one had heard from him, we started fearing the worst, but said nothing. Perhaps one of the most painful things about growing up is realizing that rather than go away, the things you don't talk about lurk in dark corners and grow.

August rolled around and Xavier drove to the other side of the island to start college in Mayagüez. I started thinking about life as a runaway train that accelerates every time you think you'd like it to slow down a little. I knew Xavier would end up dressing nicely, working at an office somewhere, and leaving his parents' barrio behind like his sister had done. I just hoped he'd stick around and not move to Florida or New York like everyone with a good degree did.

Tavo had applied to a few community colleges, but they all said no, so he started sending out fake résumés to get a gig, but every place either ignored him or replied with a no quicker than any college ever had. Tavo was the only person I knew who loved the ocean more than I did, so an office gig would've made his soul shrivel and die a slow, agonizing death. Instead, he woke up every morning, grabbed his board, and headed to the beach. He was a natural at every sport he tried, but surfing was the thing he loved most. He had his own crew for that because even though every island boy's heart belonged to the ocean, none of us were into surfing.

Tavo never spoke of dates or boyfriends and we never saw him with anyone, but we all wished he'd find someone. I understood him because I had my own secrets. His father, a tall gringo named Richard who'd met Tavo's mom in his native New York, sold insurance to American businesses for a living and had a drinking problem. After coming out to us sophomore year, Tavo had shown up at school with a busted lip. We knew Tavo hadn't come out to his parents, but his dad must have heard about it from someone. We said nothing because family is sacred and what happens at home is no one's business unless you want it to be. But when it happened again a few weeks later, a black eye that time, we paid Richard a visit one Saturday morning when we knew Tavo would be at the beach. Richard never put a hand on Tavo again.

Paul had moved in with Cynthia, the girl he'd been dating for three years. They were always fighting and calling it quits, but inevitably ended up back together, sometimes mere hours after a big ugly fight. We sort of understood them. Paul was moody, so he gravitated toward someone similar to him. We doubted anyone too stable would be able to put up with him. Some folks like Paul took meds at school to keep them mellow, but Paul exploded whenever his mother or Cynthia brought up that possibility, usually after some nasty incident. In any case, Paul started college that August as well, but he went to a private school that never turned down anyone whose parents could afford tuition.

He called me every day, kept bringing up stories from high school, talking about those days as if they had happened decades ago, like it was a magical time to be cherished. Funny how sometimes you can't wait to get the hell out of a place — only to miss it like crazy once you do. He was the angriest of us, the one with the shortest fuse, but also the most vulnerable. His mother worked for an American company doing something all over the Caribbean, so she was able to provide, but she was never home. Paul needed us in his own way.

I started college in my town, at the University of Puerto Rico at Carolina, a small public institution. I didn't have the numbers to go into business administration, but UPRC had a program where they let you in as a "general" student so you could take easy classes and then use your first-year grades to apply to a degree program with them. Natalia, my girlfriend, was a third-year student at the same place and she had used the program to get into nursing. She had taken so many classes that she was going to graduate in three years instead of four, and then hoped to get into a graduate program in the States. We often talked about moving there together.

The last time we had that conversation, I'd made some stupid comment about some people being born to be peacocks while my friends and I were born to be parking-lot pigeons, and she nearly ripped me a new one. *You can have a house in a good neighborhood and not have to worry about not having health insurance or being broke all the time. You don't have to spend the rest of your life working construction. You don't have to stay in a place where corruption and crime and...and even the weather seem to be...en contra de ti. You don't have to stay where you're born. People aren't trees. We can move around.*

Natalia was always talking about how patriarchy was a cancer, that it was the thing that had kept her mother and aunts from going to college. She had taught me about the roles women had been pushed into throughout history, and one of those was being everybody else's refuge. I realized I had started thinking about Natalia as my sanctuary and knew it was wrong.

She was much more to me than a place where I felt safe. I felt protected. I knew, because I had grown up deeply immersed in bullshit macho culture, that if anybody said anything to her or touched one of her curls, I'd be throwing hands, that I had to be the one who offered support, the strong one, but it always felt like it was the other way around. So, I spent many nights at the little apartment she rented with a friend in the back of a gas station in Isla Verde, and nodded along as she explained things to me, made plans for the future, dreamt big. And in the meantime, I worked construction and felt like I was growing up faster than I had wanted.

But the thing about Puerto Rico, especially if you're poor, is that there's a lot going on — death, drugs, gangs, violence — so you either grow up quickly or you don't get to grow up at all. When you live in a place that's just a hundred miles long by thirty-five miles wide, only security gates separate you from the good stuff. For Paul, that wasn't really an issue, because despite not having a husband, his mother made good money. He lived in a world where people slept safely and kids got to pick what university they went to without worrying about paying for it. For me and Tavo, things were tight but okay. It was different for Xavier and Bimbo. But we were brothers despite our different backgrounds, and suddenly not seeing each other every day was taking a toll.

That's why when I heard someone honking the horn outside my mom's house, I got excited even though I knew it could be for someone else. It was only a couple weeks after classes had started for me, so I wondered if Xavier was back or if Paul had taken the day off for some reason and decided to visit. It couldn't be Tavo, because he always asked you before dropping by. It was a formality he got from his gringo blood.

I stood up, walked to the little window in my room, which faced the front of the house, and peeked outside. I saw Bimbo sitting behind the wheel of his shit-brown Dodge Neon. He was nodding his head to a reggaetón song. The bass was shaking the little car's doors. I'd never thought his round face would make me so happy. I ran out to meet him.

"Where the fuck have you been, man?" I asked as I made my way to the driver's side of the car.

Bimbo opened the door and stepped out. We hugged. I felt like crying again for some reason. Then I felt like an idiot for wanting to cry.

"I was locked up," he said.

The words made no sense for a second. Then they clicked in my brain.

"You were what?"

"Encerra'o, cabrón. En la casa grande, papi. In jail. Let's go get some food and I'll tell you all about it. Are Xavier, Tavo, and Paul around? I'm working on getting a phone again..."

Bimbo had spent his early years between various cities in Florida and Barrio Obrero, which wasn't much better than Xavier's neighborhood except for the fact that it wasn't considered a "residencial." He spoke a weird mix of English and Spanish. In fact, Bimbo seemed to prefer the mix to either language by itself.

"Xavier is in Mayagüez until Friday, but Tavo and Paul are around. Let me text them. Where we going?"

"El Paraíso Asia and you fucking know it."

3

GABE

—

El Paraíso Asia

Altagracia

Revenge

If someone fucks with one of us…

A hurtful silence

So, you got locked up? No wonder you look like shit," said Paul.

"I better fix that," said Bimbo. "Don't want folks thinking I'm related to you."

The crew was back together, and so was the banter.

We were sitting under some red paper lights and an AC vent that had been collecting dust for a decade.

El Paraíso Asia was Bimbo's favorite restaurant. A Chinese joint that was somehow the best place for Chinese food and also the best place if you were in the mood for Puerto Rican fare like tostones al ajillo. The joint had been in business for generations, and everything they made was great. I was digging in to my plate of fried chicken with fried rice and a side of tostones al ajillo (also fried) when Paul finally asked Bimbo how he'd gotten locked up.

"Baby mama drama, papi," said Bimbo, his lips glistening from the oil of the tostones.

"The hell does that mean?" asked Paul.

"Remember Jessica?" asked Bimbo.

"The woman you had a baby with and then she told you you'd never see your kid again and took you to court and you wanted to murder everyone while the whole thing was going down and we couldn't even talk to you? Nah, I forgot about her," said Paul.

"You talk so much shit you should call your mouth your asshole, P," said Bimbo with no meanness in his voice. "Well, after they killed my mom, I kinda forgot about Jessica, the baby, and that whole child support thing. I worked with the construction folks Gabe hooked me up with for a week or so, but then I stopped going. It was too fucking hot and humid out there, and all I wanted to do was stay home and get high until my mom's face stopped floating in front of me, you know?"

We all stayed quiet.

Bimbo took a deep breath and went on. "Anyway, I stopped paying and the bitch came at me through El Departamento de la Familia instead of reminding me with a text or something. The usual sh—"

"You got locked up for not paying child support?" asked Tavo. "My cousin Rubén has half a dozen kids with different women, and the son of a bitch doesn't pay any of them. Getting thrown in jail for that in this country is next to impossible, man."

"Well, not exactly," said Bimbo. "I mean, they don't arrest you and take you to jail. They sent me letters, you know. I went to court. Tried to explain the whole thing. I thought the judge would cut me some slack with my mom getting killed, but...you know, I was really sad and nervous and wanted something to calm me down, so...I showed up high and drunk. I don't remember what happened, but apparently, I told Jessica to go fuck herself and then told the judge to go fuck himself. A guard grabbed me to kick me out and I swung at him. That's how I ended up in jail. Oso Blanco. They can only keep you for six months for shit like that, but when my sis found out, she...somehow convinced my uncle Pedro to put up the bail money, so they let me out and here I am."

"So, you just got out?" I asked.

"Nah, got out a week ago, but—"

"And you're only letting us know now, you fat fuck?" asked Paul.

"No…well, yes—but listen," said Bimbo. "I had to take care of some stuff first. Plus, I got no phone. It got cut off when I got locked up and stopped paying it. Point is, I met a dude inside. José Luis. A Dominican. Good guy. We shared a cell and talked a lot. He got caught writing bogus checks for ghost employees for a company that didn't exist, but he has all kinds of things going on. One of them is hooking up Dominican women with single boricua guys, yeah? They hook up, live together for a while so they can get to know each other, and then get married so the woman can get citizenship. Then, a quick divorce. It pays twenty keys, man."

We looked at each other.

"You're really gonna do that?" asked Tavo. Bimbo smiled slightly. I didn't think citizenship was that easy to get, especially if you got divorced right after, but said nothing.

"¿Te vas a casar con una dominicana?" said Paul. Paul was always sliding back into Spanish whenever he was scared, drunk, angry, or surprised. In other words, often.

Since Tavo's family hadn't moved to Puerto Rico until he was ten, he'd never really picked up Spanish, and we mostly talked in English for his sake. We had all picked up English skills elsewhere, and we loved that it made our conversations feel private at school, but we still switched back and forth. Paul did it more than the rest of us. Luckily, Tavo had gotten used to it and almost always got the gist of things.

"I'm already living with her," said Bimbo. "That's part of the stuff I had to get squared away."

"Where are you living now?" I asked.

"Same place," said Bimbo. "My sis is living with her new boy-friend. I have the house to mys—"

"What's her name?" asked Tavo.

"Altagracia."

We looked at each other again. Altagracia was the name of a

Dominican house cleaner who had appeared in a comedy show on local TV when we were kids. She was always the butt of the joke in every skit.

Puerto Ricans always make fun of Dominicans, which is stupid because we're all in the same brown boat, but some boricuas feel superior to them even though we're second-class citizens from a colony where we can't vote in US elections. At least our colonizers hand us a blue passport when we're born. That gives us a chance to get off the fucking island, which leaves more space for the Dominicans who come in yolas to our shores, looking for the same better life we seek in the US. Las gallinas de arriba se cagan en las de abajo, pero todas son gallinas, my abuela used to say. The chickens on the top branch shit on the chickens at the bottom, but they're all chickens.

"¿En serio, cabrón?" asked Paul.

"I'm serious. She's not bad-looking, either," said Bimbo. "We have to talk to each other a lot, you know? So we have a story to tell when they ask us, because if they think we're faking it, they won't give her the papers and they'll send her ass back to la República Dominicana and probably throw me in jail for trying to fool Uncle Sam. So, we're practicing our story. You know, where we met and what we like and all that shit. I think she likes me. We'll see how it goes."

"Tú estás loco pa'l carajo, Bimbo," said Paul. Tavo laughed and spat rice. Even he could understand that. Bimbo just nodded.

"You've always known I'm crazy, papi," said Bimbo with a smile. "Tú sabes cómo nosotros lo hacemos. Now, if you fucking pigs are done with your food and asking me questions about my love life, how about we get down to business?"

"What do you need, man?" asked Tavo.

"Not here," said Bimbo. "Let's get into Gabe's car."

We picked up our plates, threw away our trash, and waved to the woman who worked as a cashier and translator at El Paraíso Asia, although she mostly used her hands and we had never heard her say a single word in Mandarin or Cantonese, not that we'd know the difference.

We walked to the parking lot and got into my car. Bimbo climbed in the front with me, and Tavo and Paul got in the back. I turned the car on and started the AC because late summer in the Caribbean gives you two choices: AC on full blast or death.

"So, what's this serious business you wanted to tell us about?"

The red neon letters that hung above El Paraíso Asia reflected on his eyes and made him look sick and strong at the same time. Bimbo didn't reply straightaway, just looked at each of us. He had something in mind, something I was sure had to do with his mom, but I was also pretty sure none of us wanted to hear it. You can fool yourself into thinking bad things will stay away if you don't talk about them, and we were all experts at doing just that. Hablar del diablo lo hace venir porque decir las cosas las hace nacer. Talking about the Devil makes him come because saying things brings them to life.

Bimbo cleared his throat and started talking.

"I drove by Lazer the day after they let me out. There was a skinny motherfucker working the door. He was standing right where my mom used to stand. It was...weird. Anyway, I'd never seen that dude in my life, so I know he's new there. I wanna talk to him."

"You wanna talk to him because you think he knows something about your...about what happened?" asked Paul.

"About my mom," said Bimbo, anger creeping into his voice. "About the motherfuckers who killed my mom. Yes. And y'all can talk about her, say her name. María. I say it a million times every fucking day. María. María. María. I'm gonna hold on to her until the day I die. Not talking about her murder does nothing to bring her back."

"What do you have in mind, man?" I asked Bimbo.

"Easy," he said. "We show up late and wait around until Lazer closes. Then we follow this guy to his car or his house or whatever and have a talk with him."

"Will this talk involve violence?" asked Tavo. "You know I don't like violence. It...it brings bad karma, man."

"I don't fucking know, man," said Bimbo. "I guess it depends on what he says."

"I don't think we should waste our time following some dude just because you—"

"I don't give a fuck what you think, Paul," interrupted Bimbo. "I don't give a fuck what any of you think. You either come with me or you don't. It's that simple."

Leave it to Paul and his fucking mood swings to be the first to be all in at María's wake and then the first one to step back when it was time to get to work.

"Tranquilízate, cabrón," said Paul. "En este carro, tú no tienes enemigos. I know you're angry as hell. I'm angry too. We all are. Thing is, following that dude and asking him questions can get you—us—in a lot of trouble. We don't know who he is. Cynthia says I should stop—"

"Ah, now it all makes sense," said Bimbo. "Cynthia says. Well, I told you, I don't give a fuck about what Cynthia says and I don't give a fuck about whatever trouble I can get into for asking questions. Trouble is waking up and not having my mom there. Trouble is worrying about my sister day and night because my mom was the only one who could keep her happy and under control. Whatever 'trouble' this motherfucker wants to bring my way is fine by me: He either doesn't know a thing or he knows exactly what I want to know."

"Fuck you, man."

"Nah, fuck you, P."

"There are ways to go about revenge," said Tavo, jumping in the middle. "We need a bit more info, Bimbo. That's all."

"I was locked up, so don't pretend you motherfuckers have spent more time thinking about this than I have. If you came to me and told me someone shot your mom in the face, I'd be down for whatever you want to do. I'm not gonna sit here and beg your asses to back me up," said Bimbo. "We've never done that, remember? We don't have to.

We stick together no matter what. Every time someone has come at you for being gay, Tavo, what have we done?"

The silence that followed Bimbo's question hung around us like a thing everyone disliked and no one wanted to touch. Finally, Tavo spoke.

"You've beaten their asses."

"We've beaten their asses," echoed Bimbo. "And do you know why we — and that includes you — have beaten their asses, Paul?"

"Because Tavo is one of us, and if someone fucks with one of us —"

"They fuck with all of us," Tavo and I finished like choirboys reciting a prayer.

"Exactly," said Bimbo. "And what did we do when that guy with the nose ring put his hands on my sis?"

"We beat him so bad he spent two days in the hospital," I said, remembering the way his face had looked after we were done. I had an image of the guy turning to the side because he was gagging and then spitting out a bunch of bloody teeth.

"And why the hell did we do that, Gabe?" asked Bimbo. "Why did we almost kill that motherfucker?"

"We did it because if someone fucks with one of us —"

"They fuck with all of us," said Bimbo.

He was right. I thought about it and I couldn't let him go alone. I could help keep him focused. I could keep him from doing something dangerously stupid. I could be the voice of reason, especially if Tavo didn't want to go.

"I get what you're saying, man, but this —"

"Hold your horses, T," said Bimbo. "I'm not done. I'm only getting started. We never go looking for trouble and you know it. We don't go out looking for violence or whatever. Those things find us. They always have. And we have never backed down. It's what we do, right? Think about it. What did we do when those huge motherfuckers pulled a gun on Gabe at the beach when he was selling jewelry? What did we do when we were at that bar that looks like a boat from the outside and those six guys got into it with Paul? What did we do that time I got caught shoplifting and the two security goons wanted to teach me a lesson? What did we do when we were partying at Babylon and four guys from some cruise decided to pull a knife on you and called you a faggot?

"I could spend three hours asking you questions like that and you would have to reply with the same thing again and again because you fucking know what we did. You know we did what family does. This is no different. You fuckers come with me or you don't, but I'm not asking you twice."

"I'll come with you, man," I said. I said it not because I wanted to but because I knew it was the right thing to say, the only thing to do after Bimbo had spoken his piece. Spoken the truth. I did it because I knew Bimbo would've done the same for me and because María had given me a place to hide from the ghost of my father and set a plate of food in front of me without even asking. I said it because no one else had said it, and their silence was starting to hurt.

"I'm with you, brother," said Tavo. Paul stayed quiet, but he looked at Bimbo and nodded. That was all he needed to say.

4

GABE

—

The meeting
A lot of questions
A shitty plan
The mood pendulum
Something awful living inside it

That Friday night we met at Bimbo's house. Xavier was home from school, and he didn't even need a little speech: I told him Bimbo had asked us to go along with him, and he said, "I'm there." It made me think about the oddness of their friendship because they loved each other like brothers despite being opposites.

Bimbo was a mess in school, and Xavier was all about doing better than those who went before him. Bimbo never talked about leaving Barrio Obrero, but Xavier always spoke of working hard and getting a house somewhere nice. Bimbo was a chubby guy who loved weed and greasy food; Xavier was in college because he was a gifted athlete. Bimbo sold drugs from time to time and seemed to be happy to follow in his mom's and uncle's footsteps; Xavier was all about upward social mobility and getting a legit job.

Still, they were outsiders, and that had been enough to make them brothers. None of us had more to lose than Xavier, who was doing exactly what he wanted to do with his life, and he'd been the first to say *I'm there* without hesitation.

We parked on the narrow street — Barrio Obrero's streets were all narrow — and as soon as we climbed the dilapidated concrete-and-metal stairs to Bimbo's apartment, I remembered the smell of coffee or food wafting down to greet me each time I visited, a sign that María was in the kitchen.

Remembering María made me think of how some people exist in the periphery of your universe without ever taking center stage. María had been like that, one of my best friends' moms and a woman I saw regularly and who basically took me in for a while, but she'd never been at the center of my life the way her son was. Her death had turned her into something else, a glue that held us together.

As soon as Bimbo opened the door, I remembered he now had someone living with him.

Altagracia was a thin dark woman with a doobie wrap on her head. She was wearing purple yoga pants and one of Bimbo's black T-shirts, judging by the way the thing covered her down to mid-thigh. The neck was so big on her that her left shoulder was hanging out of it, revealing a black bra strap that dug into her skin and made a tiny bridge of fabric between her shoulder and her collarbone. She was a collection of angles under big brown eyes.

She stood by the kitchen door and waved at us when Bimbo made introductions. Her slim hands matched the rest of her slender figure. Then she mumbled something to Bimbo, told us to have fun, walked silently into Bimbo's room, and closed the door.

"So, she's wearing your shirts and sleeping in your room?" asked Tavo with a smile on his face.

"Things are going well, papi," said Bimbo. "Don't hate the player, hate the game."

We sat around the tiny living room and waited for Bimbo to stop asking Xavier about school and life on the other side of the island, like he had moved to another country and not a place two hours away. Finally, he realized we were waiting for him.

"Shit, you're all expecting me to give you some instructions or something?" Bimbo laughed. We all cracked smiles. It seemed like he was fine just talking and not addressing things, and I realized that was also true for me. This didn't feel like a meeting where we'd have fun; it felt like a business meeting where we'd discuss the future of a company at the verge of collapse.

"Not instructions, you fat fuck, just some...guidance, you know?" said Paul. There was no humor in his voice. "Aquí nadie sabe qué carajo vamos a hacer con este tipo...o qué se supone que vamos a hacer si de casualidad te dice lo que quieres saber. It's like you expect us to help you stalk some random guy you saw working at the club and then stand behind you while you...what, slap the fucker around?"

Bimbo looked at Tavo as if apologizing for Paul's Spanish. "I haven't told you what we're gonna do with him, because I have no idea how things are gonna go, Paul," he said. Not *man*, not *P*; Paul. There was a difference there. "We're gonna watch him first, but if he works there, he probably knows something, especially if he's also dealing. We'll wait for him to leave, follow his ass, and ask him who he's working for and if he knows anything about what happened to my mom. That way we'll know more about the whole thing. Or not. I don't fucking know how it'll play out, you know?"

"So, what happens if he doesn't wanna talk?" I asked. I wanted to take control of the conversation because Paul's face was scrunched up and his tone had been enough for me to know he was in one of his moods. That pendulum had swung and he was now thinking this plan was dangerous and stupid. I didn't want this to turn into a fight. I didn't want Tavo to worry too much. I wanted to feel like we were on the right track to...something, and to feel less nervous.

"That's why I'm bringing you beautiful motherfuckers with me." Now Bimbo's smile was somehow that of an angel and a demon at the same time, and his answer was a sharp reminder that things could go bad.

"So, if this dude gives you some names...we're gonna go find some other guys?" I asked, wanting to know how things could play out. I wanted to know if bad could get worse and then maybe go all the way to fucked. Then it hit me; my nerves and discomfort came from the possibility of an angry Bimbo messing with a guy who was completely innocent.

"Yup."

"Find some other guys?" asked Paul. "What does that mean? Tonight? Tomorrow? Why am I the only one who has an issue with not knowing what the hell we're doing? It doesn't—"

"Listen, hermano," interrupted Xavier. "It sounds like this is just the start," he said. Despite being smarter than us, he always went along with everything anyway. It's the way he was built. For every time we'd helped him, for every small act of kindness between friends, he felt like he owed us his life, and we loved him for that. "The goal is to get info. Or so Bimbo says. We're there for backup in case the guy gets stupid. No biggie. No need for complicated instructions now. That will come later, at least if this guy gives Bimbo some names."

"So, we talk to him. Cool. And what are we gonna do if he gives you some names? What's the 'later' Xavier's talking about?" asked Paul. He sounded a bit calmer. Resigned.

"We already talked about that, Einstein: We get the names, we go find those guys," said Bimbo. "And, no, it doesn't have to be tonight, so relax."

"And what happens when we do find them?" asked Tavo.

"We're gonna kill them," said Bimbo.

There it was.

The silence that followed Bimbo's words was so dark and deep I was sure there was something awful living inside it.

5

ALTAGRACIA

—

Pressing darkness
A knife going up and down in the dark
Escaping Jarabacoa
Ghosts at the bottom of the ocean
Nightmares inside the moon

We're gonna kill them."
Bimbo's voice reached Altagracia as she sat near the window, blowing a stream of cigarette smoke into the night. She had no idea what Bimbo was talking about, but she didn't care. Men kill. Men lie. Men steal. Men fight for no reason. She was born into it, lived through it, and thanks to her brother, had escaped it just in time. Now she was living in the midst of it again, and she wanted no part of it. Unfortunately, her brother was sure this was their big opportunity, and she couldn't say no to him.

Bimbo was a sweet guy, and losing his mother had clearly unhinged him, but Altagracia knew he wasn't a killer. She'd always been able to "see" inside people. Her grandmother Ana had passed on a gift to her. There was something about bad men, a darkness that lived inside them, that she could see. Bimbo didn't have that in him.

Altagracia had learned about bad men early on. She was born in the outskirts of Jarabacoa, where her parents had worked in a hotel.

Her mother spent her days around the pool area, serving drinks and bringing food to tourists from all over the world, mostly Europeans. She would always complain about the comments male tourists made and hated when some of them got handsy with her after a few drinks.

Her father worked in the afternoons and late into the night, playing games on a stage or at the disco with drunken tourists. He'd never gone to school, but could have simple conversations in English, German, Italian, and French. He'd taught Altagracia some English early on, but then things had changed. Her father had started drinking, and when he lost his job at the hotel, he started vanishing for days at a time, coming back smelling like death and with dark bags under his eyes.

He also started hitting them like they were to blame for whatever had driven him to drink in the first place. Altagracia and her mother took the hits whenever they couldn't hide. Sometimes, when her father had been gone too long, she could feel his violence approaching, so she would walk for hours and hide at her grandmother's house.

Doña Ana, Altagracia's grandmother, always took her in and made her feel protected. Sometimes her mother came along, but Doña Ana would always get on her case and encourage her to leave her husband, so she came only once in a while.

Altagracia's brother never went with her. He had always been braver than her, stronger. If her dad was drunk enough, her brother sometimes managed to get the best of him. Dad would just come back angrier than the previous time. Altagracia kept having nightmares in which her father came to them in the middle of the night carrying a machete and chopped them into little pieces, starting with her brother.

Altagracia was fourteen when her father lumbered into her room at some ungodly hour and clumsily climbed into her bed. When he touched her, Altagracia realized he wasn't there to hit her. The touch was different, its intent something Altagracia hadn't understood, his hands going places her mother had told her no man should touch.

She told him he had the wrong bed. She said it sweetly, not wanting to startle him and make him mad. But he didn't listen and his hands moved faster, his thick fingers pinching her soft flesh.

Altagracia told him again, louder this time.

He didn't listen.

She screamed.

He covered her mouth.

She could feel the darkness inside him pressing against her, the stench of the dead rising from his mouth as he pressed it against her neck.

Suddenly, her father stopped. A pained gargle escaped his rotting mouth. In the darkness of her room, Altagracia saw her brother standing next to her bed. His hand went up and the knife he was holding caught some of the light that came through the window from a moon so full Altagracia had no doubt it was pregnant with nightmares.

Altagracia watched the knife go up and down, up and down. There were strange wet sounds mixed with her father's grunts. Then her father went quiet and stopped moving. She never screamed, her fear, anger, and confusion a thick chunk of something lodged in her throat.

The aftermath was ugly. Someone turned on the light. There was blood everywhere. Altagracia's mother screamed and cried. Her brother yelled at her for not kicking their father out long ago, for not doing what he himself had done — and not doing it the first time that man had put his hands on them. Her father, slumped facedown on the floor with one leg under her bed, lay unmoving atop a dark pool of blood.

Altagracia knelt next to her father, put her mouth to his, and did what she had to do to make sure his angry ghost wouldn't haunt her mother. The thing that came squirming out of his throat smelled like burnt hair and death. She swallowed it with tears in her eyes, feeling her father's evil scratch her throat and land in her stomach like a hot rock.

They didn't have much, which was good because they didn't have much time to pack. Altagracia packed some of her clothes in the backpack she used for school and grabbed the sacred book her grandmother had given her from its hiding spot in her closet. She was sad that she wouldn't be able to keep learning from the book, that she wouldn't get more knowledge from her grandmother, but she was happy to be leaving her father.

They left as the sky was beginning to turn that strange shade of gray that announced the dying of the night. Their mother refused to go with them. She wanted to protect them from the cops. She couldn't leave her aging mother behind. There were a lot of tears.

Altagracia and her brother walked for two days almost without stopping. They finally made it to the house of a man she'd never seen before. Her brother knew him. He asked for a big favor. They talked in hushed voices in the kitchen while Altagracia pretended to sleep on the man's bumpy, itchy sofa.

The next day two men came to pick them up in a brown truck and drove them all the way to the coast. They hung out at the beach all day, watching the tourists run in the surf and eat snacks from the stands that lined the beach. That night they walked to some rocks that had been placed there to keep waves away from the tourists and hopped on a boat as the sounds of merengue and bachata reached them from nearby bars.

Her brother explained that they were going to Puerto Rico. They had a cousin there who would find him work. Their cousin was the reason they were able to get on a nice boat instead of one of those yolas most Haitians and Dominicans were forced to use, and in which so many of them died, the dream of a better future still fluttering around in their heads. They were going to be okay, he told her. She believed him.

It was dark all around them, and the boat moved a lot, doing an angry dance on top of waves that made Altagracia feel like they were going to capsize at any moment. Altagracia felt sick, but she closed her eyes and tried not to think about sharks and all the dead people at the bottom of the ocean.

Morning came and the boat stopped. The men talked about pretending to fish and told Altagracia and her brother to stay hidden while it got dark again. After a few hours of fitful sleep, they got up and drank some coffee. When it got dark, they started moving again. After a while, the boat stopped and they were asked to come out. They were far from shore. Altagracia could see lights in the distance, but not in front of them. She thought again about sharks, about other things that lived in the ocean. Doña Ana's voice came to her then, telling her she'd be okay, that she would make it to shore, that she and her brother had done the right thing.

A man in a small boat emerged from the shadows and they drifted closer. He took them all the way to shore, dropping them off at the beach without a word and then speeding away. Everything had happened so fast that Altagracia didn't have time to process it, to give in to her fear. They finally came to a road. Her brother made a call on his cell phone and they waited hidden behind some uva playera bushes. Her brother kept telling her they would be okay.

About twenty minutes later, a blue van showed up. Her brother grabbed her hand and they got in the back of the vehicle without a word. It smelled like sweat and burnt plastic, but before she knew it, they were walking into a strange house with a big smiling man with a shaved head and a lot of tattoos just slightly darker than his skin. That, according to her brother, was their cousin Mateo.

That was five years ago. They'd gotten their own place since. Altagracia had worked at a few restaurants nearby, always getting paid under the table because she and her brother didn't have any papers. Then she started offering her services to people. She told them what she saw or answered questions about the things that troubled them. Some insisted on giving her money. Others brought food or clothes for her.

It was enough to get by. She even made enough to rent a small room next to a local pharmacy and hang a sign on top of the door that read LECTURAS/LIMPIAS/AMARRES/TRABAJOS.

Her brother...well, he made money. She knew he was up to no good, but he was good to her, and that was all that mattered. He got her work only at places where he knew the owners and made sure they were always respectful to her, which was more than their own father had given her.

She didn't much care about what her brother did while he was gone. Men were mostly awful, but if they weren't awful to you, it was hard to judge them for it. That's why when he'd talked to her about this opportunity, she didn't say no.

Altagracia didn't understand all of it, but she knew someone had killed Bimbo's mom, and her brother needed her to pretend they were going to get married so she could get her papers. She was supposed to make it look like they were in love, which had turned out to be very easy. Her brother checked in on her, kept saying this was their chance, so she should be a ghost and try to exist only for Bimbo. It felt weird, but whenever she thought about saying no or backing out, she remembered her brother next to her bed that last night back home, knife in hand and ready to protect her against a demon.

We're gonna kill them.

Her father had taught Altagracia a little English, but he'd also taught her a very valuable lesson: Men are dangerous and stupid. She would listen to Bimbo and report back to her brother. He would make sure everything was okay, he always did.

Altagracia exhaled another plume of smoke through the metallic window slats and thought about turning into a ghost, a silent entity floating through the world, safe from the dangerous thing that lived in all men and unafraid of the nightmares she knew hid inside the moon.

6

GABE
—

All stories are ghost stories
On the hunt
Heavy rains
Colombian neckties
Cracked skull

Old San Juan was our home. It's where we went to have a good time. We drank and partied there. We went there and laughed, argued, and even bled on its streets—or made others bleed. When the latter happened, we knew there was a good chance it wasn't the first time that spot had seen blood. Old San Juan's cobblestone streets were full of history. The colonial homes—some in ruins, some residences, and many turned into bars, food joints, and stores for tourists, selling vejigante masks, little bottles of rum, T-shirts, and everything you could think of with a coquí or the Puerto Rican flag on it—were reminders of how the Spaniards had taken over and forced their God, laws, architecture, and language down the country's throat.

On those streets, the steady stream of gringos clad in cargo shorts and flowery shirts unloading from cruises and filling our bars with their sunburned skin and superior attitudes reminded us that we were still a colony and there was nothing we could do about it. Despite all of that, we loved Old San Juan. It was a place full of ghosts and memories. It was the place that made us.

We took Xavier's car, a 4Runner in which we fit almost comfortably. Xavier and Bimbo rode up front. Tavo, Paul, and I shared the back seat. Squeezing in was always a dilemma because Bimbo was a big dude, but so was I.

I'd played baseball at school for years, but then something...made me quit. In high school I tried basketball, but a kid went down hard going after a rebound and crashed into my right knee. I had needed physical therapy and spent the last few games of our junior-year season on the bench. At therapy, we did a lot of leg extensions, leg presses, and eventually squats, so my legs grew. I liked it, so I gave up basketball and started lifting so the same would happen to the rest of my body.

Xavier kept the radio off as he drove. The sound of rain hitting the car was enough to keep us distracted. There were rumors of a storm coming.

The ride was short. As we crossed the Dos Hermanos Bridge into Old San Juan, I realized no one had said a word since we'd gotten into the car. There's that easy silence that often crops up when friends spend a lot of time together, but this wasn't it. This was like the silence in the car outside El Paraíso Asia, a kind of silence in which something lurked.

We parked in the Doña Fela parking garage. Lazer, the club where Bimbo's mom had been shot, was two blocks down on the street that runs right in front of the garage, Calle Covadonga. As we slammed our doors and regrouped, Tavo and Paul started to talk about a night we'd been kicked out of a bar for getting into a fight, but everyone had gone silent again by the time we exited the structure and faced the rain.

We jogged up the street toward Lazer, staying close to the buildings, ducking the weather. We were all tense, too alert. Xavier kept doing that head shake thing he did when he was worried, and Tavo kept pulling out his phone and checking it even though he had received no new calls, texts, or notifications. Every time he put the phone back in his pocket, he wiped it against his jeans first. Bimbo was quiet, too, but there was something in the way he hurried along with his head down that suggested determination.

When I looked at Paul, he was already looking at me, as if trying to make eye contact and ask me a question that never left his mouth. He kept putting his hand in the pockets of his jeans, taking them out, running them over his slightly wet face and hair, and shoving them into his pockets again. I wondered if he was nervous about what could go down, annoyed at the rain, or worrying about what Cynthia would think of what we were doing if she ever found out.

Reggaetón was pouring out of Lazer's front door. Besides a little bachata and some techno and hip-hop now and then when too many gringos showed up, it was all the club played. The sound of the bass was a massive heartbeat that gave the street life. I could feel it shuddering through my chest.

There was a short line out front, broken up because people were using the cover of the awnings and entryways of other businesses, all closed now, to stay out of the rain. At the door, right under a black vinyl awning with LAZER emblazoned on it, a skinny brown dude with a fresh fade wearing black jeans and a black T-shirt was quickly running a metal detector over people's waists and taking cursory glances at IDs before letting them in. We got in line.

I tried not to look at the floor in front of the club. I imagined María's blood would be gone, but the sidewalk was rough and I was worried I'd see a darker spot or something. I thought about her big smile in the Disney World picture they put up at the wake, the same smile she'd given me every time I showed up. I was trying to feed my brain something good, but all I could think about were those two spots where whatever they had used to fill the bullet holes in her face had sunk a bit. What if María had tried to run away and fallen right where I was standing?

My abuela had passed away two and a half years earlier, but I spent a lot of time with her before that. She was a bruja. In her house, there was a bathroom full of candles, a bathroom no one was allowed to use because that was where the spirits lived. She always mumbled weird prayers when we drove past a cemetery because she said the dead stuck around.

She also used to tell me creepy stories and then end with: *Todas las historias son historias de fantasmas.* All stories are ghost stories. The memory sent a shiver down my back despite the heat and the vapor the rain was drawing from the hot street. I could feel María's ghost there and suddenly didn't know what to do with my feet.

We shuffled forward to the last awning before Lazer's and talked about getting tripletas after. A minute later, the guy at the door signaled for us. Bimbo ran forward and stood in front of the skinny guy. He pulled out his driver's license, showed it to him, and lifted his arms to the side. The dude barely looked at the ID. He waved the metal detector over Bimbo's right side and then his left and quickly waved him in. He did the same with each of us. Just inside the door, Tavo leaned into Bimbo and asked him if that was the guy he'd seen when he drove by earlier. Bimbo nodded.

It was late and the rain had surely kept some people home, but there was a good crowd inside. Around thirty bodies circulated between the bar and the dance floor. Everyone looked tired. Some looked like they were trying to have fun but failing miserably. Clubs always remind me that we're all sad animals looking for something to lift us out of the mud we lived in and make us think being alive was worth it.

We pulled up to the bar and bought some Medallas. Puerto Rico isn't the US. Here you become an adult the moment you get your driver's license at sixteen, and the legal drinking age is eighteen, not twenty-one. Being a fucking colony is bad, but women can still get abortions without going to prison and we can drink earlier, so I guess we haven't lost every battle.

We dug our elbows into the bar and settled in. Xavier leaned forward and we pressed our heads together as much as we could. Xavier yelled over the music and told us about life in Mayagüez. He loved the freedom of having his own place and only attending classes from Monday to Thursday. He found the classwork manageable, but hated the two-hour drive he did on Thursday afternoons to come stay at his parents' house and again on Sundays to go back to his place. He complained about paying for gas and joked with Paul about bringing his laundry home for his mom to do every weekend.

Once Xavier was done, Tavo leaned closer to me and asked why I hadn't moved in with Natalia yet. He and Natalia were good friends, and Tavo was convinced she was the love of my life.

"That woman can change your life, dude," he yelled into my ear, making my eardrum tickle. "She's a hard worker, responsible, and has a good head on her shoulders. You'd be a fucking idiot to let her go and you know it." Between his family's moves all over New York and eventual jump down to the island, Tavo had missed a lot of school, so he was older than the rest of us. However, he seemed wiser than that to me, like maybe moving around a lot had forced him to start thinking about things earlier in life.

When it came to Natalia, I knew Tavo was right. I nodded. But I didn't like to talk about Natalia much. She made me feel emotions I'd never felt before and had me thinking about stuff I'd never thought about. The domesticity of it all still made me squirm.

Whenever Natalia spoke about getting into a program at some university in the US, and the two of us moving away together, it was like she was making me choose between her and everything else I knew and loved. I secretly hoped she wouldn't get into any program, so I wouldn't have to deal with that decision. That disloyalty made me feel like shit, but I ignored it like most other nasty things in life instead of dealing with it, until my brain moved on to something else.

The word *destierro* translates into "exile," but that translation doesn't really work. The *des* prefix means "to negate" or "the opposite of" whatever follows it. The *tierro* comes from *tierra*, which simultaneously means, in this context, "land, earth, and home." Destierro is to have your home negated, to be ripped from the place where you belong, to be uprooted from your land. The history classes I'd paid attention to in school had shown me that Puerto Ricans have a long history of migration, of destierro, but every time they leave, they become something else. The Puerto Ricans born in New York are Puerto Ricans, but they also aren't: they're Nuyoricans. Those who spend their lives in Florida or Chicago are also something else, some hybrid that bears the anger of the island plus all the bad stuff they face because they're too brown, too foreign, even if they're American citizens.

I didn't want to become that. I wanted to stay where I was born, to somehow help fix the mess I'd grown up in. Moving away felt like giving up to me, like becoming another desterrado, living in exile in a racist country that had kept my homeland a colony for too damn long and would forever treat us like second-class citizens.

I wanted to be with Natalia, but I also wanted to be *here* with these guys, drinking beers and looking for trouble.

I'd once heard someone say that you don't need a huge army to take over the world; you need three or four crazy motherfuckers who really love you and are willing to do whatever had to be done. These four were my crazy motherfuckers, and the world was ours to take.

After an hour or so, the traffic into Lazer slowed down enough for them to close the door and post a massive Black dude with a Kimbo Slice beard on a stool right inside the door. The skinny dude who'd been checking IDs turned off the metal detector, spoke to the big man on the stool, and then walked past us toward the back of the club. He disappeared down a little hallway that opened up next to the bathrooms.

A moment later, Bimbo said he was gonna try to score from the guy to see if he was running a side hustle and disappeared down the short hallway that led to a patio where people went to smoke or make out or yell into their phones away from the music. The little indoor patio was a remnant from when the place had been an actual house, a place where some Spaniard — and later some wealthy American — probably smoked fat cigars while the blood of colonialism tainted their souls.

Light from the back patio poured in and then died as Bimbo closed the door.

"I hope that dude gives him a name or whatever because I wanna get this over with," said Paul. He didn't sound angry, just in a rush.

"Da fuck is wrong with you, cabrón?" I asked him, trying to find a perfect balance between Paul being able to hear me over the music and no one else hearing what I had to say. "María was killed right outside that fucking door while working and you can't be here without complaining?"

"María got shot because she was dealing drugs, not because she was working the door," said Paul. "Y'all need to keep that shit in mind. The people who killed her are the kind of people who have no problem doing a drive-by, okay? You know the streets have levels. This is on another level, not ours."

Paul had never given a shit about levels or consequences or anything else. This was Cynthia talking through his mouth. It bothered me. It made me mad that maybe the motherfucker had a point. It also reminded me that I wanted to be there, but I was also thinking about Natalia, and that I'd feel just fine if Bimbo decided to drop the whole thing. Maybe I was worried. Maybe I was scared. Maybe Paul wasn't wrong and that was the thing that pissed me off the most.

Tavo put his hand on Paul's shoulder and spoke before I could tell Paul to go fuck himself.

"We know that, P," said Tavo, his voice loud but calm. "Remember when you thought that guy who worked with Cynthia kept hitting on her and we destroyed his car and scared him so bad he never went

46

back to the office? That was stupid. I mean, we probably fucked up his life for a while. You should've kept your cool, but when you didn't, we went with you. This is like that. We're not here because we want to; we're here for Bimbo. He'd do — shit, has done — the same for us."

Paul nodded just as Bimbo poked his head into the room and jerked his head toward the exit. We gulped down the rest of our beers and followed him.

Outside, the air stuck to our skin. The rain had slowed down a bit and the smell of stale, sun-cooked urine wafted up from the walls of historic buildings as we walked. In front of us, the skinny guy from the door was hunched over, heading down the same sidewalk, his body pressed close to the wall to protect himself from the rain. I looked around. There were a few people about, all of them moving quickly, but no one was behind us.

We kept on cracking jokes, collectively — and subconsciously — agreeing that not saying a word as we followed the guy would make us look shady. The skinny guy shook water off his arms and took the next parking garage's stairs to the third level. We followed him inside. Xavier pulled his keys out of his pocket. Just a group of friends heading to their cars.

The skinny guy pulled out a key fob, and the lights of a green Supra flashed red like the eyes of a demon. Outside, the rain grew heavier, the sound of it a constant murmur that drowned out everything else.

"Oye, primo," said Bimbo to the guy, breaking into a trot again. The guy stopped and turned. He looked calm.

"Dímelo," said the guy. He probably thought Bimbo was going to say something about his car. Or maybe he remembered him from Lazer and thought Bimbo just wanted to score again.

Bimbo walked up to him and asked him if he knew Roberto.

"Roberto?" asked the guy. "No." Skinny flicked his eyes to the rest of us and turned to get into his car. He'd been around enough to smell bad news. Bimbo moved forward and pushed him from behind. Hard. The guy slammed against the car and dropped his keys. He immediately turned, already reaching for his piece. Bimbo threw a right hook. It was bad and glanced off the guy's left temple, but it was enough to make him turn his face in my direction.

The guy still had his hand down, pulling his black shirt up. I threw a right that caught the guy in the chin. I'd stepped into the punch and put everything behind it. A clack erupted from the guy's mouth, and he fell against the car and slid down a bit. He was stunned, but not out. Bimbo grabbed his right arm, which was now under his shirt, and yanked it back. I grabbed the left one and did the same. Both hands were still mercifully empty.

"Check him!" said Bimbo.

Tavo stepped forward, threw both hands at the guy's waist, and pulled a big black gun, very much like the one Bimbo had placed on his dead mother's chest.

"What da fuck are you doing?" said the skinny guy in English. Probably another New York or Florida transplant. Or maybe he had just heard Bimbo speak in English and decided to switch.

"Who do you work for?" said Bimbo.

"Who da fuck are you?" asked the guy, his voice full of bravado I knew I'd never be able to muster if I found myself surrounded by five guys. "Let me go!" he screamed. He tried to shake us off. We held him harder, pushing his arms against the car.

"I said—"

Tavo jammed the gun into the guy's cheek, right below his right eye.

"No screaming," said Tavo. "We all keep cool and you'll go home in a few minutes, yeah?"

The rain roared like a beast. I looked to the side and saw curtains of water falling down hard. The storm folks had been talking about was coming, and this was nothing but a taste.

"Who do you work for?" Bimbo asked again before the guy could say anything else.

The guy looked at Bimbo with hatred in his eyes. "I'm not saying shit, bitch. Your boy didn't have a gun to my face, I'd be kicking your fat ass. Both of you. You want my money? Take my money!" He thrust his hips forward. He thought we wanted his roll.

Bimbo looked back at Xavier and Paul. "Pick up his keys and open his trunk. See if this motherfucker has a lug wrench in there or something."

Paul didn't move, but Xavier bent down, picked up the keys from the floor, and shuffled to the back of the car.

"This is what's gonna happen," said Bimbo as the guy tried to shake us off again. His skinny body was going nowhere with Bimbo and me holding his arms. "I'm gonna ask you who you work for again. If you say anything other than a fucking name, I'm gonna hurt you. Then I'm gonna ask you again. We're gonna do that as many ti —"

"Fuck you!" said the guy. "¡Ayuda! Me están asalt —"

Tavo pressed the gun harder into the guy's cheek. That shut him up.

"I said no screaming," said Tavo. "And we don't want your fucking money. Pay attention and answer the damn questions so we can be done here."

Xavier came back carrying a short black lug wrench. It was the kind that looks like a crowbar instead of a plus sign. Bimbo asked Xavier to switch places with him and grab the arm he was holding. Xavier placed the lug wrench on the grimy floor and took Bimbo's place. Bimbo made sure Xavier had a good hold on the arm before letting go. Then he moved forward and picked up the wrench. He stood next to Tavo in front of the guy and asked him again, "Who's your boss?"

"I said fuck y —"

WHACK!

Bimbo had quickly lifted the lug wrench and brought it down on the guy's head. It wasn't a killer blow, but it was hard enough to surprise me and stun the guy. A second later, blood started dribbling from the guy's hairline, just a shy trickle of dark red that seemed almost afraid to roll down his forehead. He looked dazed for a moment. Then he screamed.

Bimbo shot his left hand out and covered his mouth, slamming the back of his head against the curve of the Supra's roof in the process.

"Shut the fuck up!" said Bimbo through gritted teeth. "If you scream one more time, I'll hit you so hard your brains are coming out your ears. You hear me? Now tell me who you work for."

I looked at Bimbo. They say the eyes are the windows of the soul. If that's true, Bimbo's soul had taken a vacation.

"I'm not gonna tell you shit, you fat fuck! You're a dead man. You're all fucking dead!" His eyes jumped wildly to each of us and then back to Bimbo, but he wasn't screaming.

Fear had crept into the guy's voice, so he was making up for it with threats. He was overpowered, disarmed, and now bleeding. We were holding him down and he had a gun pressed against his face, and there was nothing he could do about it. Still, somehow, the stupid macho bullshit he'd grown up in, and the code of silence the streets had taught him, was blocking his common sense.

"Gabe, you're way stronger than this bitch," said Bimbo, looking at me. "Pull his arm to the ground."

I yanked the guy's arm down. He resisted. Bimbo took a much better swing this time and hit the guy in the balls with an uppercut that bent him over with a cough. Xavier and I took advantage of that, pulled him to the ground, and forced him to get on all fours. The guy groaned some more, inhaled deeply a couple of times, and then snapped out of it. He looked up at Bimbo and blurted something unintelligible. His threat flew out of his mouth in a little dart of blood and hatred. Bimbo didn't respond.

Then the guy stopped looking at Bimbo and turned his head toward me. The hatred in his pupils dug into mine. And I felt it way down. Knowing someone would kill you if they had the chance is a strange feeling. The guy tried to pull his arm away, but I held tight. I had control of my whole body and about sixty pounds on him, every one of which I was using to keep his open hand on the floor. Plus, Xavier had his other hand and Tavo still had the gun on him, now pressed against the top of his skull.

"That's enough, man," said Paul. "We're just here to talk to h—"

"Shut the fuck up," said Bimbo.

Bimbo placed his right knee on the ground and twisted his body toward the guy's hand. He pushed my hands up, grabbed the guy's wrist right below my hands, and pulled it forward a bit, forcing both of us to move a little in the process. Then, without asking him about his boss again, Bimbo lifted the lug wrench over his head and brought it down on the guy's fingers.

The metal clanked against the ground. Then Bimbo did it again. I swear I heard the guy's fingers crack on the second hit. For a moment time had stopped, as if the sound of the second hit had ruptured something crucial in the world and thrown us all into a different reality.

The guy was quiet.

The sound of the lug wrench hitting the floor still rang in my ears.

Tavo still had the gun pressed against the guy's head.

Xavier and I were still holding down the guy's hands.

The rain was a living thing right outside the garage, a thing determined to drown the world.

Then the guy howled. Just like before, Bimbo covered his mouth, but this time the sound was much louder and we were all in a weird position, so the scream slithered around Bimbo's hand and bounced off the garage's walls.

"Shut up or I'll hit you again," said Bimbo.

"Someone's fucking coming!" said Paul. We all looked at him. His eyes bounced between us and the stairs.

Tavo pulled the gun away from the guy's head, lifted his own shirt, placed the gun in his pants, and stepped back so he could see beyond the van that stood between us and the stairs. We stayed quiet, looking at Tavo. "I don't see anyone," he said.

"I swear I saw someone on the stairs," replied Paul. "A guy. He was peeking out, trying to hide."

We stayed put and waited for Tavo and Paul to say something else. They both kept looking toward the stairs. The sound of the rain grew louder in the silence. Then the guy made a weird sound and I realized he was crying. I was surprised he hadn't yelled for help while we all thought someone was coming.

"See anyone, P?" I asked. Paul shook his head without turning to me. Tavo pulled the gun out and placed it against the guy's head again.

"Who's your boss?" asked Bimbo, his voice calmer now.

"Papalote, okay?" said the guy, looking up at Bimbo imploringly. He had a snot slug shimmering under his nose, and his eyes were wild and full of tears. "I work for Papalote. Fuck!"

Paul made a sound like a deflating balloon. Bimbo looked at him and then at me. Papalote — a word some Spanish-speaking countries use for "kite" — was the drug kingpin of La Perla, Puerto Rico's trafficking epicenter. He was our version of El Chapo Guzmán or Pablo Escobar. He was the guy mentioned after every massacre in San Juan. He'd been behind a triple homicide at a big hotel a few years earlier and his name had been everywhere.

Last year, a massacre attributed to him had been on the news for days. Nine people in a small apartment. Two had been women. One was eight months pregnant. The killers gave everyone Colombian neckties — cutting right under their jaws and pulling their tongues through the hole. They'd sliced the pregnant woman open and done the same to the baby. Papalote was a fucking monster. He was also named as a suspect on the news whenever the feds grabbed a significant amount of kilos coming or going from Miami.

But he was untouchable in a way only unlimited power can make criminals untouchable. He was never seen anywhere. He never left La Perla. However, his hands were everywhere and he saw everything. This was bad. This was like jumping in a puddle and finding out it's deeper than the Mariana Trench.

Bimbo stood up with a grunt. The guy went back to sobbing. The rain started sounding like a warning.

"Okay, now let's get the fuck outta here," said Paul. We looked at him. His eyes were ricocheting between us and the stairs. He'd been quiet, staying out of it from the start. He'd spoken only when he thought someone had approached, and that wasn't like him.

"Shut the fuck up and give me a minute, man," said Bimbo. He turned to the guy again. "There was a woman working the door at Lazer before you came along. You know who killed her?" asked Bimbo.

The guy shook his head. The blood from his hairline was now a tiny river dividing his face. The mix of blood, tears, and snot made him look awful. I felt bad for him and hoped we could end this soon so he could take care of himself.

Bimbo stepped back and then kicked the guy in the face. His head flew back, but we were still holding him down. He made a noise, but it died in his throat when his head snapped. Bimbo moved forward again and stepped on the guy's shattered hand. The sound that came from his mouth was more of a wet groan than a scream.

"The woman? Her name was María," said Bimbo. "She was my mother." The last two words were full of static. Grief had broken Bimbo's voice. He sniffled. "You know who killed her?"

The guy was looking at Bimbo with something other than fear and hatred in his eyes. I don't think there's a word for what I saw there.

Bimbo ran his hand under his nose and sniffled again. Then he cleared his throat like a man who hated the feeling that had lodged itself inside him. "I'm going to ask you one more fucking time, man, and if you don't——"

"Luiso," said the guy. Bimbo stared at him. "All I know is there's... there's a guy named Luiso. He hooks everyone up with guns when they go out on a job. Maybe he knows! I fucking swear that's all I know, man. I swear." He sobbed. "Just...just let me go. Please."

"Not yet," said Bimbo. "Where can I find Luiso?"

"I...I don't know! I swear. I fucking swear, man."

"A number," said Bimbo. "You have a number? Know someone who does?"

The silence that followed was different. Sometimes you don't have to be great at reading people to know when they're lying. The guy's eyes darted down to his shattered hand. Then he lowered his head before looking at me again.

"Just fucking tell him, man," I said, speaking to him for the first time. "He's gonna kill you with that thing if you don't." I signaled with my head to the lug wrench in Bimbo's right hand.

"I...I don't know. I don't have a number, I swear. Maybe Tito knows how to get in touch with him."

"Who's Tito?" asked Bimbo.

"Big guy at the door. The one with the beard? I've seen them together. That's all I know!"

"Let him go," said Bimbo. Xavier immediately let the guy go. I didn't. What if he had another gun somewhere?

"Let him go, Gabe," said Bimbo.

I looked at the hand I was holding down. The middle and ring fingers were slightly crooked and much bigger than they'd been before. The skin covering them looked very red, almost starting to turn purple. It was his right hand, and it didn't look like he was about to do anything with it anytime soon. I let go and moved back.

Bimbo stepped forward and said, "Hey."

The guy looked up at him while falling back a bit to sit on his ass. He cradled his busted hand.

Bimbo lifted the lug wrench and brought it down across the guy's face. It was fast. The guy made a noise like he was choking on something and tried to put his hands up to protect his face.

Someone said, "Fuck." Thunder cracked somewhere far away, the sound softened by the rain. The guy moved, as if to scoot away. Bimbo hit him again, turning his head sideways. Hands can't stop iron.

Bimbo hit him again.

The guy went down on his right side. His face was a bloody mess and his nose didn't look the same. He mumbled something and blood poured from his mouth. I saw a couple of teeth in there.

"What da fuck are you doing, man?" said Paul. "Let's get the fuck outta here!"

Bimbo ignored him. He moved closer to the guy, lifted the lug wrench above his head with both hands, and brought it down on the side of his head. There was a loud thud and a crack. The guy twitched. The side of his left eye sank in a little and his eye closed. He shivered the way guys do in the UFC when they get knocked out.

I didn't want to be close to him, but I couldn't move. I looked at Bimbo, standing there with the wrench in his hands. The wrench went up like a dark prayer, hovered for a moment like the worst promise ever, and came crashing down again on the guy's head like the sword of some avenging angel.

"You're...you're fucking killing him, dude," said Tavo. His voice was low and scratchy.

"Did you hear the fucking name that came out of his mouth? If he identifies any of us, we're all dead," said Bimbo. He looked at all of us like we were idiots for not understanding his actions. "You motherfuckers don't know the streets like I do, so shut the fuck up."

The streets have levels, we always said. We'd said it when Bimbo got caught selling drugs at school the first time. We'd said it again when he got caught the second time and they kicked him out until all of us and many of our parents came to school to demand counseling and help as a solution, not throwing him out. We'd had it every time we got into a fight because we knew that beating someone's ass was a great way of making sure they never messed with you again but it could also be a quick trip to the grave if they were someone's kid, or cousin, or had an older brother who was hard.

We'd said it whenever someone we knew suddenly vanished and then we learned they had moved to the States to hide from people who wanted them dead. We knew Bimbo was deeper into the streets than any of us, that he had been born into it, thanks to his mom and uncle. He was right. Still, this felt very wrong. Death very rarely feels right.

"Listen," said Paul, bringing his hands up. "I get it, man, I really do, but killing him isn't—"

Bimbo turned back to the guy, who was making a strangled sound that seemed pulled from a nightmare, and brought the lug wrench up and down again. There was a loud crack. The guy's head was now more deformed on the side. He had a crew cut and I could see his skull had caved in just like the side of his eyeball had.

It reminded me of Bimbo's sister's dolls when we were kids and I'd stay at his house to hide from my father's ghost. We would steal her dolls and squeeze their heads, momentarily turning them into deformed monsters. Then we'd let them go just to see how long it'd take for the dent to pop back out. I knew the guy's skull wasn't going to return to its original shape. He was beyond fucked.

I was about to say we had to go, but Bimbo had other ideas. He brought the lug wrench up and hit the guy again and then again. It was quick. Blood started coming from his eye. He had stopped moving. The pool of blood was about to reach my shoes. I moved back. The guy's head was a misshapen mess. Under his eye, bone fragments were poking up from the flesh and blood like small boats in an ocean of gore.

"Fuck! Fuck this," said Paul. "We need to go. Now."

Tavo placed his hand on Bimbo's shoulder and pulled him back. "That's it, Bimbo, no more," he said. "We need to go."

I managed to pull my eyes away from the floor and looked at the guy's torso. He wasn't breathing. His hands weren't moving. There was no sound coming from his mouth. He was dead.

7

GABE

—

Death is always there
The rain won't stop
A prayer to Elegguá
The darkness swallows a gun
Worrying about Papalote

Death is always there and it can show up at any moment — a bullet, a bad fall, a heart attack, a car accident — but when it shows up like this, it eats a piece of your soul and rents a room in your nightmares.

Bimbo dropped the lug wrench. It clattered against the floor and made us all jump.

"No," said Xavier. "Pick it up, Bimbo. It has your prints all over it."

Bimbo bent down and picked up the lug wrench.

"That's it," said Paul. "We need to move. Now!" He took a few steps back, turned, and started walking. His movement shattered the invisible thing that was holding us in place.

I knew La Puntilla didn't have cameras. It was an old parking garage and they'd never gotten with the times. Everyone knew about the nonexistent CCTV because people talked about how convenient that was if you managed to find someone to fuck but couldn't take them home or afford a motel. It was a stupid joke, but the moment Xavier mentioned prints, that was the first thing that came to mind: Cameras. Prints. Hairs left on a body. Blood on our clothes. Witnesses. It was easy to end up in prison for a small detail, a tiny oversight.

I looked down at my hands. They were clean. I looked down at my pants. There were drops of blood near the cuff of both legs. I looked back the way we'd come. I was surprised not to see bloody footprints behind us. I had moved away from the growing puddle of blood just in time. A shiver ran down my spine despite the oppressive heat, the humidity from the incessant rain, and the smell of exhaust in the garage.

Tavo was walking next to me. He was still holding the gun.

"Yo, T, the gun," I said.

He glanced down at his hand. He looked like he couldn't believe what he was holding. He held the gun away from himself as if it carried some disease. Then he lifted his shirt and made the gun disappear.

We were walking quickly away from the body. Bimbo was moving strangely. I saw he was trying to jam the bloody lug wrench down into his pocket and covering the other half with his shirt.

We heard voices on the stairs.

"Fuck, fuck, fuck." It was Paul again. He was pale, and there was a film of sweat coating his forehead.

"So, you guys wanna get some food?" asked Tavo. Talking was the right thing to do.

"I'm in," I said. At that moment, I thought I'd never feel hungry again.

The voices moved away. The people coming up the stairs had stopped on the second floor. We walked faster.

We made it down the stairs and out of La Puntilla. It was raining hard. We ran toward Doña Fela.

No one screamed and we didn't hear sirens in the distance. Still, I was having a hard time filling my lungs, like there was something cold wrapped around my chest, preventing me from taking in enough of the warm, wet air.

By the time we reached the entrance to the Doña Fela garage, we were soaked and breathing hard. We probably looked strange, five dudes moving through the garage like they had the Devil on their backs, but we were dying to get into Xavier's car and as far away from the dead guy as possible.

His shattered skull.

His legs twitching.

The growing puddle of blood.

The bone shards poking through the mess.

The images kept flashing in my mind, and every time they did, my brain tried to tell me it wasn't real, that I had imagined it all. Sometimes lying to ourselves is the only survival mechanism that makes sense.

Xavier unlocked the doors and we climbed in. He pulled out of the parking spot and made his way down the wide ramp to the exit. He had left the ticket in the car, so he grabbed it and paid at the meter. No one said a word. No one offered to chip in. No one told him where to go. Our collective breathing inside the car was the only soundtrack to the nightmare we'd just experienced.

Bimbo pulled out his phone and started looking for something as Xavier drove west on Covadonga. The car's wipers were going fast, pushing sheets of water off the windshield, the window immediately blurring the world again after each swipe. Xavier and Tavo were athletes, so they got their breathing under control before the rest of us.

"Are we just...going home?" asked Xavier.

"Yeah," I told him. I wanted to be as far away from San Juan as possible. Living on a tiny island isn't a problem until you start wishing you could put a thousand miles between you and some nightmare.

"Oh, Elegguá, tus ojos brillantes lo observan todo porque estás destinado a ver todo ahora y para siempre," said Bimbo. He was reading from his phone. "Elegguá, te pido que vigiles detrás de las puertas, en cada rincón, en todas las encrucijadas y los senderos de mi vida porque en cada espacio puede acechar el peligro, uno de mis enemigos o alguna maldición." No one knew what the hell he was going on about. He was creeping me out.

"What are you doing, Bimbo?" asked Tavo, his voice tense. Bimbo ignored him and kept reading.

"Elegguá, tú eres un orisha justo, lleno de vida y sensible como los niños—"

"Hey, Bimbo!" said Tavo. "What the hell are you doing, man?" I guessed not knowing what he was saying had made Tavo even more confused than the rest of us. Chaos is one thing, but chaos in a language you don't speak is chaos multiplied.

"It's...it's a prayer, man," said Bimbo. He reached into the top of his T-shirt with his right hand and pulled out the red-and-black beads that always hung from his neck. "You know, for protection. We don't want that guy's ghost to haunt us."

"Haunt us?" asked Paul. "What the fuck are you talking about?"

"We killed him," said Bimbo. "Maybe you don't believe in that stuff, but I do. I've...I've seen things. And my uncle told me stories that would give you nightmares. I don't want this guy's ghost showing up in my room in the middle of the—"

"No, no, no," said Paul, shaking his head. "Stop. *We* didn't do shit; *you* killed him. I didn't even touch him. You smashed his fucking brains in with...with the—"

"That's right!" said Bimbo, interrupting Paul. "*I* killed that motherfucker. So you all can go to sleep at night, okay?"

The ghost of what he'd said hung inside the car like a bad smell. For a few seconds, the pelting of rain and the desperate swishing of the windshield wipers were the only sounds. Then Bimbo looked down at his phone and started reading again. "Elegguá, sabemos que eres bueno, que eres justo, pero también sabemos que es mortal tu ira cuando eres ofendido o molestado. Sabemos, oh Elegguá, que puedes ser tan bueno como un ángel y tan malo como el diablo."

We know, O Elegguá, that you can be as good as an angel and as bad as the Devil.

Whatever Bimbo was doing was the opposite of what we needed. I imagined the guy bleeding on the ground, his ghost floating over him, swearing he would haunt us all. I wondered if I'd start hearing noises when I was alone in the house. I wondered if I would have to go with my girlfriend to get one of those limpias she and her mom regularly got with some blind woman Natalia claimed was a witch.

Estamos rodeados de fantasmas y todas las historias son historias de fantasmas.

It was my grandmother's voice, as clear as if she'd been sitting next to me in the car. We're surrounded by ghosts and all stories are ghost stories. She was right.

"Stop, man," I said. "Just...stop. We need to figure out what we're gonna do."

"Yes," said Xavier from behind the wheel, his eyes still on the road in front of us. "What's gonna happen when they find the body?"

"Well, then it's a good thing I took care of that for you." Bimbo paused, searching our faces for some acknowledgment but probably getting only horrified, clueless expressions in response. "Dead men don't identify people, okay?" Bimbo continued. "So, there won't be a gatillero sitting outside waiting for you the next time you leave the house. Why? Because I killed that motherfucker, so I guess you can thank me for protecting your sorry asses."

"Okay, but...," said Tavo, "what if someone saw us, and Papalote's men come after us when they find the body?"

The name brought back the uncomfortable silence that had submerged us since the man was first mentioned. It was a monstrous silence. Saying Papalote's name was like saying death, and none of us wanted to think death was coming for us.

Estamos rodeados de fantasmas.

"Nah, we're good," I said. "There was no one around—"

"Bullshit!" said Paul. "I told you I saw someone near the stairs, looking at us. I'm sure they were there. They peeked from behind the wall like they were trying to stay hidden. Then we made a big deal out of it and they went away or something."

"Whatever, man," I replied. "A drunk person. Maybe someone who had the wrong level. Or they heard that guy screaming and took a quick look but wanted none of it. Whatever. We were pretty much covered by that van. All we have to do is lay low for a while and it'll be fine."

"Laying low sounds like a good idea to me," said Tavo. "But what happens next? Bimbo has the name he came looking for, but we're not going after Papal—"

"No, we're going after the guys who pulled the trigger and killed my mom," said Bimbo. "All we have to do is ask the dude with the beard how we can get a hold of—"

"Aren't you satisfied with killing that g—?"

"I killed him because I had to, but he didn't kill my mom. I killed him because he could put everyone in this car in the fucking ground, not because I wanted to. Now we're going after the guys who did it."

Guys. Plural. Always. I got it, because it was usually a driver and a shooter, maybe two shooters if you wanted to make sure you got the job done, but we had just left a body with a shattered face in a pool of blood in a parking garage, and the thought of adding two more to the list made me feel sick. What if I had to do more than punch a guy and hold his arm next time? What if they got to their guns before we could do anything about it? And this was Papalote and his people, which meant we could end up...I already knew where we could end up.

I tried to push those thoughts out of my head, but doing so took me to the crushed skull we'd left behind...and then that guy showing up in my room in the middle of the night to drag my ass to hell, his head busted like that blond dude from *Pet Sematary*.

"Slow down when you go over the bridge, X," said Tavo. "I need to get rid of this fucking gun."

Bimbo unlocked his phone and started reading again, but he kept his voice low. His mumbling wasn't much better, and I found myself paying attention and recognizing a few words over the constant sound of the rain.

Elegguá.

Orisha.

Muerte.

Protección.

As we went over the Dos Hermanos Bridge, Xavier slowed down. Tavo lowered his window a bit and looked around. A spray of water came into the car and sprinkled my face. Tavo hurled the gun out over the water. We saw it disappear into the darkness and the rain. I wondered how many guns were down there, how many weapons used to kill people rested under that bridge, which looked so great during the day. Then Xavier stepped on the gas and Tavo wiped his hands. "There, one less thing to worry about."

"This is the country of don't say shit and mind your business. I'm not worried about prints on the gun," said Paul. "What I'm worried about is Papalote."

8

GABE

—

The storm is coming
Haunting memories
Estamos rodeados de fantasmas
A prayer to Santa Muerte
A death

I woke up to noises in the kitchen and the smell of coffee. The brain fog in my skull wasn't enough to cover what had gone down a few hours earlier, and the ugliness peeked through it like a shark's fin protruding from the muddy waters of my brain.

I thought about turning around, finding the cool side of the pillow, and falling back into oblivion for a while, to force that stupid shark to return to the bottom, but my mom had the TV on and that was it; I was done sleeping.

Sitting up, I ran my hands over my face. I prayed that Bimbo's explosion of violence would make him realize one dead guy was enough and that last night turned into the kind of thing you remember from time to time but never talk about.

Like Gisela.

She had gone to our school and was a year younger than us. She was pretty, a popular sophomore, and full of life. She'd had a huge crush on Tavo. He didn't pay attention to her, which was something we came to understand only years later.

Gisela had trouble at home, and one sunny Sunday morning, she jumped out of her seventh-floor balcony, and the pavement in the parking lot below didn't give a flying fuck about her youth or good looks or the possibility that I had a crush on her that was as bad as the one she had on Tavo, or the fact that maybe life had a few sweet surprises in store for her.

Nah, the pavement shattered her body, but for almost half an hour the impact didn't kill her, a broken doll who was conscious enough to realize there was no undoing that fatal jump. The idea that maybe regret had come over her while she was lying there always made my stomach feel like something dropped into a very deep hole.

They couldn't move Gisela, because lifting her would've made her insides spill out, so her death became a spectacle. Neighbors came out. People screamed. Parents pulled their children away. Gisela's mom ran down to her and passed out a few feet from her dying daughter.

We were hanging out at the beach when it happened. We'd walked there from Tavo's house. Our phones started blowing up. We ran to Gisela's building, which was only about six blocks away.

When we got there, it was chaos. Folks going somewhere or returning home stumbled onto the gruesome scene and were reminded that death is always near. Someone puked under a tree and moved on to escape the too-real nightmare. I didn't stick around after the cops and the ambulances showed up. None of us did.

The next morning, we pretended to go about our business at school until the principal stopped everything to say some words about Gisela over the PA system and then offer help. We moved around and talked and went to class as if her ghost weren't hanging in every damn hallway and classroom, and we tried to convince ourselves we were unchanged, that we were still young and strong and happy and indestructible. But we knew we weren't.

That night my mom sat down next to me at the kitchen table, and touched my face like she was trying to sand the sadness off it.

"¿Estás bien, mijo?" she asked.

Three words.

They broke me. I wasn't okay.

I cried. I cried until I bent in half.

The question didn't really need an answer. My mom just stayed there, her hand on top of my head like a silent blessing. She did the best thing she could have done and kept quiet, but got up and held me, and it felt like she had started holding me the day my father died — and never let go.

After a few minutes of that, I was done. So was she. I stopped crying and took a deep breath. She squeezed me one last time, as if to push some of her strength into me, and walked away.

Gisela's death became the first thing we instinctively knew we couldn't joke about. Everyone talked a little softer and drank a little harder and tried a few new pills, but no one partied on balconies for a while and no one judged her best friend, Mónica, when she came to school high for a couple weeks and then her parents took her out and sent her to rehab. Then time did its thing and no one talked about Gisela again.

Everything that had happened with Bimbo since his mom's murder pushed these thoughts to the front of my head again. I didn't know where the skinny guy from the parking garage would fit into my life. He wasn't my friend. I didn't even know him. But some other people would mourn him.

My thoughts had grown heavy, uncomfortable, so I shook my head to try to shake off the ghosts.

Estamos rodeados de fantasmas.

Fuck. My grandmother had been right.

I got up, used the bathroom, and then walked to the kitchen. As soon as I walked in, my mom started talking.

"The lady says the tropical storm is a hurricane now," she said.

"That's what, the tenth this season? I've lost count. I hope the sucking tube gets this one too."

The sucking tube—el tubo que chupa—didn't exist. Historically, Puerto Rico has been relatively lucky in terms of escaping big hurricanes, so people say there's an invisible sucking tube hanging somewhere over the island that sucks storms north and keeps them from hitting us.

While the weather lady rambled on about the Category 1 hurricane, I grabbed a cup from the cabinets on top of the sink and poured myself some coffee. The cup had little green leaves on it and fancy cursive words that read *It's the little things in life.*

Mom moved nervously. She kept looking at the TV and then at me. The lady on the screen was going on and on about possible trajectories. I tried to focus on what she was saying, looked at the screen. The name of the hurricane appeared at the bottom.

MARÍA.

Sometimes life's sense of humor is like a knife to the heart.

I was swallowing my second sip of coffee when I heard my phone ping in my room. I left the cup on the table and went to grab the phone from where it was charging on the floor next to my bed. I expected it to be Natalia. I didn't know what time it was, but she had ESL classes every Saturday morning. She wanted to develop her English skills in case she was accepted into one of the nursing programs she'd been applying to in the States. About six months ago, she'd asked me to speak only English to her...and never again tell her she had a Sofía Vergara accent.

The text wasn't from Natalia. It was from a number I'd never seen before. It read CALL ME BIMBO. It was enough to make me smile. I'm sure the humor of his text was lost on Bimbo.

Calling him was not something I was ready to do. I wanted to finish my coffee first and then take a shower. I called him anyway.

"Gabe," he said.

"What's up, man?"

"You busy this afternoon?"

"I want to be, if I'm being honest," I said. He didn't say anything. I thought I'd lost him for a second, then heard his breathing. "Listen, I—"

"No, I get it," he interrupted. "I'd rather be busy myself, but I need to talk to all of you and make sure that we're all on the same page. Last night was...heavy. I understand if y'all want to stay home and let me handle this shit myself."

I didn't know if I wanted to go along for this ride. In my mind, I could see the guy's crushed skull bleeding into the grimy floor of the parking garage, his legs kicking out a bit as death came to drink his last breath. I could see the tiny shards of bone poking from his cheek right underneath his eye. Walking away would be the smart thing to do. I knew it, and I could hear Natalia's voice saying it in my ear. One night of following Bimbo on his quest, and I'd witnessed a fucking murder. That was enough.

Then I saw Bimbo playing video games with me, keeping me entertained because he was used to not having a father and I was a new member of that club. I saw him going with me during our sophomore year when my mom came home crying because the pool guy at one of the houses she cleaned had tried to force himself on her. I'd wanted to kill him, but ended up having to pull Bimbo away from the guy after he kicked him in the head and the dude passed out and started shaking.

I saw Bimbo swinging on two gringos at once because Tavo had misinterpreted their friendliness and asked one if he could buy him a drink and they called him a slur. I saw Bimbo—chubby Bimbo with glasses—with bloody knuckles after many fights that had nothing to do with him. I saw Bimbo coming to visit whenever I was down because he had a car before the rest of us did. I saw Bimbo there, filling the hole left by my father. I saw Bimbo my friend, my brother, always there. The one thing I didn't see, the one fucking thing I had no recollection of or couldn't imagine, was Bimbo complaining, making excuses, or sitting one out because it had gotten ugly.

The answer was out of my mouth before I had time to think it through.

"I'm with you, hermano," I said. I meant it. It scared me. It was the right thing to do. Bimbo would do anything for any of us, and doing the same for him was the only option.

"Thanks, G," he said. I heard him exhale. Knowing I'd seriously considered bailing made me feel like shit. "Thanks," he said again, like someone turning the knife sideways after stabbing you. Then he hung up.

I placed my phone back on the floor and stared at the bookshelves I had on the wall right next to the bed. It was a cheap black thing I'd bought for thirty bucks and put together myself when Mom got on my case about the stacks of books piled up against the wall. She always had a way of using the word *animal* to mean much more than you'd think. It'd dig into your thoughts until you felt dirty and worthless. Most of the shelves sagged before the thing was full. It was mix of crime novels by writers like Jim Thompson, some old novels my dad had owned, and a lot of horror paperbacks by writers like Richard Laymon, Stephen King, and Bentley Little.

There was a space in the middle of the third shelf, where I had a small altar. My grandmother had helped me set it up. There was an incense burner there, pictures of my grandparents, a little statue of Santa Muerte that Natalia had bought for me at the botánica her mom always went to, and a statue of San Lázaro that had been on my grandmother's night table until the day she died. I wasn't very religious, or at least not so religious as Bimbo with his necklaces and prayers and candles, but like every other kid who'd grown up immersed in the chaos of the Caribbean, I believed there were forces out there that could help you or help ruin you. I sent out a prayer to God, Santa Muerte, my dad, and whichever saints and Orishas happened to be around and listening: *Please, let this shit end well.*

I went back to the kitchen to finish my coffee. My mom was still there, listening to the news and scribbling some chicken scratch on a torn piece of yellow paper. She was heading to the grocery store before María showed up. Once the news mentioned the word *hurricane,* everyone would run out and the shelves at every grocery store on the island would look like something out of a zombie movie. My mom hated that and liked to get there as early as possible. She'd come back with cans, batteries, and bottled water. I was sure her diligence, and her worry, had something to do with losing my dad.

"Hijo, voy a comprar agua y eso. Te veo luego," she said. She came over and kissed the top of my head before grabbing her keys and heading out. I turned off the TV, finished my coffee thinking about the way Natalia's lips would taste after she drank coffee, and took a shower, hoping the warm water would wash away the previous night.

After the shower I went back to bed and turned on my little TV. The plan was to watch something and kill time before meeting up in Old San Juan, but I fell asleep. I woke up to the sound of my phone. I thought it was Natalia, but I was wrong again. She was probably still in class. Tavo's name was on the screen. I picked up, sure he needed a ride for tonight.

"Gabe," he said. There was something in his voice that scared sleep's ghost right out of my system and made me sit up and grab the phone tighter.

"You good, man?" I asked. "Need a ride for tonight?"

"No," said Tavo. "Listen, man, they...they killed Xavier."

9

GABE

—

The walls of El Morro
Henry's story
They sliced his neck
El camino lo abre Elegguá
Sharks

We were sitting on an east wall of El Morro. It was one of our favorite spots in the city, the place we went to when there was nowhere else to go, when we needed to plan something important, or when we just wanted to sit close to the ocean. Tonight was different, like we were caught in a storm that wouldn't move on.

In front of us, impossibly blue, was the Atlantic Ocean, teasing us with the vast, unreachable world that existed on the other side of it. To our left was El Morro, a huge monument to colonialism. The wall we sat on — as I'd learned after many school projects and Puerto Rican history classes that ignored everything from the Taíno genocide by the Spaniards to the US takeover that kept us a poor colony all the way to the present — had been built sometime in the 1600s.

Right underneath us was the Santa María Magdalena de Pazzis Cemetery, which everyone just called the Old San Juan Cemetery. A national treasure, the cemetery was where plenty of important Puerto Rican figures had been laid to rest. José Ferré, the brother of Governor Luis Ferré, and Sor Isolina Ferré, the Mother Teresa of Puerto Rico, were there. So were the songwriter Rafael Hernández, and Dr. José Celso Barbosa. But my favorite was Pedro Albizu Campos. Albizu Campos was a warrior for Puerto Rican independence. A poster of him adorned my bedroom wall next to one of Bob Marley. Many of Albizu's most famous sayings resonated with me, someone who hated living in a colony: Cuando la tiranía es ley, la revolución es orden. *When tyranny is law, revolution is order.* Si el voto cambiara algo, sería ilegal. *If voting changed anything, it'd be illegal.*

I loved the cemetery and knew all its stories, like the fact that in the northeast corner, there was a tomb known as la tumba de la bruja, where people of various religions performed rituals in the middle of the night. Now, however, the cemetery brought me no comfort. It was a place full of ghosts who couldn't save us.

Like everything else in Old San Juan, the cemetery had been built too close to the water. Over the years, the waves that lapped at the cliff that gave El Morro its vantage point had eaten away at the terrain below. As a result, you could sometimes find dark holes on the sea cliff and remnants of old caskets poking out from the dirt. After big storms, it wasn't rare to see debris from graves floating around in front of the darkness of the reef. Local fishermen refused to fish there, and folks refused to venture out in small boats because there were many stories of boats vanishing. Everyone had heard tales of sharks feasting on human remains right off the shore. And we had all heard that there was something beyond the reef that was responsible for the missing boats, but no one had a name for whatever it might be. Either way, we had a good idea who was responsible for the bodies.

To our right, separated from Old San Juan itself by another huge wall, was La Perla, Papalote's kingdom. La Perla is what gringos call a shantytown or a slum, but it had made some improvements over the last two decades or so. It was beautiful to look at; a cluster of colorful houses—pink, yellow, blue, red—built literally on top of the ocean. Between them, like giant cavities in a shiny smile, were abandoned homes and gray, stained, graffitied ruins. The neighborhood showed up in popular music videos and looked picturesque from atop our wall. It was a place tourists loved to see. It was also the center of the heroin trade on the island and a deadly place unless you belonged there or understood how to navigate it.

A year or so back, Xavier, Tavo, and I had been on our way to Calle San Sebastián when we came upon three drunk assholes rocking flip-flops and polo shirts with popped collars yelling at someone on the ground. The man on the floor had a long beard and he was screaming in English. We knew him. He was a homeless junkie born and raised in Florida named Henry, who was always around when we went to Old San Juan. He liked bumming cigarettes from Xavier and telling us stories about his previous life as a captain for hire for wealthy people.

We liked Henry and hated bullies, which is a bias you develop when you grow up as an outsider, so we walked up to the three and told them to leave Henry alone or we'd knock their teeth down their throats. The trio quickly moved away.

The moments right after saving someone from a beating are awkward. Henry thanked us in that slow, mumbled frog croak that heroin users develop. We told him it wasn't a problem, then we stood there, not knowing if he needed a doctor or if we should just help him up and carry on with our night. Finally, Xavier told Henry he was in the mood for coffee and we should all head down and get something at the little café in Plaza de Armas. Xavier was a good guy, so I went along with it, knowing the coffee lie was all about feeding Henry instead of giving him money that would end up as more heroin in his veins. Henry nodded.

A few minutes later, with an orange juice and a muffin in front of him, Henry brought his hands up and started to pick at his food while Tavo, Xavier, and I sipped our coffees. I'd seen many busted hands — from accidents, from working construction, from fighting — but Henry's hands were unlike any I'd seen before. Besides the grime and broken yellow nails, there was dried blood on them, and a bunch of scratches that looked like they were infected, and he had dark spots all over his palms. He was picking at the dark spots and grimacing. I asked what was wrong with them.

Henry told us that, years before, Papalote had stolen a horse from someone just to let them know he could. The animal had then died or been shot—Henry wasn't clear on this. Regardless of how the beast died, the fact remained that Papalote was stuck with a huge carcass on his property that was quickly decomposing under the ruthless sun. To solve the problem, he drove to one of his places of business and offered the first four junkies that came to get their fix fifty bucks a head to pull the dead horse out to the reefs bordering La Perla and tie him out there for the crabs and other sea creatures to feast on.

Fifty dollars is a lot of money for a junkie, and being on friendly terms with a drug lord seemed like a good idea, so Henry and three others quickly agreed. Equipped with their questionable strength and a couple of ropes, the foursome set out to accomplish their mission. Unfortunately, once in the water, they learned two things: waves are much stronger than they look and walking on a reef is easier said than done, especially when you're dragging a dead horse while flying on smack and aren't used to walking on jagged rocks.

The four men managed to get out there and tie the horse down to the reef, but it took them much longer than they'd thought. By the time they had figured everything out, the sun was going down and the tide was coming up. They were about to return to shore when Henry saw something come out of the water, something that wasn't a crab or anything else that was supposed to be out there. He stood and watched, sure that it was either a trick of the light or a joke, but then realized it was neither.

It was a thing that looked like a man. He ran. They all ran. If walking on a reef is hard, running on it is impossible, so Henry and the rest of the men fell and landed on top of sea urchins a few times. The black spots he was picking at on his hands were spikes still buried in his flesh. He had been picking at them for two days and said he had managed to get most of them out. Then he said he hoped the ones that were really buried in there would come out by themselves.

We thought Henry had finished his tale, but we were wrong. Henry used his wrecked, shaking hands to break his muffin in half, pour sugar on each portion, and wolf it down. Then he killed the small bottle of juice in three swigs and recapped it before talking again.

"Papalote was waiting for us when we got to the shore. He'd been watching us work, making sure we'd done what he was paying us to do. I'm sure if we hadn't, all four of us would've gotten a bullet between the eyes. Anyway, he told us to get in the bed of a truck parked just up the hill from the little beach down there at the end of La Perla. He drove us to one of his two bars down there. When we got to the place, he made us climb down from the truck and told us to walk in. Then he sat down, gave us some beers, and offered us a gig.

"He needed more stuff handed to the reef. He said the horse was a little test, but that we would be bringing bodies out there. He offered to pay us in heroin, so we all agreed on the spot. Then he stood up and did a thing with his hand. A second later, each of us had a fucking gun pressed against our temples. He said we were now his employees, and that we had to keep our mouths shut. If he found out one of us had told anyone about our new arrangement with him, he'd kill us and find some other 'fucking junkies'..."

At some point during Henry's story, Tavo, Xavier, and I had leaned forward. Yes, Henry's brain was full of chemicals that made people see things. No, we didn't think we could trust everything he'd just told us. But his words lined up perfectly with the stories we'd been hearing since we were kids about something living right beyond the reef in front of La Perla. They say there is a bit of truth in every story, and what Henry had told us made that possibility grow into something we weren't sure we could process.

"So, what's out there?" I asked Henry. "What eats the bodies? What is this thing you said kinda looked like a man?"

Henry looked at me. He had green eyes that I was sure had helped him with the ladies or the guys or whatever he was into back when he was a captain for hire. Now they looked like counterfeit gems flashing with all the things he'd lost.

"Stuff you're better off not knowing about, my friend," he said.

One thing I knew about junkies is that they often have to be somewhere else; that they are stuck in a perpetual state of movement driven by their eternal quest for the next fix, and Henry was no different. Before I could ask him anything else, he muttered something about needing to go meet a friend by a parking garage. He dabbed at the blood on his hands with the napkin they'd given him with his muffin, stood up, and thanked us for the food and for giving him a hand with the three guys who were messing with him earlier. Then he waved a bloody hand and took a few steps away from our table. Tavo, Xavier, and I were looking at one another, full of questions, when Henry turned around and looked at us with those green eyes I was sure had once shone like shallow, clear ocean water.

"Fourteen years as a boat captain, and I never stepped on an urchin," he said. "Now look at my hands." He raised his ruined palms to us. His picking hadn't improved them at all. "Just...stay away from fucking drugs, guys."

I remembered that story vividly because it had been weird and bloody, like the best and worst stories San Juan had to offer. But I also remembered it because we all smoked weed regularly and had at one point or another tried shrooms or pills or done a line at a party, but we all stayed away from heroin. After we told Bimbo and Paul the story Henry had told us, they didn't crack any jokes. The fact that they had also stayed away from heroin was a testament to the story's power. Strange how ruined lives can sometimes effortlessly dish out salvation.

I thought about the dead guy in the parking garage and then

thought about Xavier. He'd died alone. He died afraid. He wanted none of this shit.

Then I thought about the cops: Would they come around asking questions? Then I remembered the news from that morning: There had been twenty-two murders over the weekend. We were done crying. A strange mix of nerves and anger had replaced the hole of sadness that had occupied my chest since I got the phone call about Xavier. The whole damn country couldn't have a single day without someone's life lost, someone being killed. The cops wouldn't come by asking after Xavier. No one gave a shit.

"Do you know what happened?" asked Paul. He looked calm, but his bloodshot eyes and shiny, puffy face told another story.

Tavo had done his best to fill us in when he arrived, but it'd been too much for him, and all he managed to do was cry and make us join in. Hugging those guys up on that wall reminded me of doing the same thing at María's wake. The smile on her picture came to me. I wished we could smile soon.

"They killed him. Right in front of his house, man. They…they sliced his neck. He bled out. A neighbor found him in the morning as he was leaving for work." Tavo's voice cracked again.

They sliced his neck.

He bled out in front of his own fucking house.

Those words did something to me. Death is death, but when the particulars are vague, it's easier to deal with as a concept, to comprehend, to stash away somewhere between "everyone dies" and "shit happens." This was different. Deliberate. Intentional.

Everyone was quiet for a bit. Tavo sniffled and the sound of the ocean in my ears became everything.

"They sliced his neck?" asked Bimbo. His voice was lower. He seemed to be handling the thought with kid gloves.

"Yeah, man. Fuck. And…and they took his eyes." Tavo took a deep, trembling breath. I understood what each of the words he'd said meant, but together they made no sense. There had to be a mistake.

Tavo inhaled shakily again and tried to speak while looking at Bimbo, but managed only to make a noise and choke on the words trying to crawl their way out of him. Then he exploded in tears, sobs bursting from his throat like a monstrous cat trying to claw its way out of a hole. I placed my hand on his shoulder and gave it a rub.

"Fuck," said Paul. "Fuck, that's some dark shit. Too dark, man. His eyes! Estaban tratando de mandar un mensaje..." He looked at Tavo and switched back to English. "There's no fucking way what they did to Xavier and what Bimbo did to that guy in the parking garage aren't related—"

"Listen," Bimbo interrupted Paul. "It doesn't fucking matter if I was the one swinging that lug wrench, okay? This isn't about me anymore. This is about all of us. They killed Xavier because they caught him alone. What if they come for you next, P? What then?"

Paul stayed quiet. The muscles on the sides of his jaw were working hard, sending small ripples down his face. I imagined him trying to crush his grief, guilt, and anger between his molars.

"What the hell are we gonna do now?" Tavo was broken. He was the one who kept us in check, and seeing him looking like a lost kid was enough to break me all over again.

"First we need to calm the fuck down," said Bimbo. "Then y'all need some guns. If Xavier had been packing, he wouldn't be—"

"Are you sure about that?" asked Paul.

Bimbo turned to him, and for a second I was sure he was going to take a swing. If they fell off the damn wall...

"I'm not sure of anything, P," said Bimbo. "What I know is that my mom is dead and now Xavier is dead and any of us could be next. Now...well, now I'm gonna kill them all and—"

"Kill them *all*? Who's 'all'?" asked Tavo. Bimbo had been looking at Paul while he spoke, like he was explaining something, but he turned and looked at Tavo before speaking again. His eyes softened, but not much.

"The dude with the beard. He might know who we need to talk

to. The guy who gets folks guns. I'm sure he knows who pulled the trigger. Once we know that, I wanna take them out."

"Listen, man," said Tavo. "The motherfuckers who shot your mom deserve to die. I get it. But what happens after? We got some info from a guy in a parking garage, and a day later, Xavier is fucking dead. He...he didn't fucking deserve what they...You really think putting two more motherfuckers in the ground is gonna be the end of it?"

Bimbo put his hand on Tavo's shoulder and looked out, his eyes scanning La Perla. "The men who pulled the trigger are gonna pay for what they did. I don't know why Papalote wanted my mom dead, but I'm gonna kill the motherfuckers who did it. I have a plan, a way of making them look the other way while we do it. I'll do that part alone if y'all don't want to —"

"No. You're fucking crazy, man. I'm out," said Paul. We all looked at him.

"You should let him fin —"

"Nah, it's all good," Bimbo interrupted me. "For real, it's fine. I get it. I'll do the thing myself if I have to. I was angry about my mom, but now I'm angry about my mom and about Xavier."

"I already told you I'm with you, man," I said. I had no idea if my words were meant to comfort Bimbo or to show Paul he was a coward and a lousy friend or to let Xavier's ghost know I was going to make the assholes who killed him pay for what they had done. I didn't care. Everything felt out of place.

"I'm out." Paul brought his hands up. It looked like he was trying to tell a bunch of dogs to stay put. He took a few steps back and shook his head. "Y'all are crazy." He pointed down at La Perla. "I get it, Bimbo. I really do, but this is too much for us. You've always said the street has levels, and now you wanna go all the fucking way down to the last fucking level and take out Papalote's guys with...what, a little help from your uncle and the three of us? Tú estás loco pa'l carajo, tipo. Nah, I'm out. I can't do this. I'm sorry."

Paul turned around, took a few steps, bent down to place his right hand on the wall, and jumped down. He disappeared for a second. The sun was going down fast, and the world, like our souls, darkened. No one spoke. Paul's head appeared again. He kept walking, making his way up the hill and away from the wall. He never looked back.

The voices in my head were going crazy.

Xavier was dead.

Two more guys.

When the hell had that become part of the conversation? That was impossible. I had to talk Bimbo out of it.

"This...this plan you have," said Tavo, taking another deep breath. His voice made me focus on something other than the static in my head. "I wanna hear it. I can't let you two take this on alone, but unless you have a solid plan...I don't know, Bimbo, this is a lot."

"It is a lot," said Bimbo.

I wanted him to say more. I craved some kind of reassurance. I wanted to hear him say his uncle had an army ready to go to war and we could sit this one out. I wanted Paul to come back and apologize for being an asshole and say of course he'd stick with us — with his brothers — no matter what.

Instead, Bimbo stayed silent, his eyes scanning the colorful houses down below. Tavo looked out at the ocean, angry under dark clouds. I knew he felt about it the same way I did. Or maybe he was thinking about going back to New York, about leaving all this mess behind. I looked at the horizon, that blurred line behind which the rest of the world was always hiding, always waiting, and saw the last sliver of sun go under. Not even the sun wanted to stick around for this.

There were some people still out and about, a mix of families with kids ready to go home and the folks who were just getting to Old San Juan for one last night of partying and drinking before the storm hit. Both groups belonged to a different world than ours. We were part of something awful now, something none of us could take back. Something that felt impossible to fix. The darkness, usually a comfortable thing that signaled good times, now felt like a threat.

Bimbo put his hand deep in the right pocket of his jeans and pulled out some colorful beads. Necklaces. Red and black. He untangled them and gave one to Tavo and one to me.

"What's this?" I asked.

"El camino lo abre Elegguá," he said. Then he looked at Tavo. "Elegguá is the Orisha who opens all the roads. He moves silently and gets things done. We're gonna do the same. This is for protection. Even if you think it's silly, please wear it."

Tavo and I brought the necklaces over our heads at the same time. Bimbo bent down and placed another necklace down on the wall.

"That one was for Xavier," he said. He had one more. He didn't say anything about it and placed it back in his pocket.

We stood there for a few minutes, looking down at the necklace, not wanting to accept what it meant. Xavier was gone. The pain was so big it bled into every thought I had.

After a while, Bimbo spoke. "You still think about that story we heard about something out there eating corpses after big storms, Gabe?"

"I do, B. All the time."

"That's how it always is. Someone is always trying to eat you, you know? We're surrounded by sharks even when we're on land."

I had no idea what he meant by that, but I didn't like the sound of it.

"There's a hurricane coming," he said. He was right. Above us and over the ocean, the sky looked angry. "They...they named it María. It'll probably stop everything and make the whole island go dark for a few days if not weeks or months. Like always. We're gonna become the sharks in that darkness. We're gonna be sharks for my mom, yeah? For Xavier."

"Yeah," said Tavo and I. That was it.

10

GABE

—

Natalia

Tears

A thing to burn

Six heads in a trunk

Burn them to the fucking ground

After leaving Old San Juan, I found myself on my way to Natalia's place. Once I realized where I was headed, it made sense. I felt dirty, like there was something dark and grimy stuck to me, and I didn't want to take that home. I also didn't want that thing to come with me to Natalia's place, but I knew that if anyone would be able to make me feel better, it'd be her.

Natalia had a way of getting to the core of things that affected me. She talked and explained and asked questions until she revealed to me some inner truth that had been hiding from me all along. She often surprised me in the process, the way she could be ridiculously smart and somehow make me smarter when I was with her. It's not that she put ideas in my head; more like she knew how to remove the debris that often clouded my thinking and had the tools required to pull out what lived underneath.

But she also worried, so I had to make it sound like we were in control. I had to convince her that this was the right thing to do. And I hoped I'd convince myself in the process.

None of it worked.

I saw Natalia's big brown eyes and her pretty face surrounded by a mess of black curls and I broke down.

"They killed Xavier," I said. The words felt like chunks of my heart tumbling out of my body.

Natalia pulled me in for a hug. Her hair smelled great; one of those fragrances with a name I can never remember. I found myself weeping again. I was born and raised hearing that men don't cry, but that's bullshit. For people who cry regularly, it can be a way of exorcising small demons, a way to cope with the ugliness of the world. For those who bottle things up, tears always feel like blades running down your face.

We were standing right outside her door, but it started raining, so we made our way to her small kitchen table and sat down. When I looked at her face, I realized she was crying too. Before she could ask me anything, I found myself telling her what had happened. I left out the part where Bimbo bashed that guy's brains in with a lug wrench. Then I was done. I was empty, all cried out. Sadness had shown up again and placed a sleeper hold on my anger.

For a few minutes, Natalia was nothing but sweet. She touched my hair, placed her head against mine, rested her hands on my shoulders, and kissed the top of my left ear while holding me. She told me everything was going to be okay. It felt great. Then — and a part of me knew this was coming — she asked me what we were going to do next. The worst thing about smart women is that they smell the stupidity on everyone else. I knew lying to her would be useless. She would find something in me and know I was lying. So, I told her the truth, and watched Natalia's eyes change. I could see a hurricane brewing in her pupils, and suddenly every word out of my mouth sounded incredibly dumb.

"So, who was it?" she asked. Her voice had quickened. The rain became stronger, like an echo of Natalia's alarm against the windows.

"Who was what?"

"Cut it out, Gabe," she said, her eyes burning mine. "You said you got some info from that man in the parking lot. So, who did it?"

"Papalote." Lying to her was useless.

"¿Papalote? ¿El bichote de La Perla ? That Papalote?"

"Yeah."

Natalia looked away from me and inhaled. Then she lowered her head and exhaled like she was trying to push something out of her body.

"Papalote kills people, Gabe. He kills a lot of people. The things he does always end up on the news. When I started college, he was on the news for a few days because they discovered his people were using Dominican women as mules, and many were dying from the amount of drugs they were forced to ingest before getting thrown on a boat. A couple months ago, they found six heads in the trunk of a car right outside La Perla. Before that, it was that massacre in that nightclub. And don't forget the Colombian necktie thing! He kills women and babies, Gabe. He—"

"Yo sé—"

"No me interrumpas, carajo," she said. "This is bad. This is very bad. You'll all end up dead."

My silence spoke volumes, and Natalia didn't like a single word I didn't say.

"Ustedes son estúpidos. Don't do this. I know you're all sad and angry, but this isn't a dumb movie. There's no...cómo se dice...escenario? Scenario?" I nodded. "There isn't a scenario where this works, Gabe. Vengeance isn't an option. You're gonna get hurt. You could put your mom in danger. You could put me in the danger!"

"So, what's the option? Call the cops?"

"No, and you know it. The option is forget about it and move on."

I said nothing again.

"Nosotros hemos hablado de esto mil veces, mi amor," Natalia said, her voice softening a bit.

"What happened to English only?" I said with a smile. Humor had always been my coping mechanism when things got heavy with her.

"Good point," she said, but she didn't smile back. "We've had this conversation before, mi amor. We have talked about how you and the boys are always out there, and I'm not saying you're looking for trouble, but trouble...you know, it seems to find you. It scares me because you act like a kid but you're a man and you need to understand that the world is...unforgiving. You guys are convinced that you're...how do you say indestructibles?"

"Indestructible."

"Ah. Anyway, you think nothing and no one can mess with you or hurt you, but Bimbo's mom was shot in the face and died...probably thinking about her kids, on a dirty...acera? Sidewalk! A dirty sidewalk. And now Xavier. *That's* real life."

She paused for a second, but before I could respond she plowed on. "You guys always start swinging the second you feel...provoked, and you come up with the stupidest ideas I've ever heard. This one is the stupidest of all! You act like youth is a...a thing to burn..."

"I know, you're right." I usually said things like that to get her to stop tearing me a new one. Everything I did with the guys seemed logical until Natalia and I talked about it. Then it started looking dumb, and I hated that.

"No, don't say I'm right. I know I'm right. This is about our future...or you not having one. Do you think I like spending my Saturdays taking English classes? En verdad, las odio. No, but I do it because I want to get into a good graduate program and get out of here. Get *us* out of here. But your little plan for revenge is not going to get you anywhere except into the...cementery...and you know it."

"Cemetery. Sin la *n*."

"¡Que se joda! Are you even listening to me?"

"Yes."

Natalia had started pacing, but she came over to me and grabbed my face between her hands. They were warm. "I *need* you to listen to me, Gabriel. I want you to be alive, with me, and I want you to move to the US with me like we've talked about…So, stop doing stupid shit." Outside, the wind picked up and the rain made a whooshing sound.

I could promise her that, yes, I was going to stay away from this whole mess, that I'd figure out a way to move to the States with her. Instead, I offered up a weak smile. Lying is one thing, but not telling the truth is a different story.

Natalia took my smile as an answer, thankfully, and leaned over to hug me again. Natalia was a castle as much as she was a woman; a strong thing that made me feel safe. She released me from her arms and stood up, still smiling. It reminded me of María's smile in that Disney World picture they'd had next to her coffin. Then I thought about Xavier's relaxed smile. Those two smiles had been extinguished. I'd never hear Xavier laugh again. I'd never hang out with him or hug my brother again.

That wasn't okay. I had to make someone pay for that. I smiled back at Natalia as hatred, grief, and anger threatened to make my heart explode. She was right about me seeing youth as a thing to burn, and I was going to use it to burn those responsible for María's and Xavier's deaths to the fucking ground.

11

GABE

—

Gas station symphony
An awful nightmare
Two small coffins
A pool of blood
The world shatters

I stayed with Natalia that night. She and her roommate Keyla had lax rules about letting guys stay over. It boiled down to keeping the bathroom clean.

Natalia was paying for her studies with a part-time gig as a research assistant at the university, and Keyla, her housemate, worked at a clothing store at Plaza Las Américas during the day and shook her ass in reggaetón videos at night. Their combined efforts got them a small two-bedroom joint on the second floor of a house in Isla Verde that backed up against a gas station. Across from the gas station was Avenida Isla Verde, and on the other side of it, the tall buildings that lined Isla Verde beach.

I was focusing on every sound to keep my mind occupied. Natalia's relaxed breathing was inviting me to try to sleep, but I feared what was waiting for me on the other side of consciousness.

The barely concealed holes in María's face.

Xavier's empty eye sockets looking at me as he bled out.

The tiny pieces of bone erupting from the guy's face on the garage's floor.

Things from beyond the reef, ready to devour anyone who tried to leave the island.

Suddenly, Xavier's mom was standing in front of me with a gun in her hand, the barrel pointed at my face. "You did this," she said, and as soon as she pulled the trigger, I felt my body falling.

I woke up with a start.

It was still dark out, but I could hear the cars zooming down Avenida Isla Verde on their morning commute. Natalia had to go meet her mom. They were going to get some more bottled water and canned food. I had to leave. I used the bathroom and splashed cold water on my face, making sure everything was pristine before I left. Then I kissed Natalia and escaped down the stairs before she could lecture me, again, to be careful.

I was deep in my thoughts when I pulled up in front of my house.

Then it hit me.

There was something on the door.

Graffiti. Some kind of symbol. Black. It looked rough, like someone had drawn it in a hurry with a big marker. The dark lines made two jagged rectangles; one almost as wide as the door and a second one, smaller, on top of that one. A cross with lines inside it sprouted from the middle of the smaller rectangle. There were small coffins, or what looked like coffins, on each side of the cross. I had no idea what the graffiti meant, but with everything that had happened in the previous forty-eight hours, it couldn't be anything good.

I simultaneously wanted to make sure my mom was okay and to get back in my car, hit the gas, and keep going.

Mom won out.

I stumbled into the house without realizing I was holding my breath.

There was someone on the floor in the kitchen.

My heart stopped.

My mom's body was sprawled on the floor, facedown, a small pool of blood around her head. Her hair was in a bun, which meant she'd been getting ready to go clean a house.

A strangled scream escaped my throat as I ran to her.

They'd killed my mom.

They'd fucking killed my mom.

I knelt next to her, my knees slipping on her blood, and turned my mom around, my tears blurring her face. I expected to find empty eye sockets, but her face looked relatively untouched.

The soft rise of her chest shook the world.

"Ma!" I called to her. "Ma. Ma. Wake up, Ma!" The two letters became a prayer.

She moaned and moved her arm.

"Ma!" I was trying to hold her still, but my hands were shaking.

Her eyes fluttered open.

She was alive.

The world stopped shaking.

I bent down and held her, my face against her head, my tears falling on her hair.

A moment later, she touched my face.

She said my name.

I was not alone.

12

GABE

—

The attack
More wind and rain
A white car
A father's ghost
Aviso de huracán

O nly one guy, but I told you, someone else was waiting in a car outside." My mom was sitting across from me at the kitchen table, holding a bag of ice to the swollen gash on her head.

"And he said something about a package?" I'd asked her at least half a dozen questions already, but I needed to know everything that had gone down. It was raining outside, the wind making the mangroves behind the house whisper. The wind had continued to pick up. Hurricanes don't just show up; they start telling you they're coming way before they get to you with gusts of wind and heavy rains.

"Yes." She took a long sip from her coffee mug, and I could see that the ugly lump on the side of her head had blown up to the size of a baby's fist, but at least it'd stopped bleeding and looked like she wouldn't need stiches. "The man was holding a small box and said something about signing for a delivery. As soon as I took the chain off, he kicked in the door and I stumbled back. When I looked forward, he had a gun. He told me not to scream, asked me if there was anyone else in the house. When I said no, he pulled out a phone with his other hand, made a call, and said, 'He's not here.' Then he came up to me...I was standing right there, and he...he hit me in the head with the gun. It hurt. Then he hit me again. Harder. I remember the feeling of something running down my forehead, and then the world went black and...There's nothing more until I woke up and you were here."

He's not here.

I was lucky to be alive. A tightness squirmed its way around my insides. They'd come for me, and my mom had almost gotten killed.

"What about the car?" I managed to choke out.

"What car?"

"You said there was someone waiting in a car outside."

"It was a white car," she said, clearly losing her patience with me. "That's all I know. Once he kicked in the door, I stopped paying attention to anything else."

A white car. Two men. I needed to know as much as possible.

"Gabriel..."

My mom usually called me Gabi, mijo, or Gabo. If she called me Gabriel, I was in trouble.

"What are you involved in now, Gabriel?"

I hesitated. How much could I tell her?

"Yo no soy pendeja, mijo," my mom said. "Does this have something to do with María's death?"

It wasn't really a question, since she already knew the answer.

My mom reached across the table and grabbed my hand. "Don't be stupid, mijo. I know you love Bimbo, but think about Natalia. Think about me."

"I am thinking about you. I'm gonna get you out of here to —"

"No," she said. "I'm not leaving my house."

"But —"

"But nothing. This is where I've lived most of my life. This is where you were born. Your father is still here. I'm not leaving."

Your father is still here. I knew my mom, and fighting with her was not going to get me anywhere.

"But how — ?"

"Stop." She let go of my hand. "I won't open the door to anyone. But I'm not leaving."

"I'll fix this," I said. The words rang hollow, a pantomime of what they should really mean.

My mom took the remote control from the middle of the small table, where she always left it, and turned on the TV. On the screen, the same woman from the other morning was pointing to a storm and talking about increasing wind speeds.

"La cosa esa viene pa'ca, mijo," my mom said. *That thing is coming this way, son.*

I paid attention to the TV. The lady kept gesturing with her hands in front of a screen displaying a massive hurricane.

"El Centro Nacional de Huracanes emitió ayer por la mañana un aviso de huracán para Puerto Rico ante lo que parece que se convertirá, si continúa la trayectoria esperada, en el paso del huracán María por la isla..."

Every year we would hear many warnings throughout hurricane season, but sometimes those warnings carried the dark weight of certainty.

I tuned out, thinking of ways to protect my mom that didn't include killing a bunch of people, but kept looking at the screen. Puerto Rico was a tiny, slightly rectangular green speck between the Dominican Republic and the British Virgin Islands. In front of it was a lot of blue and then a round beast, white and massive. The lady kept talking as the beast went from white to a mix of blue, yellow, orange, and red at the center.

María, when nameless, had hung low in the Atlantic, howling its way across the ocean. Then it got meaner, faster, stronger, and now it was pushing up against the Virgin Islands. If it swung up soon, it'd pass just to the north of us, bringing a lot of wind and rain, but nothing too serious. If it didn't swerve up soon, we were in trouble.

She'd tear the street to pieces and we'd be without water or electricity for days, with the heat stuck to our bodies and my mom's tiny radio spewing out stories about destroyed homes and dead people. Rivers would turn to morgues, carrying folks away, and trees would come crashing down even weeks later. It reminded me of my father every single fucking time.

María was a monster, clearly ready to feast.

13

GABE

—

A veve
Barón Samedi
The god of death
Stained sidewalk
María is coming

Fuck. That's a veve," said Bimbo as he slammed his car's door.

"A what?"

"A veve." He frowned, pointing to the weird markings on my front door. "Voodoo shit, man. Happened to my uncle…Anyway, people use them in their rituals."

"What did your uncle do about the veve?" I wasn't sure I wanted to know the answer.

"Uh…" Bimbo had a strained expression on his face, like he was trying to remember something he'd forgotten to study. Even though he never gave a fuck about school, he still always looked a little guilty when it came time for tests. "Uh…I think Uncle Pedro said the loas were the only thing keeping him safe. He was worse than my mom was, and you know she was always lighting candles and praying and putting fruit and rum in that altar she had in her room. Anyway, every loa has one of those and…" Bimbo had pulled his phone out and was typing and moving his finger around on the screen. Then he tapped on something and turned his phone around. "This one is for Barón Samedi."

"And who the hell is Barón —?"

"A very powerful loa." Bimbo turned the phone around so he could read. "Says here he's the god of death. He takes souls into the underworld," said Bimbo, grabbing at his neck and holding his red-and-black necklace with the fingers of his left hand while still reading from his phone. "This is some dark shit, man. Says here Barón Samedi is feared because he's the master of the dead. I...Listen, we can read about it or do something about it, and after what happened with Xavier and now with your mom, I think we should do something about it."

Bimbo's eyes opened a little more than usual. I could tell he'd just had an idea.

"Get in the car," said Bimbo, climbing into the driver's seat.

"Why? Where are we going?"

He closed the door without answering. I felt the pull of the house, telling me to get back inside and ride out the storm with my mom. A gust of wind rocked the car as if on cue. Then something wrapped itself around my lungs and squeezed. The black markings on my door — the veve — made me question everything: Would I put my mom in more danger if I stayed? Was she at a greater risk all alone?

They'd come close. Way too fucking close. And they knew where I lived. They had to be dealt with. Burned to the fucking ground.

I got in Bimbo's car. It took me five minutes to realize we were going to Xavier's house. Bimbo was driving like a maniac, the radio blasting El Gran Combo, filling the silence between us with an energy that felt alien to my ears.

Something stirred in me when we turned onto Xavier's street. I'd been there a million times. I'd sat at his table, shared meals with him and his parents. I'd camped out on his couch countless times when we were too broke to go out, watching something on TV or talking and showing each other dumb stuff on our phones. I'd gotten high in his room and talked about the future, made plans, made no plans, imagined an adulthood in which our friendship remained untouched. Now I was here again, but I would never get to hang out with him.

We pulled up in front of Xavier's house, a squat one-story building with beige walls marked with dirt and rain stains and an off-white garage door that had clearly been hit by more than one car. Then I saw the house's door. The same drawing I'd seen on my door was there, the two coffins like eyes peering into my soul.

"Vete pa'l carajo," I said. Bimbo grunted an acknowledgment.

We sat there, the sun going down behind Xavier's house, the sky full of angry gray clouds, and stared at the black lines on the light brown door.

"Let me guess," I said. "You have a plan?" It came out drenched in sarcasm. Bimbo didn't pick up on it, or if he did, he ignored it.

"Last night after y'all left, I went back to Lazer by myself. I had a few beers and waited for the big dude with the beard to leave. I followed him home. I know where he lives. We're gonna pay him a visit."

"We? You gonna call everyone?"

"Nope, just you and me," he said. "Tavo is taking this super hard and I don't think we should bring him along for this, in case it goes south, you know? And Paul walked away from the whole thing. It's you and me for this. You in?"

For the first time since we'd been sitting there, Bimbo peeled his eyes away from Xavier's door and looked at me. When I looked back at him, I didn't see my friend, didn't find the person I remembered growing up with. In his place was a wounded man, an angry man, a desperate man. Bimbo looked older, somehow bigger. Not chubbier or more muscular, but like he'd become a grown man in a few days, shedding whatever vestiges of childhood he'd managed to hold on to while going through his teens and into his early twenties. I wondered what he saw when he looked at me.

I was ready to do whatever it took to keep my mom, myself, Bimbo, Tavo, and even Paul safe. I was ready to make someone bleed for Xavier. That last thought made me open the car door and step out.

"¿Pa' dónde tú vas, cabrón?"

I closed the door without answering. This was too personal to put into words.

I crossed the street and then the strip of grass between the curb and the sidewalk and started looking down. About six feet away from me, there was a dark brown stain on the sidewalk. It covered a large patch of concrete, reaching the edge. Xavier had bled to death there. His blood had pooled underneath him and then poured over the end of the sidewalk and into the grass. He'd taken his last breath right there.

I walked up to the stain, knelt beside it, and placed my right hand on top of it. Tears ran down my face, but the anger inside me didn't let me think about them. My friend — my brother — was gone, and they had tried to do the same to me.

Bimbo placed his hand on my shoulder and I heard him snort snot back into his skull. I'd lost a lot, but he'd lost more. Around us, the wind picked up. It wasn't an angel or Xavier letting us know he was there with us.

"María will be here soon, man," said Bimbo.

"I know. You still wanna pay that dude a visit tonight?"

"I do," he said. "We're gonna use the hurricane to our advantage. We're gonna take care of this while the whole country's locked inside and in the dark."

"We are?"

"I told you, hermano; we're gonna be sharks."

"Sharks. I like that."

"Get up. We have work to do."

I looked at my hand on top of the stain left by Xavier's blood and got up.

14

GABE

—

Sitting and waiting
Questions with teeth
Violence erupts
The world goes dark
Two Davids, one Goliath

Bimbo had saved an address on his phone's GPS. It took us less than twenty minutes to go from Xavier's house to the big guy's place, the one I'd come to think of as Kimbo Slice.

He lived in a small one-story house on the street behind Magnolia's Café, a shitty bar on Avenida Central we'd been to a few times. The grass in front of the place looked like a small jungle. The house almost looked abandoned, but the closed door, intact windows, and trash can sitting near the sidewalk made it clear someone was living in it.

We parked a block down on the opposite side of the street. Bimbo lowered the windows and killed the engine. We sat in silence for a while. A few cars came and went. A big blue van. A red Celica so low to the ground I wondered how it'd managed to navigate the potholes that plagued our streets. A white Lumina that threw weird, shaky colors out of its left back taillight because it was half full of water. "How do you know he'll be home tonight? What if he's spending the hurricane somewhere else?" I asked.

"I *don't* know, but we'll find out soon."

We were sitting there and hoping the man would come home at some point before the world cracked.

We sat and waited some more. I looked at the houses. Most of them had either storm blinds or wood panels nailed over the windows. Above us, thick, sagging power lines were waiting to fall. I thought about my father, whose accident was not so unique as I used to think. How many people would be electrocuted and die this time? How long would it take to fix the grid? I daydreamed about Natalia and me living someplace cold, where winter storms leave snow on the ground and naked branches reach up to an empty gray sky while the power lines sleep underground like fat worms and everyone was safe and warm at home.

Bimbo talked about his sister for a while. She wasn't doing well. María's death had hit her hard and Bimbo feared she'd found a way to hide from the pain that included a syringe. To my surprise, he said things were still going great with Altagracia. She was funny, he said. A good listener. And a great cook. Sancocho. Mangú. Habichuelas guisadas. Bimbo was eating well, and he was happy about it. They were really getting to know each other. He was sure they'd nail the interview and he would get his twenty bands. Between that and the insurance money he'd get from his mom's death, he was going to be able to afford a place somewhere else. When he was done talking, we sat in silence.

But then I realized he was quiet only because I hadn't asked him anything, and that silence morphed into a series of questions with teeth. Outside the car, the street was empty, the sky was an angry mess, and the wind picked up and made the trees dance. Bad things were coming and the world knew it.

I sat there, looking at the trees and missing my father a lot. Maybe if he'd been home with my mom today, I wouldn't be on the edge of a panic attack, wondering if she was okay. It all filled me with the kind of anger that feeds on itself, and that anger was telling me Bimbo was to blame for everything. He'd dragged us into this. He was obsessed with vengeance. Maybe I could get him to stop. Maybe I could say something to make him change his mind. But I said nothing because I knew there was a crack in his heart that nobody could fill. Sometimes the only thing holding a friendship together is the stuff you don't say.

I thought again about Natalia. I thought about a day in the future where we could all get together and party without thinking about murdering people or about our murdered people or Papalote's long shadow haunting us. None of that fixed anything, but it distracted me and made my anger deflate a bit.

A few minutes later, a lady went by us walking her dog, surely wanting the little furry thing to do its business before the hurricane locked them in. The pooch stopped and took a dump almost in front of Kimbo's house. The lady pulled a tiny green poop bag from her pocket and placed it over her hand before bending down to pick up the dog's turd. She gave us the evil eye while doing that. I understood her: two dudes she'd never seen before sitting in a car in her neighborhood right before a hurricane. Our presence couldn't lead to anything good. She was right. Still, it was a reminder of what Bimbo and I had encountered a million times before because of who we were, how we dressed, and how we looked: someone willing to look down on us while literally holding a fistful of warm shit. Every time Natalia started talking about moving to the States, things like this came to me. I didn't want someone asking me if I had papers or saying people like me coming over was ruining *their* country. I didn't want people mocking Natalia's accent or mine. I didn't want to deal with any of that shit.

About twenty minutes later, with fat raindrops on the window and just as I was about to tell Bimbo the wind was getting bad and we should head back, a clapped-out brown Camry drove past us. One of its belts was screaming like a tortured banshee. It pulled up in front of Kimbo's house.

The driver killed the engine and the door swung open. It was

Kimbo. More than stepping out of the car, the man unfolded himself as he exited. Sitting down in the darkness of Lazer, he'd looked big. Standing next to his car, he looked like a giant. Kimbo had to be at least six foot five and carried around a lot of muscle, all of it protected by a thick layer of fat.

Kimbo hunched his shoulders against the rain and moved his huge body to the door as quickly as a small man would. He opened the door and got inside.

"What now?" I asked.

"Now we wait," said Bimbo. "Let him get comfortable for a couple minutes. Then we'll go up and knock on his door."

"Knock on his door? What, like we're selling trash bags or some shit? What happens when he opens the door?"

"We'll both swing on him at the same time," he said.

His answer was so stupid it made me chuckle.

"I don't know what movies you've been watching, mi hermano, but punching people doesn't work like that. Plus, he looks like you could hit him in the face with a brick and he'd smile at you before eating your fucking head in one bite."

"The hell you been pumping all that iron for, man? Not gonna be doing any calendars or anything with your ugly-ass face and those glasses, so you might as well put those muscles to good use."

I smiled. It still felt good, our kind of normal.

The rain began to fall in sheets that moved with the wind like a living thing. The trees' wild dance was waking up the ghosts of too many bad memories inside me.

"You ready?" Bimbo asked.

"No," I said while thinking of the dark bloodstain in front of Xavier's house and the little coffins on my door. My mom was alone behind that door right now. "But let's do this."

We got out of the car and started jogging toward Kimbo's house. The lady had vanished around the corner long ago and there was no one else out and about. It looked like the kind of place where everyone knows the best course of action is to always mind your own fucking business anyway. A few houses had lights on inside, but we hadn't seen anyone walk by their windows. In Puerto Rico, most windows are covered with exterior bars, and folks like to have curtains on the inside, especially if they're on the first floor. It's an attempt to keep out the world.

A white car rounded the corner and we were caught in its headlights for a moment. We both looked.

"Keep moving," said Bimbo without turning around.

The car moved a little too fast for a residential area and soon passed us, its headlights illuminating raggedy front yards, trash cans, and the few cars that were parked on the street. I looked at it just as it was braking to turn right at the end of the street and noticed the left taillight, half-full of water, casting a soft, shaky red light into the street.

It clicked.

A white car. The same white Lumina that had passed us half an hour ago.

Were we being watched?

I heard Paul's voice in my head: *I swear I saw someone on the stairs.* I wanted to say something to Bimbo, to put the same fear I was feeling into him so he'd turn around and maybe we could drive away. But we had reached Kimbo's house and Bimbo was raising his fist to knock.

Adrenaline flooded my system.

We waited for a minute. Nothing happened. Bimbo knocked again. A few seconds later, the door flung open.

I'm five foot nine. Standing there looking up at Kimbo, I felt like a kid in front of the school's biggest bully, about to call his mom a bitch. How the hell were we going to swing at the same time? It's not like we could do a countdown.

Bimbo wasn't saying anything either, and I wondered if he was too scared. Was I supposed to take over? I moved my left foot forward a bit, rotated my torso, and threw a perfect right cross.

It caught Kimbo in the chin. His jaw clacked. Electricity ran down to my elbow. His beard felt like I'd scratched my fist against a steel wool pad. He took a step back but was still standing. Fuck.

Bimbo stepped forward with his own punch, but it was more like a push that landed on Kimbo's chest. Kimbo moved back and shook his head. Bimbo took another step. Kimbo tried to slam the door closed. It hit Bimbo's foot and bounced back. I threw another cross, aiming higher this time. Kimbo moved out of the way. Nothing will fuck with your balance — and your plans — faster than punching air with all you've got.

Momentum pushed me forward.

My jaw clacked and then the world went

d

  a

   r

    k

I heard what sounded like a tired horse dying from an asthma attack. I jolted, realizing it was me, sputtering on the floor. The world was still dark, and I could feel something hard pushing against my face. My glasses. The cold plastic pressed against the side of my face, somehow unbroken. A small win. I opened my eyes to an alien world.

Off-white tiles.

A pair of black boots on the ground a few feet away.

A second pair of shoes — gray sneakers — were levitating close to the door's threshold, their heels banging against the wall. Bimbo's shoes.

I placed my hands on the floor and pushed myself up. The world spun. Sounds other than labored breathing began to register. Grunts, mostly. Then flesh smacking against flesh.

I managed to get my right knee under my body and my left foot on the floor. The world kept spinning, and my whole face pulsed, like when your hand or foot falls asleep and you finally start to get circulation in the area again. I shook my head, which made everything worse for a second, and looked up.

Kimbo had lifted Bimbo up and pinned him right next to the door and now had both his enormous hands wrapped around my friend's neck like he was trying to press him through the wall. Bimbo's face looked like a balloon ready to pop. He kept trying to push Kimbo's hands away from his neck, slapping at his forearms and scratching at his face. Bimbo was breathing hard now, spittle was flying out of his mouth. I thought about getting up and jumping on Kimbo's back to get him to release Bimbo, but realized my position behind him was an advantage.

Instead, I crawled behind Kimbo, steadied myself, and kicked him in the balls from behind like my life depended on it.

Kimbo grunted and released Bimbo. I expected him to grab his nuts and topple over like a tree. He didn't.

Instead he just snarled.

There was no time for thinking. I swung again, putting all my weight behind the punch. Kimbo raised his arm and my punch bounced off his meaty flesh. He lunged and grabbed me by the shirt, swung me around like a rag doll, and slammed me against the wall on the side of the door opposite of where he'd been holding Bimbo.

Air exploded out of my lungs, and the back of my head bounced against the wall. The room filled with little stars instead of darkness this time. I reached out and grabbed Kimbo's wrists to try to keep his hands off my neck. Getting my ass kicked was bad, but dying in this monster's house was worse.

I saw movement on the floor. Bimbo, scooting toward the door. Then he kicked it shut. Kimbo didn't release me, but he looked toward the door. Bimbo brought his hand up to Kimbo's leg. He was holding a gun. It was the same one he'd placed on his mother's chest—blocky and black. He pressed it against Kimbo's right knee and pulled the trigger.

The sound was not as loud as I'd expected. Maybe my ears were still malfunctioning from getting knocked out. Kimbo let go of me, crumbling to the ground with a guttural scream.

Bimbo rolled out of the way and stood up on wobbly legs. He was breathing like he'd just run a marathon in front of a pack of angry dogs. He stepped toward Kimbo, who was trying to roll onto his side, and kicked him in the face. Kimbo said something through gritted teeth. Bimbo kicked him again, catching him in the mouth. Kimbo turned slightly, still mumbling something, and Bimbo kicked him in the temple. That made the big man relax with a moan and then go still. Bimbo kicked him in the head again, the sound like someone punching a melon and failing to break it open.

"You okay?" Bimbo was winded and sounded scared.

"No, I'm not okay." My jaw, face, and the back of my head felt hot and swollen.

"I know. You went down hard. Your legs twitched. I thought this motherfucker had killed you."

Bimbo was right; I'd gone down hard and could now feel pain dancing to my heartbeat and too much warmth on my jaw. However, it felt like he was throwing it in my face, as if getting my lights turned off for a few seconds by a man who looked like he could beat an adult gorilla was something to be ashamed of.

"Killed *me*? He had you up against the wall, dude. You looked like your eyes were about to pop outta your skull. I saved your life."

There were an infinite number of things Bimbo could have said and done right at that moment, and the one he went with made all the difference in the world to me: he smiled.

"Good point," he said, rubbing his neck with his left hand and then reaching into his shirt to hold his beaded necklace.

"You and Elegguá."

"My ass. What now?"

"Now we tie him up."

15

GABE

—

Duct tape and blood
Chasing a ghost
Bullet to the face
The wind gets stronger
Some words haunt you forever

Bimbo moved past me, still holding the gun neither of us had talked about bringing. I followed him into the kitchen, where there was a small yellow fridge that seemed to have been pulled from the 1980s next to an old gas stove with a faded blue towel hanging from its door handle. A small wooden door stood to the side, and Bimbo opened it and slipped into the garage.

As Bimbo rummaged around out there, I went to the fridge and opened the freezer. There were things wrapped in foil and a few large sandwich bags with what looked like frozen beans. Then I saw a bag of breaded chicken tenders and grabbed it so I could put it to my face.

From the other room, Kimbo made a sound and my stomach dropped. He'd taken a bullet to the knee and a few kicks to the head, but he wouldn't be out long.

Bimbo came back in from the garage, holding a roll of duct tape with some pieces of a spiderweb clinging to it.

"You know why this shit shows up in all the movies?" he asked.

I shook my head while pressing the bag of frozen chicken tenders against the side of my face. "Because it works. Let's do this before he wakes up."

I placed the frozen tenders on the kitchen counter and touched my battered jaw.

We approached Kimbo the way new zoo employees probably approach a tiger someone just shot in the ass with a tranquilizing dart.

"Turn him on his side and wrap some of this shit around his wrists. Then you can get his feet. I'll keep the gun on him just in case."

His idea sounded like shit to me, but I got to work. I hated that this had become a thing: me not liking what crazy idea came out of Bimbo's mouth and then going along with it anyway. Thinking back, maybe it had always been a thing for all of us. I wanted no part of this, but even more than that, I wanted to feel like I wasn't alone. Alone like Bimbo would be if I walked out on him. Alone like Paul was probably feeling after walking away from us.

But it also had a lot to do with feeling like we were in a deep hole and had to do whatever we could to climb out. I knew I couldn't live the rest of my life looking over my shoulder, waiting for my eyes to get plucked. And they knew where my mom lived.

I turned Kimbo on his left side. Blood from his knee had soaked through his pants and pooled around his legs on the off-white tiles. I wanted to move him, and myself, away from it. He was as heavy as he looked. His right hand stayed under his body, which made it impossible for me to do what Bimbo had asked me to do. As soon as he noticed, Bimbo stuck the gun in the back of his pants and helped me out.

The thing about massive dudes is that you can't bring their wrists together behind their backs. We figured that out pretty quickly. I held his arm out of the way and we dropped him on his back. Still, his gut was in the way, and he was too wide, so we looped the duct tape around his left wrist a couple of times and then left a strip in the middle and did the same with his right wrist. We did it about twenty times because I was sure the material between his hands wasn't enough to hold him. His feet were easier. Despite the thick beard, so was covering his mouth.

With the angry giant wrapped in duct tape, we grabbed him under the arms and dragged him over to an ugly beige sofa. It took some effort, but we propped Kimbo up against the sofa in what passed for a sitting position. The sofa had two blue-and-brown cushions on the left corner. I thought about grabbing one and placing it under his leg to catch some of the blood, but decided against it. He was somewhat secured, that was enough. We stepped back from him. Bimbo and I went to a small table in what was probably the dining room — nothing more than a table in the corner — and pulled out two chairs.

"You never told me where you got the gun," I said to Bimbo as soon as I sat down. Then I got up, went to the counter, and retrieved the bag of frozen chicken. The dull pain on my jaw was becoming a very different animal. I applied the frozen bag again.

Bimbo looked at the gun in his hand instead of at me when he answered.

"My uncle gave it to me. Right after they killed my mom. I told him what I was planning to do and he said he'd help me out, but that I had to keep my eyes open and carry a piece just in case."

"Glad your uncle is giving you a hand," I said through the side of my mouth that wasn't under the frozen chicken. Bimbo didn't respond. I didn't exactly mean it as an insult, but his uncle was a dealer, Barrio Obrero's bichote, a man with a lot of power. Someone who was already on the level. Plus, María had been working for him when she got killed.

"Listen, man, this is…it's a fucking lot—"

"I get it," Bimbo interrupted. He sounded angry. Then he stayed quiet, his eyes still on the gun. I waited. Kimbo made a sound. We turned to him. He was moving around a little, like a giant in a kids' story waking up from a deep slumber. He moaned again. Blood trickled from his mouth. Probably from Bimbo's kick. I was sure the conversation was over, but Bimbo spoke.

"I just need to get the motherfucker who pulled the trigger," he said. "Or, you know, the fucker who pulled the trigger and whoever was driving him, but——"

Kimbo mumbled something behind the duct tape, and we jumped a little. His eyes were daggers. I half expected him to rip the duct tape and charge at us. Bimbo stood and walked up to the big man on the ground. He was holding the gun again.

"If you tell me what I wanna know, I'll walk out of here and you'll never see me again," Bimbo said in Spanish. "If you don't, I'm gonna put a bullet in your head and walk out of here like nothing happened. We clear?"

Kimbo didn't nod. He didn't mumble or try to snap the duct tape around his wrists like it was toilet paper. Instead, he sat there, slumped against the sofa. Outside, the wind was starting to howl. The sound of trees shaking and water pummeling the world was making me even more nervous. If we didn't hurry, we'd be stuck at Kimbo's when María arrived.

Bimbo lifted the gun like he was about to shoot. Kimbo moved his legs to push himself up to the sofa, but his eyes went wide and he screamed behind the duct tape. Had he forgotten about the bullet in his knee?

"Hurts like crazy, don't it?" asked Bimbo with a smile. "I'm glad it does. You tried to kill me, motherfucker." Bimbo didn't say anything about walking up to the guy's door, knocking, and then trying to punch his teeth down his throat without provocation. Kimbo stared at him, breathed deeply a few times, and calmed down. Unlike the guy at the garage, Kimbo was a professional. This was not good.

"I'm gonna pull the tape off your mouth. That way you can catch your breath and tell me what I wanna know, okay?"

Kimbo took another deep breath through his nose and nodded. Bimbo stepped forward, still aiming at Kimbo's face, and pulled the tape from his mouth. Kimbo's gasp told me the duct tape hadn't done any favors to his beard.

"It's Tito, right?"

The question brought the name back to me. Tito. The guy in the parking garage had said his name. I hadn't remembered that. He was Kimbo now.

Kimbo nodded.

"I'm looking for your friend Luiso," said Bimbo.

Kimbo looked at him and absolutely nothing ran across his face. He was clueless or resigned, or both. Or maybe he was even more of a pro than I'd thought.

I expected Bimbo to pull back the hammer on his gun like they did in the movies or make some other gesture to force the information out of Kimbo, but he just inhaled slowly like a frustrated father dealing with a fussy toddler. Asking things again and again was getting to him.

I understood. I'd once gotten high with Tavo and we'd watched a movie in which a criminal went around looking for the $70,000 someone owed him. He beat up and killed a lot of people trying to get those seventy keys, but everyone thought he wanted double that because that was what he and his partner had stolen before his partner betrayed him and ran away with all the money. I didn't remember much about movie, because we were so high we had to look down to see airplanes, but I remembered the man getting angry because he only wanted his original cut and had to keep repeating himself. Bimbo was experiencing the same awful mix of anger and frustration.

Bimbo moved forward, replaced the tape on Kimbo's mouth while still holding the gun, and then moved back. Then he kicked the shit out of Kimbo's bleeding knee. The big man opened his mouth and screamed, ripping the tape from his mouth in the process. It was loud enough to reach the neighbors. Bimbo jumped forward and put the gun to Kimbo's head. He shifted into deep, wet breaths.

"I'm going to ask you one more fucking time and then I'm going to shoot you in the face unless the next thing to come out of your mouth is how I can find this Luiso."

Bimbo's tone was enough to convince me. It also convinced Kimbo because the big man said: "Ese cabrón está muerto."

Luiso was dead.

"Dead? Are you serious?" Bimbo asked in Spanish.

"Yes."

"If you're lying to me —"

"Think I wanna die for some motherfucker? Shit went down a month ago," said Kimbo. "He was handing off some guns and the buyers didn't wanna pay. They emptied their clips on his ass and took off with the metal. Happened right behind that Cuban restaurant in Isla Verde. Shit even made the news. Check on your fucking phone if you don't believe me. Luiso Martínez. That was his name. Go on, look it up!"

Bimbo stood there, gun still aimed at Kimbo's face, and said nothing for a while.

"He used to sell everyone guns, right?"

Kimbo nodded, his brow furrowing. He wasn't sure where the conversation was going.

"So, who's doing that now?"

Kimbo thought about it for a few seconds and then chuckled. "I don't know what beef you had with Luiso, but he's dead. You need some guns, I can get you guns. Lot of people can get you guns. Luiso wasn't the only one."

"So, you sell guns too? You kill people? Is that part of your job?"

Kimbo kept quiet.

"You work for Papalote? Say something or I swear I'll pull this fucking trigger."

"No," said Kimbo.

"No to which fucking question?"

"I sell guns, but I don't kill people," said Kimbo. "I beat fuckers up, but that's it. I work for whoever pays me."

"I respect that."

Kimbo stayed quiet again.

"I'm María's son," said Bimbo.

For the first time since he woke up, Kimbo's features shifted. Of course he knew who María was. Did he know who killed her? I was about to ask him, but Bimbo beat me to it.

"Did you kill my mother?"

"No. I fucking told you: I don't kill people. Your mom was cool. She was nice, made me laugh. Everyone liked her. I swear."

It sounded like a real answer because he didn't hesitate and even with a gun pointing at him was looking at Bimbo straight in the eyes.

"Do you know who pulled the trigger?"

"No," said Kimbo, but he didn't sound like before. His tone was different. He was nervous for the first time since the whole thing started.

"You sure? You knew her. You worked with her and you know people who sell guns and kill for money," said Bimbo. The hand holding the gun had been steady, but it was shaking now. I feared he'd blow Kimbo's brains all over his shitty sofa. I didn't like Kimbo, but I didn't want to be two bodies deep into this thing and not a single step closer to knowing who had killed María and Xavier.

"I knew your mom," said Kimbo. "I liked her." His voice was deep, calm. "She was good, but she'd been fucking around, bringing her sellers into San Juan, and San Juan belongs—"

"That's a fucking lie!" Bimbo screamed. He looked at me. The gun shook a bit more. "My mom was selling at Lazer! That's it!"

Was María up to something else? In the days following her murder, we learned a lot, but in life you rarely get all the pieces to the puzzle. *She'd been messing around and bringing her own sellers into San Juan.* That was big. That changed everything. I hoped it wasn't true.

Kimbo opened his mouth to say something else, but Bimbo interrupted him.

"Have you worked for Papalote before?" asked Bimbo.

"If you work in San Juan, you work for Papalote. Even if you don't know it," said Kimbo.

"Da fuck is that supposed to mean? Just answer yes or no."

"Yes."

"So, you know some of his people, right?"

Kimbo mumbled something.

"What did you say?" asked Bimbo.

"I said I do," said Kimbo.

"Who does he send out to kill people? Who are his favorite gatilleros? One, three, ten; I don't give a fuck how many names you know, just give them to me."

"For what? You can't kill—"

Bimbo hit Kimbo in the face with the butt of the gun.

"Fuck!"

Bimbo hit him again and then placed the gun on his forehead. "Tell me or I'll pull the trigger right now!"

"Ra...Raúl y El Brujo...That's all I know," said Kimbo. He sounded as bad as he looked.

That was it.

Two names.

It had cost us a body and getting our asses kicked, but we got two names. It was over. We could leave.

"Only two guys?" asked Bimbo. Of course, he wanted to know more.

"They're Papalote's go-to men," said Kimbo. "They're the ones who take care of things outside La Perla. They're...untouchable. Like ghosts. No one sees them coming or going."

"Where can I find Raúl and El Brujo?"

"In La Perla," said Kimbo. He sounded defeated. "I swear that's all I know, man. If you walk out of here now, I swear I've never seen you, okay? I won't—"

"They both live there?"

Kimbo stopped as if he didn't know what Bimbo was talking

about. Then the names came back to him, understanding making his features shift. He nodded, blood and snot pouring from his nose and down his chin. My own jaw was throbbing. I ignored it.

"Did they kill my mom? Tell me the truth and I won't kill you."

"I don't know who killed her!" said Kimbo. "Fuck, man, I could've been out there next to her when she was shot. I'm just telling you what I know."

"You don't know shit," said Bimbo. "Tell me this: Did you run to her when she was shot? Did you try to save her? Did you call an ambulance? Did you—?" Bimbo's voice broke. His breath caught in his chest. The gun shook against Kimbo's forehead.

"Tell me what you fucking did, cabrón!"

Kimbo didn't say anything. His silence told us what he'd done; he'd run away. He heard shots and bailed.

"You're a fucking coward," said Bimbo, his glasses sliding down his chubby face as he held on tight to the gun. Kimbo said nothing. His eyes were on Bimbo and he was breathing like he'd just run a marathon. It was good to finally see him scared.

"Listen," said Kimbo, "I had nothing to do with María's death. You have to believe me. She was fucking around in Papalote's turf and—"

"Shut the fuck up!"

Bimbo moved sideways, reached over Kimbo, and grabbed a cushion from the sofa. He pulled the gun away from Kimbo's forehead, pressed the cushion against his face, placed the gun on top of it, and pulled the trigger.

The world dropped beneath my feet and I had to hold on to the table.

"Bimbo, he didn't do anything—"

"That's right, he didn't do shit," Bimbo said while standing over Kimbo, his hand still pressing the gun against the cushion as blood ran down the side of Kimbo's neck and onto his chest.

There were tears running down my friend's face, but he was someone else now. I once again felt like a few decades had gone by without me realizing, and it dawned on me: Bimbo felt everyone involved was to blame.

But this was wrong. He couldn't kill people like that.

I wondered what Bimbo saw on my face. I hoped my swollen, throbbing jaw did enough to hide the horror that was surely plastered there.

"This asshole didn't do shit, Gabe, and my mom died on that sidewalk."

"I know, man," I said. I wanted to get the fuck out of there. "But, listen, you can't —"

Bimbo put a hand up. For a moment I was afraid he would turn the gun on me if I said no or started lecturing him about killing people. Kimbo hadn't done anything, that was true, but after the bullets flew and María hit the sidewalk, I wondered who did. We all think we're braver than we are.

Nothing would make it right, nothing would bring his mom back, but sometimes we don't want a solution; sometimes all we really want is a place to put our anger.

And sometimes we make excuses for the people we love just so we can allow ourselves to keep loving them.

"Okay, no lectures. How you wanna handle this?"

"There's something I have to —"

Someone screamed outside. A woman. Could they see us from outside? There was a window on the wall past the small table where we'd been sitting. It had a deep blue curtain covering it. I went to the window, moved the curtain a bit, and peeked outside. It was raining sideways, the water coming down in sheets that moved like a rushing ocean. I couldn't see anyone. I moved to the left. The woman who'd been walking the little dog was standing on the sidewalk across the street. The wind was blowing so hard her pup was a couple inches off the ground. She was pulling on its leash. We couldn't drive away now.

"I think we're stuck here," I said, turning to Bimbo. Every time I spoke, my jaw told me to go fuck myself. I pressed the frozen chicken against my face again. It wasn't that cold anymore.

"Good. I have something to do."

Without another word, Bimbo went to the kitchen and started rummaging around and opening drawers. I looked back outside. The lady and the dog were gone. The trees were bending this way and that. I thought about my father. A lot of people were going to die soon.

I turned around and faced Kimbo's body. Another dead man. His ghost was probably right there, floating next to his body and coming up with ways to make us pay for what we'd done to him in his own home. I'd told Bimbo to shut the fuck up, back when we were in the car after he killed the first guy, but now I was hoping he had another prayer ready, one that would keep Kimbo's ghost away from us.

Then I remembered Bimbo had fired the gun twice inside the house.

"Listen, man, you pulled that trigger twice," I said. "You think we should—"

"No one heard a thing. It's too loud outside. And even if they heard something, no one's coming. No one gives a shit. María's coming. Everyone will be locked inside."

Bimbo liked saying the hurricane's name. His mother's name now belonged to a dark, powerful force he hoped would hide us and help us do what needed to be done.

"For real. If you heard shots next door in the middle of a storm, would you go check?"

He had a point. I said nothing.

"Look, the only thing anyone cares about right now is María, so relax. We'll be here for a few hours and then we'll bounce."

Relax. I couldn't. Not so close to Kimbo's corpse. Our second body. Based on Bimbo's plan, it wouldn't be the last one.

Estamos rodeados de fantasmas.

Some words are so powerful, so true, that they haunt you forever.

Bimbo went back to looking around for something in the kitchen.

A thousand thoughts flew around in my head. I thought about getting the fuck out of there and walking away from this whole situation — even if it meant walking home in a goddam hurricane.

I pictured some cops asking me about two bodies and not being happy with my answers. I heard Natalia's voice, telling me this is exactly what burning my youth carelessly was all about. And I thought of my mom, alone as the winds rattled the house's bones. I had to protect her. She only had me to count on. And I only had her.

"I got what I need," said Bimbo. I looked his way. He was holding a big serrated knife.

16

GABE

—

Severed tongue
Silence the ghosts
The sound of the hurricane
Casting out a spirit
The wind wants to devour the world

What's that for?" I asked.

Bimbo pointed at Kimbo with the knife.

"What the fuck are you gonna do with that?"

"Protect us, Gabe," he said. He moved toward Kimbo's body.

"Protect us? He's dead. What are you — ?"

Bimbo sat on the ratty sofa next to the body and took a deep breath. "I asked you to come along because…because you know what's up. You believe in ghosts. This is what this is about." He raised the knife and shook a bit. "I wasn't ready for the dude at the parking garage, but this time I am ready. Altagracia said that if we do this, he won't haunt us."

The fuck? I thought, and without another word, Bimbo lifted the cushion that covered Kimbo's face. The room had gotten darker since we'd come in, but the yellow bulb in the kitchen spat out enough light to see Kimbo's face. The bullet had pierced his skull below his left eye. It had come out the back, leaving a ragged mess on the sofa I tried to ignore. The lower half of his face, his neck, and his chest were covered in blood.

Bimbo used both hands to open Kimbo's mouth and then put his fingers inside it. Looking at Bimbo digging around Kimbo's mouth, I was dumbfounded, but I couldn't think of what to say to make it stop.

Bimbo made a grunt of frustration and got up. "His tongue is too slippery with all the blood and shit," he said. "I need something to —" He didn't finish. He bounced up and went to the kitchen again. He grabbed the small blue towel that hung off the stove's door handle. With that in hand, Bimbo returned to the sofa and opened Kimbo's mouth again.

Bimbo grabbed Kimbo's tongue with the towel and pulled it out of his mouth. Then he started going at it with the knife. Part of me was screaming silently about how fucked up it was, but another part knew I wasn't going anywhere, and I wasn't about to start an argument with Bimbo. I didn't know what I was dealing with.

Either Kimbo's tongue was very hard or Bimbo was weaker than I thought because it took him forever to cut through the damn thing. There wasn't much blood involved, probably because Kimbo was already dead. I was thankful that the sound of the wind and the downpour pummeling the windows drowned out the rhythmic squish of blade on muscle.

Bimbo finally stood up and dropped the tongue on the floor.

Bimbo placed his foot on top of the severed tongue, opened his phone, and read another prayer. I was too confused, worried, and, in a strange way, scared to make sense of everything he was saying, but I got some of the words.

Protección.

Silencio.

La nada.

El más allá.

Justicia.

Callar los fantasmas.

Silence the ghosts.

The room suddenly got even darker, but it wasn't the kind of dark that comes from a storm or a dark cloud covering the sun. This was thick, almost tangible, like a new presence in the house.

Everything I'd been thinking about before collapsed, and the only things that existed were the room around me, the sound of the hurricane outside, Bimbo's voice, and Kimbo's body.

After he finished reading from his phone, Bimbo went back to the body, bent over a bit, and spat in his left eye and then in his right.

"Con el poder que me otorga ser hijo de Elegguá, te gobierno," said Bimbo. "Soy tu señor, tu amo, tu dueño, y con estas palabras te envío, para siempre, al más allá. ¡Ahora lárgate, espíritu!"

Someone — or something, because the sound was definitely not human — screamed. Inside or outside, I didn't know. It sounded like it was right by the front door. A moment later, the darkness that had filled the room retreated. Something cold slipped into my heart. Outside, the wind howled as if it wanted to devour the world.

17

ALTAGRACIA

—

Doña Ana

Juracán

Hay demonios en el viento

Useless prayers

The darkness has teeth

Doña Ana was scared. Outside, the wind shrieked like a demon. It rattled the storm blinds she had managed to put up with the money her daughter gave her last year so she could go to the dentist. She needed protection, so she spent the money wisely and took the tooth out herself with the help of a little rum and a lot of prayers to Babalú-Ayé, the Orisha who cures illnesses and helps you deal with pain. And they're good storm blinds. She knew they would hold, but the sounds the house made told her the walls could be a different story.

In her mind, Doña Ana had already died three times. She imagined the roof caving in and crushing her even before the winds started. The lady on TV had said they were expecting a lot of rain, and she knew water tends to accumulate on her roof. For the thousandth time, Doña Ana wondered why Dominicans built flat houses instead of using gable roofs like they did in the States.

The wall behind her cracked and Doña Ana's heart did a somersault. As soon as the wind started, she pictured her second death: a heart attack caused by her anxiety. She even felt a bit of pain in her left arm. That's when she went to her bedroom and grabbed the rosary she now held in her right hand. She was on her third Hail Mary. It wasn't helping.

Dios te salve, María, llena eres de gracia, el Señor es contigo.

Doña Ana wondered why she hadn't left. She could've followed Altagracia when she went to Puerto Rico. But she hadn't. People here needed her healing powers and medicine. Altagracia had left, but Doña Ana was at home, and she felt more alone than ever. She prayed harder as an image of Berto, her dead husband, popped into her mind. Then she sent her thoughts to Altagracia, asking for strength and giving what she had to give.

Three hundred miles away, Altagracia felt Doña Ana's presence in her room. The tips of her fingers tingled and her breath caught in her chest. Doña Ana was scared and Altagracia could feel it. She closed her eyes and sent her thoughts to her grandmother. *Relax.* You'll be okay. *Te amo.*

Altagracia wondered if her thoughts were strong enough to reach her grandmother. She wondered if her grandmother could tell she was lying.

Bendita tú eres entre todas las mujeres, y bendito es el fruto de tu vientre, Jesús.

Doña Ana kept praying, but her mind was focused on Altagracia's words. Everything would be okay. She believed her. The girl could see things even better than she could.

The wind screamed and Doña Ana missed her dead husband more than ever. Berto was always getting books from the library, mostly about history and baseball. If he knew there was a hurricane coming, he'd get more than usual. "No vamos a tener TV, viejita," he'd say. He was the one who told her about Juracán, the Taíno god of chaos. She knew Juracán had turned into *huracán* and eventually into *hurricane*. The idea of the entire world calling these storms something that came from a Taíno god had always pleased her, especially because she could speak only about a dozen words of English, but now she knew why the Taíno had seen the wind as an angry, destructive, bloodthirsty god.

Her mother had told her stories of hurricanes from her childhood. She had been convinced bad things came with the wind. She spoke of howling demons running down the mountains of her youth, drowning people in rivers and making others vanish forever. She grew up knowing that people died in hurricanes, which was normal, but the skin on the back of her neck went up whenever she heard about disappearances in the news after a storm. Every hurricane she had ever been through had made people disappear without a trace, and she knew there had to be something to her mother's stories.

But those were not the stories she feared the most.

Doña Ana's mother had also told her about babies being born with hooves or with mouths full of teeth during a storm. Her mother, Isabel, had been raised in the mountains, surrounded by small farms, where they spoke of calves born with six legs or two heads during the night of a hurricane or the day after one. And then there were the stories of the folks who went missing and then were found again, their bodies missing their eyes or entire limbs, their torso slashed open and their insides missing. Those were the stories Doña Ana feared the most, the ones that she tried her hardest to forget about, to inject with enough doubt to kill them, though she never could. Now, with the sound of the house like a huge breaking bone all around her, all the stories were alive inside her, and prayer was all Doña Ana had to combat them.

Santa María, Madre de Dios...

The wind howled again, a sustained scream that surrounded Doña Ana's small house and seemed to enter her skull. Everything shook. Her heart skipped another beat. She wanted to be with Altagracia. She wanted to be somewhere else.

...ruega por nosotros, pecadores...

* * *

Altagracia smoked and looked out the window as the tears rolled down her face. She could see Doña Ana at home, her hands wrapped around her old rosary, her mouth moving in silent prayer. She could feel Doña Ana's fear, and it was killing her. There was a darkness coming and she knew it. The darkness came with every storm. Sometimes it was small and left quickly, but sometimes it was big and stuck around, feeding on the pain and destruction. This time, the darkness felt bigger and stronger than ever. In her mind, Altagracia saw that darkness approach Doña Ana and swallow her. Her tears reached her chin and fell from her face. Outside, the rain danced in the wind, and the trees shook with the power of the storm, the power Altagracia knew would hurt her without ever touching her.

Behind the house, something hit the ground with a loud thud. A tree, she thought. No, said her brain; a chunk of someone's house.

A body carried by the wind.

A demon.

Juracán's foot.

...*ahora y en la hora de nuestra muerte. Amén.*

Doña Ana's kitchen was at the back of the house. When she and her neighbors had gotten together to build it, she'd been adamant about the placement even if everyone else had kitchens at the front of their homes. She'd explained she hated to receive people with the smell of food, which was true, but she had wanted the kitchen in the back because she loved to grab her coffee and toast, heavy on the butter, every morning and then open the little door that looked out at the mountains behind her home. Doña Ana liked to pray at night and would regularly fall asleep while doing so, but she considered those mornings a true moment with God. She would look at mountains, inhale the clear air or smell the rain, and sip her coffee while thanking God for another day aboveground. The only bad thing about that door was that the Dominican man who'd installed it had somehow gotten a door about a quarter inch too narrow for the frame her neighbors had made. Sometimes, when the wind got nasty, the door would fly open and slam against the house's wooden wall. Doña Ana heard that now.

BAM!

In a second, the howling from outside was inside, the power of the storm invading her home.

Doña Ana was sitting at her small table, holding her rosary as hard as she could and praying with all her heart. The sound made her forget where she was on the rosary. She looked toward the small door in her kitchen. Beyond it, there was nothing but screaming darkness and curtains of water falling sideways, beating the house with millions of tiny fists.

Doña Ana got up. She had to close the door or everything would get wet. She took a step toward the kitchen and stopped. The darkness from outside was moving into the house. It looked like the air was solid and bulging past the threshold. As Doña Ana watched, trying to make sense of it, the darkness stretched and began acquiring a somewhat humanoid form.

"Hay demonios en el viento."

Doña Ana heard her mother's voice as clearly as if she were standing next to her, just as her granddaughter Altagracia heard her now as she was meant to die. The thing in the kitchen was so tall its head almost reached the ceiling.

Doña Ana heard a noise that wasn't the wind or the rain. She looked down and realized she had dropped her rosary. She started praying again, the first thing that came to her.

"*Padre nuestro que estás en el cielo...*"

The figure kept growing, its dimensions surpassing anything human and pushing the idea — the desperate hope — of it being a person out of Doña Ana's mind.

"*...santificado sea tu nombre...*"

Then the thing moved forward, coming at Doña Ana with the speed of the wind, the otherworldly howl of the hurricane, the screams of the demons Juracán brought with him, cutting Doña Ana's prayer in half.

The last thing Doña Ana saw was a mass of piercing blackness filling her vision.

Her last thought went out to Altagracia.

The last thing she heard was an inhuman wail.

The last thing she knew was that she was going to be one of those people who disappeared during a hurricane, never to be seen again.

18

GABE

—

Wet chaos
Prayers to San Miguel Arcángel
A man made of shadow
Paranoia
Life is weird

Bimbo and I sat in the dead man's living room, listening to the sounds of windows rattling like they were possessed.

I'd texted my mom and Natalia, told them I was riding the storm out with Bimbo. Both of them replied with some combination of *Take care* and *Save your battery*. I burned with shame.

We lost power about half an hour later and sat in the dark without saying a word. I wondered if the thing Bimbo had done with the tongue, and the sacred words that followed, had been enough to push Kimbo's spirit into the afterlife forever, or if his angry ghost was in the room with us, sewing curses on our souls with the threads of our own sin.

Outside, it was wet chaos. The wind roared for hours, occasionally changing its pitch, and I had to stop checking my phone to conserve battery.

There was another wild scream at some point, and Bimbo started praying again.

"San Miguel Arcángel, defiéndenos en la lucha contra lo que nos amenaza. Sé nuestro amparo contra la maldad y las acechanzas del demonio. Que Dios manifieste sobre la maldad su poder. Esa es nuestra humilde súplica, Arcángel, que tú, con la fuerza sagrada que Dios te ha otorgado, arrojes al infierno a Satanás, a los fantasmas y a los demás espíritus malignos que vagan por el mundo y quieren hacernos mal. Amén."

"Amén," I said, not even thinking about it.

There was another scream outside, something like a big, angry animal in pain.

I looked out Kimbo's window.

Sheets of rain slammed against the glass, but I could see something across the street. A figure. It looked like a tall man made of shadow. I wondered if it was my father. His spirit, maybe doomed to go wander, trapped in an endless line of killer hurricanes. The wind didn't seem to affect the shape. Then the figure turned into thick black smoke that María blew away in a second.

I blinked back, smoky shadows still imprinted behind my eyelids.

Next to me, Bimbo was still praying, eyes closed. Part of me was relieved: He wouldn't be able to corroborate what I'd seen. The other part of me was left wondering if I was going crazy.

At some point Bimbo got up, turned on the flashlight on his phone, and went deep into Kimbo's house. I didn't follow him. The darkness around us shrieked with howling wind and breaking branches. A few trash cans dragged through the street, hitting cars nearby. A foul smell kept crawling up my nostrils, rising from the body. We come into the world a mess, and we go out the same way.

I sat in the dark and prayed nothing happened to my mom or Natalia or Bimbo's car and that the power cables that were on the ground were dead.

After a while, Bimbo emerged from the darkness without his phone. He was carrying a duffel bag with big flowers on it. He placed it on the table and sat down.

"What's that?" I asked.

"Guns."

"This guy's guns?" My chest squeezed into my throat like some sort of half-drowned rodent trying to escape under a crack.

"Guns this fucker was going to sell. We're gonna need them. They're our guns now," he said.

María kept ravaging the world. My mom and Natalia kept popping into my thoughts. I wondered if Tavo and Paul were okay. I wanted the fucking hurricane to be over so I could get back home and tackle whatever came next. Being in Kimbo's house felt like being trapped in the world's smallest prison.

I asked Bimbo a question that had been bothering me.

"What are we gonna do with the body?"

"Leave it here. You hear that thing outside? It'll be days before they find him."

"You sure about that?"

"Listen, we're gonna be fucked for weeks if not months. No power. No water. No food. No medicine. They'll send food and batteries and bottled water, and we won't get any of it because the government is full of assholes. You know how it is. No one will pay attention to anything but themselves for a while. Cell phone service will be a mess for days. Nothing will be open. It's hitting hard enough that there'll be a curfew, like always, and the fucking pigs will be doing their best to stay off the streets and protect their own asses.

"By the time they find this guy, he'll be crawling with worms. They'll be more concerned with cleaning up and moving on than with solving the case. Plus, he probably has a record, so no one will look into this too much. When was the last time you saw anything on the news about cops solving one of the massacres we have every week?"

The question hung between us. The door rattled an answer I couldn't decipher. The cops never solved shit, it was true, but this felt different because it involved us. Paranoia. It was a tiny ghost with a squeaky voice whispering things in my ear. Bad things.

Bimbo sniffled and wiped his nose with the back of his hand. He'd been crying while he was gone. Maybe he'd gone looking for the guns or something else, but maybe he'd just needed some time alone, away from Kimbo's body and his stench. Away from me. I didn't know what to say. I was sitting next to a guy who'd put his neck on the line for all of us dozens of times and apparently was also a bloodthirsty monster.

A memory came to me. Bimbo and I playing video games in his room after my father's death. *Street Fighter II.* Out of the blue, he'd said to me, "Don't think about it too much. Don't try to understand it. Life is weird. Carry a knife, love like you mean it, and move on." Then he'd smiled. I tried to take it as a joke, but his words dug deep. They were still there, somewhere inside me.

Bimbo sniffled again. I wondered if he thought the howling wind outside was his mother telling him something.

19

THE HURRICANE

—

The ocean roars
Ghosts cling to whatever's left
Babies with horns
Bloody rituals
A house of bone and rain

The ocean roared. Rivers overflowed, the raging mud-colored water becoming a violent monster that tore through homes, demolished bridges, and left entire families scared and isolated. Or dead.

Power lines went down everywhere, their electric cargo suddenly let loose on the world. The grid, old and weak, had been on its last leg for decades, and María left every corner of the island in the dark.

People flocked to shelters. Churches, government buildings, and city arenas filled with desperate souls. Then the shelters ran out of cots. They gave people bottled water and little else. People were scared, angry, anxious. Tempers flared. Fights broke out. Everyone felt useless and at the mercy of something violent and hateful that they couldn't control.

Hospitals ran out of beds, painkillers, suture thread, and gauze. People kept coming. Some missing fingers after weird accidents, some bleeding from head wounds caused by projectiles, some carrying their dead children, spouses, brothers, mothers. Their grandparents. Their neighbors. Their friends. The doctors and nurses did what they could. It wasn't enough.

The ghosts of those killed under the weight of the wood, bricks, cement, and plaster clung to whatever was left. They were all angry and desolate. If anyone rebuilt where they'd died, there'd be hauntings.

The wind yanked out air-conditioning units that had hung underneath windows like rusty fruit. Wind and water entered the gaping holes left behind and destroyed sacred mementos, ruined walls, and soaked the floors.

The ocean swallowed boats and destroyed houses built too close to the shore. In places like Dorado, Santa Isabel, Luquillo, Fajardo, and Loíza, sharks, dolphins, and other sea creatures washed up on shore, dead and, more often than not, horribly mutilated. Most of the carcasses had chunks missing, and some showed large teeth marks. Those who lived in the coast knew that they'd have to walk the shore once the storm had passed because on top of the horrible smell, the dead creatures always brought bad luck.

Trees broke or were ripped from the ground with their roots still wrapped in dirt. Palm trees bent until they could bend no more and then they snapped, their coconuts projectiles that crashed against homes and shattered windshields and windows. Plants were obliterated. Crops vanished. Papaya and banana trees were the softest, so they were the first to go. The wind hollered across the decimated fields, the sound drowning the wails of the farmers who had, once again, lost everything.

In the mountains of Jayuya, a girl was born at around 10:45 p.m., after her mother went into labor right after dinner. No one had a signal. Their landline was dead. Their street had turned into a raging river. They couldn't go to the hospital. The woman's younger sister helped her through the birth. The baby girl emerged—wet, purple, angry—and screamed. She looked healthy. While cleaning her, her aunt noticed her mouth. The newborn girl had rows of tiny pointy teeth all the way to the back of her throat. The baby's father had never been in the picture, so the woman's sister had to take care of it. She took the baby to the garage and used a tire iron to bash its soft head in. It was rough and her hands shook, but it was what needed to be done. She left the baby under a tarp to bury her in the morning.

That baby wasn't the only one.

In a small house near the beach in Loíza, a Black woman gave birth to a premature girl with a three-inch horn protruding from the right side of her forehead. She suffocated it against her sweaty chest as the father cried in a corner and prayed to a god that had always ignored him. The wind carried the sounds of the mother's screams over the mangled animal carcasses that littered the shore.

And in Guánica, a mother lost her life when the baby inside her used a mouthful of razor-sharp teeth to chew its way out. The woman's partner, a much younger woman, used a kitchen knife to murder her newborn son. Then she took off her golden cross, stuffed it in the baby's bloody mouth, and sat in the dark to wait for morning.

The same story repeated itself all night. Newborns with small mouths full of teeth like piranhas. Babies with horns. Squirming fetuses with claws as large as their tiny pink bodies. Newborns coming out of the womb speaking in tongues. They were all killed by someone who was supposed to love them or who at least loved their mothers. Many had crosses or rosaries stuffed in their mouths. Others were subjected to bloodier rituals by those who knew the power that had made them was older than the god those who used the rosaries and crosses prayed to.

Practitioners of Voodoo, Mesa Blanca, santería, and Palo Mayombe performed rituals to keep the demon that came with the storm away. Some heard its scream and some didn't, but they all felt its presence.

In Carolina, a woman saw a figure standing in front of her window. It looked like a very big man made of black ink. Her seven dogs went berserk and tore into her. She died screaming their names, begging them to stop, feeling the pain of their betrayal in her heart as much as the pain of their teeth on her flesh. No one heard her. No one would check in on her for a while. The dogs calmed down as soon as the figure vanished, but continued to feed on her for days.

The same happened with farm animals, sometimes with deadly results. Anyone who managed to survive such an attack would later recall a dark figure and a strange, piercing shriek. In other parts of the island, people with no pets also saw the same figure. Some died. Some lost their minds. Some took the nearest sharp object and drove it into an eye socket or slid it across their throats.

It was everywhere, destruction. There was screaming and crying and fear and blood and merciful murder and brutal death in many homes.

Accidents happened. Flesh blossomed into deep wounds everywhere. Blood flowed. Pain, fear, grief, and panic reigned.

The island became a playground for death, a place of death and angry ghosts, a shuddering house of bone and rain.

The wind howled.

The wind howled and howled.

20

GABE

—

Rows and rows of tiny teeth
On the road again
San Miguel Arcángel
Nothing but anger and shitty plans
Sometimes God is your copilot, but it's the Devil who takes you home

Finally, the wind began to die down. At some point Bimbo said he needed some rest and vanished farther into the house again. I couldn't sleep. The idea of it seemed ridiculous, so instead I pondered death and how we do things in life that push us closer to it. Alone in the dark with Kimbo's corpse, I felt like I was standing at the edge of a bridge while stuffing my pockets with rocks. My heart ached for María and Xavier, but as much as I wanted this to be the answer, I couldn't convince myself we had done the right thing.

I eventually dozed off while looking out the window. My arms rested on the table and my head on top of them. I dreamed of Natalia pregnant, her favorite dress pulling tight against her waist. She beamed at me, rubbing her belly, now bigger than it was just seconds ago. Then her beautiful, serene smile vanished, the sockets of her eyes sliding into her hollowed-out cheeks as she handed me something wrapped in a soft, bloody blanket. Our child. I looked down, moved the cloth away from the baby's face.

The baby's eyes stayed closed at first, the pruned skin pinching its facial features. I stroked its cheek softly, then moved my hand to its red lips, which instinctively opened. But instead of fluttering around in search of milk, the mouth opened wider, revealing countless rows of tiny teeth and unnaturally red gums. And then a silent scream as its bloody tongue dropped to the floor.

Bimbo said something behind me and woke me up. I had no clue what he'd said.

"What was that?" I asked.

"I said we should try to get the hell outta here," he said. "The rain's still bad, but the worst part is over and if the car is okay, I'd rather hit the road before anyone else leaves their house, you know?"

I stood up. Leaving sounded like the best idea ever. Our phones had no signal and I needed to make sure my mom was okay. I also needed six aspirin for my jaw.

Bimbo handed me the duffel bag from the table and made for the door without looking at Kimbo's body. I had to look one last time. The severed tongue looked like a dead slug.

We ran to the car. The wind had knocked down a few trees and several posts, so I kept my eyes on the ground in case there were any power lines.

Everything was wet and it smelled like rain, plants, and destruction.

Bimbo's car was okay. Seven or eight feet in front of it, a fallen tree covered half the street. We got in with one last look around and Bimbo turned the ignition.

We had to navigate a broken world, but made it out to where trees weren't an issue anymore.

I was surprised to see we weren't the only cars on the road. I wondered what had forced all these other people out into the tail of the hurricane. Were they worried about loved ones they couldn't reach?

Were they running away from something? What could they need so desperately?

I turned to look behind us. The little ghost in my ear was telling me I'd see red-and-blue lights if I turned around, that the cops would be on our asses even if María had destroyed everything. There were no red-and-blue lights, but there were a few cars there. A big white van. An ambulance with the lights and siren off. A small blue car with one big wiper trying to keep water off its windshield.

Then I saw it.

It was only seven or eight cars behind us. I didn't have to look too hard to see what it was, because my buddy William had driven one like it for years. A white Lumina. I knew its left taillight was full of water. The tiny ghost in my ear grew a hand the size of Kimbo's and wrapped its cold fingers around my heart. I turned back around.

Grab a gun? Tell Bimbo we were being followed? Remind him Paul had seen someone on the stairs and then someone had sliced Xavier's neck open and then plucked his eyes out? I did none of the above. Instead, I turned back to see if the car was still there. It wasn't. The tiny ghost with the squeaky voice and the big hand didn't let go of my heart.

Bimbo's eyes were firmly fixed on the road. His hands kept squeezing the steering wheel like he expected to get juice out of it.

"What's the plan now?" I asked.

I had a vague idea of what he wanted to accomplish. I didn't know exactly how we were going to go about it. They say ignorance is bliss, but that doesn't apply to times when not knowing what's going to hap-pen means you could end up staining a sidewalk with your blood.

"Now we wait a few days," said Bimbo. His voice was different. He spoke like his mouth was in the car but his brain was far ahead of us, maybe in the future, putting a bullet in another skull.

"Okay," I said. "We wait a few days…and then?"

"I'm still figuring that out. I have to talk to my uncle. I'll tell you soon."

I turned around again. There was an old SUV behind us and a yellow pickup truck in the other lane. No white Lumina. My heart felt a bit better, but the tiny ghost was singing a song about prison and telling me Bimbo didn't have a fucking clue. It was also reminding me Kimbo had said María had been trying to take over Papalote's turf. Could that be true? If it was and Bimbo didn't know, he was leading all of us to our graves with nothing but rage and shitty plans.

Maybe it was my turn to think, to come up with the next step. We had some information and two names. Raúl and Brujo. Also, a location: La Perla. We had what he needed, what Bimbo had said he wanted. Maybe he and his uncle could take care of this alone. Maybe it was almost over. I tried to convince myself of this, but Bimbo hit a pothole, and the guns in the duffel bag rattled against my right ankle. A whole bag full of death.

"You still have your necklace?" Bimbo asked.

It took me two seconds to figure out what he was talking about. I reached into my shirt and pulled out the red-and-black beads. "Yeah."

"Good," he said. Then he sniffled again while reaching up to grab his own necklace.

I wondered about this god of his. Elegguá. An Orisha, according to Bimbo. I didn't know him, but I also didn't know God. Some bigger power, right? Anything worked.

San Miguel Arcángel. Bimbo's prayer came back to me as I watched the wipers push rain around on the windshield.

"Hey, what was that San Miguel Arcángel thing back there?"

"I talked to Altagracia a few days ago. She knows about this stuff. Learned it from her grandma. I told her my uncle used to pray to San Miguel Arcángel. She said San Miguel Arcángel is the commander of God's angelic forces or some shit. If you call on him with prayer, he comes with a sword in his hand and fights off the darkness. He's the guy who protects us from evil. You know, like the ghosts of those two motherfuckers."

"Not Elegguá?"

"Nah, Elegguá just…clears the road, man. I told you, he moves obstacles outta your way and protects you, but he doesn't fight evil the way Altagracia said San Miguel Arcángel does."

"So, Altagracia prays to angels and saints from different religions?"

"We all do, man. Puerto Ricans. Dominicans. Cubans. Voodoo. Santería. Palo. Trust me, man, everything you've ever heard is true. God. Elegguá. Shiva. Whatever. You can pray to whoever has the tools to help you out."

"Makes sense." I wished it did.

I'd love to say we drove into the rain, but it felt like something else; it felt like the rain was swallowing us down.

21

GABE

—

Little coffins
Only six bullets
The tiny ghost of paranoia
More rain
Estamos rodeados de fantasmas

It was still raining when Bimbo dropped me off at home. As I opened the car door, Bimbo told me to take a gun with me. I shook my head. After what we'd been through, I wanted to keep death as far away from me as possible. Then Bimbo pointed at my door and said, "Do it for your mom, man." I didn't have to look back, because the little coffins from my door were tattooed on my brain.

I grabbed the duffel bag from the floor and opened it. There was a lot stuffed in there. Most of it was black or dark gray, but there were also some flashes of pure metal. I grabbed the first thing that looked wieldy and pulled it out.

"A revolver?" asked Bimbo. "You sure about that? There are other things in there that have more—"

"This looks easy to use," I said. The gun I'd grabbed was heavy and had a long barrel with a black grip that had a red line going down the back of it. Bimbo grabbed it and played with it for a minute. I looked around, fearing a neighbor might see us out there with a bag full of guns, but the street was deserted. There were a few downed trees on the street and more thrown across the sidewalks. I thought about my father and again wanted to rush in and check on my mom.

"Ah, you have to touch here and here to open the barrel. Si yo fuera tú, cogería algo más grande y con más balas, cabrón. There are only six bullets in there, and that's it." Bimbo pulled the duffel bag to his lap and rummaged around it for a bit. "You sure that's what you want?"

I nodded. "I'm good with this," I said. The thing was as heavy as hell. What I didn't say was, if I needed more than six bullets, I was fucked anyway, so having more wouldn't make a difference. The gun definitely didn't feel like a guarantee, but it felt like something. "No... safety or anything?"

"Nah," said Bimbo. "Probably means you have to pull the hammer back all the way for it to shoot. Empty it and figure it out."

I nodded again. Bimbo placed the duffel bag back on the floor.

"No, empty it. Like, fucking listen to me and make sure the thing is empty. Don't point it at yourself or—"

"I got it. Gonna check on my mom." The moment I said it, I regretted it. He was going home to the ghost of his mother.

"Stay safe, Gabe," he said. "Take care of your mom. I'm sure she worried about your ass all night. I'll try to text you once we have a signal again."

The cold-blooded killer was gone and the Bimbo I knew was back. Then I realized I was sitting there holding a gun we'd stolen from a man he'd killed—a man who had barely played a part in María's death. Bimbo would never be the same. Neither would I. The same probably went for Tavo and Paul. I missed them—and Xavier, whom I was sure I'd miss the rest of my life—but a part of me was glad they hadn't been with us for this killing.

Bimbo drove off, the sound of his tires heavy in the soaked street.

I walked into my house and remembered there was no power. I yelled out for my mom, fearing she wouldn't answer and that I'd find her in another pool of blood, this time too much of it, all coming from a sliced neck or a bullet hole in her head.

"Estoy en la cocina," she said from the kitchen. I went to her and hugged her for a long time. She told me about the rain and the wind. Her eyes looked tired. I knew she hadn't slept all night, worrying about me, worrying about the house, and thinking about my father. Sometimes lost love is like a disease that sticks around quietly and flares up from time to time, making the world a bit dull and rekindling the flame of that fucking pain that refuses to go away.

I didn't say much, and told her I hadn't heard from Natalia when she asked. Then she said she was going to make coffee on her little gas stove. I told her I needed some rest.

I made my way to my room and hid the gun in my closet. Then I lay down and stared at the ceiling. As I tried to get some sleep, I thought about Kimbo and about all the destruction outside and the chaos that was still to come, but the gun was the thing that haunted me the most. I couldn't see it, but its presence was kind of a living thing. It meant something could and would still happen, that the more time I spent with the gun — and doing things that made me feel like I needed the gun — the greater the chances of me having to use it. I didn't want to kill anyone; I didn't want another ghost.

Estamos rodeados de fantasmas.

The rain picked up again and I drifted off into a fitful sleep with those words echoing in my head and the sound of the rain beating its tired fists against my window.

22

GABE

—

Coffee
Boxes full of screws
Facing a monster
El ojo del Diablo
We carry trauma

I woke up sweaty and disoriented. It was still raining. I went to the bathroom. Only a trickle of water. Enough to wash the last remnants of sleep that clung to my face.

My mom was still sitting at the kitchen table, coffee in hand. She was playing around with her small radio, trying to find a signal carrying some news. The smell of coffee was soothing. I grabbed a mug and got some from her areca. I took a sip, and the warmth reached my stomach and tricked me into thinking everything would work out.

I pulled a chair over and joined her at the table. She looked okay, really. My father and she had shared a million conversations at that table. He'd gotten her that little radio after he couldn't figure out how to fix her old one. The screws from that were probably somewhere in the garage. My father always pulled stuff apart and tried to fix it. When he failed, which happened almost every time, he saved the screws. "Might need just the size and then I won't have to buy them," he'd say. I don't think he ever used any of them. We cleaned out a few things after he died—his clothes, a few old boxes covered in mold he kept in the garage—but we couldn't bring ourselves to throw out his tools and all those jars and little boxes full of screws.

My mom was getting frustrated. There was nothing on the air. Radio stations would come back relatively quickly, but it'd still take a while. Looking at my mom reminded me of the relief I'd felt after thinking she was dead. It also reminded me I needed to paint over the thing on the door.

"I saw it get here, Gabu," my mom said with her eyes still on the radio.

"Saw what?"

"The hurricane," she said. "On the news. The lady kept going on and on about people who lived on the coast needing to find shelter away from the ocean. Pictures of empty grocery store shelves and long lines at the checkout appeared on the screen. I know we've seen it all before, but it made me feel like we were facing a monster. There was something...different about María." My mom stopped talking and looked at the wall as if whatever she wanted to say next was written there.

"Different how?"

"I don't know. Its shape. Its size. Something. It looked...evil? I don't know. El ojo del Diablo. That's what your grandma called it. Remember how she used to stay with us anytime a hurricane came? She'd always wait for you to go to bed and then she'd sit there with panicked eyes and her arthritic hands wrapped around her old rosary. She always said hurricanes bring something."

I stayed quiet because there was nothing to say.

We carry trauma from every fucking hurricane. My mom had seen more than me, and her face showed it. I didn't blame her. In the United States, every time a kid walks into a school with a rifle and kills a bunch of other kids, the government talks about gun reform and then nothing happens. In Puerto Rico, something similar happens every time a hurricane destroys our shitty electric grid: The government talks about the need to fix it while putting patches on it to get it back up and running, and then they forget about the whole thing until the next hurricane leaves us in the dark for a few months. Looking at my mom's face, I knew she was thinking about the heat and the water problem and how much food we had, but also that she was thinking about dead people. She was thinking about the demons her mother said lived in the angry winds. And I knew she was thinking about my father, just like me.

23

GABE

—

Bruised sky
Bones breaking in the wind
The silent screams of a ghost
Inside a punished chapel
Boricuas de pura cepa

They always say the sky looks bruised after a hurricane, and that's exactly what it looked like after María. After finishing my coffee, I stepped outside to check on the door and look around a bit, maybe walk around the block. One look up at the battered sky and I realized my mind was also bruised from the attack we'd just survived, and my soul felt sore from the tension and fear that had packed the preceding hours.

I pictured my mom in the house alone with the ghost of my dad when the hurricane came. I bet she was watching the lady on the news talking about shelters filling up, businesses closing up, and warning people to stay away from the ocean no matter what.

Then the power went out. Absolute darkness enveloped her. In the absence of the TV's sound, the racket of the wind surely swallowed the world around her. I wondered if my father's ghost had offered her some comfort, and hated myself for being with Bimbo when I should've been with her.

Our house backed up against a mangrove, and the sound of snapping branches always reminded me of a fight, each snap like a bone breaking in the wind. I wondered what my mom thought of it.

In a hurry and working with stuff we'd saved from our neighbor's trash two or three years earlier, my mom and I had managed to nail down some planks to protect our windows before María came, but a few were too rotted and she decided the small windows in the kitchen would have to survive without protection. I wondered how many times she looked out that window, thinking about me and praying.

I started walking around a bit to silence my thoughts.

Our street had faulty drainage, like many places across the island, and there was a small lake in front of our house, its surface constantly moving from the rain that was still falling. Beyond it and along our street, the trees looked naked, which is really unnatural for a place stuck in a perennial summer, where everything is relentlessly growing and constantly in bloom. Now everything seemed dead or dying. A hurricane's winds, especially a Category 5 hurricane's winds, are awful, but the wounded silence you find when the storm is over is almost worse. I stood there and listened. I wanted to hear neighbors yelling or something, but even the animals were silent, as if the previous vicious attack had driven fear into their tiny bones and they were scared of making a sound and bringing back whatever the fuck that thing had been that had destroyed everything around them.

Across the street, the houses looked like they'd taken a wet beating. Some had leaves plastered all over them, and at a yellow house where an old man who never talked to anyone lived, I could see a branch sticking through a window. The thousands of folks across the island who lived in small wooden houses built without permits had probably done much worse than busted windows. Category 5 hurricanes pummel cement and mess up paint, but they obliterate wooden homes. Whatever it is that's doing the hurting, it always hurts the poorest folks the most. I thought about Xavier and his parents. Their house had a crappy roof that leaked every time it rained. I wondered if it had withstood María's winds.

I hated the sight of the world, but I stayed outside under the rain because I was craving anything other than the darkness of the house and the silent screams of my father's ghost and my guilt.

There were branches on the ground and leaves stuck everywhere. No one else was out. I wanted to cry out, to yell. I wanted to wake up the world. But I couldn't bring myself to do it. The aftermath of a hurricane always drives silence into you, as if instead of being in the world, you're inside a punished chapel, a place where uttering a single word would be akin to screaming an insult.

I turned around and walked back to my place. As I approached, I saw the door. The veve was still there, the tiny coffins on its sides like strange eyes looking at me. They knew what I'd done the night before. They knew everything. Maybe they were trying to tell me I was next. Weirdly, the gun in my closet felt like a chunk of hope. I walked in and closed the door.

The first thing you do when the power goes out during a storm is start thinking about when it will come back. That's not the case after a hurricane like María. No, you know the power is out and it will be a long time before it comes back, so it's better not to think about it. I went to my room and grabbed my phone. I had 61 percent battery, but no signal. It could be a few days before we got a signal back. I wanted to hear Natalia's voice, to hear her tell me she was okay. If the signal didn't come back soon, I'd try to drive to her place.

In the kitchen, the faucet coughed and made a sound like someone dying of thirst. Nothing came out. It was okay. We were alive. We still had a roof over our heads. We'd done this before. We would do it again. We were boricuas de pura cepa, and that meant we'd do whatever it took.

24

NATALIA

—

The best thing is not to go out
Secrets up in the mountains
Quick, merciful ends
Taking a hammer to the sky
Provincial

Natalia sat on her balcony, wondering how many people in the mountains were digging holes in their backyards, tears in their eyes.

Hay cosas sin nombre que viajan con la tormenta. Después de que pasa un huracán, lo mejor es no salir. "There are nameless things that travel with a storm. After a hurricane passes, the best thing is not to go out."

Natalia stared at her scrap of ocean, remembering her grandmother's words. Beyond the gas station, the line of deep blue framed by two tall buildings whose wealthier residents surely got a marvelous, uninterrupted view of the Atlantic.

Moving into this place with Keyla was a good financial move. The place was close to everything—the panadería, the beach, her mom, the cemetery where her grandmother was buried—but those buildings blocking the ocean always bothered her. Bothered her because they reminded her of what others had, of all the things she didn't have, and all the things that seemed designed to push her down. Man, weather, God. Fucking spirits.

There are things without a name that travel with a storm. After a hurricane passes, the best thing is not to go out.

Natalia's grandmother had repeated those words to her time and time again. Every hurricane season, in fact. Every year between the beginning of June and the end of November. From time to time, if Natalia was busy doing something else or when she became a teenager and her grandmother's old stories were boring and she rolled her eyes at them, her grandmother, Iris, would tell her additional stories that always sounded like warnings.

People went missing after hurricanes, Iris would tell her. They would vanish as the hurricane raged, taken away by the unnamable thing that came with the wind and rain. The old and the sick would sometimes open the door and walk out into the rain willingly, never to be seen again. In farms across the island, goats and cows gave birth to two-headed offspring or writhing masses of flesh and hair with extra limbs and exposed organs. The wrath of rivers in the mountains turned ungodly, swallowing small boats and houses that stood too close to their banks. Children would speak in tongues. Old folks would start talking to friends and family members who had been dead for years as if they stood in front of them. People who lived alone would die mysterious deaths at home, their bodies broken by something that left no evidence behind. Someone in the family or neighbors would eventually find them, their bodies rigid, their faces frozen in horror.

As with many other things, Natalia had believed the stories when she was a girl, thought they were bullshit when she became a teenager, and had returned to believing in them once adulthood had settled in a bit and she started looking at her family's history. She'd been back home during her first year of college when an old friend invited her over for some food. They were sitting out at a table in her friend's backyard when Natalia spotted a tiny weather-beaten wooden cross on the ground. Her friend told her it was her little brother's grave. He'd been born with a horn in the middle of his forehead during a hurricane nine years before. Her father had bashed his soft little head in with a brick, tied a rosary around the infant's neck, stuffed another one in his mouth, and buried him out there in the wet earth so that whatever thing was still around the day after the hurricane could take its poor, unbaptized soul with it.

The story shocked Natalia, but she kept quiet. Her friend, an Afro-Caribbean second-year student named Zoé who had taught Natalia a lot about navigating college, saw something in her face and touched her shoulder. "Every culture has things like this. You know, things that seem...brutal to other people. We have this. We've always had it. This and the things in the reef off La Perla and whatever lives in that cave in Jayuya where the government has the place fenced and protected. It's no worse than a lot of our history, which is ugly." Her words didn't match the smile on her face.

After that encounter, Natalia came up with an idea for an oral history project, and spent the next six or seven weekends going up and down the mountains, asking the folks she'd known all her life about their experiences during and after hurricanes. She ended up with a list of thirteen missing people, which was a lot for her relatively small mountain town of Jayuya, and seven babies who'd been born with "la maldición," the curse, or that were, as an old man put it, "bebés de la lluvia," rain babies.

The events her grandmother had told her about, which sounded like old-lady stories, were all true. Now, as Natalia sat on her balcony staring at the torn sky and the angry sea between the buildings, those stories were about to start again, like after every other hurricane, in the newspapers and on her phone. They would start pouring from the small speakers of her radio as soon as someone came back on the air, too, all of them wrapped in innocent words like *missing, disappeared,* or *presumed dead.*

Everything she'd learned while interviewing people for her oral history project had awakened something in Natalia, a thirst for knowledge that sent her to the library and the Internet. She started devouring books about folklore and then magic, rituals, and Caribbean history. The breadth and scope of everything she'd previously ignored became a heaviness in her soul, which she felt she could only cure with knowledge. Since then, learning more had become her obsession. She wanted to help, so she stayed the course, graduated with her BA, and then kept going so she could become a nurse to get paid while helping people, but she has also studied everything she became curious about.

First it was history. Then it was religions like Christianity, Buddhism, Voodoo, Hinduism, Santería, Palo, Rastafarianism, and Islam. Then she studied sociology and politics. Then she became obsessed with philosophy, its history, and the way human thought had been shaped and reshaped countless times. Then she discovered feminism, diaspora studies, and the dark, hidden side of colonialism, American history, and the lingering wound known as post-colonialism.

The more she learned, the more she wanted to know. That unquenchable thirst for knowledge was behind her desire to escape. Puerto Rico was too small to contain her. She wanted to experience life elsewhere. She wanted to save money and visit Madrid, Venice, New York City, Tahiti, Paris, El Salvador, Cuba, Sri Lanka, London, Tokyo, Nairobi, Argentina, Brazil, Germany, Switzerland, and Uruguay. She wanted to visit the pyramids and to see the Nazca Lines from the air. She wanted to drink the world and everything it contained. And she wanted Gabe to come along with her, to experience a different world so he could become as curious as she was...

There are nameless things that travel with a storm. After a hurricane passes, the best thing is not to go out.

Natalia checked her phone, knowing it wouldn't have a signal. She knew Gabe and his mother were fine, but still wanted to hear from him. And she knew if the signal didn't come back soon, he'd show up at her place. It was the way he was built.

Natalia kept looking at the dark slice of sky right above the ocean.

She'd heard someone say the sky after a hurricane looks like it's been in a fight, like someone took a hammer to it while it was dark and left it all mangled and angry. They were right. Natalia thought about a bloated corpse hanging over the island, something abused waiting to fall down and crush them all. While a part of her wished the sun would return and the power would come back on, a smaller part of her relished the destruction because it reminded her of how everything in Puerto Rico was sort of broken, how even the most basic things seemed to constantly malfunction, and of course, how she had to leave. There was just too much to lose by staying. How much would be taken from this place? How much would they lose?

She would leave with or without Gabe, but she'd prefer the former. Gabe was good, pure in a strange way that had something to do with his simplicity and the way he'd filled the hole left by his father's death with love for everyone else in his life. She knew that people like that, people who loved unconditionally — recklessly — and with everything they had, were rare. But Gabe was also a bit stupid, provincial. He loved her perfectly, stupidly, just as he loved his mom and his friends. He thought that was enough. Natalia knew it wasn't.

25

GABE

—

Getting water
Colonialism hurts
Corpses stand up
More reasons to move
Lying

The heat was awful. It stuck to my skin as if it were trying to strangle me. I could feel sweat running down my face and sides. Despite that, it felt good to be out of the house.

"They have no idea when the university is going to open again," said Natalia. "We might lose the semester or push the end of it back a few weeks. And I haven't heard anything about my English classes." The lady in front of Natalia turned around and looked her up and down, apparently angry that Natalia had spoken English during such a Puerto Rican moment: We were standing in line behind a water truck.

Natalia had more information than me. My mom's little radio had picked up a local news station on the third day after the hurricane, but they focused more on the lack of government response and how long it was taking to get aid from the US to Puerto Rican shores than on anything else. The thirst for independence dripped from their words, and I understood it. Being fucked when you're a small republic is almost understandable, but being fucked while being a colony hurts a little

154

more because it reminds you that colonialism is like being the child of a neglectful parent.

"What else did you hear?" Natalia had stopped talking, and I wanted her to keep going.

"I can get two stations out on the balcony," said Natalia. "They've been saying María was it, the hurricane we'd talk about for years. A lot of people are dead or missing. Entire mountain towns are completely unreachable because of landslides. The hurricane destroyed houses everywhere. Things just…collapsed. They said there are teams working on the electricity around the clock, but it won't be enough. Water will hopefully be fixed sooner." Natalia looked around. The lady who'd given her the evil eye was screaming a man's name into her phone.

"We've done this before," I said. "We'll do it again."

"This isn't like before," said Natalia. "This was…the Big One. Hospitals are struggling with too many patients, lack of power and medicine, and injuries. The shelters weren't ready for the number of people they received. They don't have enough food or beds. The rain was as bad as the wind, and there were floods all over. The damages are estimated to be in the billions, Gabe. The people on the radio were saying it will take years to bounce back from this one."

I noticed Natalia's English had improved. A lot. When she wasn't focused on minimizing her accent, she spoke well, her words flowed. But listening to her made something crumble inside me. I felt sad, hurt, and useless. Hurricanes feel like a personal attack because they take away things like your power or your ability to move around or go to the places you want to go to, but they also feel like a collective attack. María had killed people—my people—and demolished my country. Every destroyed palm tree, every obliterated house, every missing person hurt in that part of my heart that was tied to the island I called home, the place that watched over my birth and saw me grow up. Everything Natalia was saying bothered me. The thing that was bothering me the most, though, was the one selfish thought that kept coming back to me carrying Bimbo's words: *No one will pay attention to anything but themselves for a while.* Everything was fucked, but I was starting to feel safe, and that made me feel good...and feeling good was making me feel awful.

"My friend Tamara went back to the hospital where she works the second day after the hurricane," said Natalia. "She was assigned to help in the morgue because they'd run out of space. There was some problem with their emergency power system and it took about three hours to get it running after the power went out. A lot of people died. Others were brought in either dead or dying as soon as the wind stopped. The morgue filled up quickly, and they knew more were coming..."

The little paranoid ghost whispered in my ear about Kimbo. Natalia must've seen something in my face because she suddenly changed the subject. It wasn't a good change.

"Have you called Xavier's parents?"

Guilt kicked me in the chest. Natalia could've asked anything else, but she cared about people, so she asked about those who had been hit by something worse than a hurricane. I shook my head and couldn't find the strength inside me to say no or look Natalia in the eye.

"You should call and check on them."

Natalia had a soft, raspy voice that, in the best moments, made me think of cigarette smoke rolling over velvet. In the worst moments, she sounded like my fucking conscience. I nodded, dreading even the possibility of getting Xavier's mom on the phone.

"You never finished telling me about Tamara," I said, eager to change the subject.

"Lo que pasa...I don't know if I want to talk about it?" It was weird to hear Natalia end a random sentence in a question mark, and that worried me.

"Whatever it is, you can tell me. You told me to share the weight sometimes, remember?"

She smiled and then looked around. She moved a bit closer and dropped her voice.

"Tamara said she was...waiting. You know, for the power to come back or whatever, and then she started hearing noises."

"Noises?"

"From the...from the dead people. ¿Cadáveres?" She said the last word as quietly as a secret.

"Corpses," I said. "I guess you can say bodies too."

"She heard noises coming from the corpses. Like they were... complaining or...¿Gimiendo?"

"Moaning."

"Complaining or moaning or something. A lot of them. And then they stood up. She said it was fast, like someone had pulled them all up. One moment they were...you know, down, and the next they were all standing up. She screamed and heard people screaming somewhere nearby and then the bodies just...dropped back down. It happened with the dead folks they hadn't brought to the morgue yet too. I don't know, it sounds like a horror story. Anyway, she left and hasn't been back to the hospital since."

It was hot, but something about Natalia's story sent a chill down my spine. I understood why she hadn't wanted to talk about it. I felt for Tamara because, hard as I tried to convince myself whatever she'd seen came from her tired brain and not the real world, I knew better.

I could see in Natalia's eyes that she wanted to move on, to leave the story out there, untouched, in hopes that having shared it would help it go away, so I asked about her mom and how she and Keyla were coping in their tiny place. They were okay. No damage other than some water getting in. They were taking walks along the Isla Verde beach in the afternoons. She said the breeze felt great and there were lots of people out there with kids and dogs, all of them trying to keep the cabin fever at bay.

We eventually made our way to the front of the line and filled every container we had brought with us with warm water from the truck. It smelled like pool water after a chlorine treatment, but it'd have to do.

We put everything in my car and I drove Natalia back to her place. We talked about restaurants we liked on the way there. I was glad she didn't want to talk about anything deeper. Or about Tamara again.

Once I had helped Natalia carry all her water up to her apartment, I told her I was going home to take the water to Mom so she could take a bath. Then I kissed her. Keyla wasn't there, but there's something about not showering in four days that kills your craving for intimacy.

"Mi amor," said Natalia. My love. That was the only thing she ever called me other than my name or Gabe. Those two words allowed her to get my attention. Always. I looked into her eyes and found doubt there. I hated it. "Are you okay?"

I was definitely not okay, but replying with the truth would be too much. "I'm okay," I said. "Ya estamos del otro lado." *We're already on the other side of this.*

I couldn't look at her when I said it. Natalia grabbed my face and kissed me again.

"The thing with the power going out and not coming back for weeks? That's just another reason to move, mi amor. There are places where this shit doesn't happen. We can go there. We can have a place for our moms to go to when things get bad here. Remember that, okay?"

I nodded again, kissed her one more time, and started walking down to my car.

"Where did you spend the storm?"

The question stopped me in my tracks. I thought she had believed the story about spending it at Bimbo's place.

"With Bimbo, why?"

"It's okay if you don't want to tell me, but I'd like to know. You must've been doing something very important to leave your mom alone and only check on me with a text." She sounded angry, but was trying to keep it under control. I wanted her not to be angry at me more than I wanted to keep our secret.

"We visited a guy. We got two names."

"Dos nombres…"

"Los tipos que mataron a María."

"Do they work for Papalote?"

"Yes."

"And you guys are going after them, right?"

"I don't—"

"Don't lie to me, Gabriel. Please."

"Yeah."

"No. Please. Don't do it." There it was. Her voice; my fucking conscience.

"We'll be fine. Bimbo has a plan. I don't even think I need to, you know, do anything else. Nothing's gonna happen to—"

Natalia shook her head and closed the door. My heart shattered. I felt like a kid who'd just let his parents down. I thought about knocking on her door again, telling her I wasn't going to do it. It wouldn't work. She'd read the lies on my face. She'd get even angrier.

The first thing I did as soon as the car was running was plug my phone in so I could keep the battery full. The screen lit up and I realized I had a text from Bimbo from seven minutes earlier: ill pick you up at 7 okay

Ill. Yeah, the whole country was ill. We were far from done. I drove away, thinking about dozens of corpses suddenly standing up in a dark morgue.

26

GABE

—

Another veve
Talking to Henry
The Lord is my shepherd
La Garita del Diablo
We're all haunted

The sun plummets into the sea quickly in the Caribbean. When the power's gone, the arrival of night feels like a threat because you know the heat will stay, the animals will make an inescapable racket, and you'll have nothing to do but try to fall asleep and wait for sunlight while sweating your ass off. The governor had put in place a six p.m. curfew for three days after the hurricane. Now it was over and we could move around. It made me wonder if Bimbo had been planning stuff and simply couldn't make it happen sooner or if this was something else. I wasn't sure I wanted to find out.

I'd heard from everyone within seventy-two hours of the hurricane. It had been mostly short texts because people wanted to save battery, but I knew everyone was okay. My guess was everyone had texted everyone, but I was still surprised when Bimbo pulled up with Tavo riding shotgun. Both got out of the car to hug me and ask about my mom. If Tavo saw the thing on the door, he didn't say anything. Maybe Bimbo had already told him.

"So, where are we going, man?" I asked Bimbo.

"We're gonna try to find old Henry."

I had half an idea about why Bimbo would want to see the addict. I hoped we didn't find him.

Riding in the back of Bimbo's shit-brown Neon as he drove down Old San Juan's streets, I kept thinking about Henry's story of the reef. As far as I knew, Henry was still alive, as of at least two or three weeks earlier when we had seen him walking by Calle Sol. That meant he had kept Papalote happy all this time and, if his story was true, that he had spent the last three years dragging bodies out to the reef and tying them there for the creatures to feast on.

Everything outside my window was as bad as thinking about Henry and whatever was out there on that reef. Old San Juan is always a little shiny and a little decrepit, a little touristy and a little dilapidated. It is a city that mixes the best and worst that history has to offer. Now that mix had tilted to the bad side because the hurricane had also done its thing here, peeling the paint off some of the newer houses, spreading trash all over the place, destroying plants, ripping signs apart, and plastering leaves on walls. Seeing my beloved stomping grounds battered like that hurt my soul, and it made me think about how awful things had to be in smaller towns, places in the middle of the mountains that had lost contact with the rest of the country, and in places where houses were made of wood slats and zinc sheets.

Bimbo had stopped and was about to make that turn when he said, "Oh fuck." I looked at him and then looked in the direction he was looking. In front of us was the house that sat on that corner. It had a tall wall around it that had been painted pink at some point. There was a large Barón Samedi veve painted on it. Right underneath it, there were two eyeballs. They were just round things with black pupils and tails like a tadpole, but it was clear that they were eyes. My blood ran cold, but before I could process, a voice pulled me back to the present.

"There he is!" said Tavo.

Henry was carrying a couple of grocery bags over his shoulder while heading north on the right side of the street. Bimbo rolled down his window and talked to him. Henry told him he was on his way to a van the government had set up near El Morro. They were doing health checks and offering free meals and bottled water since the third day after the hurricane. Henry said he was starving. He looked like he was about to topple over.

"It's okay, man," said Bimbo. "I'll drive you there. Hop in. I have a question for you."

Henry climbed in the back with me. He said hello to Tavo and me, even managing a smile full of rotted teeth. His smell quickly filled the car. His mouth, hair, and skin were worse than the last time I'd seen him, and he looked a bit thinner, if that was really possible.

"So, what's up?" he asked Bimbo. "You guys okay? That was an ugly one. I've seen a bunch of hurricanes, but this one was different. I swear I heard demons howling in that fucking wind. Dead serious. Sixteen years ago or so, I was working on a boat for some music producer. We were off the coast of Labadee, in Haiti. A storm was about to hit us, so I pushed as close as we could to the shore to try to get some protection for the boat. Everyone but crew and I had already left for a hotel. We saw fire on the shore. A big one. There were some folks moving around it, dancing or something. Anyway, point is, the wind started blowing and the rain became a nightmare. We lost a lot of visibility in a matter of minutes. But the fire on the shore didn't go out. Something big and dark was covering half of it. Something...like a person. A very big person. Then we all heard it, the howling. It was louder than the wind, and the wind was loud as hell. I heard that shit again, the night of the storm."

Some stories are like really cold nights in that they seem to suck all the sound out of the air. In the wake of Henry's story, none of us spoke. We were all thinking about floating bodies out near the reef, the remnants of the dead caught in the ocean's mad, angry dance.

There are nameless things that travel with a storm.

Where had I heard that? Natalia. Her grandmother used to tell her that. I remembered it because it echoed things my own abuela used to tell me. Old women are often right about the most important things in life...and in death.

"Yeah, it was bad," said Bimbo. His voice brought me back to the car, and to Henry sitting there, full of stories and pain and a craving that would eventually destroy him. "But we're okay," Bimbo went on. "Glad to see that you're getting hooked up with food and water. About damn time this government did something right. Anyway, listen, I have a question for you." Henry nodded. Bimbo kept going. "I'm looking for two dudes who work with Papalote: El Brujo and Raúl. You know them or know where I can find them?"

Henry moved around in his seat like he was uncomfortable. I'd seen him passed out on the street, so I knew comfort wasn't the issue.

"Why you asking me this, man?"

Bimbo pulled the car into a spot on the side of the street and turned back to face Henry.

"Those motherfuckers killed my mom right here in Old San Juan."

Henry's eyes went wide, the green flashing in them momentarily. "Your mom...she was the one who worked at Lazer?"

Bimbo nodded. "I know you ain't supposed to be talking about Papalote's business. You're a smart man. That's why you're still alive, but all I need to know is where I can find them. I swear. I'll pay you. No one will ever know you talked."

They kept looking at each other, but neither of them said anything else for a minute. I guessed Henry was looking for a lie in Bimbo's eyes. I know he found only pain and anger in there.

"My mom's name was Judith," said Henry. "Cancer took her two years after I started working on boats. I was in Curaçao working for some rich singer when it happened. It broke my heart, not being there. Felt guilty about that shit for years. I'm glad she never saw me...you know, like this. We didn't always get along, and she wanted me to do something different with my life. You know, like being a lawyer or some shit. She didn't think living on boats and taking rich folks to gorgeous beaches was really a career. But I loved her anyway, and I know she loved me. Moms are special like that, like...they will hurt you from time to time and you will hurt them a bunch of times, but the love is there because they fucking brought you into this world. Killing someone's mother? That's fucked up, man. I'm sorry."

"Thanks, Henry," said Bimbo. "I'm sorry cancer took your mom."

Henry took a deep breath and then looked at me. "Gabe, Xavier, and Tavo here helped me out real good a couple years ago. They stepped up to some punks beating the shit outta me. I'll never forget that. Not a lot of people willing to put their neck on the line, you know?"

Henry stopped talking, took another deep breath, and looked around as if he expected to see one of Papalote's men right outside the car, waiting for him to say anything out of place just so they could put a bullet in his skull.

Then he cleared his throat and finally spoke. "Papalote usually spends his days at La Garita del Diablo, one of his two bars. The big one. It's right down there in La Perla. Pretty popular place at night. You can get your booze and anything else you want there, and people like that. He lives right next to it. Big white house that looks out of place. Motherfucker even has a tunnel under his house that takes him all the way to beach. We've been asked to bring in packages from small boats a few times.

"Anyway, El Brujo and Raúl are always coming and going from that fucking bar. If you need to find them, that's your best bet. El Brujo is almost always there, making sure the sales run smoothly. He's a bad dude. You don't even wanna know why he got that nickname. Motherfucker doesn't even carry a gun now, but no one messes with him.

"Anyway, I know he lives right next to the little chapel they got over there because some people go to his house to get his...services or whatever. Witchcraft shit. People bring him, like, animals and fruit and other stuff. At night you can hear chanting sometimes, too, some language I've never heard before. I want no part of that. I might be living on the streets, but I still walk with Jesus. 'He leadeth me beside the still waters. He restoreth my soul: He leadeth me in the paths of righteousness for his name's sake.'"

Henry took a deep breath. His smell was becoming too much. I wondered if he talked to God when he was high. Maybe that's why he kept shooting heroin, to sit with God in a cloud and tell him all his grievances to his face. Or maybe that's the only way he could see his mom again. I wondered how he dealt with his life while also being religious and if the things he did to get his fixes haunted him daily and filled him with the special kind of guilt religious people often feel, especially if they were raised by religious parents. Of course, a lot people do things worse than Henry: abuse their partners or kids, attack people for being gay or a different color, rape, traffic...and half the time, they did it all with God's name dancing on their lips.

"Anyway," said Henry. "I...I guess I don't know exactly where Raúl lives, but I've seen his truck parked all over the place on that street, so I'm guessing it's somewhere nearby. He's the one who usually...supervises us when we have to take one of Papalote's packages out to the reef."

"What's out there, man?" The question was out of my mouth before I thought about asking it.

Henry looked at me. The thing in his eyes was somewhere way past fear. "Things you don't ever want to see, Gabe," he said.

"So, the stories are true?" I asked him.

"Of things living beyond the reef? Yes. Those stories are true. And those things work with Papalote, so y'all better do whatever you need to do and get the fuck outta there quickly, hear me? And if you managed to do it, don't ever go back."

"We'll do that, man," said Bimbo. "Listen, one last thing: Does Papalote live alone? Is there an army in his house? A few pit bulls he never feeds or something like that?"

"Nah, he has a woman who lives with him now. I don't know her name. She has a daughter. Papalote ain't the father, I don't think. He took them in or something. I've seen the woman come and go, but I've never seen her daughter, so I don't know if that part's true, but I've heard Raúl talk about the girl."

"Okay, so a woman and maybe a girl, but no men, right? You said they're no longer —"

"I told you all I know because of your mom, and because I owe these dudes, but that's it. That's all I've got, man. I don't know anything else. I was only in that house once, making a big delivery. That's it. Maybe there are some men in there and maybe there aren't. That's all I got. Eso es lo que trajo el barco, as the Cubans say, yeah? Now I have to take care of some things."

Henry cleared his throat and then opened the door and got out of the car. Bimbo told him he'd take him to where he was going, but Henry waved him off as he readjusted the bag over his shoulder. "I don't wanna be seen with y'all, no disrespect. Do what you gotta do with that info. I hope I see you guys on the other side of this. Good luck."

You know shit's about to get dark when not even junkies want to be seen with you.

27

REBECA

—

The man who was darkness
Retribution is holy
Ancient prayers to a dark god
Bloody sacrifice
Killing an angel

The woman had dark eyes that never seemed to blink. It was a scary thing, a thing that made the woman look a little less than human, or maybe a little more. The woman didn't give her a name, but she welcomed Rebeca into her place of business, a little room next to a pharmacy with a sign on top of the door that read LECTURAS/LIMPIAS/ AMARRES/TRABAJOS. Rebeca had found her the way everyone seemed to find things that weren't readily available in this world; the woman was someone a friend of a friend of a friend had once met or worked with or something. The point was that the woman seemed to know what Rebeca needed as soon as she walked into her tiny house.

The woman was sitting at a table, her hands on top of a black book. When Rebeca walked in, the woman put her head to the side and looked at her, reminding Rebeca of the way her childhood dog would look at her when she whistled. It was only a small tilt of the head, but it signified much more. Then the woman said, "You're here about your daughter." She said it in Spanish, with a thick Dominican accent.

Rebeca nodded because not saying anything and simply agreeing is the only thing you can do when someone throws the truth at your face, especially if it's a truth you didn't expect them to know. As she approached the dark woman, Rebeca tried to make sense of it all. It could be that the friend of a friend of a friend had heard from one of those friends that Rebeca was looking for something and that something had to do with her daughter. Or it could be that she had grief etched all over her face and the woman was able to read the lines there, the dry riverbeds that anguish had carved into the corners of her eyes and the sides of her mouth in a few short months. A tiny voice in the back of Rebeca's head told her to turn around and leave, to stop looking for vengeance, that nothing good would come of talking to this strange woman even if she was somehow able to help.

"Relax," said the woman.

Rebeca inhaled deeply and nodded again. In life, we can be surprised both by the stupidity of our fellow humans or by the way they seem to have an understanding that lets them know your innermost thoughts, your darkest desires, your deepest pain. This woman could see into Rebeca and Rebeca knew it, could feel her unwavering gaze go past her skin and dig into her soul.

"Show me your story. Think about what you've been through. Show me," said the woman.

"Show you?"

"Don't speak. Think. Feel."

Rebeca knew her story wasn't unique. She knew the country — the world — was a mess, a godless place in which children died from neglect and abuse, went hungry, fell into the hands of human traffickers, and suffered from horrible illnesses that took them into the darkness despite the fact that they could easily be saved with a pill or injection that wasn't available — or affordable — wherever they lived. But that wasn't her story, her daughter's story. Rebeca knew she lived in a country that did a great job of pretending it wasn't the Third World. Her daughter had a great pediatrician, a lot of toys, a loving family, and went to a decent school. No, her daughter's story was different. She belonged to the group of kids who are pulled into the darkness not by illness or neglect but by the hand of man.

Or maybe it had been a demon.

Remembering hurt, but the pain was always there, so Rebeca allowed it to flood into her mind, to rip her insides apart once again. The woman wanted her to think about it, to show her, and that's what she was going to do. She closed her eyes and relived all of it.

Someone had broken into Rebeca's house in the middle of the night. A shadow, an evil spirit, a thing that moved in the darkness, a thing that was darkness; whatever you want to call it, but it had acted like a man, looked like a man, and run like a man.

It happened fast. There was a sound. Footsteps outside her bedroom door. Too heavy to be her daughter. They tugged at the corners of Rebeca's consciousness. Feet on the floor. Movement. Anything out of the ordinary woke her up. It was an ability she'd suddenly acquired the moment they came home from the hospital with her daughter wrapped in a blanket and looking out at the world with her unfocused little eyes.

The sound of footsteps was followed by the sound of the bedroom door creaking. By the time Rebeca had sat up in bed, understanding had dawned on her and it was too late. There was a figure in the room. Half of it submerged in shadow, the other half standing in the light that came from the hallway. The figure was holding a gun. A manly voice started giving orders and asking questions.

Don't move.

Don't scream.

I will kill both of you if you don't do as I say.

Where do you keep the money?

Where do you keep your jewelry?

Rebeca's husband was next to her on the bed. He was sobbing. Fear was making his body shake. The man didn't want to kill them, or at least that's what he said. He wanted money, jewelry, laptop computers, phones. He wanted whatever could be turned into money quickly. After the initial wave of fear subsided, or after Rebeca managed to learn to ignore the ringing in her ears, she realized it wasn't that bad. All they had to do was give the man all they had and he would be gone, back into the violent night from which he'd come. But that didn't happen. They didn't have time. A figure moved in the doorway, casting a small shadow on the man's arm, allowing darkness to swallow the gun but not its threat.

"Mommy?"

A single word. The last word. The man who was darkness turned. There was a boom and a flash that birthed a nightmare. A small body hit the floor. A scream ruptured the night. The man who was darkness said something and then he ran, his legs going over the small body. Rebeca heard him tumble down the stairs. She jumped out of bed, her husband right there next to her. Both were screaming now. Both were crying. Both knew the one thing they truly didn't want to know with a certainty that threatened to crush them. The man who was darkness had taken from them the one thing that mattered and left everything else behind, everything he had said he wanted, the stuff that didn't matter.

The cops came. The ambulance came. Family came. The neighbors came. The newspeople came. No one had answers. Nothing could be done. Death had visited them and ripped them in half and no one in the world could do anything to make it better.

There was a short investigation and then Rebeca and her husband stood under the midday sun and cried some more as they lowered their daughter into the ground inside a small casket.

For weeks there was nothing but silence and pain. Around her, the world crumbled and lost all meaning. Rebeca focused on breathing because she was convinced the pain in her chest would kill her if she let it take over, if she allowed it to make her stop breathing. It was all wrong. It was way too soon. Reality had turned into a nightmare so bad Rebeca's brain had never allowed itself to entertain it. Rebeca

and her husband kept crying and hugging family members and praying and screaming. Their house filled up with an absence too huge to
withstand, so they went to a hotel. They drank. They fought. They
comforted each other. They ate takeout that tasted like nothing while
listening to people on the TV talk about things that didn't matter.
None of it made a fucking difference. The cops didn't give a shit. They
had a case number, but every time Rebeca called, she received the
same response: They were working on it and had nothing to report,
no new leads, nothing. No one had seen anything. The world went
on. The news forgot about their daughter. Their family and friends
returned to their lives.

Rebeca wanted to find the man who had killed her daughter, but
the man who was darkness had been nothing but a brutal slice of night
and as such he had returned to the night, vanished into shadows, never
to be seen again. Rebeca and her husband were left alone, trapped in
a maelstrom of anger and fear, drowning in the aftermath of a stupid,
senseless act of violence.

Like most other crimes in the country, the death of her daughter
was filed away and never solved. The cops started talking about the
case going "cold" whenever she called. Then they stopped picking up
the phone and returning her messages. That's when Rebeca knew she
had to do something. She knew that finding the man would be impossible, like trying to punch the mist that some mornings floated over
her mother's backyard up in the mountains. That's when she started
asking around.

She wanted to contact her daughter, to ask her what she should do,
to have her help her from beyond the grave. She'd seen shows about
things like that. She had read a few books about ghosts talking to people and giving them answers. Her mother said it was all true. She said
that the veil between the world of the living and the world of the dead
was very thin and that many people had the ability to lift it and facili-
tate communication between the two sides.

Someone at work told Rebeca about a man who lived by the beach in Condado. They said the man did strange things and had weird powers and then they gave Rebeca a phone number. She called. He picked up. They met. The man made Rebeca drink some coffee that tasted like burnt cigarettes and puddle water and then he looked at the dregs at the bottom of the old yellow cup and told her something about an upcoming financial opportunity. Rebeca got up and left, leaving the man behind, screaming about payment and saying she'd messed with the wrong brujo.

One bad experience, Rebeca knew, didn't mean she should stop looking. Everything in life was always about trying, failing, and trying again until you got it right or died trying, so she kept asking around, going from one botánica to another and then from psychic to palm reader to bruja to another psychic all across the island. No one talked to the dead. No one could help her find a man no one had seen.

Finally, at a botánica in Río Piedras, an old Cuban woman with a thick accent and a cigar hanging from her lips that she seemed unwilling to touch told Rebeca about the dark woman. A special woman. She said the woman dealt with gods older than the island itself. She said that, for the right price, this woman could get her what she wanted. Rebeca said price wasn't a problem. After all, the one thing she couldn't afford to pay was the only thing she had already lost. The old woman wrote a number from memory on the back of receipt and blessed Rebeca before sending her on her way.

Rebeca had called the woman the day before the hurricane. The woman asked her no questions and told her to call a few days after the storm depending on the state of the roads. She said a big one was coming. She had been right, and here was Rebeca, four days after the hurricane, tired, sweaty, and remembering everything.

"Now tell me about your daughter," the woman with the dark eyes said.

Rebeca opened her eyes. She'd been deep in her memories and suddenly felt like ten seconds or ten minutes could've gone by since she'd walked into the woman's tiny home.

"My daughter was killed," said Rebeca. "A man killed her. He broke into my home to steal and shot her. I want him dead."

"You already showed me all that," said the woman. "And I don't kill people. Tell me something about your daughter. Something you didn't show me."

"I don't want you to kill this man," said Rebeca. "I want you to help me get in touch with my daughter. I know she will help me find him."

"You don't want that. Don't pull the little one into your darkness and hatred. She already crossed over. She's happy there. Let her be."

Rebeca had no idea what to expect when she walked into this house, but having this woman tell her to drop her plans wasn't something she was willing to put up with. Everyone was always telling her how to act, what to feel, what to wear. "It comes with being a woman," said her friend Sandra every time Rebeca complained. She was done with it.

The woman with the dark eyes lifted her hand. The hateful words that were about to burst out of Rebeca's mouth died on her tongue. Their carcasses turned to dust. She swallowed them.

"I said to let the child be, not to forget about retribution," said the woman. "Retribution is holy, and you are certainly entitled to it."

Rebeca felt like the woman had been inside her mind, like she had seen her thoughts. It made her feel uncomfortable. The heat inside the woman's dark house felt oppressive, like a million tiny hands pressing against her skin all at once. It'd been that way everywhere since the hurricane knocked the power out. She hated it.

"Tell me something about your daughter and I'll help you."

Rebeca gave in. "My daughter was my everything. She was my world. She filled me with joy. I loved her more than anything else —"

Tears came and her words caught in her throat.

"Good," said the woman. "You're a good person and you loved your daughter. You deserve retribution."

"How can I get...retribution if I don't know this man's face or name?" asked Rebeca.

"You don't have to," replied the woman. "Strong hurricanes always bring something with them, a presence that rides in the wind and comes down with the rain. This presence knows everything. If you feed it and say the right prayer, it will do your bidding."

"This presence will…it will kill the man I'm looking for?"

"Maybe," said the woman, her eyes impossibly dark and unblinking. "This presence will give you what you want or show you what you need to see if you feed it. It depends. Take a seat."

Rebeca realized she hadn't moved, as if entering the house any further would put her within reach of something monstrous. The monster she feared was exactly what she was looking for. She moved toward the table and sat across from the woman.

"How do I feed this thing?"

"This thing is older than any of us," said the woman. "This thing has been around since our ancestors started filling the sky with invented gods. To feed it, you must offer it blood. Flesh blood. And you must recite an old prayer in a language very few people speak now, a tongue that has been lost to time. Are you sure you want — ?"

"Yes, I'm sure," interrupted Rebeca. "The blood offering, how big does it have to be?"

"The bigger the sacrifice, the bigger the reward," said the woman.

"How do I find it?"

"You don't," said the woman. "You summon it."

"And if I summon it, what will it do?"

"I already told you. If you summon it and it comes, there's no telling what it might show you or do for you. Old gods are moody."

"As long as it gets me what I need, I don't care about anything else."

"Close your eyes and think of your daughter again," said the woman. Rebeca obliged.

"Now repeat after me: Ehe maytubi Javasasgot igomoro."

The words were strange, but the woman spoke them loudly and clearly. Rebeca repeated them.

"Ehe maytubi Javasasgot igomoro." The syllables felt funny, like something she'd said in a previous life or a set of sounds that were somehow familiar to her tongue.

"Memorize it. Don't write it down. Don't tell anyone or you will pay. Ehe maytubi Javasasgot igomoro."

"Ehe maytubi Javasasgot igomoro," said Rebeca again, ignoring the threat the woman had thrown her way. She had no idea how she could write words she had never heard before in a language that had been lost to time, but she nodded in agreement, her eyes still closed.

"Ehe maytubi Javasasgot igomoro," said the woman again.

"Ehe maytubi Javasasgot igomoro," echoed Rebeca.

"Ehe maytubi Javasasgot igomoro."

"Ehe maytubi Javasasgot igo—"

Rebeca felt the table shake, its wooden legs rattling against the floor next to her feet. She opened her eyes. The woman's eyes were entirely white. Her arms were on the table, still resting on top of the black book. Behind her was a strange shape floating in the air, a dark deeper than any dark Rebeca had ever seen, like an inky mix of liquid and smoke. She felt like she was looking into an opening in space.

"Your pain is big enough," said the woman. Rebeca looked at her. Her eyes were normal again, still unblinking. Behind the woman, the darkness had disappeared.

"If you call it, it will come," said the woman. "Now go. Remember the prayer and forget you were ever here."

Rebeca was surprised by the abruptness of the visit's end. There was something in the woman's voice that Rebeca couldn't fathom arguing against, so she got up.

"How much—?"

"No payment," said the woman. "You've lost enough to know the most important things can't be bought with money."

Rebeca had nothing to say. The woman was right. Again.

Rebeca thanked the woman, stood up, and walked out of the tiny house. Outside, she crossed paths with a young woman with a beautiful head full of curls. The young woman smiled at her, and Rebeca tried to reciprocate, but her mouth felt dead and the strange words in her head were occupying all her attention, so she merely nodded and kept walking as the young woman entered the house.

On the way home, looking at the devastation the hurricane had left behind and wondering how long it'd take for the trees to grow full and green again, Rebeca thought about the sacrifice the woman had talked about. *The bigger the sacrifice, the bigger the reward.* All she wanted was for the man who'd killed her daughter to die. There wasn't a single thing in this world she wouldn't sacrifice for that slice of cosmic justice. *The bigger the sacrifice, the bigger the reward.* Rebeca knew where she was going to get the blood.

As soon as she got home, Rebeca pulled her phone out and turned on its flashlight. She walked into the kitchen and went to the knife block that sat next to the coffee maker, untouched. The block was made of a dark, reddish wood that was probably very expensive and came from some jungle the folks who sold it were tearing to shreds. It housed a few knives, none of which Rebeca used. They weren't bad knives; she just like her old knives better.

Rebeca reached for the top knife on the left side of the block. The biggest blade on the block was a chef's knife. Its edge was sharp and reflected the light from Rebeca's phone perfectly. They'd never used it, so it had to be sharp.

"Ehe maytubi Javasasgot igomoro," said Rebeca while turning around, shutting off her phone's flashlight, and walking toward the door again.

Rebeca walked out of her house, knife in hand, and turned right.

"Ehe maytubi Javasasgot igomoro."

Juliana. That was her name. Rebeca's neighbor. Rebeca's angel and savior. She had shown up two days after her daughter was killed. She brought food. She held Rebeca while she cried. Since then, Juliana had been like an anchor. She listened to Rebeca. She still held her while she screamed and cried. She prayed with her. She brought food to her. Juliana did everything Rebeca wished her husband had done.

"Ehe maytubi Javasasgot igomoro."

Rebeca walked up to the door and slammed her left fist against it. It was dark, and the insects and coquíes were going crazy, but without power, nothing was running, so she knew if Juliana was there, she'd hear the door.

"Ehe maytubi Javasasgot igomoro. Ehe maytubi Javasasgot igo—"

The door flew open. Juliana stood there, holding a candle. She looked surprised for a moment and then smiled. Rebeca brought the knife up and forward. The blade hit her angel, met the slightest resistance, and then penetrated her soft belly.

Juliana made an *oomph* sound and then sucked in air like she'd just popped her head above water after a long dive.

"Ehe maytubi Javasasgot igomoro."

Rebeca couldn't let Juliana scream. She pulled the knife out. Juliana bent over. Rebeca grabbed her hair, turned the knife sideways in her hand, and ran it across her friend's neck.

The spatter of blood could be heard over the racket of the insects and coquíes.

"Ehe maytubi Javasasgot igomoro."

Rebeca looked around. She'd done it. The sacrifice. A big one. There was blood now. A lot of it. *The bigger the sacrifice, the bigger the reward.*

"Ehe maytubi Javasasgot igomoro."

Juliana was curled into herself on the floor, making noises that made Rebeca think of a small bird thrashing around in a muddy puddle.

"Ehe maytubi Javasasgot ig—"

There. At the end of the small walkway to Juliana's door. Darkness. Impenetrable darkness. She'd done it.

"Ehe maytubi Javasasgot igomoro," said Rebeca again, now with renewed vigor. How long did she have to keep repeating the strange prayer? She didn't know. She didn't care. The woman had never told her when to stop. *The bigger the sacrifice, the bigger the reward.*

"Ehe ma—"

The thing moved. It covered the distance between where it had been floating and Rebeca in less than a second. It was bigger now, and shaped like a very large human. A very large human made of shadows and with a black hole for a face.

The darkness came closer to Rebeca. She forgot the prayer. The world in front of her went out of focus. The figure was looking at her. It had no eyes, but Rebeca knew it was looking at her. She could feel it. She thought about her daughter, about the man who had destroyed the most precious thing in the world and then vanished into the night, about the blood pooling at her feet.

The thing made of night lifted something resembling an arm and touched Rebeca's face.

Rebeca saw her room, the man, the gun exploding. She saw the man running out of her house, the man waking up in a small apartment, the man breaking into another house. Then she saw the man walking into a building. The figure in front of her was standing behind the man. He turned around. The man made of space flew at the man who'd killed Rebeca's daughter and swallowed him. He was dead. Rebeca smiled.

Rebeca opened her eyes. The black figure was gone. She turned around. The door was still open and the candle her friend had been holding lay extinguished on the floor, but Juliana was gone. And there was no blood on the floor. The figure had drunk it all. Rebeca felt lighter. The pain was there, but the man was dead and that made her feel like justice had been done, and a bit of justice was sometimes enough to keep you going.

28

GABE

—

Creepy stories
A dark figure
Sidewalk ghost
Vengeance
A gun isn't enough

You're not supposed to trust a junkie. Everyone knows that. But sometimes you're so desperate that trusting a junkie is just one more bad decision after the others. Maybe it's your only option.

We were leaving Old San Juan behind, the whole city as dark as the night that opened up beyond the reach of the car's headlights. All I could think about was the story of things living right beyond the reef. We all grow up surrounded by creepy stories. Some are made-up tales about kidnapped children and awful accidents told by our parents and grandparents to keep us safe and afraid of the world. Some are made up by our friends to scare us just for the fun of it. Some are always around, like the kid who died crossing the road without looking both ways, the student at your school who vanished mysteriously, and the one dilapidated house in every neighborhood, which is either haunted or the house of a witch. As you grow older, reality pushes those stories out of your head. But sometimes those creepy stories find you and invade your life again. And the second time around, you're old enough to know they're not just stories. Fear was our constant companion and we dived down to a level of the streets that was new to us.

"So, what now?" asked Tavo.

"Right now? Nothing," said Bimbo. "I'm gonna get you guys home and that's it. Tomorrow we'll get you a gun and see if we can find Raúl. If what Henry told us is true, it shouldn't be hard."

"And what happens if we find him?" I asked. I was afraid I already knew the answer.

"If we find him, we're gonna take him for a ride and ask him a few questions."

Fear does weird things to you, and I could feel a lot of fear inside me. They knew where I lived. They had killed Xavier. The list of stuff making me uncomfortable had been growing steadily since this whole thing began. Everyone has different coping mechanisms, and one of mine was anger. Hearing Bimbo's bullshit response made me snap.

"Shut the fuck up, B," I said. "What you fucking mean to say is that you—we—are going to torture him and then kill his ass. Am I right? Did I get it all?"

Tavo opened his mouth as if to say something and then closed it without uttering a word.

Finally, Bimbo spoke. "That's exactly what we're gonna do, Gabe," he said. "But you don't have to come along if you don't want. It's cool. Same goes for you, T."

The world had collapsed, but bad things don't stop just because there's no power and no water. We had to be like those bad things, like the bad people who made them happen. If we didn't put an end to this, more of us would die. How long did we have before they came for Bimbo? For Tavo? For me? What if they decided to come back and kill my mom? What if they had followed me and knew where Natalia lived? Prayers to keep ghosts from haunting us wasn't going to be enough to save any of us, and Bimbo sure as hell couldn't do this alone.

"I'm in this with you and you fucking know it," I said. We'd dug too deep. We'd already gone too far. Papalote could end us at any moment. He could end everything we loved. Not doing what we had to do would be like signing my mom's death warrant. I wasn't going to do that. "Been with you from the start and I'll be with you until it's done, but no more...no more bullshit. You have to let us know what we're gonna do."

"You got it, man," he said. "I can see you're worried. It's all over your ugly face. You thinking about your mom, aren't you? "

I was fucked. We were fucked. I nodded.

"She's gonna be okay," said Bimbo. "We're gonna make sure of that. We're gonna make sure everyone is okay."

We drove on in silence. The world around us was empty. We saw few cars and there were no lights anywhere. I imagined everyone at home, trying to sleep through the heat or huddled over tiny radios like my mom and me. I wondered how many people across the island were up to no good. We hadn't even seen a cop car since Bimbo picked me up.

No one said a thing as we approached the house with the veve and crude eyeballs graffitied on its wall.

By the time Bimbo pulled up in front of my house, I was ready to jump out of the car. I hadn't stopped loving him or Tavo, but being stuck in there with them, surrounded by a murky, battered world, had gotten on my mood. I wanted to be in Natalia's arms, with the AC on, listening to her dreaming up a better future for both of us, a future somewhere else, a future in a place where things actually worked.

I opened the door and Bimbo asked me to bring him the duffel bag from the trunk. I couldn't believe he still had all the guns with him. I had a hard time dealing with having one in my closet, and he was rolling around the city with an arsenal in his car. It was dangerous and stupid, but I decided not to say anything because I knew whatever I'd say would come out even worse than I intended it to be. Also, I already had a gun, so making me get the duffel bag in front of my house instead of waiting for them to be in front of Tavo's house felt like he was testing me.

"Nah, we already played with guns enough out here. Someone might see you this time. Do that shit later," I said. I expected Bimbo to say something or argue, but he didn't do either of those things.

Instead, he smiled. "You're right, Gabe," he said. "I'll pick you up tomorrow, yeah?"

"Sure, B," I replied, already walking up to my house, trying to burn off the graffiti on my door with my eyes. It wasn't working.

I opened my door and stepped in without looking back. I heard Bimbo's car as he drove away. As the sound of the motor vanished, the sounds of night in the Caribbean took over. The cacophony of insects was almost overwhelming. It was a sound that told me there was an entire wild world out there, and that it would devour me if I gave it half a chance. Then I heard something in the mangroves behind the house, a painful wail unlike anything I'd heard before.

The hair on the back of my neck stood up despite the stifling heat. I walked to the little window in the kitchen and looked out. Total blackness. For a moment I thought it could be Tavo and Bimbo, trying to be funny, so I went back to the door and opened it to look outside. The darkness was less dense in the street because there was open space there and not everything was swallowed up by the pummeled trees and because a bit of moonlight had broken through the clouds.

The neighbor across the street had two palm trees in front of his house. They were only a couple of thick sticks poking the night now, their tops blown off by the hurricane. Even in the darkness, I recognized them, but something was off. There was something next to the palm tree on the right, the one farther from my door. I stood there and allowed my eyes to adapt to the gloom.

I realized I was looking at a man. Someone was standing across from my house, not moving, looking my way. There was no one else out there and there were no cars running anywhere on the street. Plus, it was late. Then the coffin on my door flashed in my head. Someone—maybe more than one person—had come up to my house in the middle of the night and painted that thing while my mother slept inside. Someone had caught Xavier right outside his home. They'd taken his eyes, and for the first time, I hoped with all my heart that he was dead by the time they did that. It was a thing I hadn't thought about before, and I hated it. I also hated myself for not having thought about it before. And for not being there when they killed Xavier.

I closed the door and went to my room to get the gun. I was going to kill the man outside. That would send them a message.

The gun was exactly where I'd left it. When I picked it up, it felt heavier than the last time, as if it had fed on my intent. There's something strange about holding a thing that can obliterate a life in a second. Having the gun in my hand scared me and also made me feel a bit better; this was the only protection I had. I recalled what Bimbo had said about having to pull the hammer back all the way for the damn thing to shoot. I would do that right before opening the door.

I got to the door and pulled the hammer back. The clack it made was much louder than I'd expected.

As soon as I flung the door open, I knew the man was gone. But he'd been there. I hadn't imagined it. A dark figure. Like the one I'd seen just before my father died. The spot the figure had occupied was now just empty gloom next to a thrashed palm tree. I walked outside and looked around. It was too dark to see much, so I kept walking.

Half a block later, I turned to go back home and saw a man standing on the sidewalk about ten feet behind me. Was he planning on killing me? If so, why hadn't he pulled the trigger yet? I felt like I was looking at Death, and I knew my gun was not going to stop it.

I took a step forward. If this man was going to kill me, I wanted to look him in the eye and whisper a curse the second I went down. If I was going to kill him, I wanted my face to be the last thing he saw.

There was something in the way he held his head, slightly tilted to the left, and the shape of his shoulders that looked familiar. It was like looking at a silhouette of a famous person or cartoon; the thing isn't there, but your brain has everything it needs to fill in the blank.

My brain screamed. My feet pushed forward as if they craved a different truth than the one flooding through me. I took two more steps and was too close to keep lying to myself.

The man on the sidewalk was Xavier.

But the man on the sidewalk couldn't be Xavier, because Xavier was dead. I was looking at Xavier's ghost.

Todas las historias son historias de fantasmas.

The beating of my heart became so loud all the sounds of the Caribbean night around me faded into the background.

This meant something. Xavier stayed there, silent and looking at me. Then I blinked and he was gone, the sidewalk deserted, the place where Xavier had stood now empty.

Sometimes you see a puddle, and the water looks clear. Then someone steps in it or a car drives through it, and all the crap that was at the bottom explodes and muddies the puddle. The same thing happened to my thoughts, as if someone had used a very long stick to stir the sludge at the bottom of my brain, the part that is too close to the heart for its own good.

Xavier's death — his murder — hit me all over again. It was enough to bend me over a bit. The part of me I couldn't control was finally accepting his death, breaking off the piece of my heart Xavier would always own and throwing it to him on the other side of the veil. Then a wave of fear washed over me. I feared for my mom. I feared I would lose Natalia if I kept on being an asshole and making bad decisions. I feared my future would run away from me if I didn't step the fuck up and grab it by the horns, grab it with the same hands I was using to hold on to the previous stage of my life...and to a dead man's gun. I feared that my friends would end up just like Xavier. I feared the graffiti on my door was a sign for Barón Samedi and that he would come find me. I feared I would walk into my hot, dark room one night very soon and I would find Barón Samedi there, his face painted white, his wild eyes on me, letting me know he was going to take me to the land of the dead.

Sadness filled the space where everything else had been. I'd seen

Xavier, but I would never hug him again. We would never go camping again. We would never listen to each other dreaming out loud. My brother was dead, and seeing his ghost wasn't going to change that, so seeing his ghost had to mean something.

Vengeance.

The thought popped into my head fully formed, with the song of pain screaming in its veins. Vengeance. It was what we all wanted and what we needed to do. Xavier's ghost wanted vengeance, and we were going to deliver it to him.

Anger allowed me to stand up straight and start walking home. They say anger is poison to your soul, but I think it feeds other parts of you. It can be like gasoline for your soul, but also like cocaine for your spirit.

By the time I'd made it back to the house and walked in, the anger had deflated and my thoughts slowed down. I had just returned the gun to my closet when I heard another inhuman wail coming from the mangroves. I had to save my phone's battery, so I sat there, surrounded by night, straining my ears, trying hard to listen and identify anything that was out of place, anything that didn't belong to the usual cacophony of night in the mangroves. For a few minutes, every insect was a monster, every coquí was screaming a little warning, every sound was an omen that promised a death that would come only after someone took my eyes.

Suddenly, the gun didn't feel like enough.

29

GABE

—

Black holes for eyes
Nothing works
Love outweighs hate
More tiny coffins
A return

In the aftermath of a hurricane, waiting becomes a state of mind, and time loses its meaning. I was waiting for something to happen and none of it was good. I needed to go somewhere, to do something, to focus on something other than Bimbo, the men we would attempt to kill, and the graffiti on my door. I needed to forget the strange sounds of the previous few nights and the little radio, with the man who sounded like he would rather be anywhere else than talking about missing and dead people.

It was all too much, so I got in my car and drove to Natalia's place.

Natalia felt like another island to me. Solid land. Her voice pushed the images of Xavier with black holes for eyes and Kimbo rotting in a small living room out of my head. We ate strawberry Pop-Tarts while sitting on the tiny balcony at the back of Natalia's place and looked at the folks who came to the gas station to fill up, try to get milk for their kids, or to see if they could cop some ice.

Natalia was sad. The lack of classes and work was getting to her. Also, that morning she'd learned that someone had killed Keyla's uncle. The dude was married and had a kid who had been very sick recently. Keyla's uncle had bought a new generator because the kid needed it to breathe, and some assholes had shot him in his own backyard to steal it. They'd gone as far as unplugging it and pushing it closer to a wall, but then they'd either gotten lazy because it was heavier than they'd expected or gotten scared and had abandoned the thing not ten feet from Keyla's uncle's body.

I understood Natalia's sadness, but I felt only anger. Keyla's uncle hadn't even made the news. No one was coming to save us. Still, I kept my mouth shut when Natalia started saying this was just another sign that we needed to move to the US.

Natalia mistook my silence for an invitation to continue, as if my lack of words meant I wanted more of hers. She obliged.

"This place offers nothing but heartache, mi amor, and every time a hurricane comes, all the bad stuff we're used to pushing down all the time bubbles to the surface and it...me encojona. De verdad, ya no lo soporto."

I knew what she meant. I'd felt it too. The country was messed up. Everything Natalia was saying was true. However, the idea of leaving made me feel worse than all those things combined. Home was home, and I didn't want to leave. I didn't want to move away from my mom and my friends. The infrastructure was garbage and crime was through the roof and there weren't many opportunities for us, but something about the island called to me. Not something; many things. Old San Juan. Guánica. Isla Verde. El Yunque. The places where we went camping. My friends. Our music. Everything here, the beautiful mix of races that birthed a small, angry, courageous nation with a unique identity. I hated the same things Natalia hated, but my love for everything else outweighed it.

The conversation put me in a weird mood, and the day was too damn hot and humid, so after chatting about nothing for a while, I left Natalia to her sadness, looking at the ocean between the buildings, and went home.

I plugged in my phone and dropped it on the passenger's seat while I drove. When I got home and unplugged it, there were two missed calls. Both from Paul. I turned the ignition again, plugged the phone back in, got the AC going, and called him back. It rang only once before he picked up.

"Hey, Gabe."

"How you doing, P?"

"I'm...not good, man."

"What's wrong, brother? How can I help?" I asked. I meant it. With all the chaos, my anger had dissipated a bit. With no power, no water, and families still trying to reach folks who lived up in the mountains, a million bad things crossed my mind.

"I don't know."

"Talk to me, man. What's up?"

"Someone...someone painted something on my door. Some kind of symbol or something."

I was sitting in the car, so all I had to do was look at my own door to know exactly what he was talking about. However, I didn't need to, because the image was tattooed in my brain. Paul was scared, and I understood him.

"Let me guess," I said. "It's a cross with some tiny coffins on the sides and —"

"Yes! That's it, man. No tengo idea de qué es esa mierda. Cynthia said they marked my house to let me know they know where I live and that they're watching me. She left to stay with her parents and told me to call you guys and figure out how to get myself out of whatever shit you started."

"Whatever shit we — ?"

"You know, her words, not mine."

"Yeah...Listen, they put that on my door too," I said. I decided not to tell him about the same thing being painted in front of Xavier's house. That would push him over the edge. I could imagine him freaking out.

"So...¿qué carajo está pasando? What is this? What the hell does it mean? Was Cynthia right?"

"The only thing you need to worry about right now is that they know where you live."

The silence on the other end of the line spoke volumes. I could hear Paul breathing, could almost hear the gears in his head turning. He surely had questions—and recriminations—but there was too much noise in his brain and he couldn't get those things out. I gave him an opportunity to do something to feel better about it.

"We got two names. The dudes who killed Bimbo's mom. We're gonna see if we can get one of them tonight. Or, you know, figure out where he lives and then grab him at some point soon. We're meeting at Bimbo's house this afternoon. You should come. That shit they painted on your door? It's called a veve. Bimbo knew a bit about it. The one you have—the same one that's on my door—is for Barón Samedi. He's the...he's a god. One of those old gods we got from Africa that doesn't fuck around. He deals with the dead. These guys are sending us a message. I can't tell you exactly what it is, but it's nothing good."

"I...I can't have this, man. If they know where I live, they could kill me like they killed Xavier. They could...¡le pueden hacer algo a Cynthia, cabrón! I need her back here with me. Things were going great and now this. This...this is shit."

He was right. He was more right than me. They could definitely do something to Cynthia. The same went for my mom and Natalia. They were planning on doing something to all of us. We had to end it before they could.

"You're right. That's why we're gonna end it. Help us. Only way we make this shit go away is by killing them first."

Again there was silence on the line. I could hear Paul on the other end. Breathing. Worrying. Thinking. Imagining bad men approaching Cynthia just like I'd imagined them breaking into my house and doing something horrible to my mom. Again. Just like me, Paul was thinking about Xavier on the sidewalk in front of his house, the flesh of his neck turned into a deep red mouth with no teeth, his eyes empty black holes full of death's black, silent scream.

"You guys are going tonight?"

"Yeah. Tavo's coming too," I said.

"Can you pick me up?"

The question surprised me, but it was what I'd been hoping for. Paul being with us was the right thing. He was joining us because he was scared and wanted to get Cynthia back to their place, but also because he hated the motherfuckers who killed Xavier as much as the rest of us did. I was angry at him, but he'd also lost a brother.

"Be ready at five. I'll text you as soon as I get on the road."

30

NATALIA

—

The woman with the dark eyes
Death does what it wants
Cryptic words
Broken windows and toppled trees
The future

Natalia sat in front of the woman with the dark eyes and wondered for the millionth time what could be written in the black book she always had with her. It was thick and looked old, but there was no writing on its cover or spine.

"More than my book brings you in today," said the woman.

Natalia had been extremely uncomfortable the first few times she'd come to see this woman, all of them with her mother. The woman was young and had a thick Dominican accent. She never blinked and often answered questions before being asked. With time, Natalia had come to accept that in the same way she'd come to accept the strange things that went on in the mountains where she was born. It still bothered her from time to time.

"I want to know if my boyfriend will be okay," said Natalia.

"Think about him, about what he's involved in right now. You've never asked me about him before, so something new is happening. Show me."

Show me. The woman always said the same thing. It was unnerving. It was a clear statement: I can see inside your head. Still, people — including Natalia and her mother, although they now visited separately — came to her. They came to her because she could help them, because she knew things. They came to her because she revealed truths to them and offered guidance through the world's dark passages. None of it made sense, but it was all true.

Natalia thought about the things Gabe had told her. *They killed Xavier.* She thought about Gabe's fear and the way he and his friends were always throwing themselves at danger as if their youth was a thing to burn, something they could waste. She knew nothing she said would stop Gabe, but she hoped she could help him somehow. If that was possible, the woman would know how.

Natalia closed her eyes and focused on Gabe and his fear, the way his warm tears had felt on the tattooed sun on her shoulder. She thought about Bimbo's mom, killed outside the club where she worked. She imagined Gabe's desire to help his friend, the way she knew he wanted to dish out justice at any cost.

"The young man you love is going blind into a dark room full of monsters," said the woman. Natalia opened her eyes and looked into the woman's unblinking eyes. The woman looked worried, maybe even a bit scared. Fear wrapped itself around Natalia's heart like a cold snake.

"Will he — ?"

"Don't ask that. Death does what it wants and the future is unknown. All we can do is try to navigate our way there in the safest way possible."

Natalia had been thinking about that question all the way here, and now it was the one thing she wasn't allowed to ask.

"Don't worry too much," said the woman. "He has something following him. Probably a grandparent or parent. And a dark, playful old god that goes by many names. I think he will be okay. Especially if you help him. He's too...trusting. He's caught up in someone else's life. But he will do whatever he wants, so you should worry about yourself."

"About myself?"

"You're troubled. You've been thinking about the dead. You feel its presence. You feel the thing that came with the storm. Sometimes to think of something is to call it, and you don't want to call this."

There are nameless things that travel with a storm. After a hurricane passes, the best thing is not to go out.

"I have. I know…things happen in the mountains during hurricanes. Bad things."

"Bad things happen everywhere, miss. The world was designed that way. We work hard to bring good into the world because evil always comes by itself. Stop worrying so much about it. There are big changes coming for you. The changes you want. Prepare for those. The matters of the dead are better left to the dead, child."

"Is there anything I can do to help him?"

"That's up to you," said the woman, her eyes open and unfocused. "Listen to your inner voice. And listen to him. He might not tell you things, because he wants to protect you from the darkness he's immersed in, but if you listen to what he says, you might hear what he doesn't say."

The woman's words were cryptic, like always. Talking to her was like trying to solve a riddle, but Natalia had seen her words click into place time and time again, both for her and her mother. She would think about Gabe's words, and she would find a way to help him. She wanted him around for the changes the woman spoke of.

Natalia got up, thanked the woman, and left. She had learned not to ask about payment. When the woman wanted something, she asked for it. If not, she shared things and sent her away.

On her way back home, Natalia drove slowly, soaking up the damage María had done: Broken windows. Toppled trees. Puddles of brackish water everywhere. Destroyed plants. Power lines on the ground. Branches piled on the side of the road. It would all fade away eventually, until the next one came. Natalia wanted out. She wanted to live in a clean place with nice streets and less crime.

After a hurricane passes, the best thing is not to go out.

The words came again, like always. Gabe had also told her to stay inside. He also said he was going to La Perla tonight. And that they had spoken to Henry.

Something clicked in Natalia's head. She signaled and turned onto a small street. She drove around the block and then headed to Old San Juan. She didn't know how to help, but she had an idea.

31

GABE

—

Brothers reunited
Gloomy and muggy
Cojones
Shaky yellow light
The van

I parked two blocks down from Bimbo's place. Barrio Obrero is not a pretty neighborhood, but the hurricane had made it worse. Bimbo's street normally looked like any other street in his neighborhood: narrow, dirty, packed with small houses built almost on top of one other, with power lines crisscrossing everywhere and cracked sidewalks you can't use because there were cars parked on them. María had knocked down those power lines, peeled old paint from the homes, destroyed all the plants, and ripped away all cloth awnings and many metallic ones, leaving them stuck to the houses in a mangled mess that looked like they were thrown carcasses of strange animals.

Paul and I walked down to Bimbo's place and climbed up the stairs to his door, feeling the movement of every rickety step under our feet as we clambered up. Bimbo opened the door for us before we'd had a chance to knock. The groans coming from the stairs had tipped him off.

Bimbo paused when he saw Paul. I was so glad that Paul was

willing to help us that I hadn't stopped to think about how Bimbo would feel.

But Bimbo's face didn't betray anger or hatred. Instead, a smile broke his mouth open and they hugged. They didn't even talk about that day on the wall of El Morro. As soon as we walked in, they started talking about the hurricane and asking each other how they'd been.

Tavo was already there when we walked into Bimbo's tiny living room. He smiled weakly and went back to the sofa. Paul joined him. Bimbo pulled out a chair from the three that were pushed under the small round table standing between the living room and Bimbo's kitchen and sat down. I joined him there.

It was gloomy and muggy and Bimbo's place smelled like unwashed bodies and old cigarette smoke. I wondered if Altagracia smoked. She was apparently in Bimbo's room because the door was closed and there was shaky yellow light coming from beneath it. I wanted the smell to be from her, because if it was from Bimbo's mom, then it meant we were inhaling the smoke that had once been inside a dead woman's lungs.

We sat around making small talk. No one wanted to start that conversation, because it felt like jumping into the ocean knowing there were sharks. Except this time, Bimbo was ready for the question.

"I want to get to Raúl first because it seems easier. We know he hangs out in that tiny beach at the end of La Perla and supervises the junkies that take the bodies out to the reef for...whatever the fuck Papalote has going on out there. There's four of us, so two should be looking out for trouble and two should ambush Raúl and throw him in the back of one of our cars. Once we have him, we have to keep him down and get the fuck outta there quickly."

I was going to ask him how he planned to pull that off in Papalote's backyard, with a man who had a gun and would not hesitate to use it, and in the presence of junkies who would identify us for the price of a fix. Tavo started talking before I had a chance to open my mouth.

"You think he's gonna be alone?" asked Tavo. "Going to La Perla is the easiest way to get them, but don't you think they're gonna have some kind of protection? Wouldn't someone else have gotten to them by now if they didn't? We're not picking off some old lady at the mall's parking lot, man. This is—"

"I talked to my uncle about this," said Bimbo. "He thinks we'll be fine because no one will expect us to walk into the mouth of the lion like that. Nadie tiene los cojones que tenemos nosotros."

Cojones. Balls. Cojones are great and all, but they're what you need to carry out a solid plan, not something you use instead of one.

"Listen, Bimbo, I don't think that's a plan," I said. Everyone looked at me. Tavo nodded his agreement. It made me feel like I wasn't alone. "We need to check out the place first and we need to know if there's anyone else keeping an eye on the whole thing with the bodies. Focusing just on the fucker we need to get into the car is an easy way to get killed."

Bimbo was looking at me, but there wasn't any anger in his face. He looked like he was waiting for me to go on. I did.

"We should split, yeah? Two groups aren't enough. We need more eyes in more places. Someone should stay at the top and look down at La Perla, see if there's anyone following us after we drive in and make our way to the little beach where we think this asshole is going to be. Someone should also keep an eye on La Garita del Diablo to see what everyone else is doing while the other two are down there getting shit done. And even if the coast is clear, getting the guy won't be easy. You know he'll be packing, and we don't know what'll happen if the guys he's with—"

"We're gonna wait until they're out on the reef," interrupted Bimbo. It didn't sound like he was trying to argue with me; he was just filling in blank spaces and helping me along.

"Great," I said. "We also have to make sure no one sees or hears us. It's not a long way from the tunnel to that beach and then back to the tunnel, but those are narrow-ass streets, so stepping on the gas isn't an option. How the hell are we gonna throw the guy inside a car and get out without anyone spotting him…struggling or whatever?"

"I'll get us a van," said Tavo. We all looked at him.

A figure appeared in the dark hallway beyond Bimbo's kitchen. Altagracia. Beyond her, the door to Bimbo's room was open. There were a bunch of large candles on a small coffee table in the middle of the room. Their light was bathing the room in a wavy yellow glow that spilled into the hallway and danced up the walls. Altagracia smiled at us and waved shyly.

"Everything okay?" asked Bimbo.

"Yeah," she said, and her accent made me think of delicious mangú. "I just wanted some water."

Altagracia grabbed a glass that was already on the counter and filled it from one of the five or six gallons Bimbo had on the kitchen table.

"Where the hell are you gonna get a van?" asked Bimbo.

"Don't worry about that. I'm on it," said Tavo.

"You mean now?" I asked.

"Gimme…twenty minutes?"

We kept looking at Tavo, waiting for more, but he was done talking. He looked at Altagracia, who had finished her water and was fiddling around on her phone while leaning against the counter. A moment later, Altagracia moved away from the counter, her face still buried in her phone, and returned to Bimbo's room.

"Okay, you do that," said Bimbo.

Tavo stood up, went to the door, and walked out. We heard the stairs groaning under his weight.

"Now, who wants to stay on top and who wants to hang out at La Garita del Diablo?"

"I'll go with you to the beach," I said. It was the right thing to say, mostly because Bimbo and I had done every other horrible thing together. I also didn't trust Paul enough now to let it be him down there, and a part of me wanted to protect Tavo from whatever mayhem could unfold. I'd seen Bimbo's clumsy punches in the parking garage, and at Kimbo's house, and it was clear he needed me. He had enough anger and hatred inside him to get the job done once he was in a position to do so — two corpses were proof of that — but his skills wouldn't get him to that point without help. He was heavy and awkward, and every plan he came up with was shit. Yeah, I had a lot of reasons for wanting to be down there with Bimbo, but it also had to do with me. At some point, merely going along for the ride had turned into craving vengeance for Xavier and for my mom. Xavier had died alone, and the guilt was eating me alive. Killing the motherfuckers who'd put him in the ground would be the only thing that could make me feel better. Protecting my mom…well, that was just as personal.

"Good," said Bimbo, looking at me and nodding, his eyes saying thank you and letting me know he understood why it had to be me down there with him.

"I wanna stay on top," said Paul. I wasn't surprised. It made sense. At any other time, Paul putting himself as far away from danger as possible would've made me angry or at least it would've forced a cruel joke out of my mouth, but I was still surprised he was back at all, so the cruel joke died and the smell of María's smoke buried it somewhere near my esophagus.

"Tavo can take La Garita del Diablo," I said. "We've been there a few times. He can grab a beer and pretend like he's waiting for someone."

"Great," said Bimbo. "Let's do this."

"Wait," said Paul. "I came here with Gabe. Shouldn't I have a car if I'm gonna stay up there by myself?"

"You can take mine," said Bimbo. "I'll ride with Gabe in the van if Tavo gets it."

"What happens if he doesn't get it?"

"It's Tavo, man. He'll get it," said Bimbo. "And I hope he does it quickly. If Raúl's going out to the reef today, he'll do it when the sun is going down."

32

GABE

—

The Lord of the Crossroads
The Devil's Sentry Box
Into La Perla
Knock the motherfucker out
A confession and a promise

Twenty minutes later we got a text from Tavo. He was downstairs. With a van.

The van was white and looked familiar. When I climbed inside, it dawned on me: It was Beto's van. I'd have to ask Tavo how he got it. Beto, a friend of ours, used it to help his girlfriend get her drum kit to gigs and to carry his father's equipment to tattoo conventions all over the island. He never let anyone borrow it.

The van smelled like mold and didn't have shock absorbers. There was nothing in the back, which made me wonder how we were going to keep Raúl under control back there. We didn't have rope or duct tape or anything else. We were unprepared and relying on a shitty plan and cojones, a combination that made the whole thing feel a bit like a suicide mission. At least we were going to have eyes in more places that just by the water. It felt good to have Tavo and Paul along for the ride.

I fished my phone out of my pocket and sent Tavo a text: you good? How did you get this thing?

I looked at the screen until it went black. No reply. That meant nothing. Or it could mean everything. I felt something slither into my thoughts, something cold and wet. I shook my head, knowing it wouldn't take care of the slithering thing, and looked out the window to fill my head with something else. It didn't work. The thing was still there. Why was I so scared? This was stupid and dangerous, but I was with my brothers. We'd been through a lot of shit. We —

Henry.

Fuck.

This whole thing was happening because of information we'd gotten from Henry. I know there are many paths to addiction and I judge none of them. Same goes for homelessness. Hell, every person in the world is anywhere between three and ten bad decisions away from losing everything. No, the problem wasn't that Henry was almost always high and wandering the streets with his veins full of warm visions. The problem was...no, the problem was exactly that. How much could we trust him? How much of what he told us could we trust? Anything Henry missed, any small detail he could've forgotten, could get us killed.

"You're quiet," said Bimbo. "That means you're thinking. Whatever you're thinking, stop. We're here to do something, not to think about it." I didn't reply, but what he'd said was simply ridiculous. Bimbo stayed silent for half a minute and then spoke again. "Listen, man," he said. "I'm sorry about putting you in danger the other day. That was dumb. I want all these motherfuckers dead, and sometimes that's all I can think about, so I'm sorry if I don't have all these awesome plans I know you wish I had, yeah?"

"Don't worry about it," I said. This was not the time to start an argument.

I looked down at my phone again. Still no reply.

There was almost no traffic on our way to Old San Juan. There weren't many places to go, and people were tired, broke, hot, and angry. María had broken the world, and people wanted to stay home so they could feel like it was all far away. La Garita del Diablo would be open because bars in San Juan know that the darker things get, the faster people turn to booze to keep the demons at bay...or to invite them to dance. After every hurricane, gas stations, panaderías, and places that sold liquor always opened first. Baile, botella, y baraja, right?

Bimbo was driving fast. He'd said he wanted to make it there with some sunlight left. The van moved, clacking with every pothole we hit. I imagined it breaking down under our asses or a tire popping when we were down in La Perla, leaving us stranded. Which would mean we'd die. Quickly. I brought my hand up to my neck and touched the necklace Bimbo had given me. It felt more immediate and alive than the god my mom often talked about, which was the same one she'd blamed for killing my father. The beauty of syncretism is that, in times of need, it offers a lot of options. Heading to the ocean while thinking about death and the possibility of something monstrous living beyond the reef, the idea of an old god, one that had suffered changes and survived the awful trip from Africa and then managed to refuse assimilation, brought me a sick kind of comfort. I picked up my phone, opened Google, and typed "Elegguá" in the search bar. I clicked on the third result and read.

Elegguá, also called Lord of the Crossroads, is an old African deity which is sometimes represented as a small Black child and sometimes as an old man. Elegguá represents the beginning and the end of life. Elegguá is the Orisha responsible for opening and closing the paths of life, and people who want to have a difficult pathway opened to them pray and make offerings to this Orisha.

Elegguá likes to be celebrated by children, enjoys offerings of guava and pork, and is sometimes known as the trickster because he has the attitude of a child and likes to play practical jokes on people. Similarly, because of his childlike nature, this Orisha is known to enjoy sweets and toys, which are often placed on his altar. While many people take Elegguá's child-like nature to mean the Orisha lacks power or isn't important, the opposite is true. Elegguá is an extremely powerful Orisha who is known as one of the warriors and —

"What are you reading?"

I looked at Bimbo. "Nothing, man," I said. "Just glad to know Elegguá is on our side for this."

A smile broke across Bimbo's face, the corners of his mouth curling up and displacing the anger and anxiety I'd seen etched into his features before.

"Hell yeah he is," he said. "He's gonna help us be sharks, man."

We drove in silence. Then we crossed into San Juan and turned right after passing the Castillo San Cristóbal. Much smaller than El Morro, San Cristóbal is a fortification the Spanish built to protect against land-based attacks on the city after they got their asses handed to them by the English and then the Dutch. I couldn't remember the years of those battles to save my life, but remembered the part about getting whupped and how they realized they needed to cover their backs against land attacks. San Cristóbal was where the legend of la garita del Diablo came from. La Garita del Diablo was the name of the bar where Tavo would keep an eye out for us, probably while trying to ignore the sound of the generators they had undoubtedly set up in order to run the place, but it was also an actual place with a hell of a spooky history.

San Cristóbal, just like El Morro, is surrounded by garitas, or sentry boxes. One of the sentry boxes at San Cristóbal is located farther away than any other and is somewhat removed from the fortification itself. The sentry box, which can be seen from the top of the fortification, protrudes into the ocean, hanging over some black rocks that are constantly getting battered by the angry Atlantic. According to the legend, soldiers didn't want to be assigned that sentry box at night because eerie sounds could be heard there after the sun went down.

There are many versions of the story, but the basic facts remain the same: A Spanish soldier went to that sentry box one night to keep an eye out and was never seen again. Those who wanted their world to make sense said he had a lover in town, a Black woman, and he'd decided that running away in the middle of the night was easier, and faster, than trying to quit. Even though Spaniards had been involved with — in other words, had regularly abused — Black women since they started bringing enslaved Africans to the island, interracial relationships were taboo, so the story of the soldier running away made sense.

However, that story isn't the one most people believe, especially those who have been to that sentry box at night. Those who knew there are things in the world that are beyond our comprehension believed the man had been taken by the Devil. Some versions of the story mention that a few soldiers had said they'd heard screaming. Others claimed they'd seen dark demons emerging from the water at night and that they had surely taken the man. Those rumors were enough to give the sentry box its name, the Devil's Sentry Box, and to make it a part of Puerto Rican folklore forever.

While thinking about the story as we climbed Calle Norzagaray on our way to La Perla, something clicked in my head. The story of the Devil's Sentry Box sounded like a typical Devil story about a dark, creepy, remote place where, obviously, the Devil roamed, but when you threw in the rumors of demons emerging from the ocean — one of the things we were supposed to be close to very soon — the legend started looking a lot like a misinterpreted reality.

"Call Paul," said Bimbo. "Tell him to park near one of these businesses. If he can't find a spot, tell him to park in El Tótem or wherever and then get his ass back to the far side of the wall."

I called Paul and told him what Bimbo had said. He hung up without a word. Despite being the one staying at the top, which put him as far as possible from danger, Paul was obviously scared. The veve on my door — on our doors — popped into my head. My confidence had been shaken a bit, but we were moving and doing things, and that had kept me from focusing too much on what the future held. Thinking about the veve was like driving a van packed with explosives into the basement garage of my confidence. I was just waiting for it to blow.

"What about Tavo?" I asked. I was still waiting for his reply, still worried about how he was feeling about what had gone down at Beto's place.

"Tavo's fine. He knows what to do. He's smarter than all of us put together. He doesn't need instructions."

Bimbo had a point. Having Paul with us felt good because it meant one less hole in our group, but having Tavo with us made me feel better because he could come up with things on the fly and always seemed to have a solution for everything. The van we were in was proof of that.

To our right, the houses of La Perla looked like they were ready to slip into the ocean. María had hit them hard and they looked rotten, their melted vibrant colors less lively than usual. Beyond them, the yellowing ocean stretched all the way to the setting sun. There was an entire world on the other side of that water. It was the world Natalia wanted us to conquer, to be a part of, but my brain didn't let me focus on that. The reef was much closer than the horizon, and if there was something there, we were going to get close to it. We were also going to put ourselves very close to an evil man with a gun.

"So, we're just gonna drive in like we're on our way to a bar or to cop and then...what, make it all the way down to the beach?"

"Yeah," said Bimbo. I expected more. Nothing came. His dark eyes were glued to the road. His right hand kept squeezing the wheel as if he were trying to get something out of it. "You brought your gun?"

I hadn't. The gun was a presence for a while, something I couldn't stop thinking about, an unmoving entity saying nothing very loudly from the darkness of my closet. I'd thought about it from time to time and planned on bringing it with me, but then I'd talked to Paul and forgot about it.

"Nah, I forgot."

"It's okay. I got mine," said Bimbo. "But I don't think we should use it."

I agreed. *Boom.* Big noise. Small place. Bad idea.

Kimbo came to mind.

"You want me to try to knock the motherfucker out, don't you?"

Bimbo sucked at planning and at fighting, so it stood to reason. Part of me already knew he was going to rely on me. That's why I'd volunteered to come down with him to the worst fucking part of our mission.

"Only if you think you have what it takes, nerd," he said, looking at me for a second with a mischievous smile on his round face. That this motherfucker could keep smiling with his mom and one of his best friends in the grave and on our way to commit terrible acts was a testament to either his lack of a moral compass or his absolute disregard for our health, or it was proof that some people are born with good souls, and no matter how much shit and pain and blood and death life shovels on top of them, they'll always be that way.

The van rattled as we turned right on Cemetery Street and headed down to the short tunnel that keeps La Perla separated from the rest of Old San Juan. Bimbo rolled down the windows and put his left arm outside the car and his right one on top of the steering wheel. I placed my right hand outside the window and my left one on top of the van's gray dashboard. La Perla has its own set of rules, and we didn't want to call attention to ourselves, so we were doing our best to comply with the rules and look like two dudes in a van looking for a cold beer on a hot night or a bit of weed to help us ignore the heat.

The tunnel that takes you into La Perla leads to a short street where you can turn left and go to the cemetery or turn right and go into La Perla itself. Bimbo turned right, but it felt like we were going the opposite way.

Once in La Perla, we followed the main road, Calle San Miguel, all the way to the end, where there's a small rocky beach with a tiny patch of sand.

We saw only three people on our way there, all of them walking. The sound of generators running filled the air. Some were for businesses that would start receiving folks again soon. The rest were for people to combat María's putrid aftermath. The sun had started dipping into the water, so we were there just in time. All we had to do now was wait and see if we'd gotten lucky or not. I hoped so, not because I was looking forward to whatever chaos we were about to bring down on Raúl and on ourselves but because I hated the idea of Tavo having to go through whatever he had gone through again.

Bimbo spotted an abandoned house and parked in front of it. He left the windows down and the motor running. I was afraid it would announce us, but the roar of the ocean drowned the sound of the motor, and the buzz of the generators would surely help mask our presence.

"You ready?" asked Bimbo.

"No." It came out quickly. It was honest.

"You remember that time Tavo got in trouble soon after he came out?"

"You mean that time with the kids from that other school? The whole thing that started at the beach?"

"Yeah."

"What about it?"

"We were about to start throwing hands and I turned to you." Bimbo looked at me now. "I asked you if you were ready because you looked scared as shit. You said the same thing. No. It was bullshit. You beat a lot of asses that day."

"What's your point, B?"

"My point is you're always in your head, always thinking and shit. You're always ready because you think about stuff more than the rest of us."

"I don't think—"

"When your pops died and we started hanging out, I thought you needed help. Thought you were soft, you know? But then we all started running around together and I quickly learned you weren't soft at all. You're ready for this. You've been ready for everything."

"What da fuck are you talking about, man?"

"Life, Gabe," said Bimbo. "I think Tavo will stick around and do his thing. You know, get a job or whatever and hit the waves. Paul is gonna tie the knot with Cynthia. They'll probably have a couple kids and spend the rest of their lives throwing shit at each other's heads, but it'll be fine because they both come from money. You're different. You think too much, but maybe that's a good thing. I think that will take you places."

Bimbo and I had had a lot of deep conversations over the years, but this one was the most surprising. I had no clue he thought about me that way. I had nothing to say, and correcting him and vomiting all my insecurities inside the van felt wrong. I'd had a plan for a while. Sports. Playing ball. It was going to get me through school and into college. I was good enough. Then the coach called me into his office one day, sat next to me, and touched my thigh. Then his hand went to my crotch and started rubbing me through my shorts. I ran out of his office. I gave up on sports that day. My father asked me a few weeks later why I'd quit the team. I told him. He hugged me. I don't know what he did, but the coach never came back to school. A few weeks after that, my father was dead. I'd been drifting ever since. Aimless.

"What about you, B? You know, since you can suddenly see the future and all."

Bimbo stayed quiet for a minute that stretched out all the way to the horizon. Then he reached for the key and turned off the ignition. I was sure he wasn't going to answer, but he did.

"This is it for me," he said.

"'This'? What do you mean?"

"The streets. I'm not too smart, you know. I can probably go to college, but for what? To sit in a cubicle doing shit I hate for minimum wage for the rest of my life? Nah, I belong here. This shit is in me. My uncle used to tell me that all the time before he got killed. He used to tell me I had to stay in school, that I —"

"Hold the fuck up!" I said. "Your uncle is dead? When did that happen?"

Bimbo made a sound with his mouth that carried all the frustration in the world. He looked out at the ocean again. When had his uncle died? Did that mean we weren't going to get help from him? Did this have anything to do with his mom?

"Listen..."

I listened, but nothing else came. Every second felt too long.

"Talk to me, asshole," I said. "What's up? What happened to your uncle?"

Bimbo took a deep breath. When he started talking, he kept his eyes on the water.

"Fuck, man. That just...slipped out. It's...well, someone caught my uncle alone four months ago. At home. They...they stabbed him a bunch of times and then cut off his head."

"Are you fucking serious?"

Bimbo looked at me. His eyes answered for him. I felt like shit for asking.

"They took a pic of his head on the floor and texted it to my mom from his phone. My mom had worked with him for years and knew everyone, so she...well, she took over. She told everyone to keep doing their thing and pretend my uncle was still around. She knew whoever had done it would try to get the word out. She thought making it look like he was still alive would make him a legend or something. A ghost no one would want to fuck with."

"So, you've been lying to us? This whole fucking time? He didn't tell you about the body or none of that shit you said?"

Bimbo had lost even more than I'd thought, but I felt betrayed.

"No, G," he said. "That was all me. I'm sorry. I was going along with the whole thing because it's what my mom wanted after she took over. Then they killed her, and it just made sense to keep — "

"Bimbo, no. Did they kill her because she took over?"

Bimbo stayed quiet again, his eyes still on the water.

Fuck.

We were here for all the wrong reasons, and it was too late to call it quits.

"Does anyone else know?"

That got Bimbo to look my way. "No, only you. I was going to tell you soon, but I didn't know—"

"Fuck all that right now," I said. "This is still about your mom and Xavier, but don't forget they attacked my mom. I found her in a pool of blood. I don't want that to happen ever again. I don't want weird shit painted on my door. I don't want to walk around feeling like some asshole is gonna step outta the shadows at any moment and kill me. I don't want to be afraid of what could happen to Tavo or Natalia or Paul or you. I don't—"

"I get it. Then we have to do this."

I nodded.

"I don't think we should tell Tavo and Paul," said Bimbo. "We don't know how they'd react. This can stay between us. Like your thing with the coach."

Like your thing with the coach.

I felt cold. And angry. And exposed. How did he know? My face must've given away everything I was feeling.

"You okay, man?" asked Bimbo.

"No. How did you know?"

"The coach thing?"

"Yeah."

"You told me," he said.

"When?" I had no recollection of doing so. All I could remember was that secret inside me, eating away at me, hurting like nothing else, and making me angry at the world.

"Just…some night. We were drunk. Or high. Maybe both. I can't remember. We were hanging out at my place. The Yankees were playing someone on TV. I was going to change it and you asked me not to. I asked you why you'd stop playing baseball if you loved it so much. You shook your head and said the coach had been an asshole. I told you all coaches have to be assholes. You know, yell at you and insult you to make you better or whatever. You said he'd grabbed you. That was it. I never told anyone."

He'd never told anyone. He'd kept his mouth shut and never mentioned it even in passing. My brother had carried my secret like it was his own. I'd do the same.

"We won't tell them." I already had a heavy secret inside me; adding another one wouldn't be hard. "Let them think your uncle might help us. We need them. I feel like shit lying to them, but we can't do this alone. Why aren't your uncle's men helping us?"

"When my mom was killed, they came to me and asked me if I wanted to take over. Some of these dudes have known me all my life. I said I needed some time to think about it. Then I got sent to jail and some of them moved around or started their own thing. The few that are still around want no part of this. They think Papalote killed my uncle and—"

"Did he?"

"No."

"How do you know?"

"Because he would've taken the body and told everyone before immediately taking over. And I'd be dead."

He had a point.

"So, who was it?"

"He was trying to get something started with some Haitians. Cocaine. I think they wanted more than he was willing to pay. They got a little brave and my uncle threatened them. They kept an eye on him for weeks and came to him only when they knew he'd be alone."

"Hey, what was it you said about your uncle getting a veve on his house? You think there's a connection with who killed Xavier and attacked my mom?"

"No," said Bimbo, looking at me. "That's just Voodoo shit, but my uncle's men took care of that a few days after they killed him. My mom made sure of it. This is totally unrelated."

"I fucking hope you're right. Why the fuck are we here, B? Why did Papalote kill your mom?"

Bimbo sighed. "I think she wanted to take over Old San Juan, or at least to get more dealers in here."

I hadn't been expecting an answer. Bimbo was finally being honest with me. Kimbo had been right, and he'd died because of it. This was beyond fucked, and we were in too deep.

"What do we do now?" I asked.

"We get this done and then the rest of you don't ever have to worry about a thing ever again."

"You sure about that?"

"The Haitians are dead. Once Papalote is dead, we're done with this. Y'all will be safe. I promise."

I promise. Big words. I wanted to believe in Bimbo more than I had ever wanted to believe in anything else in my whole life.

33

GABE

—

Raúl shows up
A prayer inside a fist
Strange figures on the reef
Happy to put a bullet in your head
Four idiots winging it

W e got out of the van and walked around like we were stretching our legs or waiting for someone. Doing nothing is hard
when you don't want people to know you're doing something.

Tavo texted both of us, saying he was at La Garita del Diablo. They
were setting a few tables outside and would open soon. I looked up but
couldn't spot Paul anywhere on the wall, so I texted and asked if he
was up there. He texted back almost immediately and said he was on
his way.

"What do you think they do out here with those bodies?" I finally
asked Bimbo. The question had been in my head for a while. There
were too many stories for the whole thing to be false. Plus, everything
Henry had told us sounded legit. I wanted Bimbo's take.

"I've heard the same stories you have, but I don't know…There
might be something out there, some weird animal we haven't discovered yet or something, but I think the reef just makes it easy for Papalote
to get rid of the bodies. You tie someone out there, and between the

water pounding the reef, the fish and crabs and urchins, and the sun, I'm sure there's not much left in a day or two. Plus, La Perla is small as hell, so I don't think there's a lot of space to stash bodies in, you know? The reef fixes that problem. The thing is, I don't think people focus on the right thing when it comes to the reef stories."

"How so?"

"Well, this place is small, right?"

"Yeah, you just said that."

"And this is Papalote's kingdom, yeah?"

"Right."

I was starting to see where Bimbo was going, but I wanted him to finish. I was an idiot for not seeing it before, which made me feel bad, but listening to him, some other things were clicking in my head.

"Well...I don't think the dude is killing people down here, which means he brings the bodies from somewhere else. You know, his enemies or whatever. That's the part that got me thinking when Henry was talking to us in the car. If he was telling the truth and they're bringing bodies out there every few days, then they're getting those bodies somewhere else or this place would be emptier than the cemetery by now."

"So?"

"So, bodies are hard to get rid of," he said, his voice almost a whisper. "I think Papalote created the whole monster story to keep people away. He kills folks and feeds the bodies to some monsters that live on the reef. It's too fucking good. It's terrifying. If it's even remotely true, then the motherfucker is untouchable. Get it? He made that shit up to make himself into some kind of legend."

Yes, sure, but there had to be more to the story. We were both missing some angles. Why carry bodies all the way back here? Why do it so frequently if no one was coming around to check if it was true?

I looked at Bimbo. He was muttering and looking at his phone. He looked bigger and meaner than usual. His nickname no longer fit. He wasn't even Bimbo now; he looked like an Andrés.

Bimbo had repeatedly failed to come up with a decent plan, but here he was, talking to me about an obvious angle I had failed to notice despite developing a small obsession with whatever the fuck was or wasn't happening out on the reef. Anger was still raging inside me, but I felt okay about being down there with him. The ocean was doing its thing, relentlessly, as always. Its endless song was usually music to my ears, but this time it felt different. This time, the ocean's song was a threat pulled from its dark heart.

We kept walking around for a while. After ten or fifteen minutes, an old green pickup truck drove by us and stopped near the van. Four men were sitting in the truck's bed. As soon as the truck stopped, one of them — tall, emaciated, wearing torn jeans and no shirt, and with his brown torso full of jailhouse ink — stood up, jumped off, and said something about the light. He talked around a lit cigarette that hung from his lips, which made most of what he said unintelligible.

A second man stood up, placed his hands on the side of the truck, and jumped out of the truck's bed. It was Henry. He was talking to another man, a Black guy with a messy Afro who looked in no hurry to get down from the truck. As he talked, Henry walked toward the guy who had jumped out first, who was on the opposite side of the truck. He glanced our way and made eye contact with me. My heart stopped. Then Henry looked away and nodded. I made a mental note to look him up after this was over and give him money and buy him a meal. Then I remembered his mother's name. Judith. She'd died of cancer. I'd always respected Henry because he was a good guy, but hearing him talk about his mom in Bimbo's car had changed my perception of him. His addiction didn't matter; he was a human being whose life had been as full of grief as the rest of ours. Also, we were here because of him. We owed him. Maybe.

Bimbo stood next to me in silence, his eyes darting between the truck, the water, the men, and his phone, which he held in his right hand and glanced at every few seconds. He was waiting for word from Tavo and Paul. Both had been eerily quiet.

The driver's-side door of the truck flew open and a tall man with a fresh fade stepped out. Raúl. He was wearing orange Bermuda shorts, white tennis shoes, and a big white T-shirt. There was a gun somewhere under that shirt. He was much taller than I'd expected and his face was oddly flat. His nose sat in his face like some hunched creature. My first thought was that he looked like a frog.

Raúl left the door open and the truck running and came around to the back to drop the truck bed door. The Black man stood up with a loud groan and made his way down while holding the side of the truck, as if something hurt. The last man on the truck finally stood up. He was thinner than Henry. His jeans were almost black with grime, and the T-shirt he was wearing was a camo-like mixture of stains, sweat, and whatever color or colors it had originally been. The man's arms looked like someone had put out a hundred cigarettes on them. Despite the state of his clothes, he had recently shaved, and his hair, while messy, looked like it'd been cut in the last few weeks.

With everyone down, Raúl said something and signaled to the truck with his thumb. That's when I noticed there was a black tarp sitting on the bed of the truck with thick white twine around it. Henry and the man who'd jumped out first walked up to the truck, reached in, and pulled on the tarp. Judging by the size and the way they struggled with its weight, not to mention everything we knew, it had to be a body.

Hearing about something awful and seeing it with your own eyes are two of the most different things in the world. I didn't think Henry had been lying to us, but I'd had a hard time believing what he'd told us in Bimbo's car. I desperately tried to come up with ways of explaining away the bodies. There couldn't be monsters out there feeding on human flesh. Bimbo's theory had helped a bit. I wanted to believe the voice and to trust Bimbo, to think that this was just Papalote's two-birds, one-stone way of getting rid of evidence and building street cred.

I couldn't.

Everything was adding up. Raúl was here. Henry and the other men were here. There was a body in the truck.

There were monsters out there.

Raúl shouted something and the two men who had stayed away came to the back of the truck to help with the body. The men pulled it out of the truck and carried it between them toward the water. When they reached the water, they stopped and placed the body on the ground. The man who'd jumped out first jogged back to the truck, opened the passenger door, pulled the seat back, rummaged in there for a few seconds, and emerged with a looped rope in his hands. He put his right arm through it and shouldered the rope as he walked back to his companions.

Without another word and with no ceremony, the four men picked up the thing I was sure was a body, stepped into the water, and started walking slowly toward the reef.

"Keep an eye on him," said Bimbo, looking at Raúl while he spoke, his voice low and filled with something strange that could've been anger, hatred, anxiety, or fear.

Raúl had lit a cigarette and was leaning against the pickup next to the open door. He was staring at his phone, which he held in his left hand while smoking with the right. He barely glanced at the men dragging the corpse toward the reef and he didn't look our way either. He was supposed to be supervising the disposal of a body and he seemed more like a guy waiting in line at the bank. That spoke volumes about how untouchable Papalote and his men thought they were in La Perla. It was also proof that no cop would ever set foot down here, much less after a hurricane.

Bimbo was still next to me, his eyes jumping from the water and the men to Raúl and then to his phone in a twitchy, endless cycle.

"What's the plan?" I turned my back on Raúl because both of us standing around and looking at him was a surefire way of letting him know something was up.

"I'm gonna approach him from the other side of the car," said

Bimbo. "I want us to be on opposite sides of him. That'll make things easier if…you know, shit goes wrong or whatever. I'm gonna pretend like I'm on the phone and strike up a conversation with him. You come at him from this side. Say hi to me so it doesn't look like you're creeping up on him. I'm sure he'll be more than happy to put a bullet in your head if he feels something's off. Hell, he has the men here to take you out to the reef right now."

Bimbo smiled and then looked away as if he was rethinking his joke. The thought of Raúl putting a bullet in my skull felt more like a promise, and Bimbo was right about the men being there to take me out to…whatever was out there. I saw myself on the reef with holes where my eyes had been, just like Xavier, with small crabs crawling out of them.

"When you're close enough, I'll crack a joke or something," said Bimbo. The image of my eyeless face vanished. "When he looks my way, you put him down. We're lucky he parked so close to the fucking van."

Put him down. No big deal. Fuck. Put him down is one of those things that's easier said than done. I thought about being in the gym. My squat wasn't impressive, but my short, stocky frame was built for the bench press. It was one of the reasons I didn't mind moving away from basketball and started lifting; I was better built for that than for basketball. At least that's what I told myself to make it hurt less.

I imagined walking up to Raúl and lining up my arm so that my body mimicked the movement of a bench press. If I could put up 315 for two or three reps on a good day, I probably had enough power coiled in my chest, shoulders, and triceps to knock someone out with one punch. And my wrist and elbow could take it. I'd done my time swinging sledgehammers against walls at work. I could do this.

"Mira, dile a ese hijo de la gran puta que me llame," said Bimbo. I'd lost track of him while I stared at a palm tree and threw the perfect punch in my head. He was walking toward the truck, his phone pressed against his ear. I walked in the same direction, staying in front of Raúl.

I'm sure he'll be more than happy to put a bullet in your head if he feels something's off.

I looked out at the ocean. The Atlantic is always angry at something off the coast of San Juan, as if all the shit it's seen throughout history has made it hate people and itself. The four men looked much smaller now. They had reached the reef. I'd missed the part where the water was probably up to their necks or maybe they'd had to swim for a bit if the tide was high, but they were standing now, the water up to their knees, their silhouettes against the horizon reminding me of a sad show full of puppets that were too heavy for their strings. They were bent over and probably tying the body down. I realized no one driving by up on Norzagaray would see what they were doing because the street is built in a way that you start seeing the reef only once you've passed this point.

"Oye, hermano, tú sabes si hay algún negocito abierto por aquí pa' uno darse una fría o algo…"

Bimbo asked Raúl if there was a place nearby to get a cold beer. Raúl looked up from his phone and sucked on his cigarette before answering. While blowing smoke out of his mouth and nostrils, he pointed up the road with the hand that held the cigarette and said, "La Garita del Diablo. Cerveza fría, tragos con hielo y Medallas a peso. Lo que tú quieras, papi."

"Bimbo, cuéntame qué te dijeron," I said, closer now.

Bimbo replied, but I never heard what he said. I was walking toward them, and all my brain could focus on was one great punch. I imagined that was exactly what boxers and MMA fighters trained for, what they hoped for while getting their brains bashed against the inside of their skulls in the ring or the octagon. One knockout punch. A prayer inside a fist. A lucky shot.

I'm sure he'll be more than happy to put a bullet in your head if he feels something's off.

My life depended on this punch. Many things in life are like that. One chance and that's it. I had to get this done.

219

Bimbo said something about the ice shortage. Raúl looked at him and nodded, his phone's screen lighting the bottom of his face. I swung. Well, I didn't just swing; I pictured Xavier down on the sidewalk, the excruciating pain of his neck and eyes. I imagined the scream that died in his slashed throat, drowned in my brother's blood. I thought about his heartbroken family. I wondered if he'd thought about them and about us, maybe wishing we'd been there with him, for him. Someone had fucked with him and we hadn't been there to make it right, to make sure his blood stayed inside his body.

I thought about my mom in a pool of blood.

My eyes filled. My heart felt like a hot stone. I put every ounce of grief into my fist and threw it as if I were trying to punch a hole in the world that would allow me to go back in time. But there was no world to punch, no place for me to make that hole. Instead, my knuckles flew up and straight into Raúl's oddly flat face.

CLACK!

The impact of Raúl's jawbone against my fist sent pain all the way down to my elbow.

I'd aimed for his jaw because his nose looked like someone had shattered it already. He looked like an unskillful boxer at the tail end of a punishing career. I wanted to scramble his brain and make him shut down. I'd hit the mark despite him being so much taller than me. The momentum behind my punch threatened to throw me down to the ground, but I managed to stay upright. My knuckles exploded in pain as if someone had lit my hand on fire.

Raúl's legs quit working and he collapsed next to his truck like someone had removed his bones. Bimbo quickly bent down, lifted his shirt, and looked for a gun. He found one, showed me, and made it disappear under his own black shirt. For a moment, we both looked around, expecting a shitstorm to blow up in our faces. Nothing happened.

"Grab his legs," said Bimbo, grabbing his arms. "Van. Now."

I grabbed Raúl's legs and we pulled him up. He wasn't too heavy, but my hand screamed anyway. The punch had worked. I was stoked. My hand wasn't. Everything in life has a fucking price.

Bimbo and I did a quick, awkward shuffle to the van. Our eyes still ricocheted, looking for trouble. We scanned the water. The street. The nearby houses. Raúl. His truck. We were looking out for people, praying no one would see us. I kept thinking Raúl was going to snap out of it at any second and the whole thing was going to end up with Bimbo and me tied to the reef while crabs feasted on our faces and tiny fish nibbled at our flesh. It reminded me of Kimbo's house, which seemed, strangely, like something that had happened half a decade ago. There would be no crabs or fish there to feast on his face, but nature is brutal, so plenty of other little things would be eating him and laying their eggs in his putrefying corpse. I shook away the thought.

We dropped Raúl on the ground while Bimbo opened the van's back doors.

"Let's get him up there, and then you get in with him," said Bimbo. "If he moves or moans or whatever, pop him again, you got it? Man, that was a hell of a punch."

I nodded. Pride fluttered in my chest. Fear quickly shattered its wings. Bimbo bent over, stuck his hands under Raúl's arms, and hauled him up, but only halfway up to the back of the van. I heard him struggle, so instead of grabbing Raúl's legs again, I helped Bimbo with the man's torso.

We clumsily lifted Raúl until his upper body had gone past the van's bumper and then pushed him into the back of the van, using his weight to help us get him in there. He landed with a thud. Then I grabbed his legs and pushed them in, rolling him sideways in the process.

Before climbing inside, I glanced back out at the water. The sun was setting fast now, the way it always does in the Caribbean. The figures out on the reef were still there, now pure black against an orange-and-yellow background. But something was off and I had a hard time making sense of what I saw. There weren't four men out there; there were six. That was impossible. It had to be a trick of the light. I stopped, my hands on the van and my legs ready to get me up there, squinted, and counted again.

One.

Two.

Three.

Four.

Five.

Six.

The two new figures were taller than the four men I'd watched walk out to the reef. They were far away and the light was dying quickly, so I tried to dismiss it — some trick of the light. I could tell there was something weird about the new arrivals. Their arms were too long in comparison to the four men. And they looked much bigger around the shoulders, like basketball players standing next to skinny men.

"Gabe, get the fuck in!"

"Wait, there's —"

"Get in!"

Bimbo grabbed my shoulder and pushed me into the back of the van. He was right. I could ask Henry or maybe Raúl about the figures later. I clambered into the back of the van and heard the door slam behind me. Everything went black. I was alone with Raúl in the fucking dark.

Something clanked and then the van was moving. Bimbo was backing up. He stomped on the brakes. My body slammed against the side of the van. If he drove like a maniac, I was going to get the shit beat out of me in the back.

My eyes had adjusted a bit, so I looked around for something to hold on to. The interior of the van was thoroughly stripped. There were two plastic mounds that housed the rear wheels, and nothing but bare metallic walls above them. I placed my hands on the floor and paid attention to how the vehicle was moving to try to keep my balance. Raúl was still out. His body on the floor looked like a boulder in the dark. There was metallic black mesh separating the back of the van from the seats up front. I couldn't see much because of it, but it didn't look — or feel — like Bimbo was driving out of La Perla like a man running from the Devil.

I crawled away from Raúl and moved closer to the front. I got into a sitting position with my legs straight out and my hands on the van's floor for support.

I heard Bimbo talking, probably telling Paul or Tavo to get the hell out.

I saw images in my head.

Bullets coming through the van's panels, puncturing my body.

The van zigzagging, Bimbo dead and slumped over wheel.

The van slamming against a house.

My mom bawling at my funeral.

Natalia crying, and then moving on and finding some asshole who was more than willing to make her happy and move to the United States with her.

The fucking crabs again, this time coming out of my mouth, crawling over the bloated stump of my tongue.

More crabs, this time crawling out of Bimbo's mouth…and then Tavo's and Paul's mouths.

Raúl moaned.

I was so scared it took me a few seconds to realize the sound was coming from him and not from some part of my brain that was trying to push away the images in my head.

The same panicked fear I'd felt in Kimbo's house when we were putting duct tape around his wrists and ankles flooded my system. I wanted none of that. I moved my body forward, and when Raúl's head was within reach, I recoiled my right leg, aimed for his temple, and kicked him once, hard. He stopped moaning.

Bimbo was done talking.

"Where are we going?" I asked, almost screaming.

"My house," he said. "Slowly. No one's following us and I'm sure the dudes in the water are still making their way back to the truck. I just drove past a woman pushing a stroller and two dudes talking at a corner, but that's it." He sniffled. "I think it's too hot to be out and people just wanna get through this fucking no-power misery at home. We're good. Just make sure you keep that motherfucker quiet. Tavo and Paul are on their way to my place."

Bimbo's house. Another bad idea. No one had asked where we were going to take this guy if we managed to grab him. Welcome to amateur hour. We were all fucking idiots. The fact that only one of us had died was surprising. We were winging it on a level of the streets where people died every day for less than what we'd done so far. And we didn't even know what was really happening. Bimbo's uncle was dead, which meant we were alone. He'd lied to us about that. And apparently, his mom hadn't been as innocent as Bimbo had made her sound after she was killed. María herself had been scheming. Bimbo had also lied about that. We knew nothing, and that ignorance was going to get us killed.

Cold fingers gripped the back of my neck and I shivered despite the clammy air inside the van.

"You think it's safe to take him to your place?" I asked. "What if someone sees us?"

"We'll park nearby and it'll be dark as fuck by the time we get there," said Bimbo. "We won't use lights or our phones. Nothing. We'll bring him up like he's drunk. Then we'll tie him and cover his mouth until he knows that screaming means he'll get hurt."

"Okay." It was a stupid response, but it was the only one I had. Bimbo felt something in that word's tiny heart, something that probably sounded a lot like doubt.

"Hey," he said. "It'll be fine. We're night sharks now, remember? We have Elegguá on our side. That's why everything went smoothly."

Smoothly. We were as far from smoothly as you can get. Bimbo thought Elegguá was on our side. He thought his god was watching over us. He was wrong. We were alone. We were in danger. We had no plan. We had one of Papalote's men in the back of a van. We were fucked.

The van bounced some more. I remembered the two new figures out on the reef. They were shaped like humans, but they were too big. What the fuck was happening out there?

34

GABE

—

Submerged in darkness
Too many questions
Violent thoughts
Coward
The eager song of a hellhound

Raúl woke up again as we crossed the Dos Hermanos Bridge. We had exited La Perla without being killed, and Bimbo had stepped on the gas as soon as we hit Norzagaray again. My body bounced around a lot. No matter what I did, momentum threw me around.

I was getting back into a somewhat comfortable position after hitting a pothole when Raúl woke up, moved his arms around, and started lifting his body a bit. I lunged forward, grabbed Raúl's head with both hands, and slammed his noggin against the floor of the van a few times. It felt good.

"Don't kill him, Gabe," said Bimbo. "We need him alive for a while."

I didn't reply. This motherfucker had been killing people left and right and was now telling me to pull back? I wanted to punch him, but instead I sat down again, scooted toward the wall, and tried to put my back against the corner of the van with my feet and hands down on the floor. That position helped me stay anchored whenever Bimbo took a curve too fast or did something else to throw me around.

"I can't find a fucking spot big enough to fit the van," said Bimbo after a while. "I'm gonna drive around the block and park for a minute in front of my place so you guys can get Raúl out. Then I'll park somewhere else and meet y'all back there."

A minute later, Bimbo stopped the van. The back doors flew open. I felt like I was leaving prison. My body was tired from trying to stay put during the ride—the muscles on my arms and legs felt like I'd just finished a brutal workout. And my hand still throbbed.

Tavo and Paul were waiting for us on the sidewalk. They came over while I got down and took Raúl, each putting one of his arms over their neck. From the back, they looked like friends lending a hand to a buddy who'd partied too hard. I noticed Raúl was even taller than Tavo.

Bimbo grabbed my right hand as soon as my feet hit the pavement and put his keys in my palm but didn't let go.

"The key I'm holding opens the door," he said. I closed my hand around his fingers and felt the key he was singling out. "Get him in and settled," he said. Then he patted my shoulder and climbed back into the van.

As soon as Bimbo drove away, taking the van's lights with him, everything changed. Instead of threatening, the night felt like an ally that quickly reclaimed everything around us to protect us from prying eyes. I thought about Elegguá again, clearing the path ahead of us. That helped my fears recede a bit. I didn't think anyone would see us, and if someone did spot us, they wouldn't know what the hell we were doing, and they'd never be able to make out our faces.

Tavo and Paul were making their way up Bimbo's wobbly stairs. I looked around. Shaky yellow candlelight came from behind some windows, and a few houses had a light or two on. The thrum of small generators buzzed in the night air, right below the sound of insects. The noise reminded me of Keyla's uncle, killed over a fucking generator he needed for his sick kid. It was probably far from the worst thing that had happened since María hit, but the proximity of it bothered me. A lot. The world is a ruthless place, but seeing just how fucking callous it can be is like getting slapped by God.

As Tavo and Paul reached the top of the stairs, I remembered the key in my hand and jogged up to them. The memory of my struggles in the back of the van was like a weak ghost in the muscles in my legs. At the top of the stairs, I showed Tavo, who was closer to the door, the key I was holding and gave it to him while ducking a bit and sliding under Raúl's arms to hold him up while Tavo opened the door.

Bimbo's apartment was even darker than the world outside. As we walked in, I noticed a light under Bimbo's bedroom door. Altagracia. I didn't know how much Bimbo had told her, but if she came out and made a fuss about what we were doing, she could fuck this up for us. I hoped she'd stay in the room.

Tavo pulled out his phone and turned on the flashlight. He pointed it at the sofa where he'd been sitting earlier. Paul and I went over and dropped Raúl onto it. He landed without a sound. I wondered if the hits to the head had killed him, but then he moved.

The sound of Bimbo's breaths as he climbed the stairs was louder than the sound of the stairs themselves. He barged into his apartment with the grace of a drunken newborn giraffe, turned, and slammed the door shut behind him.

"What now, Bimbo?" asked Paul, his voice high and winded and desperate.

"Let's not waste time trying to find shit to tie him with in the dark," said Bimbo. "You and Tavo can sit next to him and hold his arms. Gabe can stand with me and we'll keep our guns on him. That should be enough to make him talk. If that doesn't work, Gabe can hit him a couple of times to loosen his tongue."

"For what?" asked Tavo.

"What do you mean?" asked Bimbo.

"You have him and that means what Henry told us is true, so you also know where to find El Brujo, right?"

"Yeah, but we need more than that. I wanna know more about El Brujo. I wanna know what Papalote is up to and what we'll have to do to get back in there and come out alive. Also, Gabe and I saw something out there on the reef and..." He sniffled and took a deep breath. "Yeah, I think this guy knows a lot of things we should know."

"Okay, so what if hitting him a couple times doesn't loosen his tongue?" asked Tavo. I'd been wondering the same thing. Also, my hand still throbbed, so I hoped the guns were enough to get him talking.

"I'm so tired of the questions, dude," said Bimbo. "If we smack him around a bit and he doesn't talk, I'll grab a fucking knife from the kitchen and make him talk. The time for questions is over. The time to say please is over. This motherfucker killed my mom. He killed Xavier, remember?"

Bimbo's words did something to me. I knew what we were doing, but the nerves and tension that came from it had more or less blocked the significance of it all. The motherfucker crumpled on the sofa, the man whose lights I'd turned off twice in the last half hour or so, had killed my brother and Bimbo's mom. I thought about grabbing a gun and emptying its clip into Raúl's head. Then I realized that would be too quick. Bimbo had said something about a knife. That would be much better. I'd skin him while making him say Xavier's name. Then I'd slash his throat and stab him in the eyes while he choked on his own blood.

The thought scared me for a second. I was afraid of myself. It's crazy to see the things getting hurt can make you wish for.

Paul stepped up. His movement called me back into the room and made me realize just how fucking dark my thoughts had gotten and how okay I seemed to be with all of it. I shook my head. We had work to do. Revenge was bigger than just Raúl. And we had to make sure we did things right so we could all stay alive.

In the shaky light of Tavo's phone, I watched Paul reach out to Bimbo. I couldn't read Bimbo's face in the dark, but I saw him reach back and give Paul the gun he'd taken from Raúl. The gun I was supposed to use while he helped hold Raúl down on the sofa.

"You sure?" asked Bimbo.

"Gabe's stronger than me. I'll be more useful holding the gun. Gabe can handle him much better if he refuses to talk or whatever."

Fucking coward.

A dog barked in the distance. Maybe it was a celebration, the song of a hellhound that could already smell the blood to come. Maybe it was a warning. Maybe it was María's ghost telling us she was proud of us.

Raúl moaned.

35

GABE

—

Childhoods buried in the rubble
Abnormal teeth around a gun
The most destructive ballet in the world
An explosion of violence
A cavern in his neck

Raúl opened his eyes and scanned the room. He looked like he had his wits about him almost immediately. He didn't scream. Instead, he kept looking around, taking it all in.

Tiny, dark apartment.

A dude latched to each arm. I wondered if he recognized me as the guy who'd popped him in the jaw and sent him into oblivion half an hour earlier.

Two guys in front of him, both aiming guns at his face.

This was either the end or something that could easily turn into the end if he made one wrong move. And he knew it. Just like Kimbo, he was a professional. He didn't cry or scream or beg. Just like Kimbo, none of that mattered, because he was going to end up dead anyway. The big difference was that this time I was expecting it.

"If you scream, I'll shoot you in the face," said Bimbo in Spanish. He'd turned his phone's flashlight on and placed the device facedown on the table. The light from the phone was shining straight up at Bimbo's water-stained off-white ceiling. It was enough for us to take care of business and not stumble around in the dark. "If you try to get up, I'll shoot you," Bimbo went on. "If you don't answer my questions—"

"You'll shoot me," said Raúl. "I got it."

"No," said Bimbo with no humor in his voice. "You don't deserve that, cabrón. If you don't answer my questions quickly, I'm gonna start cutting off little pieces of you until you die and then I'm gonna feed you to the neighbor's dog. And I'm gonna make it last. I'll pour salt on each little hole I make in you. When I run out of salt, I'll fucking piss in every wound. That's what you fucking deserve, hijo de la gran puta. We clear?"

Raúl didn't answer. Bimbo had once again turned into that other man I'd seen, the one who looked older, stronger, and scarier than the guy we called Bimbo. This was a man named Andrés. He'd kept his shit together while we got Raúl, but now everything he'd kept buried was bubbling up to the surface. An ache for justice that dissolved his sense of right and wrong. A need for vengeance so strong it made him fully calm and truly blind to consequences. Bimbo was my brother, but Andrés was angrier, and capable of every fucking awful thing he'd just said. Any vestiges of Bimbo's childhood had vanished, buried in the rubble of everything María's death had destroyed in his life. My youth was probably lost somewhere underneath the weight of losing my father and then losing Xavier.

"Do you know who I am?" asked Bimbo.

"No," said Raúl. His voice was a little lower. He'd probably heard a lot of bad things in his life, but maybe Bimbo's threats had gone above and beyond anything that had ever been hurled at him before. I'd been looking at Raúl as he spoke. His teeth were too small for his mouth and they were very pointy, as if he'd filed them down to look scarier.

"Do you know why you're here?"

Raúl shrugged. His arm tugged at my hands. I held him harder.

"I do shit that could get me in a room like this every single fucking

day. You think you're the first motherfuckers to point a gun at me?"
He took a deep breath. "I'll tell you this, of all the ones that have done
it, you're the only ones who are still alive."

That was a great line. It sounded like something pulled from a
movie. I wondered if Raúl was a stone-cold killer or a professional
bullshitter. I hoped for the latter.

"You killed a woman at Lazer a few months ago," said Bimbo. "You
remember that job?"

"No," said Raúl.

Bimbo stepped forward and shook his gun as if to remind Raúl it
was there. The gun was asking the question again. Raúl stayed quiet.

"If you don't remember, you're useless to me," said Bimbo. Raúl
stayed silent. I looked up at Bimbo. Paul was next to him, holding up
Raúl's gun. His hand was shaking a bit.

There was someone next to Paul. I recognized the figure immediately. It was Xavier. My heart skipped a beat.

"You sure you don't remember the woman you killed outside
Lazer? If you say no again, I'm going to blow your brains out even if I
have to get rid of that shitty sofa after."

Something had crawled into Bimbo's voice and turned it into
something new, like his throat had been lit, extinguished, and barely
healed, all in the last few minutes. I had no doubt he was ready to pull
the trigger. I wasn't looking forward to the mess, but I had no qualms
about the act itself.

Raúl stayed quiet for a few seconds. I couldn't see his eyes in
the scant light from the phone, but he was looking at Bimbo or was
switching between Bimbo and Paul. I did the same. Bimbo meant
every fucking word that had come out of his mouth. Paul was trying
to stay cool. He was failing. The sweat on his face gave him away. He
looked like he was about to throw up. Next to him, Xavier's ghost
stood quietly, looking at Raúl. I couldn't stop looking at him —
through him.

"Yeah, I remember," said Raúl. He probably thought saying that was going to keep him alive a bit longer. Maybe long enough to figure a way out of this. "Fat bitch working the door."

Bimbo moved faster than I'd thought possible. One moment he was standing there with his gun aimed at Raúl, and a second later he was on top of the guy, one hand pulling at Raúl's shirt and the other raining down blows with the gun's grip like he was trying to hammer a nail into a piece of wood.

Raúl tried to pull his arms up to cover his face, but Tavo and I held him down. As Bimbo hit him, Raúl gave up on freeing his arms and instead tried to lift his shoulders up and pull his head down into his chest to cover up. He kept moving from side to side to evade Bimbo's wrath, but Bimbo was too fast and had him by the shirt, so most of the blows were landing. A second later, Bimbo stopped. He was winded and breathing hard as he stepped back. Raúl said something unintelligible. Bimbo let go of his shirt.

"Open your mouth."

"What?" asked Raúl, still dazed from the attack.

"Open your fucking mouth!"

I'm sure Raúl was about to comply, but Bimbo lunged forward again, grabbed Raúl's face with his left hand, pushed it back, and squeezed his cheeks. Before Raúl could really open his mouth, Bimbo dug into it with the barrel of his gun. The gun clacked against Raúl's pointy teeth. Then the gun's barrel was in Raúl's mouth. Deep. Raúl gagged and moved his head back. Tavo and I held him harder. With his lips pulled away from the gun, I could see Raúl's teeth a little better. They were all the same size.

"I wanna fucking kill you so bad right—"

A sob cracked Bimbo's sentence in half. I'd been paying attention to Bimbo but also kind of not because Xavier was still there, standing next to Paul, impossible like a kiss from some god. I couldn't help looking at him. He didn't move or talk. His presence was enough. He was a blessing, like a guardian angel. No, better yet: an avenging angel.

All stories are ghost stories.

No one had said a word about Xavier, which meant only I could see him. I had no idea why. My abuela's blood? Maybe I was going crazy? I didn't know and didn't care. Bimbo sobbed again. It made me look away from Xavier and focus on him and Raúl.

"You know, there's nothing in the world stopping me from pulling this fucking trigger right now," said Bimbo. He sniffled and wiped his face with his left arm. The gun was still in Raúl's mouth. "But I wanna hear you say it. I wanna hear you say you did that fucking job so I can kill you with a smile on my face."

Bimbo moved back and pulled the gun out of Raúl's mouth. I caught Tavo's eyes in the dark. He was scared, but he was with us. He knew this had to happen. There was no anger in his eyes, only pain. I wanted to hug him. I wanted to hug Bimbo too. I wanted to punch Paul for being a fucking coward.

"I...I have a daughter," said Raúl.

"You think I give a fuck, cabrón?"

"I have a —"

"I don't give a fuck about what you have! You killed my mom. You're sitting there wondering why you're here and even though I asked you about the Lazer job, you still can't put two and two together because you're a fucking idiot, but that's why you're here. That 'fat bitch' was my mom. Look me in the face. She's right there. You can see her, but I bet you can't, because you probably didn't even look at her. You pulled the trigger from the car, like the fucking piece of shit you are."

"I don't —"

"Shut the fuck up! Tell me you did it. Tell me you fucking did it!"

Raúl moved back on the sofa and his arms released some of their tension. The one thing this whole fucking ordeal had taught me was that these men had an immediate clarity dawn on them as soon as Bimbo mentioned his mom, as if there was some cosmic understanding of one of the most basic rules of life: Mothers are sacred, and if you mess with one, you better not get caught or you will pay the price.

"I know it was you and El Brujo. I know —"

"I drove," said Raúl. His voice was low again, and somewhat softer. Apologetic. The words sounded like they belonged to a different man. "El Brujo pulled the trigger."

"Throwing that motherfucker under the bus won't save you now, but it's good to see that you're willing to be an asshole all the way to the end," said Bimbo. "But I don't care. If someone drives me to your house and I kill your daughter, will you spare the driver if you catch us? Would you — ?"

"Leave my daughter out of this! If you even go anywhere near her, I'll —"

"You'll fucking what? You'll fucking nothing. Shut the fuck up. I won't touch a hair on your daughter's head, you know why? Because I don't kill kids or women or shoot moms in the face. Real men don't do that shit. But you motherfuckers did. You did that and now you're here trying to tell me some fucking sad story about your daughter. I don't give a shit about your daughter. She can grow up without a father, like I did. At least she'll have a mom. My sister is doing drugs because of what you sons of —"

Another sob cracked Bimbo's sentence in half. His hand shook. He lowered the gun like he was giving up. He looked away and collected himself.

María died on a sidewalk, but her death had rippled on the pond of life, and Bimbo and his sister were still getting rocked by the waves. They hadn't had much to begin with. Now they had lost everything. Those damn ripples had also killed Xavier, affected all of us. The same would soon be true for Raúl's daughter. She was an innocent girl pulled into this by her father's actions and by someone's refusal to leave it alone. Was it worth it? Really?

I looked back at Xavier's ghost. He was looking at me. I could see the wall behind him. I'd never get to hug him again. His mother's pain was a silent scream I would hear forever. His absence would remain there, a place where something loved had once been and would never be again because some asshole had decided he had to die.

Yeah, it was worth it. Revenge is the most beautiful, most destructive ballet in the world, and you can't have a part of it without the opposite half.

Bimbo sniffled. I peeled my eyes off Xavier and set them on him. "Now tell me you did it."

Raúl stayed quiet again. He looked around the room. Then he looked at Tavo and me. Raúl was looking for a way out, a bargaining chip, a weapon. He was probably looking for God, his brain praying at a thousand miles per hour, making promises he would never keep, begging a deity that wasn't listening for one more day, one more chance to see his daughter, one dose of whatever moved him, that kept him going, that brought a smile to his face. He wanted the things he was willing to take from others.

Bimbo walked over to my side, bent down, and grabbed Raúl's arm with one hand. Then he lifted his gun and placed it against Raúl's temple.

"Give him a reason to talk, Gabe," he said. "I'm tired. I need a minute." Then he turned to Raúl and said, "You move that arm or try to grab my gun and I'm going to pull this trigger."

I moved to the side, let go of Raúl's arm, and stood up as Bimbo slid into my place on the sofa.

I stood up straight and looked down at Raúl. His eyes were on mine. There was a question swimming in there. I saw fear, a sliver of defiance, and maybe something like desperate hope in his eyes. I turned around for a second. Xavier was smiling at me. I swung.

My stance was shit, but swinging down always helps. Raúl's head snapped back. Bimbo pulled the gun away. Pain exploded in my hand. It made me even angrier.

I swung again.

My knuckles hurt so bad I had to suck in air through my teeth. I didn't know why Bimbo wanted Raúl to confess. He hadn't asked him anything more about El Brujo or Papalote or anything else. He didn't have a plan, and his emotions had gotten the best of him. The same was happening to me.

Tavo and Bimbo struggled to keep Raúl's arms pinned down to his sides.

I moved forward, placed my left hand on Raúl's neck, pushed him back just like Bimbo had when he'd stuck the gun in his mouth, and started pummeling his face.

I hit him once for María.

I hit again for Xavier.

I hit him for my mom.

I hit him for Bimbo.

I hit him for Bimbo's sister.

I hit him for the hole he would leave in his daughter's life.

I hit him for the pain he'd caused Xavier's parents.

I punched him for sending Henry out into the reef.

I punched him for the fucking veve they'd painted on my door.

I punched him and then I punched him some more because he was there and everything was fucked and it made sense.

I punched him because God had destroyed the country.

I punched him because of that fucking coach.

I punched him because I was afraid of whatever was next for me.

Adrenaline flooded my system. Maybe I wanted to die. The pain in my knuckles vanished.

I punched until my chest ached, my shoulder was tired, and my hand was numb from the pain.

Raúl's face shattered under my fist. The skin opened up under his left cheekbone and blood flowed down his face.

My left thumb was pressed against Raúl's neck and then it wasn't. His flesh suddenly caved in and my thumb slid into his neck. I looked and my thumb was in his flesh.

I stopped punching and jumped back. The darkness of the room had seeped into Raúl's face. Then I realized it was dark with blood.

"—op! Stop already! You're gonna fucking kill him, man!"

Paul's voice drilled into my ear. I had no idea how long he had been asking me to stop. I didn't care. I did what I had to do. Justice is bloodier than people care to admit. I wasn't worried about anything beyond what I'd seen and felt.

Raúl wasn't moving. He wasn't trying to free his arms or move his head around to evade my punches. A sound came from his throat. Then he leaned forward and coughed. Blood poured from his mouth. I didn't know if I was relieved he was still alive or sad that for as hard as I'd tried, I couldn't get the job done.

Pain flew back into my hand and crept all the way up to my elbow. Pain.

My lungs aching for oxygen.

Paul's voice.

I'd ignored all of it while punching Raúl, but everything was coming back at once, and reality is always like getting hit with a baseball bat, regardless of how fast it comes.

I looked down at my hand. Raúl's teeth had cut into my fingers, but that was it. My knuckles were bleeding. I guessed we were brothers now, in a fucked-up way. Blood brothers.

I looked around. Xavier was gone. I hoped he was proud of me.

"You okay, Gabe?" asked Tavo.

"Yeah," I said, though we all knew nothing was okay.

"You're bleeding."

"I know. Doesn't matter. Hold him down." They were already holding him, but I wanted to make sure they didn't let him go. I leaned forward and pushed Raúl's head to the side with my hands. I held him there with my left hand, putting my weight on top of him, and touched his neck with my right.

My fingers found the slit in his neck. It wasn't bleeding or red or hard like a scar. It was...just there, a creepy little flap of skin.

"Fuck," said Paul over my shoulder. "Cabrón, eso no es normal."

"What is it, Gabe?" asked Bimbo.

"This guy has a...an opening in his neck."

"Grab him again and I'll check," said Bimbo. "Then we'll take care of your hand." He let go of Raúl's arm before I'd even moved. I was tired and couldn't catch my breath, but I sat down again and grabbed Raúl's arm. The phone on the table was far from perfect lighting, but without him moving around and my heart rate almost back to normal, I could see his face much better. His lips were swollen and there was a bulge under his right eye. His left eye was almost shut, and the cut under it was bleeding profusely. I didn't have to look in his mouth to know that some of his pointy teeth were shattered. However, the worst thing was his nose. It was crooked, and that seemed to alter all his toadlike features even more. I'd given him a new face.

While I looked at Raúl's face, Bimbo had been checking his neck. He was so close now it looked like he was about to kiss him or suck blood from his neck like a vampire.

"Fuck. This guy has a sinkhole on both sides of his neck," Bimbo said.

"Pull that thing open again," said Tavo. "The color...it almost looks like—"

"Fuck this," said Paul. "We need to get out of here."

In response, Bimbo slapped Raúl. Not hard, just enough to get him to wake up and focus. After a minute, he came around. Instead of talking or insulting us, he started crying.

"Hush," said Bimbo, pointing the gun at him again. "Tell me the easiest way to get to El Brujo. If you don't, I'm gonna use a knife on you. What you just got? Consider that shit a warm-up."

Pummeling a man's face usually has a profound effect on their psyche, and Raúl was no different. He was broken. He'd started out as a man in control who had seen some shit, but we had turned him into a slobbering, whining mess with one functioning eye, a shattered nose, and a few broken teeth. The echo of all that damage was shrieking in my hand, almost bringing tears to my eyes and making me squeeze Raúl's arm with my left hand and merely place my right one around his forearm.

"Stop crying and talk to me," said Bimbo.

Raúl took a deep shuddering breath, and a sound between a moan and a wet cough erupted from his mouth.

"El Brujo..." Raúl's voice was different now. He was talking through busted lips. I could tell it hurt, that he was struggling to get past the pain and spit the words out. Raúl swallowed, grimaced, and went on. "El Brujo, he...he talked to your mom. He told her she had to...to start selling for him. Instead of who she was selling for. Because Lazer is in San Juan. And San Juan belongs to Papalote."

"And that's why you killed her."

"No," said Raúl. "We killed her because she was planning to take—"

"Shut the fuck up!"

There it was again. It was exactly what Kimbo had said.

"What is he talking about?" asked Paul. I'd forgotten that Bimbo never told Paul or Tavo the truth about what María was up to.

"Shut the fuck up. Both of you," said Bimbo.

I could hear Raúl swallowing and sniffing. I could hear the distant buzz of generators and the sizzling of cars on the wet street below. Over those sounds, Raúl's nose was making a strange whistling noise from time to time. Then there was something else—someone was crying.

Bimbo.

Raúl had given him the confession he wanted, so his tears didn't make sense for a second. Then it dawned on me, the significance of what he was about to do and the truth out in the open. He was about to deliver on that silent promise we'd all made with our hands on top of María back at the funeral home. Whatever god had laughed at us that day wasn't laughing now.

Bimbo wiped his face again, the gun still pointing at Raúl, and cleared his throat. "Where does El Brujo live?"

A different sound came out of Raúl's mouth. It didn't fit the scene, but Bimbo didn't care.

"Tell me where he lives, or I'm getting the knife. I won't tell you again."

"You don't get El Brujo, man; El Brujo gets you," said Raúl. "Even if you kill me, you're dead. El Brujo will find you. He sees everything. He doesn't sleep. He doesn't have a shadow. He talks to old gods like they're his friends. He's gonna—"

Bimbo lowered the gun and walked toward the kitchen. Raúl tensed up. He knew Bimbo was getting a knife. He'd called Bimbo's bluff and it'd backfired.

"Listen," said Raúl. "I'll tell you, man! I'll fucking tell you, okay? El Brujo has a house right next to the chapel, a little red two-story house. That's where he...he works. That's all I know, I swear."

"Didn't you just say he works with you?" I asked. If Raúl was lying to us and we believed him, the price could be steep. Bimbo's lies were more than enough.

Raúl turned. His face was even worse when you looked at it straight on. I was surprised he was still able to speak and that he hadn't passed out from the pain his demolished face was surely causing him. He spat at me, but the red glob never came close. It rolled down his chin and merged with the blood coming from his nose. I thought about punching him again, but my hand was screaming at me to not even think about it.

Bimbo had reached the kitchen and opened a drawer while Raúl talked and spat at me. He rummaged around inside the drawer, pulled out a knife, and walked back to us. He stood in front of Raúl and held the knife up. He looked like he was possessed by Death. The light from the cell phone reflected on the knife. It was a small serrated blade of six or seven inches. It wasn't a machete, but it was still a knife, and every muscle in Raúl's body tensed with fear. The room was hot— everything was fucking hot and humid and smelly and pregnant with the ghost of destruction and the negative energy from all the shit we'd been doing—but for the first time, I felt Raúl's body heat coming off him in thick waves and found it hard to breathe.

"Please don't kill me, man," said Raúl. He was sobbing again.

Bimbo raised the knife a few inches and took a step forward.

"Wait!" I said.

Bimbo looked at me. Raúl did the same. Hope unknotted his face a bit. Hope is a motherfucker. I looked at Raúl.

"Did you kill Xavier?"

"Who's Xavier?" asked Raúl.

"Xavier, our friend. After a night in San Juan, someone followed him. They cut his neck and took his eyes. Was that you?"

"I swear I don't know anything about that, man." Raúl shook his head. "I have no idea what you're talking —"

"Does El Brujo ever work alone?"

"What? No. El Brujo hates driving. We always do jobs together. I drive. We didn't kill your friend. I swear. Please don't kill —"

"Whatever," I said. I knew Raúl was lying through his little sharp teeth, but maybe he'd give up some other useful info. "Tell me what's in the water."

"What?"

"What's in the water. What did I see out there today? Who takes the bodies those junkies tie out there?"

"Nah, I can't tell you that."

I heard Raúl's words. Then I heard Henry in my head: *Stuff you're better off not knowing about, my friend.*

My fucking thumb had gone into that little cavern in his neck. His teeth weren't normal. I'd seen tall figures out there. I needed to know.

"Bimbo, stick that knife in his thigh."

Bimbo was happy to do it. It was quick. Raúl screamed. Paul jumped on top of him and covered his mouth. It was the bravest, most useful thing he'd done all night.

36

GABE

—

Fishes
A creepy story
A knife in the thigh
A creature outside
A dog barks a warning

Nothing lubricates a tongue quite like pain. Raúl sat there for a
minute, moaning and groaning, each neck slit now flapping like
a tiny flag with every labored breath. We all stared at him, wondering
what the hell was up with his neck. When the guy stopped moaning,
Paul removed his hand from Raúl's mouth.

I asked him again. "Tell me what's in the water or I'm going to
yank that knife out and stick it in your other leg," I said.

"Okay! Fuck. Fine," said Raúl. "We call them fishes, okay?"

"No, not okay. They were standing up. They looked like men —
big men — not fish. I want the whole story. Now."

"The whole story?"

Raúl was looking at me. I wondered if he was going to spit at me
again and stared back while thinking about Xavier. *They fucking took his
eyes!* I could hear Tavo's anguished voice in my head. It was all the fuel
I needed.

"For every fucking detail I feel you're leaving out, I'll stick that knife in you. If I think you're lying, I'm gonna cut off a piece of you. I'll start with your ears. But if you tell me everything, you might just walk out of here."

"You'll let me go?"

I nodded. Bimbo jerked his head in my direction, but relaxed once he saw my face. He knew what was coming for Raúl.

Hope is indeed a motherfucker. It was riding Raúl's veins, looking for anything to hold on to. I gave it something. I gave it a whole lifeboat.

Raúl took a deep breath, looked around the room, sat back, and groaned. "Can I get some water first?"

Bimbo didn't answer, but he went to the kitchen, grabbed a jug from the counter, and came back.

Bimbo uncapped the jug.

"Let him go, Gabe. He moves too fast, I'll blow his brains out."

I released Raúl's wrist. He pulled his hand up slowly, shaking a bit, and grabbed the jug Bimbo was offering him.

Raúl put some water in his mouth, swirled it around for a couple seconds, and then spat it out on the floor. Bimbo said nothing. Tavo moved his feet back a few inches. Then Raúl drank, stopped, drank some more, and gave the jug back to Bimbo. He hung his head down and placed his arm down. I grabbed his wrist again.

"I'm surprised the water didn't come out the sides of your neck," said Bimbo.

Raúl snapped his head up. "What did you say?"

"Those slits on the sides of your neck. What…what are you?"

Instead of answering, Raúl turned to me.

"You got your water," I said. "Now talk. The whole story. If you want to see your daughter again, tell us everything."

"Okay," said Raúl. "Papalote…his family has owned La Perla for a long time. At least…three generations. Papalote's grandpa, Ignacio, was a bichote. He was born in La Perla when the place was a stinking hole next to San Juan no one cared about. He understood why they were down there, why no one wanted tourists to see them. They were poor and dark and didn't speak English, so they didn't matter. He got tired of that shit. He got tired of his people going hungry, so he did something about it. That's why the man is a fucking legend."

"What did he do? What does this have to do with the fish?" I asked.

"You said if I left anything out, you'd stab me, and if I gave you the whole story, you'd let me go, so let me tell the fucking story!"

"Talk." I slammed my leg against Raúl's. The knife moved.

He yowled. "Fuck! Fine, man. Whatever. Where was I?"

"Ignacio," said Tavo. His face betrayed how interested he was in everything Raúl was saying. It dawned on me that we were all walking into new, possibly even more dangerous territory.

"Ignacio…started stealing with his friends, a bunch of poor kids just like him. Then he started offering protection to businesses in San Juan, made some real money and connections that way. He learned a bit of English so he could give tours to tourists. He saw what the gringos wanted when he was up in San Juan, so he figured out how to bring them down to La Perla and make money off them by opening a bar and selling cheap booze. He did that shit for years. Then came the drugs.

"He met some gringos at his bar who wanted to use La Perla as a…you know, distribution center. They never saw any cops down there. Ignacio went into business with them, supplying men, boats, and places to hide the drugs as they came and went from South America and Miami to places all over the Caribbean and the United States. When he knew how to run things, he killed his partners. Kept the dealers and connections he'd made in Mexico, Cuba, Miami, and Colombia. He took a good business and made it explode, built a fucking empire.

"Ignacio is the reason why we're huge when it comes to heroin and cocaine. He figured out that the Coast Guard wasn't a fan of hanging around the dangerous, choppy water near the reef for some reason, so he used smaller boats to do the runs. Small boats were faster and could get around the reef better. If the boats got stuck, he'd send folks out in Jet Skis or kayaks to get the shit and bring it in. He spent a lot of time out there, making sure things ran smoothly, and he got a great idea. If you fucked— Can I get some more water?"

I let him go and Bimbo handed him the jug again. He swallowed a few times. Nothing came out the sides of his neck. Whatever slits in his skin had been there didn't seem to be there anymore. Maybe he didn't even know.

Raúl handed the jug back to Bimbo and set his hand down again. "So...yeah, if you fucked with Ignacio, he'd kill you and have his men take your body out to the reef and tie it there so the fish and crabs would feast on you. Then he'd bring the body back and drop it somewhere where people could see it. You ever seen a body pulled out of the water after a few days? They get all bloated, and the animals fuck up their faces. It's scary stuff, and the smell is...something else. He scared the shit out of everyone with that. He became the king. No one wanted to mess with Ignacio. Then...well, then the bodies started disappearing."

Disappearing because someone took them. I thought about the things I saw near the reef.

"Point is"—Raúl took a breath—"Ignacio told his men to use better rope because he wanted his enemies to see the bodies, and for that he had to bring them back and display them after the crabs and shit had been at them. That was the whole point of tying them to the reef. He knew word of what he did was spreading, and the cops were quickly realizing La Perla wasn't a place they wanted to fuck with, which allowed Ignacio to run his empire without having to deal with pigs. There was gambling going on at his bar, women for the gringos, illegal cigarettes, whatever.

"His men did as they were told and got better rope, but that didn't work. The bodies kept vanishing. Ignacio told his men to use chains instead of rope, but that didn't help either. At first he thought it was... sharks. Maybe they were getting to the bodies during high tide and eating them, like…ripping them outta the chains or something. Big sharks are strong enough to do something like that, so he used more chains, but the bodies kept vanishing no matter how well they tied them down.

"Then he thought maybe people were doing it. Enemies or whatever, doing it to show him they didn't give a shit. Ignacio couldn't have that, so he made his men stay out there at night with him so they could see who was—" Raúl grimaced. "Shit, my whole face hurts, really bad. Can you let me fucking go now? I've told you enough. I need a fucking doctor."

"No," I said. "It sounds like you're just getting to the good part. Tell us who was taking the bodies—who takes them now. Then you can get the fuck outta here."

I felt no remorse about lying to him just like I felt no remorse for breaking his face. As he talked, I thought about everything I'd heard since I was a kid. The legend of la garita del Diablo seemed far more sinister now.

Raúl took a deep breath and looked around again with the only eye he could open. His face was a mess, but he looked angry now. The hope had turned into rage. I wanted him afraid, not furious. I slapped the knife with my left hand while holding his arm with my right. He howled.

"Keep talking or I'll do it again."

"Fuck! Stop! Where…where was I?"

"Something on the reef was taking the bodies, so Ignacio went out there with his men and a few boats…"

"Right. They went out, tied a body, and waited for it to get dark. They hung around with no lights or anything, but they never saw a fucking thing. They came back in the morning and went back out again the next afternoon and the body was gone. They tried it a few times with the same results; the bodies kept vanishing. Ignacio kept an eye out from the windows at the bar, but never saw anyone out there. He had his men looking at the reef from the beach, but they…never saw boats or people anywhere near the reef. It was obvious there was something under the water. Ignacio had to know, so he went out there one last time with some men, another body, and food. They waited all night and into the next day. Then he decided to move away a little, just in case. In the middle of the second night, he saw movement in the water. Something was taking the fucking body.

"Everyone on the two boats saw the splashing and creatures moving around the body. They go closer, moving as quietly as they could and using their paddles without pulling them out of the water. They saw the things taking the body, things that moved like men but weren't human. The men refused to get closer. Ignacio threatened them, but then let them go back to shore. Then he...I don't know, he became obsessed, I guess.

"Papalote likes to tell different stories to keep people guessing. I've heard him tell a new soldier that the things came to his grandpa in the middle of the night, that they went into his house and talked to him and that's how they ended up working for him, but that's not true. Ignacio started going out to the reef himself whenever he had another body. His men would tie the bodies down, but when they'd come back to shore, he'd stay on a boat by himself. He wanted to see what had been feeding on the bodies and figure out how to deal with it. He knew the fish had something to do with why there were never any fishermen out there, why he could run his business without interruption.

"Ignacio started going out there and staying out for days at a time, leaving his lieutenant in charge. After a few weeks, he came back and said he'd talked with the fish using the English he'd taught himself to do business with the gringos. He'd been taking bodies out and tying them himself and then hanging around until the fish came, slightly closer each time. One night, one of the fish came up to the boat and started talking to him. That's it. That's the story. Ignacio and the fish started working together. Ignacio gave them bodies, and they protected his business in the water and helped him get the stuff in from time to —"

"That's not the whole story," said Tavo, pointing at Raúl. "You have fucking fish gills. We all saw them."

It was something that had been dancing around the edges of my brain, but now it took center stage. It was disgusting, and incredible, but everything I'd seen and heard and the knife stuck all the way back to its handle in Raúl's leg told me it was real.

"You talked like a kid giving a presentation on something he knows inside and out." I slapped the knife again.

Instead of screaming, Raúl made a sound like he had a bird stuck in his throat and groaned like an old lawn mower trying to start. Raúl looked at me with hatred in his one open eye. The swelling had gotten worse, with blood covering his mouth and nose. I'd done that damage. The pain in my knuckles reminded me of the hardness of the bones right underneath Raúl's face and his pointy teeth and fake-looking lips. I stared back at him, wanting him to know I was ready to do more damage. I smacked the knife again. This time, he screamed.

"What do they do with the bodies?" I knew the answer, it wasn't like I thought these fish people were performing burial rites at sea, but I needed to hear Raúl say it. "Talk!"

"Look outside," Raúl said calmly, as if he was tired of talking to me.

"What?" asked Tavo.

"Outside," he said. "Go to the window and...look outside right now."

I looked at Paul. The motherfucker was looking everywhere but at me. Bimbo was the opposite. He went to the window.

"There's someone across the street," said Bimbo. "Fuck."

Raúl chuckled.

A dog barked, closer this time. It was definitely a warning.

37

GABE

—

A shanking on a sofa
A threat right outside
Watching a man die
Vanishing ghost
The soul eater

I figured the pain was going to be enough to keep Raúl somewhat under control. Also, there were four of us, two guns, and one knife buried in his thigh. Those were good odds. Instead of slapping the knife again, I let him go, yanked the knife out of his leg, and stabbed him a few inches closer to his knee. He yelled, bent over, and grabbed his leg with the hand I'd released. Tavo pulled him back. I pulled the knife out right between his hands and stabbed him again, this time on the side of the leg. I left the knife buried in his flesh and used both hands to wrench his arm back.

A shanking on a sofa. I hoped Xavier loved it.

"What da fuck are you doing, Gabe?" asked Paul. I felt like stabbing him in the leg as well. I didn't answer. He was here, but this no longer concerned him.

Raúl's arm was slick with blood. I pulled it closer to me and held him again as hard as I could.

"Who's that out there?" I asked him.

"I...I told you—fuck!—I told you you assholes had no idea what you were getting into. That's a fish. One from the water that can still stay on land for a while. They see everything. I knew they'd send someone. They take care of us living on land."

"Living on land?" asked Tavo, his eyes wide with panic. "Is that—? Are you one of those things?"

Raúl smiled. His pointy teeth were covered in blood.

It had to be a lie. He was a man. Or was he? He had fucking gills. My thumb had vanished into his neck. Bimbo had checked it out. We'd all seen it. Maybe he was a hybrid, some kind of monster that lived close to whatever lived on the reef.

"We need to kill this motherfucker now," said Bimbo. "Then I'm gonna go downstairs and shoot whoever's out there."

"No! Finish the fucking story. Now."

"The story?" Raúl chuckled again. "The story is standing out there, about to kill you all. Let me go and I'll put in a good word for you, make sure they kill you quickly."

I remembered the figure in front of my house, standing between the two skeletal palm trees. It'd vanished, but now I was sure it'd been there. I wanted to see whoever was standing across the street, but I also wanted to stay as far away as possible from that fucking window.

I wanted none of this.

I wanted a time machine.

I wanted all of us to be drinking somewhere with Xavier.

I wanted to be in Natalia's arms.

I wanted the rest of the story.

"The story. Now. Where did they come from? What...what are you?"

Raúl smiled again. I reached for the knife.

"Okay! Okay, man. You got it. A parting gift for you guys. They came from the coast of Massachusetts. They lived there for generations. Then something happened, something big, and they had to look for a new place to live. They ended up here, in the reefs outside La Perla. Some other places too. Cuba. The Dominican Republic. Jamaica. The water is always rough around the reef, so there aren't many boats around. They were comfortable there for a long time.

"Ignacio changed that. He kept going out there, bringing them bodies. Then it...grew. They started depending on it. Food isn't what it used to be out there with the pollution, dying reefs, overfishing, and all that. At some point, the folks from La Perla and the fish started mixing. My mom died from cancer. She was born and raised in La Perla. My father is out there. I told you, it's been going on for generations. That's it. I swear. That's the whole...*story*."

"So, you're one of those things?" I asked.

"No," said Raúl. "I'm a mutt. A mix. Some of us live on land, some in the water, and some in between."

"The things on your neck...are gills?" asked Tavo. He loved the water. I wondered if he was jealous, if he was dreaming of a life under the waves.

"They're pretty much useless, some of us don't even have them, but...yeah, they're gills."

No one said anything for a few seconds. This was too weird. This was bigger and stranger than we'd imagined, and if Papalote had an army of fish on top of all his men, we were beyond fucked.

"What about the guy standing in front of the house?" asked Tavo.

"That's not a guy. That's a fish, and you're all fucked. He'll probably go get some help soon. Or he'll track your asses down. I'm gonna enjoy watching you —"

"That's enough," said Bimbo.

"Are you gonna let me go or what?"

Bimbo stepped away from the window, came over to the sofa, leaned down, and pulled the knife out of Raúl's leg. Raúl yelled again, this time a wet, gargling thing that seemed to be drowning inside him.

Bimbo sort of climbed on the sofa so he was straddling Raúl. Raúl's hair was too short to grab, so Bimbo moved his gun to his left hand and used his forearm to push Raúl's head back. Raúl tried to fight him off. Tavo and I held him tighter.

"Look at me," said Bimbo. Raúl looked at him, his one eye wide and full of panic. He was breathing like a desperate animal and trying to pull his arms free. The whistling sound was coming from his nose again. I was struggling. My hand hurt and adrenaline was giving Raúl a boost.

"I thought I'd make you say my mother's name, but you don't fucking deserve it," said Bimbo. "Her name's sacred. Your fucking mouth doesn't deserve to mention her, but I want her name to be the last thing you ever hear. María."

The knife made a strange sound as it cut through Raúl's neck, like someone tearing off a piece of a wet T-shirt. Raúl made a gargling sound. Blood poured like a black mantle from his neck. Bimbo stayed there for a moment, his forearm still pushing Raúl's head back. Then he stood up.

Tavo let Raúl go and he, too, stood up like the sofa was on fire. I didn't blame him. Holding Raúl now seemed stupid. I let his arm go and got to my feet. Raúl didn't try to stand or jump us. His hands went up to his neck. He was trying to stop the bleeding, some useless, instinctive move, the innate reflex to try to stay alive. Blood kept pouring, painting his hands a deeper dark fluid in the gloom, and probably tainting us all with some unspoken curse.

Bimbo stood there, watching Raúl die, his face blank and unreadable. Raúl tried to scream or send up one last prayer—or a last fuck-you—to his god of choice. The sound that bubbled up from his throat wasn't human.

Tavo looked horrified. It was easier to watch Raúl pushing his head against his chest, his hands like black birds fluttering uselessly against the blood pouring from his neck. I wondered where my soul had gone.

Outside.

There was still someone.

A fish.

I had to check.

I turned to the window. Xavier was there again, standing near the table. He had a smile on his face. He looked proud of us. For a second, I felt the same. I hoped María had watched us too. We fucked up her sofa, but Raúl had paid, and in this world where everything hurts, sometimes inflicting pain on others is all the respite we get.

I blinked and Xavier was gone. Had he been there at all? Maybe he wasn't a ghost. Maybe he was something my brain was creating for me, a vision to help me deflect the guilt that should be crushing me, a childish excuse for my inhuman behavior.

I moved away from Raúl, trying hard to ignore the sounds he was making while knowing they'd haunt me. Paul was mumbling something. It sounded like a question.

I reached the window and looked at the opposite side of the street. The sidewalk was empty. Maybe the fish had gone to get more, like Raúl said. The thought sent a shiver down my spine.

"He still out there?" asked Tavo.

"There's no one there," I said.

Bimbo came up and stood next to me, scanning the street.

"If what that motherfucker said is true, we need to change our plans quickly."

"Change our plans? There's never been a fucking plan!" said Paul. "You've all been running around like chickens with your heads cut off, and now we have a dead guy on the sofa and some fucking creatures that eat corpses coming for us. This isn't——"

"Shut the fuck up!" I said.

"Nah, you shut the fuck up, Gabe. You told me we were gonna get these guys before they got us. You said we were going to end it. How the fuck is this making it go away, cabrón? We killed one dude and then this guy or fish or whatever he is, and now we have, what, monsters coming for us? And that's if Papalote doesn't find us first. Or this Brujo guy. Nah, this doesn't work for——"

I was on Paul before I knew what I was doing. I grabbed him by the shirt and pushed him until his back hit the wall. Each of my hands held a fistful of T-shirt. The pain in my right hand was feeding my anger, begging me to hurt someone to make the pain go away.

"Shut the fuck up!" I said again.

"Let me go, man," said Paul, his voice strangely calm.

His gun went up and rested against my left cheek.

"Now you got balls? You wanted no part of this. You were shaking like a fucking leaf while we took care of business, but now you're brave? Go ahead and pull that fucking trigger. Do it!"

"Put the gun down, P." It was Tavo. From behind me.

"Tell Gabe to let me go, and I'll put the gun down," said Paul.

Bimbo moved forward, raised his own gun, and brought it to Paul's face.

It was still four guys and two guns, but the equation had been altered, broken, messed up beyond recognition.

"Tavo asked you nicely, but I'm not going to."

Paul's face crumbled into tears. I felt numb. Had we crossed a line we could never uncross? I didn't have time to think about it. There was a dead man on the sofa, a ghost who came and went, El Brujo and Papalote were still out there, and there were some creatures that lived beyond the reef coming for us. And one of them was right outside Bimbo's place.

Paul pulled the gun away from my face and slowly lowered it while keeping his eyes on Bimbo.

"Happy now?" asked Bimbo.

"No," said Paul. "Nothing about you guys acting like assholes makes me happy. And what the fuck was that thing about your mom messing with Papalote? You told us she—"

"Stop talking," said Bimbo, giving the gun a little push.

I let go of Paul's shirt and tried to stomp down the desire to punch him.

"I'm done," said Paul.

"Paul, don't do this ag—"

"No, T, don't even try. This time I'm done for real. You crazy fucks started something you can't finish. You were in over your heads from the start, and then you dug deeper. La única opción es desaparecernos y ustedes lo saben. Forget killing Papalote, we need to just... vanish. Ustedes están locos pa'l carajo."

"Vanishing isn't an option now," said Tavo, his voice calm. "We just killed a man——"

"No, no, no," said Paul. "Don't do this 'we' shit again. Bimbo killed a man. He killed *another* man. He kills and we go along for the ride and put ourselves in danger and then what do we get, cabrón? Nothing. Only thing we've managed to do is get Xavier killed, man."

"Doesn't matter who pulls the trigger," said Tavo, raising his voice. "We're here for María and Xavier."

"We're here for them? They're fucking dead, T! Están muertos, cabrón. No podemos cambiar eso. We won't bring them back with this. Killing a hundred dudes won't bring them back. It'll cost you everything and it won't change how you feel. The thing is, no one figures that out until they've gone too far looking for it. I don't——"

"We're here to get some fucking justice because no one will give it to us," said Tavo.

"That's you! I'm here to make sure Cynthia and I stay alive and don't have to deal..."

Even in the darkness I could see the tectonic shifts turning Paul's face into a map of guilt and shame. *Cynthia and I.* That was it. The two of them. We weren't on the list. María or Xavier or any of his brothers living in peace; it was about him.

"I think you need to leave, man," said Bimbo.

"No, listen, we need to calm the fuck down and talk about this," said Tavo.

"I don't wanna hear anything this selfish coward has to say," I said.

Paul put his hands up, turned sideways, and made his way to the door, walking like he was expecting Bimbo to shoot him or me to punch him at any moment. When he got to the door, he looked at Raúl's body on the sofa and then back at us.

"Se los dije una vez y se los voy a decir una vez más: ustedes están locos pa'l carajo. Dejen esta mierda quieta o van a acabar seis pies bajo tierra."

Paul didn't wait for a reply. He turned and opened the door. The night outside swallowed him a second before the door closed.

Listening to the groans from Bimbo's stairs as Paul made his way down made me wonder how many people had heard Raúl screaming. Then I remembered no one gave a fuck. People were getting killed in their own houses for fucking generators. Bunches of people had died. There had been no reports about Kimbo. The country was broken, its soul shattered and stuck in the dark. Screams in the night were just part of the background noise.

"What now?" asked Tavo.

We looked at Raúl. He was no longer moving. His hands were near his neck, like a pair of black spiders curled around a veil of night. His chest wasn't rising. No sound came from his slashed throat and busted nose. He was dead.

Bimbo didn't answer. I didn't know what to say, so I walked back to the window and looked out. The street was still empty. Raúl was way past the point of having an opinion.

"We need to figure this out right now," said Tavo.

"Shit, I have to do something," said Bimbo while walking to his room. He opened the door, stepped into the darkness beyond, and shut the door.

A minute later, the door opened again, and Bimbo stepped out with Altagracia by his side.

"What's going on?" asked Tavo.

Altagracia didn't answer. Instead, she walked to Raúl and bent over his body, grabbed his head with her left hand, and stuck the fingers of her right hand into his bloody mouth. Then she started whispering.

"What's she — ?"

"Let her do her thing, Gabe," said Bimbo. "She knows what she's doing. Like with the San Miguel Arcángel prayer."

Altagracia's lips moved, but the sound of her words, spoken in a language I'd never heard before, came from everywhere at once, as if a dozen ghosts were whispering all around us. My blood ran cold.

The guy in the garage.

Kimbo.

Raúl.

We were deep in the water. And I didn't feel like a shark.

All stories are ghost stories, and some stories turn us into ghosts.

Raúl started shaking. We took a step back. Bimbo raised his gun. Altagracia dug deeper into his mouth and kept whispering. The sound of her strange words flew around us like a living thing. She grabbed something and started pulling. A moment later, her fingers were half-way out of Raúl's mouth, and they were pulling something from it that was pushing his mouth open.

Bimbo, Tavo, and I stood there in silence, our hearts racing, our heads struggling to process what we were witnessing.

After a bit more pulling, Altagracia extracted what looked like a black squid from Raúl's mouth. A squid made of inky black smoke. It was moving around, its tiny arms flailing. Raúl stopped shaking. She held the squirming thing close to her mouth and kept whispering. Then she opened her mouth and swallowed it. She grimaced and grunted as the thing went down her throat, making it bulge. She looked like a snake swallowing an egg.

The room smelled like burnt hair.

Altagracia stood up and addressed us.

"Deshágase del cuerpo," said Altagracia. Then she looked toward the table and seemed to listen for a second before speaking again. "Su amigo quiere que sepan que los quiere y que va a quedarse con ustedes hasta el final."

Get rid of the body.

Your friend wants you to know he'll be with you until the end.

Xavier. She could see him. He'd stay with us. A chunk of something lodged in my throat, and tears came to my eyes. I blinked them away.

Altagracia turned and walked back to Bimbo's room. The moment she opened the door, the dog barked again. It sounded like it came from the bottom of Bimbo's crappy stairs.

When the door closed, Tavo spoke. "What the fuck was that?"

"She was making sure he wouldn't haunt us," said Bimbo.

"And she was...she was talking about Xavier, right?" Tavo's voice broke when he said the name.

"Yeah," I said.

"How do you——? You know what? Never mind."

Tavo moved to me and embraced me. I returned the hug. A moment later, Bimbo was there, an arm around each of us. It was just like when we'd arrived at María's wake, except there were three of us instead of five. Both absences hurt.

"What the fuck is going on? How does she know——?" asked Tavo, pulling away.

"I don't know," interrupted Bimbo. "She has a gift. Got it from her grandma. I...don't know more than that."

"Okay, just...fuck! What now? Like I said, we need to get rid of the body."

"I know. You have a plan?" asked Bimbo.

Tavo stayed quiet for a few seconds and then said, "I do." At that moment, those were the two most beautiful words I'd ever heard.

38

ALTAGRACIA

—

Hiding in the dark
Awful screams
Faces like frogs
Swallowing a soul
A phone call

She knew death was everywhere. It had been all around Altagracia's house and drove both her and her brother out of the country. It had swallowed her grandmother. It was in many of the bad things her brother did. Now it had followed her into this house. And it was outside too. She could feel Javasasgot, the dark old god who appeared in her sacred book, everywhere. It was hungry. Altagracia thought about the broken woman who'd lost her daughter. She'd told her to feed Javasasgot, but she knew that powerful spirits were always hungry.

Bimbo had brought darkness home. He had a soft side and an undying love for his dead mother and troubled sister. This much she knew. He also spoke of his friends all the time. He said they were pure souls and told stories of things they'd done together, fights they'd gotten into defending each other. His face would soften when he spoke about them. Then it'd get hard again when he spoke of his mother and sister. Altagracia knew pain did things like that to people: harden them where they'd been soft, make them hurt in places where laughter used to live.

Altagracia was a keen observer. It was a gift that had saved her life more than once by keeping her away from bad people. The men Bimbo hung out with were not bad men. One of them, the tall blond one who spoke only English, was especially pure. Altagracia could see it, like warm light coming from his chest. Angels rarely walk the earth, but when they do, they shine like that.

Yes, Bimbo was good and his friends were good, but they were committing themselves to darkness. Altagracia knew people were often pushed to do awful things for all the right reasons, but knowing that and seeing it happen were two very different things. She'd encouraged Bimbo because her brother had asked her to do so, but now she was confused, and not knowing what her brother wanted made her feel even worse. It made her feel like helping Bimbo and his friends was the right thing to do.

When they got to the apartment that night, Altagracia stayed in her room, sitting in the dark next to the door and craving a cigarette. She could hear them out there, asking a man a bunch of questions about Bimbo's mother. And hurting him. Hurting him bad. His screams were awful. She knew if they killed him, he would haunt them all. When things got worse, Altagracia's curiosity got the better of her, so she blew out the few candles she had lit, opened the door slowly, and crawled out of the room. She sat against the wall, hidden by the shadows and a piece of the fridge, and looked at Bimbo and his friends. She couldn't call or text her brother, because they'd see the light of her phone if she did, so she knew she had to pay attention.

When Bimbo went to get a knife, Altagracia panicked and feared Bimbo would see her there and ask her why she was spying on them, but he didn't even look at the hallway. She watched them stab the man in the leg, and then, with a hand over her mouth and struggling to swallow her own screams, she saw Bimbo slice the man's throat with the same knife they'd used to get information out of him. She'd seen enough. She crept back into the room.

The story the man told was new to Altagracia, but the creatures he talked about weren't. Altagracia had grown up in Jarabacoa, far from the ocean, but she had cousins who lived on the coast in a place called Palmar de Ocoa. They made the three-hour drive a few times per year, and when they got together, they'd always tell Altagracia stories of the creatures that lived in the reefs of Bahía de Ocoa. They walked like people and had arms and legs, but they were ocean creatures and had faces like frogs. The creatures would come out at night to trade and sleep with humans from the coast. They were the reason there were never fishermen from other towns in the area, and according to Altagracia's cousins, sometimes young people would disappear mysteriously and it was rumored that they were getting old and their time had come to join the others beyond the reef.

Altagracia was still thinking about the creatures and the horrible stuff she'd seen when Bimbo came looking for her. His eyes were desperate. She'd told him enough to keep him safe, but he didn't really know what she was capable of. Something in his voice made her want to help them, to keep the darkness of the man they'd killed, to keep it from ruining their lives. She walked out with him and did what she had to do. The man's soul tasted like dirt from a garden, but she swallowed it anyway.

Then she saw a ghost standing next to the table, but it was unlike any ghost she'd seen. This one was like a dream, like the way someone would picture a ghost instead of the way they truly were. It was the friend they'd lost. He talked to her, but he sounded like the big guy with the glasses. Altagracia wondered if Bimbo's friend was conjuring this ghost somehow. She passed on the ghost's message before going back to the room.

As soon as Bimbo and his friends were gone, Altagracia called her brother, told him everything. Then she lit a cigarette and was about to sit by the window when she heard someone coming up the stairs.

39

GABE

—

The night knows things
Stuck in the back seat
Adding bodies to the list
A story of brotherhood
Making María proud

It was darker than it'd been when we got back to Bimbo's house after kidnapping Raúl, like the night knew we were out there again and it had something to prove. I once heard someone say that we're not afraid of being alone in the dark; we're afraid of not being alone in the dark, and that's exactly how I felt despite the help we had supposedly gotten from those prayers and Altagracia. I wasn't afraid of ghosts, but knowing there were creatures out there on the reef that could also be on land was too much. I got the same feeling I had every time a hurricane approached: I was trapped with a bad thing in tight quarters and there was no place for me to go, no way for me to run away. Nothing will give you a sense of freedom like looking at the ocean, and nothing will make you feel more landlocked than knowing you're stuck on a tiny speck of green surrounded by infinite blue.

Bimbo was driving and Tavo was riding shotgun. I was squeezed into the tiny back seat. Bimbo was big and Tavo was tall, so they both had their seats pushed back and were making the rear of the car feel claustrophobic. It was better than the back of the van, but not by much.

We had crossed the Dos Hermanos Bridge before anyone said anything.

"Do you really think this is going to work?" asked Bimbo.

Tavo nodded. "I think this is the only thing that can work. If we wait, those things will get us. If not, El Brujo will come for us. Surprising them now and letting those...fish know things have changed is the only way forward."

When Tavo had said he had a plan, I'd been happy...or whatever you call the lessening of that feeling of when you're in a room with a dead man with gills and wondering if monsters from beyond the reef are coming to feast on your flesh at any moment.

Every single one of Bimbo's plans had sucked, but what Tavo proposed gave Bimbo's a run for their money.

Tavo said the only way to prevent those creatures and El Brujo from putting us six feet under was to go back to La Perla, kill El Brujo, and then take out Papalote. El Brujo, Tavo said, would be looking for his partner, and if he was half as good—or as awful—as everyone said, he'd find us quickly. Killing Papalote, then dragging him out to the reef was the only way to make sure the monsters that lived there didn't come for us.

It was a choice; though by now, there was no choice.

Bimbo and I had three bodies behind us, three ghosts ready to follow us for the rest of our lives. Tavo was saying the only way out of this mess was adding two more bodies to the list, and I kinda thought the motherfucker was right. I tried to remind myself that we were supposed to be night sharks, and sharks do whatever they have to do to survive without hesitation or guilt.

Bimbo had given me his gun and then gotten another one from the duffel bag, which he still kept in his trunk. He also picked one out for Tavo, but when he tried to hand it to him, Tavo shook his head and said he refused to carry a gun because he was way too nervous and would probably kill one of us accidentally. Instead, he reached into his front pocket and pulled out a small folding knife. I wondered what he'd do with it if this whole fucking thing came down to who pulled the trigger faster or more accurately.

As we drove, I kept looking behind us, expecting a car to come at us at high speed, with the windows down and some guys with guns blasting away. Every other car I saw out there sent my heart into panic mode. I kept thinking about the white Lumina I'd seen with the water inside the taillight.

If Raúl hadn't been lying that he and El Brujo hadn't been in that car, then who the fuck had? Had Papalote put some other men on our tail? Maybe they were the ones who'd killed Xavier and painted the veves on our doors. Fuck, or maybe those things on the reef had been keeping an eye on us for a while. None of it made sense, but it also made me want to end this fucking thing as soon as possible.

We climbed Norzagaray and were reaching the turn to go down the tunnel into La Perla when Bimbo stopped and pulled to the side.

"We should walk from here," he said.

"Walk?" said Tavo. "You can turn off the lights if you want, but we need to have a car to get the hell out of there after we take care of business."

"If we drive in at this time of night, someone will be paying attention to us, and if I look shady as fuck with my lights off, we're gonna catch a bullet before we have a chance to even try to get things done."

"I know that, B, but if we try to just walk in, the same thing will happen anyway, except we won't have a chance at getting out. You didn't use this car to get Raúl, so it won't get anyone riled up, right? Plus, if Henry and the other junkies finished their part, they probably got paid, and that means they're curled up somewhere and won't be out and about until they need another fix. If we see anyone else, we'll pretend we just want to find a cold drink, yeah?"

Bimbo didn't reply, but he pulled back into the street and got us down to the tunnel and into La Perla with our windows down and his arm hanging out.

The place was deserted. There were no lights in any of the houses despite the many generators we'd heard earlier. The silence had its own deafening echo. What if we were being ambushed? How much had the junkies seen? How much had the fish seen? Bimbo's gun, which had felt like something solid and useful when he gave it to me, felt like nothing.

We got on Calle San Miguel again.

"Do you know where you're going?" I asked.

"Yeah," said Bimbo. "I know the place. We drove past it earlier. There's a little street right before you get to where we parked the van. The chapel's right there. Raúl said El Brujo lives in a two-story red house next to it, right? Can't be too hard to find."

"Where are you gonna park?" asked Tavo.

"Same place we parked earlier," said Bimbo. "I'm gonna turn around and leave the car ready to head out."

"Sounds good," I said. "But what are we gonna do if we find the place?"

"We're gonna go up to his door and —"

"No," I said. "No, no, no, B. No more of this shit. Kimbo was bad enough, man. We need —"

"Who's Kimbo?" asked Tavo.

As if on cue, my right hand throbbed, reminding me just how much damage I'd inflicted on myself while taking out all my anger and grief on Raúl's face.

"We'll talk about that later," said Bimbo. "You have a better idea, Gabe?"

I didn't. I had nothing.

"You go up to the door, B," I said. "Tavo and I will hide next to the door or behind a car or something. If he opens the door, we get in there and put him down."

"No, we won't put him down quickly," said Bimbo.

"Why?" asked Tavo before I could ask the same thing. Then the answer came to me before Bimbo could reply.

"El Brujo killed my mom. That motherfucker pulled the trigger.

The bullets came from him. I'm gonna make him pay. I'm gonna hurt him. He—"

The last word came with a punch of air. It wasn't quite a sob, but it was something close to it. Raúl had mattered because he was there, driving the car as bullets spewed forth. El Brujo was another story. He'd pulled the trigger. More than anyone else except Papalote, El Brujo was responsible for María's death. I couldn't imagine what Bimbo was feeling. I couldn't imagine what I'd feel—or do—if I found myself facing the asshole who left my mom dead with two bullet holes in the face and bleeding on a dirty sidewalk.

"I'm with you, B," I said. It meant way more than what the words implied, and he knew it.

"So am I, brother," said Tavo, placing a hand on Bimbo's shoulder. "We'll make him pay. I owe you that much and more."

"Owe me? What the fuck are you talking about?"

We had reached the same placita where we'd parked earlier. Bimbo turned and then backed up and stopped close to where he'd parked the van earlier. Raúl's pickup wasn't there. I wondered if someone had stolen it or if Papalote's people had taken it after realizing Raúl was missing and the keys were still in it. It didn't matter. He was gone, and by now, his people knew it. We had to move.

"Y'all remember Doña Elena?" Tavo asked.

"The old lady who lived on your street and rented apartments?" I asked. I had a few memories of her. She always wore flowery batas and smelled like cheap cigarettes and cat pee. Her favorite sport was screaming at us for playing in the street.

"Yeah, her," said Tavo.

"Yeah, I remember her," said Bimbo. "She was a bitch."

"Well....she, ah, she rented one of her tiny studios to a guy named Enrique when we were in tenth grade. He was a Spanish musician— guitar player. He'd come to the island to record some tracks with a band or something. Point is, he'd come out and play guitar, smoke, drink coffee, or read a book while sitting on a plastic chair in front of Doña Elena's house, right under that big tree that'd mess up the sidewalk. If he hadn't been paying, I'm sure she would've called the cops on him, but he was forking over a few hundred bucks for that little closet of a room she had on the back of the second floor, so she kept her mouth shut."

Tavo stopped talking and looked out his window. He was either reminiscing or collecting his thoughts before we went and killed another man. I had no idea which one it was, but I felt like we needed to move. The memory of the creatures I'd seen out on the reef as the sun was coming down was screaming in my head. They were still out there, which meant they could come to us at any moment.

"We need to get—"

"Let me finish," interrupted Tavo. "Enrique would smoke and play guitar and read out there and I'd see him sometimes on my way back from the beach. He started saying hi one day. Then he'd ask about the weather or the waves or something. I guessed he was lonely. I didn't mind. We started talking. His English was horrible, but he had a sense of humor about it and we hit it off. I showed him how to get to the beach and told him that was a better spot for reading. He talked to me about his favorite books. He read a lot of horror and crime novels, but also classics and knew every single book I mentioned from the ones they'd made us read at school.

"One day he gave me these two little Jim Thompson books after one of our conversations. Anyway, he talked a lot about music. You know, bands he'd played with and countries he'd visited as a session musician, always making enough money to travel and eat but never enough to really enjoy a country the way tourists do. Thing is, we enjoyed each other's company, you know? One day he saw me walking back home. We got to talking about how some cultures worshipped the sun. I told him about the Taíno sun and how I'd love to get it tattooed one day.

"Then he made an odd comment about how a body like mine deserved the finest art. I laughed, but he came closer and kissed me. He was older, but I found him really interesting and we got along really well and talked about cool shit and...well, you know. Whatever.

"Doña Elena found us. She…she caught us. In Enrique's little room. I guess we were making too much noise. The old bitch kept a key to every room. She heard the noise and barged in on us. She screamed something about God and slammed the door. I picked up my shit and jetted. I…I panicked a little. I wondered what would happen if she called the cops or whatever. When I realized I was gay, I looked up a lot of things. I wanted to know what the law said, if the things I liked were seen as illegal or whatever. There are laws against homosexuality in many places. It felt like the entire fucking world was suddenly against me.

"I worried about that shit for weeks. I think I came out to you the week after reading that I could go to jail for ten years. I'd been feeling like I had a secret that was preventing me from breathing properly, and there was no one I could talk to about it, so I had to know just how alone I really was. I was…I was afraid you guys would find out, stop being my friends. That same afternoon, while I was out talking to y'all, Doña Elena went to my house and told my parents what had happened.

"When I came home that night, still on cloud fucking nine from the way y'all reacted, feeling like I wasn't alone after all, my dad punched me in the face and busted up my lip. Then he grabbed me by the hair and punched me in the stomach. This all happened without warning, you know, like as soon as I opened the fucking door. He told me no son of his was going to be a faggot and rot in hell. My mom pulled him off me and I ran away. I slept against the wall of the cemetery that night. I went to school the next day because I was afraid things would get worse if he got a call that I hadn't been to school. I can't even remember what lie I told everyone that day. Probably that my board had hit me in the face or something.

"Then a few days went by and my dad got drunk—bad drunk, not his regular drunk—and punched me again. Hard. Knocked me out for a bit. I think that's the only reason he stopped. I remember it was a Thursday because I tried to convince my mom to let me stay home the next morning. She told me if I stayed home and someone saw me with a black eye, they would talk. It was better to go to school and make up another story about falling down or my board hitting me in the face or something.

"In any case, I went to school and then headed to the beach early the next morning before my dad woke up. I needed to be out there, in the ocean. It was the only place where I felt safe and welcome. When I came home that day, my dad asked me to sit down with him at the kitchen table. I was sure he was going to tell me that I was going to hell again, but instead he started crying. He wasn't sorry for what he did, I could tell, and he never apologized, but he told me you'd all showed up at the house, slapped him around, and pulled a gun on him—you, B, he said you pulled a gun and stuck it under his chin and that you looked 'like a crazy motherfucker two seconds away from pulling the trigger.'

"Whatever y'all looked like or did or said, I don't wanna know. I'm scared to ask. The point is that it worked. My dad was scared shitless. I even felt a little sorry for him. I felt sorry for myself, too, like I had lost a father. But I also gained four brothers, you know? I was okay after that, not alone anymore. And my father never put a finger on me again, which was great because I don't think I could've dealt with that on top of all the other shit I had going on.

"It was...I don't know what would've happened if you guys hadn't paid him a visit. That's my point. I think I might've killed him if he touched me again, or maybe killed myself, so I guess you saved my ass and you saved his. I don't know. Like I said, I owe you."

"You don't owe us shit," said Bimbo. "We're brothers. We love you, man. Remember our only rule: If someone fucks with one of us—"

"They fuck with all of us," I said.

Bimbo looked back at me and smiled. We were on our way to kill the man who had shot his mother, and he had lied to us to get us to help him, and the motherfucker still had a smile in him. A real one. He was fucked, sure, but he had a beautiful fucking soul.

I placed a hand on his shoulder and the other on Tavo's shoulder. "Listen, I love you motherfuckers, but I hate it here and want to be gone as soon as possible. Let's get this done. Let's make María proud."

40

GABE

—

Night sharks
Vanishing man
Dancing veves
Floating head
He doesn't even have a shadow

Bimbo left the car facing the opposite way and we got down. The smell of the ocean felt too big for my nose. The street was empty. Thick clouds drifted in front of the chunk of moon that hung in the sky.

Without a word, Bimbo started walking. We followed him.

When you take power away from the modern world, you silence almost everything that makes a sound. Refrigerators, air-conditioning units, televisions, radios, computer audio, old ceiling fans. As we walked to the little street where the chapel stood, we could hear only the ocean, insects, coquíes, and our own steps hitting the ground. It was the post-hurricane soundtrack, a stripped-down score that reminded me of how close we were to our primal state, and how much attention we paid to the little things that made us feel like we were part of an advanced civilization and not bipedal mammals constantly trying to find ways to fuck and kill each other.

Car lights cut through the darkness and headed our way as we turned onto the last street. My heart stopped. I waited for the sound of guns, for bullets to tear into my body.

"Keep walking," said Tavo. "Keep your cool. La Garita del Diablo is that way. If the car keeps coming this way, we can pretend —"

The car turned onto a street a few blocks down, its lights throwing up huge sliding shadows for a second before disappearing behind some houses. It was a white car. I wondered if its back taillight was full of water.

"This is it," said Bimbo. We had reached the street.

We stood there for a second, looking around and taking in the gloomy world around us, allowing our eyes to adjust to the shapes of the place. Up the street, the houses were smashed together, a blocky black mass of angles and curves that looked like a single neighbor trying to eat itself. There were cars lined up on both sides of the street, just like in Barrio Obrero, except this street wasn't big enough for sidewalks. A bit of moonlight reflected off the cars, which was helpful. The street sloped up gradually, like all streets in La Perla. Darkness covered everything, and in some stretches, it was so impenetrable that there could have been someone — or something — watching us and we wouldn't know.

The same thought came to me again: We're not afraid of being alone in the dark; we're afraid of not being alone in the dark.

Bimbo started walking again and then stopped and looked around like he was lost. Tavo and I did the same. There was no one out there. We were actors performing for no one. I tried to look out at the ocean, expecting to see some fish standing up on the reef, ready to walk toward us, but I couldn't see a thing.

Bimbo turned and entered the little street, suddenly looking like he knew exactly where he was going. We followed him.

The chapel was the second building on the left. It had a hand-painted sign hanging over the door. It was white with black letters, so we could read it in the scant light that came from the moon: CAPILLA SAN GABRIEL.

The house to the left of it looked abandoned, with gaping black holes where the windows should've been and peeling, stained walls that might've been yellow at some point but now made me think of the skin on a decomposing body. On the right side of the chapel was a small red house. There was a blue compact car parked in front of it. Shaky yellow light was coming from under the door. More light could be seen through the beige curtains that covered the only window on the first floor. Candles. Someone was in there.

"What now?" asked Tavo, his voice half a decibel above a whisper.

"Gabe, get your gun ready," said Bimbo, his voice on the same level as Tavo's. "Find a place to hide. I'm gonna knock on the door."

Fear seized my lungs, squeezing, but I looked for a place to hide.

I sent out a prayer to my mom's god.

I sent out a prayer to Xavier.

I sent out a prayer to Elegguá.

Bimbo walked to the door and knocked three times. He didn't have his gun out. He didn't wait for us to hide or look back to make sure we'd found a spot. There were no further instructions. This was it.

Tavo stood to the left of the door, pressing himself against the wall as if that would make him disappear. I took a few steps and hid behind the blue car, bending over to make sure no one could see me next to it.

A moment later, the door opened.

Yellowish light spilled out of the house and tattooed itself into the gloom of the street.

A woman stood at the threshold holding a candle. She was dark and her hair was a big black halo around her head. Her angular features shifted as the light from the candle danced on her face. She had on a long black-and-white shirt. That's all I was able to register before Bimbo moved.

He pushed the woman into the house.

The light from the candle vanished.

Something broke.

The woman screamed.

"Shut the fuck up!" said Bimbo.

I pulled the gun from the back of my pants and squeezed it. My hand screamed.

I moved.

Tavo was already there by the time I reached the door, his big frame blocking most of it. Then he stepped to the side and I moved into the house, quickly trying to process every detail because they say that's where the Devil is.

Bimbo was inside with his gun drawn and aiming it down at the woman on the floor. Her eyes were wide and full of fear. She was crawling back like a crab while still watching Bimbo.

This wasn't the way to go.

Tavo looked at me. He was holding his knife. Behind me, the door was open. Anyone walking by would see us.

I pushed Tavo farther into the house to make space for myself beyond the threshold, moved next to Bimbo, and closed the door. The smell of decay hit my nose immediately, making me cringe.

We were in a small living room. The light came from six or seven candles on a big rectangular table that was full of things. I saw a cow's skull with gristle still clinging to it, and a statue of a standing man. There was fruit and a few bottles too. Flies were dancing around everything. I looked away and took the room in.

A small brown sofa.

Six congas lined up next to the sofa, most of them pushed against the wall.

Two chairs.

A small table with a very large TV on top of it.

Walls covered in dark drawings.

What the hell had we gotten ourselves into?

"¿Quién carajo son ustedes?" asked the woman, her voice a blade. *Who the fuck are you?*

"Cállate," said Bimbo. "¿Dónde está El Brujo?" *Where is El Brujo?*

"¿Quién pregunta?" asked a deep voice that seemed to come from everywhere at once. *Who's asking?*

El Brujo was standing to the right of the table. There was a hallway behind him. The light from the candles on the table was hitting him sideways. He was trigueño, that word used in Puerto Rico for people who are dark enough not to be brown but too light to be called Black. He was tall and skinny. His head was shaved, and his nose was like a hook that had landed on his face at an awkward angle. He was wearing black basketball shorts and nothing else. His body was covered in ink much darker than his skin. There were faces, words, figures, and strange markings very similar to those on the walls. Then it clicked: Many of the drawings were lines that looked like the graffiti on my door. The man was covered in veves. He was the living death curse.

"Pregunto yo, cabrón," said Bimbo.

"¿Y quién eres tú?" El Brujo's voice came from his mouth, but also from somewhere behind me and from the floor.

"Yo soy el hijo de María."

El Brujo was suddenly in front of Bimbo, standing so close to him that the gun's barrel was pressed against his lower belly.

I never saw him move, even though he must have been over ten feet away. No, he hadn't taken a single step, and that's why Bimbo hadn't pulled the trigger.

"How the fuck——?" said Tavo.

El Brujo grabbed Bimbo's wrist with one hand, pulled upward, and pushed Bimbo with the other hand. Bimbo flew back and slammed into Tavo, which cut his question in half before it was done leaving his mouth. They tumbled backward and fell.

The gun, I remembered the gun. I aimed it at El Brujo.

BAM!

The sound of the gunshot crashed against the walls, bounced back, and punched my eardrums as the wall behind the table exploded in a tiny cloud of gray cement dust.

I'd hit nothing.

El Brujo wasn't there.

There was movement next to me. The woman was on her feet and moving past Tavo and Bimbo, heading for the door. They had to stop her. I was about to scream, but there was a flicker over my vision, and El Brujo was standing next to me. Taller than he had been.

His arm hit my forearm the second I saw him. The gun went flying. I pulled my hand back to punch him. He hit me first. In the middle of the chest. It felt like a truck carrying cinder blocks had slammed against my solar plexus.

Someone yanked me back. Pain blasted into my chest and reached my heart and lungs. A sound like a cough erupted from my mouth as I was catapulted back. My lungs deflated like popped balloons. My legs smacked against a chair, flipping me to the floor. My glasses at last hit the ground. My body curled in on itself instinctively, probably trying to protect my organs. I tried to inhale and couldn't. There was a high-pitched sound ringing in my ears, like an electrical current too close to my head. I didn't know if it came from the gunshot or the hit to the chest.

I tried to get to my feet, to stretch my body out and inhale, but managed only to get on all fours. My lungs ached. I couldn't pull air into my body. I looked around, desperate—I couldn't scream, couldn't ask for help.

The room was spinning.

The door was open.

The woman was gone.

I didn't know whether to be relieved or panicked about that, but it's not like I had time to interrogate my feelings.

Tavo was standing up again. El Brujo was close to him. Bimbo was still on the floor, grabbing his chest and grimacing. I knew how he felt. The panic was pure in my blood.

Darkness fluttered and swallowed the edges of the room. The world spun faster. I landed on my side. It was simple now. I was dying.

Air. I needed air. A tear slipped out of the corner of my right eye.

It slid down and ran over the bridge of my nose, feeling cooler than the sweat on my face. I didn't want it to end like this.

Natalia.

I wanted to see Natalia.

My diaphragm did a weird thing below my chest, and it was like a cork popping. I could breathe. I greedily sucked oxygen into my body. My heart was pounding in my ears, right below the high-pitched wail. Suddenly, I saw my glasses, right there in front of me. I grabbed them and put them on my face.

I straightened a bit and looked around the room. It had stopped spinning. Everything looked a little brighter. From the floor, I could see almost the entire room. El Brujo wasn't there. Next to the table, the veves on the walls were moving around, reshaping themselves into different versions of whatever they'd been. I saw something that looked like a heart and then a few intersecting triangles. Then some shapes came together to form the veve on my door before morphing into what looked like a pyramid with two flags sprouting from its tip.

Tavo was pulling his knife back from nothing. His eyes were wide, looking around frantically. Bimbo was standing behind him, finally on his feet and looking at the floor, probably trying to find his gun.

El Brujo stood next to the table again.

I turned, brought my knees underneath my body, and used my arms to push myself up to a standing position, but I felt wobbly and weak. I was still sucking air with my mouth, and my heart was about to explode. I tried to shake it all off somehow.

My gun. I needed my gun.

I looked around at the floor but couldn't see it.

On the table next to El Brujo, the light from the candles wavered as if a gust of wind had passed through the room. Then the cow's head started shaking, making the table rattle. All the flies took to the air at once, looking like buzzing smoke. More than hearing it, I felt the vibrations of the table's legs on the floor through the soles of my feet.

In my ears, the screeching sound was still stabbing my eardrums, my heartbeat pounding right beneath.

Tavo started walking toward El Brujo, leading with his knife, scared but also angry. El Brujo opened his arms and then his mouth.

The sound of a hundred people being boiled to death exploded from El Brujo's mouth. It was worse than the sound I'd been hearing. I covered my ears. Tavo bent over and did the same. Then the sound stopped and the same high-pitched noise from before returned to fill the void. It sounded like an alarm that played a single irritating note.

El Brujo was still next to the table, but now his feet weren't touching the floor. He was hovering a few inches above the ground, his feet pointed down and relaxed. His eyes had gone completely black and his mouth was still open, now looking much larger than humanly possible and frozen in a silent scream.

Bimbo moved into my frame of view. He had the gun and was aiming it at El Brujo. He squeezed the trigger once, twice.

BAM! BAM!

Bimbo was close. The two bullets hit their mark. A tiny hole appeared right above El Brujo's heart and a second one near the middle of his ribs on the same side. Black liquid began pouring from the holes.

El Brujo lowered his face. His black eyes were on Bimbo. El Brujo moved his arms up like he was swatting a fly, and Bimbo's hand went up. The gun jumped free.

Bimbo screamed and ran at El Brujo, but there was nothing but night air waiting for him when he reached the spot.

Then El Brujo appeared right behind Bimbo.

I moved toward them.

El Brujo punched Bimbo, a hard cross to the jaw that sent him crashing into the table. Bimbo knocked a few candles and other stuff down as he rolled onto the chair. He looked dead, like a broken doll.

Instead of falling with everything else, the cow's head went up into the air and stayed there, shaking. The light from the candles made the head's shadow dance on the wall. A huge quivering nightmare. All around it, the black lines and veves on the wall kept coming together and pulling themselves apart only to reconfigure into something new.

El Brujo hung in the air, unmoving. His mouth had become big enough to swallow a human head.

El Brujo wasn't human.

Tavo said something I didn't catch.

I looked at the wall again. El Brujo was floating next to the table, and the candles were bathing his tattooed torso with their light, but his shadow wasn't on the wall or on the floor beneath his feet. His shadow wasn't anywhere.

Tavo slammed into El Brujo, tackling him like a football player and taking him down to the floor in a heap of flailing limbs.

I was there a second later. El Brujo was sliding away from Tavo while Tavo tried desperately to hold him down. El Brujo's mouth was back to normal. Tavo pushed himself up and straddled him, sat up a bit, and brought the knife down below El Brujo's right clavicle. The blade sank in. El Brujo howled. It was a normal scream.

I bent down and threw a punch at him, cracked him in the cheek. It felt like punching a wall. For a second, I'd forgotten about what Raúl's face had done to my hand — but the pain reminded me immediately.

El Brujo pushed Tavo with one hand, and Tavo went flying back like he'd been shot out of a cannon. Impossible force. Tavo's body, impossibly fast. We had to kill him. Now. If we didn't, none of us would walk out of the house alive.

I swung again, despite every bone in my body telling me to stop and protect my hand. My fist hit the floor. There was no one there. Pain exploded along my arm all the way up to my shoulder. The sound got louder.

A hand grabbed my shirt from the back and spun me around. El Brujo's hand wrapped around my neck. He pulled me up. My feet left the ground. His eyes were entirely black, his mouth open again.

I could hear it stretching, cracking. His teeth looked larger than they had before.

I tried to pull one of his fingers back and break it, but his hand was like a vise grip. The man probably weighed less than half what I did, but he was holding me up in the air by the neck with one arm like I weighed nothing. I punched his arm, but my hand was wrecked. I swung with my left. It did nothing.

My back slammed against a wall. Right behind El Brujo, something moved. Tavo. He took a swing at his head. El Brujo took the hit, snapped his head to the side so much his neck looked broken, and then turned while still holding me. His other arm shot out and he wrapped his left hand around Tavo's neck, lifted him up, and threw him across the room.

Tavo flew across the living room and crashed against the opposite wall, right next to the sofa, before landing on the floor with a thud that made me think he was dead too.

El Brujo turned and slammed me against the wall again. The back of my head cracking against the cement. Stars exploded throughout the room. It was the most light I'd seen at night in days.

I couldn't breathe. I was dying. Again.

I tried to punch, pull, and scratch El Brujo's hand off my neck. None of it worked. I couldn't hurt him. Then I remembered his howl when Tavo stabbed him. I reached down and pulled out the knife that was still buried to the handle right above his clavicle. El Brujo grunted. The eyebrows above his black eyes knotted. I stabbed him again, closer to the neck this time. He slapped my hand away. The hit was so strong the knife went flying and my arm rang numb.

El Brujo came closer to my face. All I could register were massive pointy teeth and black eyes. The eyes of a shark. The edges of my vision were closing in, darkness bleeding in from the corners and turning the room black. The sound was as loud as ever, a single note drowning the world. My chest ached like when I'd been on the floor. The pressure in my head made me think my eyes were going to burst.

I kicked El Brujo with both legs. It did nothing. Black blood poured from the holes in his neck and above his clavicle, but he didn't seem to be losing any strength, didn't even notice.

And I didn't want to die. I didn't want to go out without avenging Xavier and María. I didn't want to die looking at El Brujo's black eyes. I didn't want that fucking annoying sound to be the last thing I heard.

I thought of Natalia.

Natalia's smile was a sliver of white in a dark world that was quickly turning darker.

El Brujo's mouth was open again, too wide to be a human mouth, the teeth too big and pointy. I wondered if he was going to eat me.

A gun.

A gun appeared next to El Brujo's head on my right side.

BAM!

The opposite side of El Brujo's head exploded. His hand released me. His body dropped to the side. I crumbled to the floor, gasping for air. I heard the cow's head bang against the table, rattling everything that was still on it. In front of me, a puddle of black was quickly spreading underneath El Brujo's head. His eyes had gone back to normal. His mouth contracting to its original size, teeth sliding into his skull. I scrambled to my feet using the wall for support. I didn't want that black blood to touch me.

I was alive. The sound in my ears had ceased. The glyphs had stopped moving. I looked to my side and it took me a second to recognize the person standing next to me, the gun still in his hand.

Paul.

41

GABE

—

Half a dozen miracles
Fear and confusion
A hurricane trapped in a human body
A mouthful of eyeballs
Broken blade

There was no time for talking or for questions. I ran to Tavo. Paul went to check on Bimbo.

Tavo was breathing like I'd been breathing a few seconds before. A thousand questions ran across his face as he looked at El Brujo's body, but they were washed out by relief. Then he registered Paul trying to get Bimbo turned around on the chair.

"Paul," Tavo coughed out, his voice like that of a tired frog.

"Not now," I said. "The woman's gone. They'll be here in no time. We gotta get the hell outta here."

"No—" Bimbo grunted. "No, no, no. Fuck!"

Bimbo stumbled over to El Brujo's body. He placed his hand on the wall, screamed, and started kicking him in the head. El Brujo's head bounced every time Bimbo kicked him. The black mess underneath him spread. Bimbo was stepping in it. I worried about what that might do to him. Sometimes things we think are dead can still hurt us. I thought about the guy in the parking lot, Kimbo, Raúl, and now El Brujo. All ghosts now, haunting us.

We needed some more protection prayers. We needed Altagracia. We needed a few gods and half a dozen miracles.

Bimbo's grunting intensified. Pain and grief and hatred and something else had become this growl he could no longer control. He kept kicking El Brujo's head. It looked like he was trying to dislodge something from his own soul by kicking the shit out of a corpse.

After a few more kicks, Bimbo bent over and started crying. Moments later, he stood up straight and looked at us. "He was supposed to suffer. This was too fucking good for him."

Bimbo bent again and turned El Brujo's body onto its back. Then he looked around, spotted the knife on the floor, and went to pick it up.

I looked at the floor until I found my own gun. Paul saw me retrieve it and lifted his up as if to let me know he was ready to use it.

It was the same gun he'd pointed at my head earlier. Raúl's gun.

Every ounce of anger I'd felt toward Paul suddenly snapped, broke free, and vanished into the dark salty air. He had saved our asses. All the bullshit that happened before didn't matter now.

On the floor, Bimbo had knelt next to El Brujo. He turned to us once more and pointed at the walls with the knife. "Look at that shit," he said. "It's like the stuff on your door, Gabe. Like the stuff on that wall we saw when leaving your place. This motherfucker killed Xavier and put that thing on your door. He killed my mom. He deserved worse."

Bimbo started crying again. He bent down and used his fingers to open El Brujo's mouth. The giant teeth were gone. Bimbo put his fingers in the dead man's mouth.

I flashed to Kimbo and knew what was coming.

"What the fuck are you doing?" asked Paul.

"Cutting off his tongue," I said. "So his ghost won't haunt us."

"What are you talking—?"

I raised my hand. Paul broke off.

"Just...let him do this."

The thing Bimbo pulled out of El Brujo's mouth resembled a fat brown snake more than a tongue. He cut it off while still sobbing. I looked at the wall. Paul and Tavo said some things, but they weren't talking to anyone.

When he was done, Bimbo stood up, placed the tongue on the floor, and stepped on it. He was praying, but I couldn't make out the words.

A moment later, Bimbo knelt again and placed his left hand on El Brujo's forehead. He used his palm and thumb to pull El Brujo's right eye open and plunged the knife into it. We heard a pop. Bimbo moved the knife to the side and yanked it back. El Brujo's eyeball and some of the stuff that was attached to it dangled at the end of the knife. My stomach did a somersault. Bimbo moved his hand and opened El Brujo's mouth, put the eyeball inside it, closed the dead man's mouth with his hand, and pulled the knife back out. The sound of metal scraping against teeth was louder than our collective breaths.

Paul turned to the side and vomited. I was happy I couldn't smell it thanks to the overpowering stench of decay. I turned away from Paul, and my eyes landed on Tavo. He was looking around, searching the walls, probably for some explanation of the shit we'd just seen. Then, simply because I wanted to know how soon we could get the hell outta there, I checked on Bimbo. His eyes were on me, begging me for something. He wanted me there. He wanted to know he wasn't alone.

Witnessing the act, gruesome as it was, was one thing; seeing my friend was harder. Bimbo was asking me if he could keep going. I nodded. Bimbo opened El Brujo's left eye with his fingers and repeated what he'd done with the right eyeball. I scanned the living room, sure that I'd spot Xavier somewhere in there with us, smiling to let us know he was happy, that we'd done well. He wasn't there. Tavo was still taking everything in. Paul was bent over, trying to spit the barf taste from his mouth.

With both eyeballs stuffed into El Brujo's mouth, it was time to go.

"Bimbo, it's done," I said. "He's dead. We need to get the hell outta here. Now." More violence would accomplish nothing.

Instead of replying, Bimbo started stabbing El Brujo in the face. The knife went up and down again and again, the black blood on it catching the light from the few candles that were still on the table.

"María." Bimbo was crying, but I heard him. A moment later, he said it again. "María." It was a prayer. Whispering his mother's sacred name in this place was probably more important than the prayer he'd mumbled while stepping on the tongue.

The blade broke with a twang. It landed on the floor and rattled a bit. Bimbo finally got up and moved to the door without a word.

42

GABE

—

Dazed
The ocean's endless song
A gate to hell
Those fucking teeth
Push back the night

There was no one outside. No nosy neighbors. No men with guns. No Black woman with a long black skirt. No mermen cannibals. That meant nothing. They could all be on their way.

We started moving toward Bimbo's car, looking around while we walked side by side, trying to stay calm and not break into a run. Bimbo had regained some strength and was walking without leaning on Paul. He looked dazed in the scant moonlight. The shit we'd just done would stick with us forever, but more of it would stay with Bimbo. I couldn't fathom moving through life knowing what it felt like to bash someone's skull in with a lug wrench or how it felt to take apart the face of a monster.

Halfway to the car, Tavo spoke, his voice a strained, scared thing. "Maybe the woman just vanished," he said. "If she was scared, you know? We can do it."

"What do you mean?" asked Bimbo, still looking around.

"We're desperate to get out of here because we're sure Papalote's men are coming, because the woman must've told someone, right? But maybe she didn't say a word to anyone. Maybe no one's coming for us. If they were, their timing is shit."

"Wait…a thin woman in a dark skirt?" asked Paul.

"Yeah, black skirt, that's her," I said.

"She ran by me as I was making my way to you," said Paul. "She didn't say a word. Caught my eye because there was no one else out and she was hauling ass. Her car was parked on the same street where I parked, because she turned the corner and a few seconds later I heard her door slam. Car looked like a Celica to me. Como el que tiene Javi. If she was there when shit started going down, she probably wanted to put as many miles as possible between herself and you guys. I don't think she stopped to talk to anyone."

It made sense. It went with what we knew about our country: No one ever saw anything, no one spoke if it could get them in trouble, and no one gave a shit about anyone else if their own safety hung in the balance. Maybe the woman had run all the way to her car and driven off. That'd be perfect. If she didn't talk to anyone — and the folks who heard the gunshots were willing to look away — maybe we still had a chance. A chance isn't much, but when you're desperate, you'll believe anything.

We stopped walking when we reached Bimbo's car. We stood there, breathing hard and listening, waiting for a bullet or a scream or a fish to come out of the darkness and drop hell at our feet.

The ocean was singing its endless song, like a whisper that carries a promise of violence you can't quite understand. A dog barked somewhere, surely another warning, this one coming either too late or at least too late for us to give a fuck about it.

Someone had turned on a generator nearby. It sounded like a big angry insect. I couldn't see light behind any window. I wondered if there was another sick kid nearby, another family hunkered down, fighting the collapse, and trying to keep their baby alive because the fucking government won't get their shit together and fix the power grid after every hurricane leaves us in the dark for months.

The crickets were going crazy, almost drowning out the generator.

It was all too much, but it reminded me we were alive. I inhaled deeply. The ocean air tasted like a miracle.

"You think we should try it?" asked Bimbo, his voice still barely louder than a whisper. He was talking to me. Something about the events with Kimbo, Raúl, and then with El Brujo had made our relationship even deeper. He cared enough about my opinion, but he also knew I wouldn't say no.

"I don't know," I said. "I'm surprised there aren't thirty motherfuckers with machine guns blowing us to pieces right now. If that woman bolted without telling anyone, and no one —"

"Henry said there are always sounds coming from El Brujo's house," said Bimbo. "God knows what sounds he meant. He even had some congas in there. Maybe people around here are used to mayhem going down at that fucking...gate to hell or whatever his house is. Did you...did you see that floating cow's head? That shit's gonna give me nightmares until the day I die."

At night you can hear chanting sometimes, too, some language I've never heard before.

Bimbo was right, Henry had said that. I'd forgotten.

"I say we move now and end this tonight," said Paul. Fucking Paul. The words out of his mouth were alienating, like hearing someone you love suddenly say something extremely stupid or racist. He'd walked away from us twice, but he was also the guy standing with us in the dark right after saving our asses. Maybe he was more than one person. Maybe we all were.

"Why...I mean, how did you show up when you did, P?" I asked.

"Because you're all stupid," he said. "I knew you crazy bastards would come with or without me and that made me worry because, like I said, you're all idiots, you know?"

No one said anything.

"I'm kidding," said Paul. "I mean, you're all stupid, that part is true — and I'm better looking than all of you — but while sitting in the car, I remembered that time those six motherfuckers got in my face at that fucking club that looks like a boat. I thought they were gonna hurt me bad, but then you guys came outta fucking nowhere, throwing punches left and right and...y'all saved my ass.

"And then I thought about how angry I was when that dude kept calling and texting Cynthia and bringing her coffee and inviting her out even after she told him she had a boyfriend. My mom said I was stupid and that if Cynthia wanted to go out with him, it was better I know about it now and not find out later. Y'all listened to me and fucked up that dude's car. You scared him so bad he quit and never called or texted again. It was stupid, but you did it because it was me. Then a car pulled up behind me and—"

"Was it white?" I interrupted.

"White?"

"The car that pulled up behind you."

"No, it was dark. Why?"

"I'll tell you later. The car pulled up behind you and?"

"Well...I got scared. After that thing we'd seen across the street and everything that guy told us...I don't know, I felt like we had to stick together, you know? I had to follow you just in case because if you came here, someone was gonna fuck with you, and if someone fucks with one of us—"

"They fuck with all of us," we said in unison.

Paul smiled. "Exactly," he said. "And they had already fucked with Xavier, so...era lo que tenía que hacer y punto. Maybe that car was there to fuck us up and maybe it wasn't, but I couldn't imagine living the rest of my life with my balls in my throat every time I saw a car park behind me or spending my days looking out the window just in case.

"It was easy to find you because the door was open and the sound from inside was crazy loud. Like a siren or something. I couldn't just barge in with the gun, because he'd just...you know, vanish or do whatever the fuck it was that he was doing, so I waited. When he was busy whupping your asses, I moved in, staying low. He was distracted with you two, so I moved in and shot him and...yeah, that's about it."

"After all we've been through and everything you said after the parking garage thing, you look pretty fucking mellow for someone who just killed a man," said Tavo with a smile.

"Nah," said Paul. "I'm fine with it because that thing I shot wasn't of this world. Did you see those fucking teeth, cabrón? Let him go back to wherever the fuck he came from."

"Good point," I said. "But there's one thing you're wrong about."

"What is it?"

"There's no fucking way anyone in the world would consider you better looking than Tavo," I said.

"Hah!" said Bimbo.

"Gabe is right," said Tavo with the smile still on his face.

The whole thing felt great. We were alive and cracking jokes. It was almost powerful enough to push back the night.

43

GABE

—

Turn off their rancor and don't let their envy touch me
Driving in the dark
Creatures from beyond the reef
A silence like a bottomless cave
Secrets

Bimbo pulled his keys out of his pocket and unlocked the car. Tavo jumped in the front. Paul and I squeezed into the back.

"Go straight back the way you came in and I'll tell you where to turn," said Tavo. Bimbo nodded and turned the ignition. The sound was like a demon screaming and I feared those who wouldn't think twice about shooting us would hear it as a call to come and take care of us now.

Bimbo rolled down the windows and started driving. The night's soundtrack spilled into the car. Then he stepped gently on the brake pedal and brought us to a stop.

"What's wrong?" I asked.

"Nothing," he said. "We need to do something first." He dug into his pocket and pulled out his phone. He opened it, typed something, and moved his finger around for a few seconds.

"Lower your heads," he said. We did as we were told because after what we had seen, debating weird stuff was a thing of the past.

"I invoke your presence, O Orisha Elegguá," read Bimbo.

"You, who are the lord of all roads, please listen to me and help me change the course of my enemies. Get them out of my way or help me remove them, O Elegguá. Make their path veer from mine, O Holy One, and if they have bad wishes, make them get what they wished upon me.

"Make my enemies powerless to hurt my family, O Holy One. Make my enemies powerless to hurt me. Turn off their rancor and don't let their envy touch me. Make it so that if they hate me, their negative energy dissipates before it can touch me.

"The only thing I ask of you, O Elegguá, is that you protect me and save me from enemies and bad friends, that everything they send my way is returned to them doubled, and that you always walk with me. Thank you for all the favors you have done me, O Elegguá. *Amén.*"

"Amén," we all said in unison.

Something stirred in my blood. It started as a tingling sensation at first, like when you smoke a lot really quickly and a wave of warmth covers you when the high hits you. Elegguá was a survivor. He was with us. Next to us was the ocean that had brought him from Africa, the ocean that had seen the arrival of the Yoruba traditions and the pain, grief, and anger of its stolen, abused, and displaced people. I felt better after that prayer. I reached up to my neck and squeezed the necklace Bimbo had given me. I would learn more about Elegguá after this was over. I would find a way to thank him.

Bimbo put his phone away and started driving again. He kept the lights off, navigating the street with the help of a bit of moonlight and the two solid lines of absolute darkness the cars on both sides of the street made.

This could be the end. The end of this thing, the end of Papalote, or the end of us, but the fucking end. I thought about Natalia, how her face had come to me when I was closer to Death than I'd ever been. I thought about how much pain and resentment she'd feel if I died out here. I thought about how I kept coming up with excuses not to give her just as much as she had always given me.

I loved her enough to grow the fuck up and tell her I'd be with her on her journey, that I would move with her if she got into a program. I could tell her that I'd get a job or try to continue studying wherever she went, but something inside me refused to accept that I could say and do those things. Now I wanted to say them, to do them. Almost dying had changed me. Fear makes your innermost truths come floating to the surface.

Papalote.

Murder.

Creatures from beyond the reef.

Those thoughts roared into the forefront of my brain and pushed Natalia back. I let them. It was a survival mechanism. I thought about the floating head and El Brujo's long pointy teeth, but Natalia's face stayed there, the way the sun stays in your eyes after you look away from it. I would make sure she and I had our time to talk things over later. This was about María and Xavier now, and I had to stay sharp.

No one talked. The silence reminded me of how everyone had stayed quiet back at Bimbo's place after he said we were going to kill people. That silence had been so dark and deep that I'd envisioned it as a ragged entrance to a bottomless cave where something awful lived. Now that something was out there, somewhere between our car and the ocean, stalking us.

"Pull into that little street coming up on the left," said Tavo. "La Garita del Diablo is right there. As soon as you turn, park and kill the engine. Shouldn't be many cars there next to the tables. If we don't see anyone, it's on."

Bimbo did as he was told. I wondered what would happen if we saw someone. The clunk of Bimbo throwing the car into Park was all we needed to tumble free.

Movies have two kinds of action scenes. In one, chaos erupts and you have a hard time keeping track of what's going on as bullets or punches fly, people move around, and editing cuts jump from one thing to the next. In the other, things slow down as someone lifts a gun or jumps off an exploding building or shoots someone.

Real life is like the first kind, especially when it involves danger and violence. The main difference is that, depending on what the film has given you, you can tell the hero will survive or save the universe or the final girl will live to be in the inevitable sequel. In real life, you don't know shit, there are no guarantees, you're scared, and the bad guys win most of the time.

We were in a movie where everything was too fast and we were too slow and the end could be right around the corner. At least the bad guy was clear.

My brain pushed back.

The guy at the parking garage.

Kimbo.

Raúl.

El Brujo.

Fuck them all. Get in, do the thing, get out. That was the plan. My brothers were with me. We had three guns and a knife. We had María, Xavier, and Elegguá in our corner.

We were out of the car and moving toward the sidewalk, Bimbo in the lead. He stopped walking and turned to us. We all stopped.

"Go around the house," said Bimbo. "There's a small property back there that Papalote has for folks who go with the women who work at the bar. They started rebuilding before the hurricane hit. They were adding more rooms or something. Anyway, it's empty. We can walk back there and climb into the back of Papalote's place without anyone seeing us. You know, as long as no one sees us going in that little space between the walls right there."

"How the hell do you know this? When were you here?" asked Tavo.

"Two days after the hurricane," said Bimbo. "Anyway, all Papalote has for a security system are some cameras, and those don't work without power. No one messes with Papalote, because of the rumors about the reef. This is the perfect time to get him."

"So, you've been planning this since before the hurricane?" asked Tavo.

"Yes," said Bimbo. "Well, not exactly. I made up my mind when we talked to Henry. I liked the idea of the cameras being down, but then I realized the timing was perfect because Henry said he moved that woman and her kid in, remember? He kicked the men outta his house because he has some chick in there with him or whatever. Maybe no one else has tried shit because they think the house is still full of fuckers with guns, ready to die. Papalote's just there alone with that woman."

Motherfucker. Bimbo had been here before. He'd scouted the place. Probably at night. Alone. That's how bad he wanted this. He was willing to die, but at least he'd done his research.

He'd played all of us and gotten Xavier killed.

Bimbo was smarter than I gave him credit for, and that bothered me. He was also braver...or maybe just more stupid than I'd thought.

"Okay, I guess that's good," said Paul. "Wasn't your uncle going to help?"

Bimbo looked at me. I said nothing. More lies were coming.

But they didn't.

"My uncle's dead."

"Did Papalote kill him?" asked Tavo, not missing a beat.

"No, it—"

"Why aren't his men here? Did you ask for help?" asked Paul, his voice higher than it should've been.

"No," said Bimbo. "Listen, this is personal. This has nothing to do with my un—"

"Why the fuck did you lie to us?" asked Paul. He looked ready to walk away again.

"I was scared. I was angry and confused, and telling y'all we'd do this alone was...Y'all wouldn't have come. I'm sorry."

"Whatever," said Paul. "We're here now. Let's end this shit."

Bimbo's face twitched in the dark. I saw happiness there. And relief. Maybe love.

"Let's move," said Tavo. "We're gonna get shot if we stay here whispering like we're in church."

We moved toward La Garita del Diablo. The place was painted red, and there were five or six tables outside with chairs piled up on top. It was weird to see no one there. It was one of the few places that was open and serving booze, which meant people should've been flocking to it. If the bar was empty now, that meant it was later than I thought. I pulled my phone half out of my pocket to check the time. 3:18 a.m. They had probably shut down around midnight, earlier if they ran out of gas or ice or whatever. I had missed five texts from Natalia. I shoved the phone back into my pocket without reading them.

On the right side of the bar was a squat building that was probably blue but looked the same color as the night sky minus the clouds and stars. On the opposite side was a big white two-story house. The only white house on the whole street. Papalote's place. Bimbo moved to the right side of the building. We followed.

The spaces between houses in La Perla are small. We stopped next to the wall and looked around. We didn't see anyone. Bimbo reached back and pulled his gun out. Paul and I did the same. Tavo didn't say a word.

Bimbo could barely squeeze his way through the side alley. I had no idea how he was going to push himself up and over Papalote's wall and into his backyard. Under any other circumstances, we'd be making fun of him. I was about to send a prayer up to Elegguá or God or whoever happened to be listening, but then I remembered how quiet they'd stayed at El Brujo's place.

Or had they?

Paul. Paul had shown up just in time like a fucking angel with a gun. I sent out the prayer with a big thank-you attached. It was shorter than the one Bimbo had read in the car, but it came from my heart instead of the Internet, and I figured that would count for something.

We followed the space between the two houses in silence. If the world was dark, this space was whatever comes after darkness. Bimbo pulled his phone out and used the light from the lock screen to move forward. I did the same. The light helped so much I didn't mind pressing the side of my phone every few seconds to keep the screen lit.

We made it to the end. The houses from the other side of the street converged there, so we couldn't walk farther. There was trash and a lot of vegetation around us. It smelled like a few rats had died there.

"Give me a hand," said Bimbo.

I thought he was being funny. Gallows humor. He wasn't joking.

I put my phone away, placed my butt against the wall, and interlocked my fingers so Bimbo had somewhere to place his foot.

Tavo saw what we were doing and stepped closer to help.

Bimbo grunted as he brought his right leg up. His foot didn't reach my hand. He stood up straight, pulled his jeans up, and tried again. Then, without warning, he used my hands as a step. The fingers of my right hand screamed in agony. I squeezed my eyes shut.

I'd thought Bimbo was going to reach for the top of the wall and pull himself over it. Instead, he lifted his left leg, put his foot down on my shoulder, and stepped on it. It almost toppled me sideways. Tavo saw it and held my arm.

Bimbo grunted again and his weight finally lifted off my shoulder. He huffed and puffed as he worked his body over the wall. We heard him land on the other side with a thud.

"Come on, P, we'll help you up," said Tavo. After helping Bimbo over the wall, Paul was a piece of cake, which was good because my hand was killing me and my palms were full of filth from the bottom of Bimbo's shoe. I hoped he hadn't stepped on any dead rats.

With Paul over the wall, Tavo offered me his hands.

"What about you?" I asked.

"I can do it myself," he said. "Move it."

Of course he could. I placed my foot on his hands and heaved myself up. I got my hands on the top of the wall and pulled with the idea of turning it into a pressing movement to get over it, but my arms weren't having it. You don't know how much the day has taken out of you until you try to pull yourself over a wall in the middle of the night.

My arms ached, but I managed to use my feet to get some extra traction on the wall and hauled myself over. Then I turned my body and slid down, holding on to the top of the wall so the drop wouldn't hurt too much.

Paul and Bimbo were waiting on the other side. Tavo landed next to me and rubbed the dirt off his hands. He wasn't even breathing hard. We used the light of our phones screens to look around.

Papalote's backyard was a long rectangular space with a natural stone floor, a pool shaped like a kidney, and a small white table with two chairs next to it. The pool was full of brackish water. There were well-kept plants in big pots all over the place. Those plants had clearly been brought inside before María hit because they would've been decimated if left out there during the hurricane.

The back of the house had a double sliding door and two windows on the second floor. There was no light anywhere and we couldn't hear anyone.

"What now?" asked Paul, his voice lower than it'd been on the street.

"We can use those chairs to smash—"

"No," I interrupted Bimbo. I'd seen those doors before. I'd installed more than a dozen while working on remodeling projects. They were solid and the glass was heavy, but they had to be carried and dropped into the rails and then clicked into place after the frame had been installed. The lock was a metal hook that slid into a hole on the door when you rotated a small handle on the inside. If two people grabbed the edges of the door on the lock side and pulled the door up as high as it'd go, the metallic hook would clear the hole on the door and you could slide the door back.

"We can open it. Tavo, come put your hands right here with me. You two get on that side and push up when we do. We want to lift it by pushing up on the glass." Tavo and I walked to the door and stood near the middle of it so we could push up close the edge.

"Push it and then go straight up when I tell you."

Our voices had adapted to us whispering and I wasn't even thinking about it anymore, just doing it. I nodded and we started pushing the door up slowly. Everyone was quiet. We kept pushing up until it wouldn't go any higher.

"Now grab the side with one hand and pull back without letting it drop." The door moved back. We'd cleared the lock with a clack. We could go in. We could enter the lion's den.

44

GABE

—

In the wolf's mouth
Sounds in the dark
Pride kills
Scales
A man possessed

The inside of Papalote's house was too dark to see anything. We were standing close to each other and couldn't make out our faces.

A sound came from the pool. We turned. Something had moved in there. The ripples it'd made were still dancing in the moonlight.

Bimbo turned on his phone's flashlight. It was like the sun had entered the room and punched me in the eyes. I covered my face and blinked away. Bimbo pointed the flashlight at the floor. The white tiles reflected back and illuminated the place without blinding us.

"You sure that's —?"

"No, T," said Bimbo. "But I can't see shit."

We were in a dining room that contained a large table with a dozen chairs and a big chandelier over it. There were more plants in the corners and on the wall behind the table. Bimbo shined the flashlight beyond that. The dining room flowed into a space occupied by a beige rug with a black coffee table sitting in its middle. On top of the coffee table sat a strange glass figure that looked like a ballerina with tentacles for arms and legs.

There were three sofas of different sizes and a television unit pushed against the right wall that contained a TV even bigger than the one we'd seen at El Brujo's place. More shiny glass figures and a few more plants occupied some of the spaces on the television unit.

"Get your phones out and keep your guns ready," said Bimbo.

Paul and I did what he said, holding the phone with one hand and aiming our guns with the other at the darkness beyond our flashlights' reach. I was itching and uncomfortable. I needed a shower and a full night's sleep with the AC blasting. But I moved deeper into the house, trying to control the sound of my steps.

The house looked empty. If they were sleeping, they were probably on the second floor. It was still hard to believe that the house wasn't full of men with guns. Bimbo was right after all. The timing was perfect. Everyone was tired, angry, sweaty, frustrated. Everyone was at home, trying to do as little as possible because there wasn't even water to take a shower. People were locked away, waiting for the country to bounce back, for things to regain some sliver of normalcy. No one being here made sense. Plus, Papalote had inherited an empire his grandfather and father had built. It was an empire that people respected and feared. Not even the cops would come for him. La Perla was a place with its own rules, and no one would dare come into it to pull anything like what we were about to pull. To put it another way, no one else was this desperate or stupid.

Soberbia. Pride. It was maybe Papalote's greatest sin, or weakness. It was something my abuela used to talk about from time to time when she wasn't talking about ghosts and demons. "La soberbia mata," she would say whenever she watched some rich person on TV showing off their house or someone on the streets with their neck, wrists, and fingers full of jewelry. Pride kills. I hoped she was right.

We made our way through a big kitchen. The sink was full of dirty dishes, and there were a few newspapers stacked on a small table. A pair of white tennis shoes had been placed next to the sofa. Other than those small things, the place looked sterile, the house of someone who was rarely home.

The stairs were to the left of the kitchen. If he was here, Papalote had to be up there. There was nowhere else to go. Bimbo started climbing the stairs first. Then he stopped, turned off his phone's flashlight, and turned to us.

"No lights. We don't want him to know we're coming. I'm gonna get up there, find him, and shoot him," he said. "Stay behind me. Kill anything that moves."

My heart was trying to kick its way out of my chest. I turned off my phone's flashlight. Total darkness took over. We stood there, waiting for our eyes to adjust. A moment later, Bimbo started moving again, his bulky frame creeping up the stairs slowly.

I kept my phone in my hand and my gun in the other. From the stairs, you could look down at the place we'd just crossed and out into the backyard. The water in the pool was still moving, and there was something dark and roundish poking out of it. I hoped we didn't have to go out the same way we'd come in.

Bimbo reached the top of the stairs and stopped again. We all froze and listened, trying to focus our senses. Enough moonlight came through that window to help us see. To the left was a hallway. We didn't know how many rooms there were, but one of them probably contained Papalote.

I realized that night sounds were distant here, and we could hear a new sound that mixed in with our attempts to breathe and step quietly: the hum of a motor. It was like a constant vibration somewhere off in the distance. A generator. A quiet one. Probably on the roof so no one would try to steal it. The quietness made sense. Papalote could afford a top-of-the-line generator that made no more racket than a beard trimmer. That's why we hadn't heard it before. That's why the doors were closed. He probably had an AC unit going. Hell, the thing probably had enough juice to run the ACs, fridge, a couple laptops, and those huge TVs we'd seen.

But the doors were closed and that's what mattered. Elegguá had removed another obstacle.

We stayed frozen, listening.

There was another sound. It was faint at first, then gone. Then it came back. We waited. It had a rhythm.

"Snoring," said Tavo. He was right.

"It's coming from there," whispered Bimbo while pointing down the hallway, his voice merely an exhalation.

There was no time to talk or come up with a plan — when had we ever had one? — or look at each other and trust our eyes communicated enough.

Bimbo moved. Slowly. We followed.

The snoring got louder.

We approached a closed door on the right.

Bimbo put his head against it and then pulled back.

He moved on.

The next door was on the opposite side of the hallway. Bimbo walked up to it and placed his head against the door. He stayed there for what felt like a long time.

Bimbo finally turned around, held his hands to his belly, and turned on his phone's flashlight again. Light poured from his phone for a second before he smothered it against his shirt. He leaned toward us.

"Turn your flashlights on," said Bimbo, so low I thought I was imagining it. "We need to see him and the lights will blind and confuse him. Let's go."

This was it.

Bimbo turned to the first door again.

I turned my flashlight on. Tavo and Paul did the same. We pressed our phones to our bodies, and I sent another prayer to everyone on my list.

Bimbo opened the door and we ran in, a burst of violent light filling the room. The room was bigger than I'd expected. In that first second, I registered a large occupied bed with a tall black headrest, a television on the wall, two bedside tables, and two doors. Some pictures on the walls. A few lamps. On the big bed, someone moved. Light blue bedsheets exploded into the air.

Papalote's surprised, squinting face popped up from behind the sheets.

Bimbo pulled the trigger. The sound bounced off the walls of the room. Papalote ducked and made himself small. Splinters flew off the headrest to his left. He was untouched.

Papalote was grabbing something from the nightstand. Paul and I pulled our triggers simultaneously, the headrest exploding right above Papalote's head. His body jerked back. Everything looked shaky.

The room was chaos. Our lights moved everywhere. The world was a fragmented mess. I tried to keep my light on the bed and my gun on Papalote.

Someone moved on the opposite side of the bed.

I saw long black hair and big eyes.

A woman.

Fuck.

Bimbo moved sideways, took a few steps toward the bed, and pulled the trigger three times. He was aiming at the form on the bed. None of his shots hit the headrest. Someone screamed and a gun went off again.

"Grab her!" said Paul. Tavo moved to the other side of the bed. The woman scooted back. Her scream was unlike anything I'd never heard. It reminded me of the sound I'd heard in El Brujo's place, but it was coming from her mouth. I feared she'd vanish and then reappear next to me with a huge snarling mouth full of big teeth. Tavo grabbed her and pulled her out of bed. Her body was covered in dark scars.

Bimbo approached the bed and squeezed off another two shots. They were as loud as the previous ones. Someone had surely heard them. We had to leave.

I moved toward Bimbo. He reached the bed and pulled back the covers. I kept my light on the bed, my gun in front of me, my finger on the trigger. Paul was right beside me.

Papalote had been hit a few times. Dark blood stained the blue bedsheets black. His torso was a mix of ink and blood. He looked at Bimbo.

"Te voy—"

"¡María, hijo de puta!" said Bimbo. He placed his gun in the back of his pants, threw his phone on the bed, and started hitting Papalote.

Bimbo moved like a man possessed, like he wanted to destroy Papalote with his bare hands. He punched and clawed at him while grunting. Papalote tried to cover himself, but he had a few bullets in him and Bimbo was relentless.

Papalote tried to turn, to crawl away. Bimbo grabbed him and pulled him off the bed. Papalote crumbled to the floor. He was wearing only boxers. Bimbo started kicking him. Papalote curled up into a ball.

I thought about María and Xavier. I remembered my mom in a pool of her own blood. I moved in and started kicking Papalote as well.

Paul joined us.

The woman screamed again. The sound pierced my ears and made me wince, but hurting Papalote was more important. This was about making him pay for everything.

We were going to beat him to death. I was fine with it.

Bimbo stopped kicking Papalote and pulled his gun out again. He was breathing heavily. He bent down and placed the gun against the side of Papalote's head.

"You killed my mom, motherfucker. Now say her name before I put a bullet in your head."

Papalote had his arms around his head. He lowered them and turned his face to look at Bimbo.

"Who are you?"

"I'm María's son," said Bimbo.

"Who—?"

"María's son! Say her name."

Bimbo leaned forward and put pressure on the gun as if he was trying to puncture Papalote's skull with it. Papalote grunted.

"Sit up," said Bimbo. "Now!"

Papalote pushed himself to a sitting position. His face was a mess. He was a handsome man with a broken cheek and a busted lip.

"María. Say her name." Bimbo put the gun in front of Papalote's face.

Papalote looked confused. Then something clicked. His expression changed. He knew what this was about.

"The stupid bitch from Lazer who wanted to take ov—"

Bimbo pulled the trigger.

The first bullet pushed Papalote's head back against the mattress. Bimbo squeezed off another shot. It hit Papalote near his mouth. There was a lot of blood. I looked away, but Bimbo kept pulling his trigger. Two more shots. Then a click. Another click. He stopped. His gun was empty. He squeezed the trigger again. I heard the desperate click and knew that if he could put a hundred bullets into Papalote's face, they wouldn't be enough.

Tavo was holding the woman on the other side of the bed. They both looked horrified. Papalote was a crumpled figure on the floor, his face a mess of dark holes and blood.

The woman screamed again. It almost bent me over.

Tavo covered her mouth.

Bimbo spat at Papalote and then hit him with the empty gun.

"María, cabrón! María!"

He was crying.

I expected him to jump on top of Papalote's inert body and keep swinging. I expected him to ask Paul or me for our guns so he could keep putting bullets into Papalote's face. Instead he stopped, stood over the man responsible for his mother's death, and said her name again.

"María."

Her name was a ritual we couldn't interrupt, a prayer to ensure Papalote's ghost knew why he'd been killed.

"¡En la puerta!" Paul screamed, pointing. We all turned. Our lights flew around. Big shadows lurched across every surface. The world tilted and then our lights shakily converged on the door, our guns aiming at the small figure standing there.

There was a girl at the threshold, holding a small hand up to her face to block our lights. Beyond her small hand, her eyes were impossibly big and entirely black. She looked scared, but didn't look like she was about to run.

"Mommy?" Her voice was a small thing under the ringing left in my ears.

Tavo released the woman. She ran to the girl and picked her up.

"If you try to run, I'll shoot you," said Paul. She looked at all of us. Her eyes were black like her daughter's. With all our lights on her, we could now see her skin better. The dark spots that covered her flesh weren't scars; they were patches covered with scales.

"What the fuck is wrong with her?" asked Paul.

"Nothing," said Tavo. "She's a fish."

"Fuck me," said Paul.

The woman's body was normal except for the scales. She looked like someone was slowly replacing pieces of her body with chunks of flesh from a large gray fish. Her face was broad and there was something different about her full lips and small, squat nose. She reminded me of Raúl. She bent her head down to cradle the girl and whisper some reassurance into her ear, and her hair spilled forward over her shoulder, exposing the side of her neck. There was a pinkish line there. When she moved, the sides of it moved with her.

Gills.

Bimbo walked past Paul and grabbed his gun. He went to the woman and placed the gun against the side of her head.

"He killed my mother, do you understand?" Bimbo asked.

The woman looked at him.

"Put the fucking gun down, B," said Tavo.

Bimbo kept the gun pressed against the woman's head.

"I understand," said the woman in English. Her voice was unlike anything I'd ever heard. It was a raspy, genderless voice that made me think she was speaking while swallowing something wet without chewing.

"I don't give a fuck about La Perla or Papalote's business," said Bimbo. "You can take over. You can have all his money. You understand what I'm saying?"

The woman nodded.

"I'm going to take him, okay?" Bimbo lowered his gun and pointed at Papalote's body. The woman nodded again.

"What are you talking about?" asked Paul.

"We need to go."

Bimbo turned to me. "That's the plan, Gabe. Just like Tavo said. We need to take him. It's the only way we'll get those things off our back."

The woman stood up straight while still holding her daughter against her body. "Those things?"

Bimbo stared at her for a few seconds before replying. "The fish. Out in the reef?"

"Oh," said the woman.

"You're one of them, right?" asked Tavo.

She turned her black eyes to him and took a step. Our guns jumped up in unison, but no one pulled the trigger.

Tavo stood there, transfixed. The woman lifted her right hand slowly and placed it behind Tavo's neck. Then she leaned forward while gently pulling Tavo toward her and pressed her forehead to his. Tavo gasped.

"Let him go!" said Paul.

The woman removed her hand from the back of Tavo's head. He looked at us. There were tears in his eyes.

"She...I don't know," said Tavo. "I mean, I do. Now. She...she showed me. She showed me."

The woman looked at me.

"Come," she said. Her lips didn't move. I approached her.

I stood next to Tavo and lowered my gun. She raised her hand again. It didn't feel like a threat.

Her fingers were cold on the back of my head. They were rough, too. Strong and wet.

The woman didn't have to pull me down as much as she'd pulled Tavo. She leaned forward. The moment our foreheads touched, the world around me vanished.

I saw fish swimming around. There was a huge underwater city around them. Tall green buildings sprouted from the ocean floor. They were so tall I couldn't see their top. The cyclopean architecture stretched as far as I could see, the edifices eventually disappearing in the water.

I felt happy. I felt that eons went by. The fish lived in perfect harmony with the ocean. Watching them was beautiful.

Then, an explosion. The fish swam faster. I could feel their fear.

The knowledge came, clear as day: Men had done this. Humans.

The tall buildings crumbled. More explosions came. Everything shook. Many fish died. Small groups swam away in different directions, their community split, broken into small bands of survivors on the run.

I saw reefs and colorful creatures swimming around. The fish rebuilt their community, now spread across the seas. But nothing was the same. They were split. They were angry. They were afraid. The water was much warmer than it'd been for them for ages. They struggled to adapt.

Then I saw an old man on a boat. He had a scar across the left side of his face. He was waiting for the fish. He brought them bodies.

Ignacio.

Then things moved forward. There was a pact. But men were never satisfied. They wanted more. Always more.

I saw Papalote on a boat. He wanted his men to be able to come and go. He wanted to rule over land and sea. He wanted to be able to bring in more product than ever. Hybrids. That's what he wanted. The men and the fish started mixing. He demanded a wife.

The woman.

Aklira.

Then I saw myself in the parking garage. And in Kimbo's house, sitting with his body in that tiny, dark living room. I saw myself staring out at an empty street from my room, standing alone on the sidewalk in the dark. I saw myself at Bimbo's place, Raúl a bloody mess on the sofa.

Xavier wasn't there. I'd made him up. I'd conjured up a ghost to give me an excuse to do the things I was doing.

Aklira had given me the gift of clarity, and it made me want to die.

I opened my eyes. Sadness sat like a stone in the center of my chest. Behind me, Tavo was still sobbing.

I looked around the room.

"How...how long was that?" I asked.

"How long was what?" asked Bimbo.

"How long was I...gone."

"I don't know what you're talking about," said Paul. "She just touched you now, just a second ago."

"Let her...let her touch you," I said.

Bimbo moved forward without another word.

A minute later, we were all standing there, our lives changed forever.

"What's your name?" asked Tavo.

"Aklira." She didn't move her lips, but we all heard it.

"Aklira," said Bimbo. "You...came from the water."

Aklira moved her head. "No. I was born on land. I changed. I can come and go."

"All of you change?" It came from Tavo.

"No. Some do and some don't." Her strange voice reached my ears loud and clear, but her mouth still hadn't moved.

"We need to go," said Tavo.

"Wait," said Bimbo. "Not yet."

He moved away from the woman and approached Papalote's body. He placed the gun in the back of his jeans and then reached into his shirt with both hands. He brought out his necklace and pulled it off his neck and over his head. Then he rolled it up with both hands, leaned closer to Papalote, and shoved the necklace into his mouth. I thought he was done, but he kept pressing deeper, using his fingers to push the necklace all the way down Papalote's throat. I thought about the stories of babies being killed and getting rosaries stuffed in their mouths.

I hoped he wouldn't want to cut off his tongue.

Tears rolled down Bimbo's face. Watching him cry with his fingers still in Papalote's mouth shook me in a way nothing else had, and we'd seen a lot.

The woman started crying. I'll admit that it was a beautiful sound.

Bimbo stopped, then wiped his face and turned to us.

"Let's wrap him up in the bedsheets and get him to my car," he said. None of us argued. Not even Paul.

Wrapping a dead man in bedsheets isn't easy, but eight arms can do it pretty fast. Once he was wrapped, Tavo and I hauled him up like an old rug and threw him over our shoulders.

As we left the room, the woman moved back to the bed while carrying the girl.

"Stay here," said Bimbo. "Please." She nodded. Her glistening black eyes were on us. The gray scales looked darker as we walked out of the room with our lights.

Aklira.

A fish. A being. Another impossible soul.

I imagined a world under the waves, a place with big buildings made of coral or stone, their walls covered in algae. It sent a shiver down my spine.

Getting Papalote down the stairs was tricky, but Paul and Bimbo helped and we got it done. Then we were out the door and walking to Bimbo's car. We weren't alone.

My heart stopped.

There were two figures standing near Bimbo's car.

A man. With a beard.

Henry.

And a woman.

Natalia.

"You motherfuckers did it," said Henry, looking at the body on the ground.

"We did," said Bimbo.

"What are you doing here, Natalia?" asked Tavo before I could.

"Helping," she said. "I —"

"Yeah," interrupted Henry. "Helping. This was all her idea. I saw you guys take Raúl. I figured he'd talk and you'd be coming back. You're all fucking crazy, but when Bimbo told me they'd killed his mom, I knew y'all would come. Then she came and found me and... tell them."

"I knew you'd talked to Henry, so I came and found him," said Natalia. "He knew what —"

"Yeah, Natalia found me down near Covadonga. She had an idea," said Henry. Natalia's eyes were on mine. I couldn't look away. "After y'all came and took Raúl, we got out of the water, and I knew no one else had seen y'all do it, because they were confused. I played dumb. We didn't stick around in case Papalote got mad, you know?

"Anyway, we parked up in Norzagaray and I called the bar from her phone. I told them I'd seen two men take Raúl and that I'd left because I was scared. I even told them about the van, except I said it was red and the dudes were whiter than snow and had blond hair. Told them y'all weren't from around here, but that I'd know you if I saw you again.

"Then I said I was down at the soup kitchen near Condado and had just seen the two dudes walking around and that the van was parked close to the soup kitchen. They hung up and we saw them roll outta here in a hurry. Everyone except El Brujo. He's been cooped up in his place since the hurricane hit, doing that dark magic shit. Anyway, that was—"

"That's why there's no one here," said Natalia. "I figured if you were going to come anyway, finding the place empty was the only way it could work."

I bent down and placed Papalote on the floor. I went to Natalia and hugged her. She was warm. I wanted to melt into her. I thanked her. She didn't respond. From behind, I heard Tavo and Bimbo thank her. Then I felt them behind me, also hugging Natalia.

It wasn't Elegguá; we'd been saved by a smart woman and a junkie.

We broke the hug. I looked at Henry.

"We'll look you up when—"

"No need. We're square," said Henry, interrupting me. "Now we need to get outta here. Y'all should do the same."

He turned to Natalia.

"Thank you," I said again.

Natalia's eyes were shiny with tears. There was a storm inside her, and she was trying to control it.

'What's wrong?"

"I…I can't do this anymore, Gabe. You almost got yourself killed. And you lied to me."

I reached out to her and she stepped back, her body saying even more than her mouth.

"No—"

"Don't," she said, lifting her arm to stop me. "I'm not waiting for you, Gabe. I won't, I won't…I…I got my letter."

Her acceptance letter. Natalia was moving. Without me.

"Gabe, let's go!" It was Bimbo. I turned. When I looked back at Natalia, she was walking away.

"You really need to go," said Henry, placing his hand on my arm.

Fuck. I needed to fix this. I had to run after Natalia, but this wasn't the time or place to fix anything. I turned and jogged back to the guys.

"Let's get him in the car." I didn't even know if Bimbo or Paul said it.

Bimbo popped the trunk. Tavo and I picked up Papalote's body and put him in the back. The trunk wasn't big enough, but it didn't matter.

I turned around. Natalia and Henry were reaching the end of the street. I ran to her.

"Are you okay? Where's your car?"

She turned to me. "I'm okay. I parked near the cemetery. See?" She smiled a sad smile that somehow shattered my soul. "Finish this, Gabriel. It already cost you too much. Finish it."

45

GABE
—

In the water
Dormant sea monster
Waiting
The fish arrive
A conversation

It took two interminable minutes to get back to the little beach at the end of La Perla. Bimbo parked as close to the water as he could and we got down. The street was still deserted; Papalote's men were somewhere else, looking for two blond ghosts and the red van Henry had fed them. Fucking Henry. We owed him the world. We owed Natalia more.

"You want to...get in the water o qué?" asked Paul as we made our way to the trunk.

"Stay here if you want," said Bimbo. "I'm gonna take this fucker out there and show it to them, tell them we're done. Maybe they show up, maybe they don't. If I don't come back, you can—"

"I'm going with you," said Tavo.

"You don't have—"

"It's dark as fuck and he's heavy. You can't get him out there by yourself. You'll drown like an idiot, and all this would've been for nothing. Plus, I'm the best swimmer here."

"I'm coming too," I said. I didn't want to, but I had to. I had to see the end of it.

"Guess that makes four of us," said Paul. "Can we bring the guns? You know, in case those things don't want to let things slide."

"It's too far," said Bimbo. "You can drop your gun into some water and it'll still fire, but I don't think keeping them underwater for that long will work. I'm leaving mine in the car. It's empty anyway."

I went to the back door and opened it. I pulled my gun out and dropped it in the back seat. It felt odd, like leaving my own story behind. Bimbo and Paul came next. Seeing the three guns there reminded me of our hands on top of Bimbo's gun on María's chest. We'd delivered on our promise. Fuck that laughing god. Tavo dropped his phone on top of the guns, and we all remembered our phones and did the same.

Bimbo and Tavo pulled Papalote out of the trunk. The sheets we'd used to wrap him were soaked through with blood. Who cared? We were going to get wet soon. The Atlantic would drink his blood.

"Think his blood is gonna bring in the sharks?" I asked.

"Not on this side of the reef," said Tavo. "If we get to the reef and you somehow fall on the deep side...that's another story."

The other side. The deep side. Where the fish lived. Did they live in caves like moray eels? Had they built an underwater city like the one the white men destroyed? Was Aklira happy that she could come and go between the two worlds? Were the fish angry at the world for what had been done to them? I promised myself I'd spend a lot of time with Natalia and then do some research when this was all over.

We grabbed fistfuls of bedsheets, pulled the body up, and walked to the water's edge. Then my brain started doing its thing. I saw a creature coming at me under the waves as we pulled Papalote's body out to the reef.

In my mind, a fish grabbed me and pulled me under, my scream swallowed by the ocean. I imagined the thing dragging me by the leg all the way to the reef and then pulling me into deeper water. My hands were covered in Papalote's blood. I could feel it, a sticky sensation I'd tried to ignore. I imagined my hands getting bloody from me trying to hold on to the reef as the fish dragged me farther into the deep. I imagined Henry's fucked-up hands. I looked around. The beach was deserted.

"Let's do this," Bimbo said as he stepped into the water, his left hand holding a corner of bloody bedsheets. We didn't stop to take our shoes off, because we knew we'd need them on the reef.

I thought about my gun in the back seat. What had I really left behind?

We walked into the water together and kept going until it reached chest level. Papalote's body wasn't so heavy in the water, but the bedsheets weren't making it easier.

"Let's unwrap him," I said. It didn't take long.

When the water reached our necks, the soft waves caressing my earlobes, I knew for sure that something was going to grab and pull me under and drag me toward the other side of the reef. The sheets we'd used to wrap Papalote up were floating next to us like some flowy, dormant sea monster.

"Think we're gonna have to swim much? I'm not a great swimmer and my shoes feel heavy as fuck," said Paul.

"I don't think so," said Tavo. "I can hear the water breaking over the reef. If you get tired or something, let him go. I can pull him."

The ocean floor dropped a bit more and we had to start swimming. My jeans slowed me down and my shoes felt like bricks. I could feel the hand on my leg before it came, the grasp. My breath came faster, my heart pounding in my chest from physical exertion as much as from fear.

Drowning would be an awful way to die. I could see a fish dragging my body over the reef's sharp rocks, my flesh opening up, my blood quickly diluting as the ocean entered my wounds.

Everyone was breathing hard, but the sound was masked by the crash of the water breaking against the reef. We were close. I kept kicking at the water and using my right hand to move forward while pulling at Papalote's right arm. I barely managed to keep my head above the surface.

"We're good!" said Tavo.

I let my legs drop. They touched sand again. My left foot landed on a rock. The reef. Now we had to climb up. Henry's pockmarked hands came back to me.

"Wait," said Tavo. He let go of Papalote and moved forward. His head was a dark shape on top of the water, which was reflecting the moonlight.

Suddenly Tavo stood up, half his body rising above the waterline.

"Gimme your arm, Gabe."

I reached up and Tavo pulled me toward him slowly. I used my feet to climb the reef, dragging Papalote behind me. When I was standing next to Tavo, he grabbed Papalote's other arm and we pulled him up onto the same rocks where we were standing.

I held on to Papalote while Tavo helped Paul and Bimbo climb up on the reef. Then we took turns pulling the body forward. When the water reached our knees, we stopped.

"Now what?" Paul said.

"This should do it," said Bimbo.

We stood there. The sound of the water over the reef filled our ears. We couldn't hear any insects or coquíes. I looked toward the car and realized it looked closer than I'd expected. Someone could show up and start shooting at us.

"You think those things are coming?"

"I know they are. They know we're here. They've kept an eye on us since this whole thing started."

A few minutes went by. We kept scanning the water's surface, listening to the ocean, and looking back to shore.

"We can't stay here too long," said Tavo.

"Fuck it," said Bimbo. "Hey! Aklira is okay." His voice was too loud. It would reach the shore and get us killed. Bimbo bent down and pulled Papalote up a bit.

A figure broke the surface about ten feet in front of us. The large dark head filled the space above the water, and my heart stopped. The rest of the thing rose slowly. It was taller than Tavo and much wider than me.

"Fuck," Paul muttered.

Another figure came out of the water, a few feet to the left of the first one. Then another one emerged next to that one. And then another. Soon we were looking at twelve or fifteen dark shapes, all of them silhouetted against the night sky, standing there, looking at us with big black eyes. I was glad we couldn't see their faces in the dark.

"Aklira is okay," said Bimbo. "She...she showed us. Everything."

The fish that had emerged first moved toward Bimbo, who was still holding Papalote. I felt every muscle in my body tense. It was even bigger than I had thought. It would rip Bimbo in two.

"Dead?" The creature looked down at Papalote's body. Its voice didn't reach my ears; it sounded inside my head. It was clearer than Aklira's, louder too. Wet and ragged, like the last water down a drain. Still, hearing a word coming from it—coming straight into my head—was mind-boggling. These fucking things could communicate.

"Yes, Papalote's dead," said Bimbo. His voice was shaky. "He killed my mom, so I killed him. Aklira is okay. And the girl is okay. She told me to tell you—"

"Who will feed us?"

"Aklira is in charge now," Bimbo repeated. "We have no problem with you. Do you understand?"

"You killed the one who feeds us."

"He had to die. And El Brujo. We killed him too. My problem was with them, not with you. Do you understand? I'm here to tell—"

"You killed the tall one?"

"We did," said Bimbo.

The fish made a series of clicking sounds that didn't resemble words. Those really came from his mouth. The difference was clear. The other fish responded with their own clicks.

"He prayed. To an old god," said the fish. "Older than us. He comes with storms. He destroys everything."

"Well, it...actually, I was the one who shot him," said Paul.

Paul was still Paul. It almost made me laugh.

The fish were silent. So were we. The ocean didn't give a fuck and kept doing its thing over the reef. I didn't know if the fish were going to kill us, but it didn't feel like they were.

The fish who had been talking moved forward a bit more. We took a few steps back. The fish bent over and grabbed Papalote's body by one of its legs, turned, and started moving away.

"Can I...come with you?" asked Tavo. We all turned to him.

The fish turned to face him.

I didn't hear anything inside my head, but Tavo nodded and looked away. They'd said no.

"I understand," said Tavo. "I do."

The fish turned again and kept moving, its big body vanishing under the dark water. The others joined him. We stood still, watching them go, feeling relieved. One by one, the fish vanished under the water. I felt better with each disappearing form, like my lungs could accommodate more oxygen when I inhaled.

"What the fuck just happened?" asked Paul.

"I don't know, but we need to go," I said. I wanted to be out of the water. I wanted my gun and to be as far from the water as possible.

We carefully walked back to the edge of the reef and jumped back into the water when we reached the edge, swimming like mad until we could stand on the ocean floor again.

We were alive and the fish had left us alone, but my brain kept screaming that something was about to pull me underwater and drag me to my death. As my jeans constricted my legs, I imagined blue darkness surrounding me as my useless screams died, my ghost joining those of the countless victims the Atlantic had claimed since humans started messing around in it, with it, across it. I was breathing hard, and that made me think of what it would feel like to drown, to feel a deep ache in my chest and not be able to suck in oxygen. I imagined taking a breath just like I did on the floor of El Brujo's place, but instead of air, my lungs filling with water, its salty sting prickling my nostrils and the back of my throat.

My feet touched the sand. I wasn't going to drown. Not on my own, at least.

We made it to the beach and stood there, letting water roll off our bodies. Tavo took off his shirt. Paul did the same. I was too stunned to do anything.

"Let's go," said Bimbo. No one argued.

46

GABE

—

A picture of violence
A desperate phone call
The limpia
Three thousand dead
An uncomfortable presence

We were in a daze when we got into Bimbo's car. I had so many questions that as soon as one began to emerge from the muddy waters of my brain, another one, unformed and hazy, would arise and push down whatever half-cooked thought had threatened to finally materialize. Outside the car, the world was still a dark mess full of broken trees and trash and power lines.

Fifteen minutes later, we stepped into Bimbo's apartment. The sofa was stained with black blood where there had been a body.

"Where's Raúl?" I asked Bimbo.

"Gone," he said. "I texted some people. I didn't want a body on my sofa hanging over shit as we took care of business."

Bimbo no longer looked like a larger, angrier, older version of himself. Now he looked like Bimbo. Something inside me recognized the need to find joy in my friend's return, but instead of ecstatic, I felt empty.

Bimbo looked deflated, Tavo sad, Paul seemingly eager to vanish.

They were all empty, just like me.

Vengeance can be the world's most powerful motor, but if you're successful, then you kill that motor and you're left with nothing.

Bimbo gave each of us a gallon of water and threw a bunch of shorts and T-shirts on the table so we could wash the salt water off our bodies and peel our too-tight, salty jeans off our tired legs.

Altagracia came out at some point, looking sleepy and with her hair up in a messy bun. She was wearing another of Bimbo's shirts. Bimbo went to her, said a few things, and walked her back to the room with his hand on her back.

I called Natalia to make sure she'd gotten home okay. I had to fix things with her. She picked up on the second ring. "Listen, babe, I love you," I said as soon as she picked up. "I'll go with you wherever you go. I just...I wanna be with you."

It was short and simple. She cried.

"I waited for you to say something like that for a long time, Gabe," she said. "You never did. Instead, you lied. You put your life at risk. You put your mom and me at risk. You did everything I asked you not to." She sighed through the phone. "I got into the nursing program at the University of Texas at Austin. I'm leaving tomorrow."

I didn't know what to say, so I said nothing. Natalia hung up. I called her back. She didn't pick up.

I sat around and thought about things. Everything from tonight already felt fuzzy. Trauma will do that to you. I hoped that with time, it would be like the way you know a stick figure is a person; the bare minimum, but no more. I thought about Paul and Cynthia. I thought about Bimbo, looking for something to keep him going. I thought about Tavo finding someone. Everyone and everything were moving all the time. I couldn't stop it, couldn't hold on to the bits I loved as it all changed and time did its thing. Natalia was my plan, my refuge, my future. And now she was gone. I'd done a lot of bad things and lost her because of it.

* * *

The predawn light felt like the most wonderful gift we had ever received. Paul got a text very early. He left when the sky above the houses in front of Bimbo's place looked like a puddle of cheap orange juice speckled with black clouds. I sent my mom a text letting her know I was okay, out with the boys. I told her we were keeping each other entertained.

Tavo left a few minutes after Paul. He said he wanted to take a shower and sleep until the next day.

"You going to the beach when you wake up?" I asked him.

"You know it," he said, his smile big enough to almost make me forget the night we'd had. I wanted to ask what the fish had said to him, but it seemed personal.

When Bimbo and I were alone, he hugged me again.

"You were with me for all of it, man," he said. "I owe you."

"You don't owe me shit, B," I said. "You would've done the same thing for me."

"I assure you, man, I fucking wouldn't."

We laughed. Then Bimbo said, "Nah, I would. For any of you. Even Paul."

Bimbo was in the bathroom and I was thinking about driving home when Altagracia appeared in the kitchen.

"Can you...give me a limpia?" I asked in Spanish. It was the first time I'd talked to her. After what she'd done to Raúl, a limpia didn't seem like a big deal.

Altagracia nodded and went to a small cooler they had on the kitchen floor. It was full of ice and contained the stuff that had been in the fridge when the power went out. Altagracia pulled an egg out of the cooler and came to me.

I was sitting in a kitchen chair. Altagracia stood behind me and started mumbling a prayer. I couldn't make out the words, but they were soothing. She rubbed the egg on top of my head in a circular motion and then down the sides of my face and neck.

When she stopped, I felt lighter.

"Sácalo de aquí que está lleno," she said. "Tíralo afuera."

Get it out of here; it's full.

I thanked her and she went back to her room. As soon as Bimbo came back, I gave him a hug and left.

I threw the egg in the gutter in front of Bimbo's place. It cracked. Instead of the transparent mucus and yellow yolk you'd expect from an egg, a black gooey mess spilled out of it. The gooey black mess was squirming, the sun glinting off it as it moved. I leaned closer. Thin black worms were moving around in the dark mess. I wanted to step on the whole thing and squish the worms under my shoe, but my desire not to touch it was stronger. I opened the car door, got in, and drove home.

I slept for a while and had a nightmare in which dark creatures dragged me into the ocean, mangling my body against the unforgiving reef. The water in my nightmare had been cloudy with my blood, but before the dream faded to black, I saw the peaks of some cyclopean place. A dreamworld I knew was real. I woke up scared and sweaty.

Downstairs, my mom was listening to the news on her little radio and sipping coffee. Seeing her was like walking into my life again, the one from before everything happened, the one from before María.

I was thinking about going down and grabbing some coffee when I got a text from Bimbo: I HAVE SOMETHING FOR ALL YOU AND HENRY LET MEET

I called Bimbo instead of texting back, just because I wondered what his life—his mind—had been like in the hours since we came back and went our separate ways. When he picked up, he sounded happy.

"Hey, G," he said.

"Learn to text, man. Your texts read like you typed with your eyes closed and using your knuckles."

"How about we meet at my place at three? That way I can give you your thing and then we can go celebrate with food."

"Cool. Paul and Tavo know?"

"I'll text them now. Not like either of them has much to do except sit at home smelling themselves and waiting for the power to come back on."

I hung up with Bimbo and checked the news on my phone. I was running low on battery. I'd have to take it slow on my ride to Bimbo's place to get some charge.

There was nothing anywhere about La Perla. There were almost three thousand dead and many more missing. Hospitals and morgues were full and no one knew what to do with the bodies, which were stacked wherever there was space and not stuffed in refrigerators because those had been full since the second day after María hit. The water we were getting was dirty and not fit for human consumption, so every news outlet had pieces telling folks to boil it. Pharmacies across the island had run out of everything. The grocery stores that had reopened had been wiped clean in hours. Gas stations were gouging prices and their convenience stores were closed because they were empty.

No one knew when the power would be restored.

I stopped reading and got dressed. I could repaint our door. I could get rid of this gun. I could sit with my mom. Everything could wait. I had to fix things with Natalia.

47

GABE

—

Brief reunion
Gunshots
The heaviest thing in the universe
A threat
Wild shot

W e were sitting around Bimbo's table again. The horrible sofa
was gone.

"I saw my neighbor from three houses down cutting some branches
and asked to borrow his hand saw," said Bimbo. "Took a while, but I
cut that thing into pieces small enough to fit into a bunch of bags I had
under the sink. I threw them in the trunk of my car and got rid of
them. Only slept a couple hours, but it was worth it. I didn't want that
in my house."

Altagracia appeared in the kitchen, her phone in hand, wearing
another one of Bimbo's shirts, as always. She waved at us with a sad
smile on her face. Bimbo asked if he should bring her some rice and a
couple of pork egg rolls. She shook her head, and Bimbo leaned in and
said, teasingly, "That's a first. You sure you don't want me to bring
anything back for you?"

Altagracia shook her head again, grabbed some water, and vanished back into Bimbo's room.

"Let's take my car," said Paul. "No offense, B, but I never wanna get in your car again."

Paul had parked two blocks down from Bimbo's place, so we started walking. For a moment, there was the rev of an engine behind us. Then gunshots.

BAM! BAM! BAM! BAM!

I hit the sidewalk. The slam knocked the air out of my lungs.

The gun went off again and again. Windows shattered. A chunk of sidewalk went up with a gray puff close to my head. Some of it came down on me. It was hot.

My heart was about to explode.

Fuck.

Two more shots rang out like an angry afterthought as an engine revved higher.

I looked up. I had to see.

A car was speeding toward the end of the street.

A white Lumina.

"Tavo!" I heard Paul scream. He was a few feet away from me, kneeling behind a blue car. He was looking past me. Bimbo was sitting a few feet away from him, closer to me, looking around with his hands over his head like he was expecting more bullets at any moment.

My ears were ringing.

I looked behind me, looking for Tavo. He was facedown on the sidewalk. There was a lot of blood underneath him.

I felt cold despite the heat. I ran to Tavo and knelt next to him. I grabbed his shoulder and flipped him over, screaming his name without meaning to.

The lower half of Tavo's face was covered in blood. There was a hole in his face next to the right side of his nose. His shirt was covered in blood. His eyes were wild, looking everywhere at once.

"I'm here, T, I'm here," I said. He knew. He looked at me. "Tavo! Tavo."

Tavo made a noise and went still. His eyes lost their focus. I screamed. Paul was next to me, leaning down, pulling on Tavo's shirt.

The air around me coagulated into something I couldn't swallow. Tavo's beautiful soul gone, his body a limp bag of bones.

I screamed again and held Tavo closer, trying to keep him with us.

Loss became the heaviest thing in the universe. Bimbo and Paul were talking, but their voices morphed into unintelligible things that floated in the air around me. I couldn't breathe. A hot rock of hate formed in my stomach, sprouted some kind of primordial legs, and climbed its way up to my throat.

I looked up, searching for something. An answer. A way out. The ability to turn back time. I found nothing but houses, peeling paint, torn awnings, naked plants.

And Xavier.

He was standing there, ten feet away from me, wearing the same thing he'd been wearing outside my house and at Bimbo's place. He was less translucent this time. The street behind him was almost blocked, as if he had become more solid, but his feet were hovering a few inches above the sidewalk, another fucking gray, dirty, cracked sidewalk just like the one he baptized at his death. Like the one where María had died. Like the one that sucked up Tavo's blood now.

Xavier had tears in his eyes. They shone under the sun. A crying ghost. It made no sense and it made all the sense in the world.

The feeling that we had failed Xavier twice slammed into me so hard I had to stop looking at him. My chest cracked, my damaged heart crumbling into a pile of haunted ruins.

My heart, so full just a day before, turned into a sad playground for the dead.

My soul was a place for hate to thrive.

My guilt was an old thing weighing down a young man's body.

Xavier opened his mouth and his voice came out, clearer than anything I'd ever heard before, a sound injected directly into my brain like the fish had done: "Mátalos a todos."

Kill them all.

"…now! Let's go!"

Bimbo. Next to my ear. His hand pointing up. I looked. He was pointing at his house.

He started running. Paul followed him. I felt lost. I placed Tavo's head down on the sidewalk and followed them, the world blurry from my tears and my lungs aching. Then I turned around. I couldn't leave Tavo there. I went back and started pulling him up. Then Paul was there, grabbing Tavo's other arm. We carried him between us just like they'd carried Raúl.

Bimbo was climbing the stairs to his place. We followed. We reached the bottom of the stairs as Bimbo entered his place. I heard screaming. We couldn't go any faster. Tavo was heavy. Paul and I did our best to get him up the stairs. Halfway up, I looked at the street and saw an old woman standing in front of a house wearing a bata and chanclas. She was looking at us. I hoped she would mind her business like everyone else in the fucking country.

We entered Bimbo's place and it took me a moment to process what I was looking at. Bimbo was close to the wall next to the hallway that led to his room. He had Altagracia there, pressed against the wall. Both were screaming.

"What are you doing?" I asked.

"She was at the window!" said Bimbo.

I had no idea what he meant. None of it made sense.

Bimbo pulled Altagracia away from the wall by her shirt, dragged her over to the table, and slammed her down on a chair. Paul and I placed Tavo on the floor where the sofa had been, his blood falling on Raúl's dried blood.

"Dame tu teléfono, cabrona," said Bimbo. He was crying.

"What are you—?"

"This bitch did it!" said Paul next to me.

"What?"

Bimbo was screaming at Altagracia to unlock her phone. She was trying to scratch his arms and shaking her head while grunting. Bimbo pulled her down to the floor, let her go, and started kicking her.

No. I moved and pushed Bimbo.

Paul grabbed me from behind and pulled me back.

"What the fuck are you doing?"

"I looked up," said Paul. "You know, like in La Perla, when I stayed up? I heard shots and thought there might be shooters up on a roof or something, so I looked up. Altagracia was at the window looking at us. She knew it was coming."

Altagracia was sobbing and trying to talk, saying some numbers. Bimbo grabbed her phone from the floor and unlocked it. She had given him her code.

"Her brother," said Bimbo. "Her fucking brother did this." He turned the phone to us. The last text was from four minutes ago: estan saliendo. *They're leaving.* The one before that read: van a salir a comer. *They're going out to eat.* At the top of the screen was a name. Rafa.

"She told her brother when we were leaving," said Bimbo. "That's how they fucking knew!"

This had nothing to do with Papalote. Or the fish. That fucking car. The white Lumina with water in its taillight. This was something else, something we'd missed entirely.

Bimbo grabbed Altagracia by the hair and asked her where we could find her brother. She didn't reply. Bimbo let her go and walked to the kitchen. Altagracia started telling us we were crazy and to let her go. Bimbo came back with a knife. It was bigger than the one we'd used on Raúl.

Paul and I pulled Altagracia to her feet and held her, each of us on one side. She was easier to handle than Raúl or the guy at the parking lot. Much easier than Kimbo. I was tired of holding people, but I was more tired of losing my friends, and if she had anything to do with Tavo's death, she deserved much more than whatever Bimbo had in mind.

She was scared, but I think part of her thought she had Bimbo in her pocket, that whatever brutality he had inside was something he couldn't let loose on her. She was wrong.

Bimbo grabbed Altagracia by the neck, placed the knife under her right eye, and told her to tell us about her brother or he was going to cut off all her fingers before moving to her toes. Altagracia wasn't a thug; she was as desperate as we were. She talked.

José Luis, the guy Bimbo had met in jail, was a friend of Altagracia's brother, Rafa. José Luis knew Bimbo wanted vengeance, so he concocted the lie about hooking him up with Altagracia so she could get citizenship and he could get some money. If Bimbo pulled off what he said he wanted to do, all Rafa had to do after was take care of Bimbo and then take over a weakened La Perla with some other Dominicans. All he needed was someone keeping tabs on Bimbo. Altagracia.

And Bimbo was all too eager to bring her home with him and more than willing to fall into their trap. But she hadn't known at the beginning. She swore. Rafa had told her it was all about the inheritance money. They were only going to take some of that. It wasn't that bad. He'd been lying. He'd come clean only a few days earlier, only to make sure Altagracia kept her eyes and ears on Bimbo and reported everything back to him.

Then we all got involved and things got complicated, but when you plan on murdering a man, taking friends with you is not a tough choice. Rafa had killed Xavier to scare us and make us think Papalote was after us, to push us to act. Listening to Altagracia say her brother had killed Xavier broke me all over again. The things we'd done to avenge him were awful, and we hadn't even done them to the right people.

"She's been...encouraging me from the start," said Bimbo. "Telling me we could do it, that everything being dark would help us. She even told me she knew it's what my mother would've liked."

Bimbo had looked deflated after we came back from La Perla, but now he was back to being bigger, to looking older and meaner.

"Tavo...we need to—"

"Soon," said Bimbo. He gave Altagracia the phone and told her to call her brother and tell him Bimbo had come back in, shot and bleeding, and died on his bed. He wanted her to tell him to come as soon as possible, that she was scared and that the money from his mother's life insurance was in the house but she couldn't find it. When she spoke to her brother, her tears were real. The shakiness in her voice from Bimbo pressing the knife against her throat was also real. Rafa bought it. He bought all of it. He didn't even ask about the rest of us. Probably thought we'd fled or were dead or dying somewhere.

"Keep an eye on her," said Bimbo. We did. She kept her own bloodshot eyes on us.

Bimbo went into his room and came back with his gun.

"This is all I have," he said. He knew we weren't carrying our guns. That part was over. Get rid of the gun and paint the door; those had been my plans for the day. This was unexpected. I looked back. Xavier's ghost was standing next to Tavo. I knew what he wanted.

All stories are ghost stories.

"We have to surprise that motherfucker," said Bimbo. "And you two better be ready, because there's no way he's coming alone."

"Do you have a plan?" asked Paul. God, I hated that word.

"I do," said Bimbo. "Get her up and hold her again."

We went to both sides of Altagracia, grabbed her arms again, and pulled her to a standing position. Maybe she was too scared to put up a fight.

Bimbo walked over to Altagracia and showed her the knife.

"Tu hermano mató a mi hermano y le sacó los ojos. Ahora yo le voy a hacer lo mismo."

Your brother killed my brother and plucked his eyes out. Now I'm going to do the same thing to him.

Bimbo pulled the knife back. He was about to stab Altagracia in the stomach.

Paul let go of Altagracia's arm and stepped in front of her.

"What the fuck are you doing, man? This isn't how we do things. We don't fucking kill women!"

Bimbo was a monster. I was ready to let him do it, so I was a monster too. Paul wasn't. Push someone hard enough and you either destroy them or unlock the monster that lives inside.

Altagracia whimpered. Paul moved back and grabbed her again. We placed her back in the chair. She bent over and hugged herself.

Bimbo moved to the back of the chair and turned it toward the door.

"Let him get in here and see her," he said. His voice was a deep thing that reminded me of the voice that had come from the fish. I didn't like it.

Paul and I grabbed knives from the kitchen. Knowing that whoever walked through Bimbo's door would be carrying a gun made my knife feel flimsy, useless. It made me understand that thing people say about bringing a knife to a gunfight.

We took careful looks out the window. From where we were, we could see Tavo's blood down on the sidewalk about half a block down. I started crying again. The day was hot and no one was out, and for that we were grateful.

"What's gonna happen if — ?"

"Don't think about what's gonna happen," Bimbo told Paul. "Don't think at all. Focus on killing whoever walks through that door. Now, stay quiet in case they can hear us…and cover her damn mouth. I don't want her to make a sound."

Paul moved behind Altagracia and put his hand over her mouth. Bimbo and I stood on either side of the door. We could hear traffic far away and nothing else. Altagracia's muffled crying could barely be heard under Paul's hand. I peeked out the window and saw a dog licking the puddle of Tavo's blood.

Then we heard the stairs groaning. A lot. And voices. They were in a hurry. At least three men.

"Altagracia?"

That had to be Rafa. Altagracia's brother. The man who'd killed Xavier and plucked his eyes out. The man who had painted a veve on my door and left my mom in a puddle of blood on the floor. He would surely come in first. I was ready to plunge my knife into him. This motherfucker deserved that and more.

"Altagracia?"

They were closer. Of course this asshole would announce himself. He was an amateur. He'd even used the same car for everything.

The door opened. A Black man with a shaved head barged in. Two men stumbled in after him. The first man lifted a gun, aimed it at Paul.

"Let her go!" His voice was full of panic and anger.

Paul ducked behind Altagracia, using her like a shield. The man's hand shook for a second and then he squeezed the trigger. The sound of the gunshot filled the apartment. My ears rang.

A moment later, Bimbo pulled his trigger. The left side of the Black man's head spat into the gloom around it. Without a sound, he fell. The other two turned toward Bimbo, their eyes wide, their faces contorted.

Bimbo pulled the trigger twice more. Two more explosions, each less deafening to my ringing ears. I didn't see where the bullets dug into flesh, but they hit their mark. At such close distance, it was almost impossible for them not to. One man fell, his silence a declaration. The other bent over, yelled something, and grabbed his left shoulder.

Paul appeared next to the man. Just like before. An apparition. A silent ghost. There was a flash, a blade catching the light for a second. Paul sank the blade in the man's neck. The man tried to scream again, but it sounded like a clogged drain. I looked down. The other man's face was half covered in blood. He'd taken one to the face.

I looked at Rafa. He had a hole on the side of his head. He was dead. It felt good. His right arm was thrown out in front of him as if he were reaching for his sister. Maybe he was reaching for all of us like some folks do as they're going out, trying to bring everything else into the darkness with them. On the inside of his extended arm, I could see the tattoo, the floating symbols. I recognized them immediately. Barón Samedí's veve. The one on my door. The one on the wall. The one on Xavier's garage door. The one on Paul's door. It was definitely him, and I was glad he was dead.

"He...he killed her," said Paul. His words didn't make sense for a moment. Then I looked at Altagracia. She was slumped on the chair, her arms dangling at her sides. Blood had soaked Bimbo's shirt, turning it dark.

She didn't deserve that.

"You two have to get the fuck outta here," said Bimbo.

"What?" I asked.

"We're standing in a fucking room with five bodies. There's no explanation for this that won't end with all of us in prison, Gabe."

"What about you?" I asked.

Bimbo lifted his gun at us. He was smiling.

"Go or I'll fucking shoot you," he said. "Five bodies is more than enough."

Paul pulled at my shoulder. Hard. I walked. We left Bimbo's place.

Tavo's blood had left a trail on the stairs. It got stronger as we ran down to the sidewalk. I refused to look at the puddle of his blood again.

"I'll text you soon," said Paul. Then he hugged me.

We walked our separate ways. Quickly. I kept expecting sirens. None came. No one gave a fuck.

48

GABE

—

A painful call
Everything will be okay
The best of us
A proper burial
A huge, scary question mark

A text came in at 10:01 p.m. TOOK CARE OF EVERYTHNG MY UNCLES PEOPLE HELPED THE FISH ARE FEED IM TAKING OVER

I called him. He didn't pick up. I called again. Then I called him again. He picked up on the third try.

"I'm with my sister, G," he said. I could hear crickets and coquíes in the back. He was outside.

"You took Tavo to the fish?"

"I did. I took—"

"Are you crazy?"

"I went with my uncle's—with some of my men. We stayed up for a while and didn't see anyone. Maybe they don't even know about Papalote yet. We did it fast. In the van. I took all of them. I told them Tavo wasn't food. I asked them to take him to their home and do whatever they do with their dead down there. I think Tavo would've liked that. Everything will be okay, man," said Bimbo. "No one gives a fuck.

Remember? They didn't give a fuck about my mom or about Xavier or about Kimbo, remember? They won't give a fuck about La Perla or about some missing Dominicans who were here with no papers. They were ghosts, and people especially don't care about ghosts. You read the news lately? Hundreds of people are missing. Thousands are dead. The hospitals are full. No one will care about this."

Maybe we'd gotten away with everything.

Maybe not.

Time would tell.

"What happens when they ask us about Tavo?"

"You're boricua, man!" said Bimbo.

"And?"

"Just play by the rules: You don't know anything, haven't seen anything, and don't know anyone who might know. They don't have a body, so they have nothing. We'll be fine. I...man, I loved Tavo."

Bimbo moved the phone away from his face, but the sound of his sobs reached me loud and clear.

Tavo. My brother. My friend. The best of us.

Something cracked in my chest, something that had been cracking over and over again recently and would never be the same again.

I didn't lower my phone or hide my sobs when they came.

I wanted Bimbo's words to be true more than anything I'd ever wanted before, except maybe getting my father back.

"Anyway," said Bimbo. He sniffled and sighed. "I gotta go, G. I'm gonna get my sister sorted and then we'll get together or something. Y'all owe me lunch."

"Take care, B."

I hung up.

The sky had turned ugly soon after. Now it was raining. I looked out the window. I expected to see a dark figure out there, looking up at me. There was no one.

49

GABE

—

Two weeks later
The beautiful thing that was broken
Questions
Darkness swallows you whole
The memory of two ghosts

It took me two weeks to get a plane ticket to Austin. Natalia hadn't replied to my texts. Keyla had finally given me her new address and then told me men were idiots who always waited until it was too late to recognize they had a good thing. Tavo would've told me the same thing.

My mom told me to go. The power hadn't come back and leaving her felt awful, but I had to talk to Natalia, I had to fix the beautiful thing I'd broken.

The airplane was packed and hot, of course. The guy sitting next to me was sleeping before we even took off. I tried to sleep and at the same time wondered if I'd ever sleep again. We'd lost too much. We'd done too much. I would need a few more limpias before I felt clean. How many ghosts can a person carry? How much bad can you bring into the world before the darkness catches up to you and swallows you whole? Vengeance is like any other drug; it destroys your life while making you feel good for a useless moment.

My abuela's voice came to me again, the way it'd come time and time again the past few days. *All stories are ghost stories.*

I thought about the ocean below us. I imagined Tavo's ghost swimming under the waves. I pictured Xavier and María smiling. We'd won. We'd avenged everyone. But we'd lost. And they were gone.

If I could get Natalia back, at least I could have something good in my life, but it didn't seem like that would happen. Maybe my stupid decisions meant I would spend the rest of my life haunted and alone, working a shitty job and watching my mom get older until I was alone with the ghosts of my parents.

I stood up to use the bathroom. Two figures were standing near the thin bathroom door. Tavo and Xavier. Real? Conjured? It didn't matter. They were mine. All stories are ghost stories. I blinked and they were gone. I gave a little smile and pushed the tears from my eyes.

ACKNOWLEDGMENTS

First, I want to thank my family for putting up with me while I was writing this book, digging into the past to revisit memories that maybe should've been left alone and getting sad, angry, distracted, excited, and violent while mentally living in this world.

You wouldn't have read this thing if two people hadn't taken a chance on me, so thank you to Melissa Danaczko — good friend, teacher, amazing agent, go-to person whenever I have a question about publishing — and to Josh Kendall, good friend and editor extraordinaire who always sees what I want to do, sometimes even before I can see it in my head. My life would be very different without you two, so a million thanks now and forever.

I want to thank Alyssa Persons, Liv Ryan, Pat Jalbert-Levine, Anna Brill, Bryan Christian, Craig Young, and the rest of the awesome crew at Mulholland for making the complicated stuff always seem easy. Also, many thanks to Gregg Kulick for another fantastic cover.

I want to thank Puerto Rico. Borikén. Mi tierra. Mi casa. Mi madre. Mi patria. La tierra que me vió nacer y que me hizo. The place where my heart lives. The place where I learned to survive, to push through, to refuse to quit. A beautiful land of ghosts and anger, of complex politics and unending resilience. Te veo pronto.

I'd like to thank every single person out there who read, bought, reviewed, or recommended *The Devil Takes You Home*. That book changed my life. The Devil and I made history together — first Latino to win a Bram Stoker Award in the novel category, second author ever and first Latino to win the Stoker and the Shirley Jackson Award for the same book, et cetera—and I don't think any of that would've happened without you, the readers who read it, talked about it, recommended it, and voted for it. Seriously, thank you. I can't wait to see what we do with this one!

I'm lucky to be part of an amazing writing community. There are too many people to list here and I will surely leave some out, but know that I didn't do so on purpose; you're just too many. Thank you to those who inspire me with their work. Thank you to those who have ever read me. Thank you to those who gave me a blurb this time around and those who came through last time. Thank you to Paul Tremblay, Alma Katsu, Becky Spratford, Cynthia Pelayo, Stephen Graham Jones, Brian Evenson, Chuck Wending, Josh Malerman, Shawn Cosby, Michael Koryta, Brian Keene, Rachel Harrison, Stephen King, Mariana Enriquez, Richard Chizmar, Daniel Kraus, Meg Gardiner, Adam Cesare, Jeremy Robert Johnson, Tananarive Due, Tod Goldberg, Rhonda Jackson Garcia, Red Lagoe, Kimberly Davis Basso, Christopher Golden, and everyone else. You know who you are. Thank you as well to the entire Twitter community and those of you who religiously take part in #FridayReads. And one huge thank-you to all the booksellers and librarians out there. You make this gig much, much sweeter. Much love to you all.

I started writing this novel back home, back in the summer of 1999. I didn't have the skills to get it all down on paper—and sometimes I think I don't have the skills now!—but I remember walking around Old San Juan alone late that summer, reminiscing, and then going down to the cemetery and thinking, *One day I'm gonna write about this.* To the crew who was there with me, to those who drank with me and fought by my side and bled with me, know this: Los llevo, cabrones.

Thank you to the music that carried me through so many days and nights. Joaquín Sabina. Bob Marley. El Gran Combo. Tom Waits. Paco de Lucía. Fito Páez. Ismael Serrano. Roberto Roena. Thank you to the ghosts for sharing their stories with me, sometimes without uttering a word. Gracias a Julia de Burgos, Luisa Capetillo y Pedro Albizu Campos. Thank you to the writers whose books were with me then and stuck with me forever. Horacio Quiroga. Stephen King. Richard Laymon. Bentley Little. Mario Benedetti. Oliverio Girondo. Harry Crews. Pedro Juan Gutiérrez. Jack Ketchum. So many others...

Last but not least, thank you once again to mi tierra, Puerto Rico. This book came from you and is for you, Borikén. It's from and for your beaches and hot nights and amazing art and hurricanes and strength. Yo, como Juan Antonio Corretjer, sería borincano aunque naciera en la luna.

ABOUT THE AUTHOR

Gabino Iglesias is the author of the Shirley Jackson and Bram Stoker Award–winning novel, *The Devil Takes You Home,* as well as the critically acclaimed and award-winning novels *Zero Saints* and *Coyote Songs.* He is a writer, journalist, professor, and literary critic living in Austin, Texas. Iglesias is the horror columnist for the *New York Times Book Review.*